I0689777

Summer in the Snowfall

Revel Pointe Romance, Volume 2

A.E. Merriweather

Published by Spoonbill Publishing, 2025.

This is a work of fiction. Similarities to real people, places, or events are entirely coincidental.

SUMMER IN THE SNOWFALL

First edition. October 14, 2025.

ISBN: 979-8991070638

Written by A.E. Merriweather.

For friendship reasons, loving partners, and romance readers

PROLOGUE

The Secret Reveler
A Blog Devoted to All Matters Reve

Dear Revelers,

It's been a wild ride. Our man Ethan Reve got hitched (cue the sound of hearts breaking across America). The Island of Sirens experience is off and running with record-breaking crowds, thanks in large part to Marin, Ethan's partner and (sigh) wife. But that's old news.

Now Revelers' eyes are on the very mysterious James Reve and his Grand Revel Library project. Unlike his half-brother Ethan, James has largely escaped media scrutiny, living in England the last twelve years, training and working as an architect. Everything has been very hush-hush the last six months, but the project is coming to an end soon. The beautiful (see aerial progress pictures below) building on-site—next to Mick & Marie's Log Cabin—will house Revel Pointe's history, honoring the life and legacy of its founder, Mick Reve. No presh, James.

Word on the street is this taciturn hunk of a man is a beast to work for, keeping ungodly hours and demanding perfection. A number of contractors have quit, causing delays. Even with his insane work ethic, there's a chance James won't finish in time for the Christmas gala. There's even been a call for extra archivists. All hands-on deck. Mayday, mayday...

His mother, Tilda Olsen-Reve, has reportedly been breathing down his neck, and James' one-word responses to reporters' questions have only made us more curious about the man behind the building. Revelers, he's holding his cards close to his chest.

Why won't he talk to the press? What is he hiding?

Talk to us, James. We don't bite. Often.

Chapter One

Summer

Nothing says sexy like medieval sewing techniques, I think as the creak of the library door pulls me from the research rabbit hole I've fallen down. This particular rabbit hole will help me add boning to the bodice of my dress for the Spring Renaissance Fair in Columbus. Normally, I dress modestly, but at the Ren Fair, my girls will be lifted to astounding new heights.

"Still here?" Lilia, my work bestie, asks as she backs herself through the door with a shoulder load of totes, ready to head home.

"Yep." I yawn, which makes Lilia yawn.

"Not fair. Don't do that." Lilia touches her rounded pregnant belly. "I'm already exhausted, Nito." Lilia, from a big Ukranian family in town, calls me Nito, Ukrainian for *summer*.

"Only three weeks of classes left," I chime, clicking off the string of Christmas lights that hang above my check-out desk.

"Huzzah!" Lilia raises her fist in celebration.

I stretch dramatically and look up at the clock. "Oh shit. I gotta go." It's already 5:30—Wednesday poker night with Dad, Grandma York, and our neighbor, Mr. Rosenberg.

"Hot date?" Lilia asks hopefully. She's been bugging me to get online and spice up my love life so she can live vicariously through me, but I haven't been on a date in close to a year.

"You know it," I joke as Lilia waves goodbye.

Out in the parking lot, I zip my puffy jacket to my chin, unlock my yellow Schwinn, and don my helmet, tucking my long bangs out of my eyes. It's getting too cold to bike, but I've been saving so much money on gas, not to mention keeping in shape. I should savor this. There were years when I couldn't ride a bike.

The sky is dark, filled with icy blue clouds moving in the distance. I pedal fast to beat the rain. As if the weather can hear my thoughts, lightning cracks across our flat town.

The rain holds out for five minutes, then the mean sky unleashes its fury before I reach the halfway point. *Perfect*. My books are going to be soaked. The rain feels like ice against my face as I sit stuck at a red light on Main, teeth chattering and torso shaking. A red pickup truck pulls alongside me. The driver rolls his window down.

"Summer York?" a masculine voice booms at me, but before I can answer, the driver has thrown his truck in park and is running around, grabbing my handlebars. It's Grainger. Grainger *freaking* McCloskey, my father's old apprentice. Grainger, the town player and the longest, most ridiculous, out-of-my-league crush I ever had. He towers over me and my bike, his dirty blonde hair tucked in a Cavaliers cap, his muscled arms and chest already showing through his soaked gray sweater—Thor disguised as a Midwestern man. I feel like a dorky eighth grader next to him.

"Come on, get in!" Grainger yells over the rain as he swoops my Schwinn from beneath me. He easily hefts my bike into the back, and suddenly I'm sitting in the passenger seat of Grainger's truck, drenched and shaking, my backpack on my lap.

I inhale. His car smells masculine—a mix of motor oil and wood. Grainger shifts gears and pulls through the stoplight, laughing, showing his perfect white teeth.

"Summer! This is perfect. I'm on my way to your house."

"You are?"

"Yeah, your dad invited me to his poker game."

"He did?" I sound inane, but Grainger rescuing me and accompanying me home has definitely been in my high-school fantasy rotation. I blush, unsure if it's proximity to Grainger or my body trying to acclimate to the toasty air blasting heat from the dashboard. He's probably saved me from mild hypothermia. *Swoon.*

"Yeah, I don't get to play often, so I jumped at the chance. I used to do pretty well at online poker, but I don't have much time for it these days."

As Grainger goes on about the weather and his work, I try to piece together what is currently happening. *Why has my dad invited Grainger to the poker game?*

My dad has had a few bad years. Mom died two years ago in a freak accident. While gardening at the back of our long lot, she tripped and fell, smashing her temple on a rock. The doctors said she likely died instantly. Dad discovered her when he came home for dinner. I was living in Cleveland then, and my sister, married with kids already, had moved to Columbus. Dad was completely alone for the first time in nearly forty years. He threw himself into work, but that was a losing game. The recession made his business of building expensive cruising boats a luxury many could not afford. He laid off employees until it was down to him and Grainger. They had just enough sales to make ends meet. In the end, it wasn't enough. He folded and retired early, and since then he's been lost. We all have. And though I swore I'd never live in this town again, I moved in with Dad, so I could look after him and so we both could save money.

Lately, Dad has been poking around my personal life, asking if there are any dating prospects in my RenFair circles, at school, in my cycling group, etc. He knows I had a crazy crush on Grainger when I was a teenager. Every time I'd visit the York Crafts workshop, it was hard not to stare. Back then I was a gangly fifteen-year-old in a scoliosis back brace, as well as a full set of dental braces, watching a sweaty twenty-one-year-old Grainger, in a varnish-stained tank top and backwards cap, sanding hulls. His forearms, biceps, and shoulders rippled like the wake of the skiffs and oars he was crafting.

Grainger was golden, a god among mortals, and it didn't matter that he knew it. I wasn't even close to his league.

But that was years ago, and now, randomly, Grainger is invited to poker? I didn't even know my dad and Grainger were in touch.

"So, what are you up to these days?" Grainger flashes an inquisitive look. "Still at the middle school?"

"Yep" is all I can think to say. I unclasp my chin strap, and the hard foam of my helmet makes a squeaking sound as I pull it from my head. I must look like a half-frozen, drowned rat.

"How is it? Seems to me it would be a bit boring after living in Cleveland. Sitting in a room with books all day." Grainger offers me his relaxed smile, one that makes girls' knees buckle. He's hot, but as a grown, twenty-six-year old woman, I'm able to actually process what he's saying to me. On one hand, he remembers that I went to college in Cleveland, but on the other hand, he thinks books are boring.

"Being in a room with books is the *best* part of the job. The middle school's okay. Not my dream job," I explain, fiddling with my helmet straps.

"So you're looking to stick around Westerville then?" He side-eyes me for the briefest of moments before looking at the road.

"Not necessarily." It's a question I've been thinking a lot about lately. I don't want to leave my dad, but I feel stuck. This place contains so many good memories with my mom, but it's also where everyone still thinks of me as the nerdy back-brace girl.

To say I was a late bloomer is a giant understatement. The brace came off my senior year after a successful spinal fusion surgery, but it might as well have been soldered onto me at that point. No one, except a few close friends, ever saw past the brace.

If I never again hear, "Wow, Summer!? You look so much better than you used to!" I think I'd die happy. I can feel them trying not to call me their least creative epithet, "Summer Dork."

I've started to daydream about my possibilities. There's the safe option of going back to school to do a Ph.D. in Library Science at Kent State. But in my grand far-flung daydreams, I think of heading further afield—my thoughts straying to England, specifically; the Bodleian Library at Oxford and a graduate trainee program. But that's too far away. Too lofty. I am not a complete coward, however.

A few weeks ago, I applied for a temporary archivist position at Revel Pointe, the storied theme park in Louisiana. I'd been watching movie trailers at lunch with Lilia, who is a total Revel Adult (a.k.a. Reveler). She even honeymooned there. When a pop-up ad announced that the new Grand Revel Library needed archivists, she encouraged me to apply. During college, I interned for three years at the Cleveland Public Libraries Rare Books and Materials in college, so I'm qualified—and I loved that job. Plus, though the position is temporary, it'd be a good resume builder.

Revel Pointe is foreign to me, but that's the appeal. Before I could talk myself out of it, I dashed off a fresh cover letter, uploaded my resume, and hit send, picturing myself in a white-columned library surrounded by boxes of animation cels and gilded scripts.

"Got big plans?" Grainger asks, clearing his throat as if saying, *Earth to Summer.*

"I, yeah, sorry. I love Westerville," I say. "But I don't think I'm ready to put down roots."

"But you already have roots here."

"That's true. And they're always a reason to come home to visit."

"Aw, come on. This place is the best." Grainger looks at me, almost too long, and I want him to look back at the road. The rain is turning to slush, and I worry his truck will slide on the slippery black ice.

"Tell me, where on Earth is better?" he asks.

"There are too many places to list, Grainger."

"Come on, we got the reservoir and the lake, and Columbus is close too. Good bands always come through. We've got it good here. Admit it."

"That's true." It's definitely a lovely place to be from, to raise a family, to lead a sleepy American life. Growing up, that's what I thought I wanted—the husband, kids, and house with the fence down the street from the elementary school—just like I was raised. Maybe I still do, but I also know I want more than that right now.

"You should come to a concert with me sometime. Maybe it'll change your mind." He smiles at me again, and I swear to god, lightning flashes, making his teeth look even whiter. *Is he asking me out?*

"Okay," I say because I'm sure he's just being nice. He can't possibly want to take me on a date. He's Grainger McCloskey, and I'm, well, me. I'm even more awkward, but luckily, he pulls into my driveway then. He retrieves my bike from the truck bed, and I wheel it to the garage, waiting as the door lifts slowly and then ducking inside. I jump when I realize Grainger's directly behind me. He has to be six-foot-five, but his shadow looms bigger, nine feet tall.

"Sorry, I didn't mean to frighten you." Water drips from his blond hair and chin, and his sweater clings to his sculpted torso. He reaches over to brush a lock of hair pasted to my forehead. "You look..."—he pauses, searching for the right words—"...different than I remember." Softness tones down his confident voice. "I've always loved the color of your hair."

I'm stunned. As in, actually motionless. My teenage self screams, *Kiss him, you fool!* but my body doesn't comply. This feels off somehow.

"Thank you?" I back up, leaving my bike against the wall and skirting around my dad's 1979 Mustang.

Inside, the house smells like chili and evergreens, which makes me feel warm and cozy even though I am not. I am cold, wet, and uncertain. Was Grainger about to kiss me before I ran inside?

My dad calls from the kitchen, "Summer, did you get caught in—" But when he turns the corner to find Grainger and me in the hallway, his tone changes. "Buddy! You saved the day." Dad throws his hands out dramatically, his smile wide and comical, unlike anything I've seen from him in months.

"That I did, Mitch," Grainger says, slapping my dad heartily on the shoulder. "I found our girl halfway home and scooped her up." They both beam at me.

Our girl? Just what exactly has my dad told Grainger? That I'm single and desperate for a boyfriend?

"Yep, my knight in shiny pick-up." I play along despite the creeping sensation that this is a set-up.

The beaming continues. My dad has always had a soft spot for romance. If there's a Hallmark Christmas movie marathon, he's there. But my life isn't a romantic comedy. Right now, it feels more like a convoluted mystery.

"Thanks, Grainger," I say, still dripping on the rug. "I'm gonna go change into some dry clothes."

"Good idea," Grainger says and then peels his sweater off right there. His broad, bare chest glistens even in the low light of the hallway. Suddenly, we feel too close. "You mind throwing that in the dryer for me?" He decides his jeans will dry fast, and Dad offers to get him a T-shirt.

We head through the kitchen, where Gran's eyes go wide at the sight of us as she stirs the chili.

The rest of the night is strange. We eat and drink beer while Grainger tells us about his new deck chair designs, the wood he's sourcing from Brazil, the almost perfect season his rowing crew had this year, going into great detail about his teammates, and it's all very impressive. He tells us about his plans to build his dream house on a plot of land at Spring Creek Lake. He goes on almost nervously through dinner, saying more words than I've ever heard him string together before.

"Sounds like a good, solid plan," Gran says, but I hear skepticism in her voice. She doesn't like braggarts. Dad keeps asking Grainger more questions about himself even though he probably already knows the answers. *This list of accomplishments is for me.* I want to melt into a puddle of embarrassment.

When we finally start the poker game, Grainger's competitive side awakens like an angry badger. He doesn't like that we play Texas Hold 'Em for twenty-five-cent chips, insisting it makes the game too easy to win and proving it by winning the first three rounds. When Gran wins the fourth, Grainger sulks a little. It's almost comical when he crosses his tanned arms across his chest, which stretches out my dad's old Browns T-shirt.

Toward the end of the night, I win a round, and Grainger congratulates me, putting his hand on my knee and squeezing. I squirm in my seat. He smirks and winks at me, right in front of my Gran and Dad, but they don't let on they've seen anything. Maybe this emboldens him because he leaves his hand on my leg for a few more seconds. *What the hell is going on?!*

"Well, I'm exhausted." I push away from the table and note the conspiratorial look between my dad and Grainger. "I think I'm done for the night, sorry." I'm built for quiet nights with my family or a book, not a Hemsworth coming on strong, especially one who actively ignored me for over a decade.

"Aw, come on!" Grainger practically yells. "It's only nine o'clock!"

"Sorry, it's a school night." I give Gran a look that says, *Save me!*

"I've got an early morning, too." She sweeps the cards back into a pile in front of her. She's always got my back. The living-room clock chimes, and Grainger relents.

I retrieve his sweater, still warm from the dryer. Once again, when I turn around from our laundry closet, he's standing right behind me.

"Thanks for having me over tonight," he says quietly.

"Of course," I say, though it wasn't my idea. "My dad loves you."

"He's great. Always been so good to me." Grainger's blue eyes soften, and he pulls the sweater over his head. This sweet Grainger is almost irresistible. "I miss working in the shop with him." He bites his bottom lip, looking like an outdoor fitness model.

"I think he misses it too," I say and hold the door frame awkwardly. I pull my long braid forward over my shoulder and touch it like a security blanket. I doubt he's about to kiss me right here, with my Gran and Dad in the kitchen, but he leans toward me anyway. "Well, good night, I guess."

Before I can retreat, he pulls me in for a long hug. His heart beats powerfully against my face. He smells like our dryer sheets. His back is hard underneath my palms. In my teenage imagination, I knew exactly how this moment would feel, an out-of-body yet a very-much-inside-my-body experience. Now I don't know what to do with my hands.

"I'd really like to take you out sometime," he says, laying his chin on the top of my head.

"Really?" I pull back, needing to see his eyes. They look earnest, so I say, "I mean, okay. Yeah."

"Good." He grins down at me. "How about this Saturday?"

I pretend to consider this offer, but I have nothing planned, and I've fantasized about Grainger McCloskey asking me on a date countless times in my life.

"I think I'm free," I say. This is literally my teenage dream come true, but up close, Grainger is a puzzle, an Adonis with some missing pieces.

Lying in bed later, trying to read my biography of Queen Isabella, I run the night over in my head. I can't place why I feel so uneasy about Grainger's interest. Why am I not more excited? Maybe I've been so shut down the last few years that I don't know how to, well, just *be*.

Chapter Two

Overnight the storm has painted Westerville white. The first snow of the season is always the best one, full of Christmas nostalgia. Students will be slipping around the sidewalks in their new boots and shrieking at snowballs smashed against their winter jackets.

As I pass through the living room, I see that Dad has brought up from the basement the retro white Christmas tree that we decorate with my nieces and nephew every year. I love our tree-trimming ritual, but it's tinged with sadness now.

In the kitchen, Dad sips coffee and reads the news on his tablet as usual.

"Tree time?" I ask.

"Hm?" He looks up sleepily. "Oh, yep. Tree time. This Saturday work for you? That's when your sister's free."

"Maybe. I don't know, Dad... because your ol' pal Grainger McCluskey asked me out."

"Oh?" Dad sips and feigns disinterest. "That sounds real nice. Going out for dinner?"

I place a piece of multigrain bread in the toaster and shove the lever down. I don't want to let him off so easily. "He didn't say. Maybe you *two* can decide on the venue?" I grab my travel mug and pour steaming coffee into it.

"What are you getting at?" Dad turns, watching me put my lunch together. "He's a catch. I know you think he's handsome."

"Everyone thinks he's hot, Dad. Including Grainger." I smile and face him. "But admit it, you set us up last night."

Dad holds his breath, puffing out his cheeks. His thin gray hair sticks up in a peacock spray at the back. His eyes look left and right, a goofy cartoon reaction. "We needed a fourth player. Mr. Rosenberg is recovering from hip replacement surgery this week."

I narrow my eyes at him and open the fridge to grab the raspberry jam. "I'll call him and change it to Friday. We need to get that tree up."

"Would it be so bad?" he asks timidly. "It makes sense to me. You've known him forever. He's a solid guy, Summer."

"Solid? He's dated everyone in town. I'm probably all that's left."

"Be kind."

This puts a point on it for me. It's something my mom used to say. Whenever we girls would be moody, gossipy, or pessimistic, which was a lot of the time, Mom would say, "Be kind." Such a simple sentiment. But it worked. Still does.

Why not give Grainger a chance? He *was* my first crush and probably the best looking man in all of Ohio, if not the country. The thought of actually kissing him, and anything further, makes me nervous, which may also explain my reticence. Truth is, I haven't had sex in a long time—a ridiculously long time. Between losing mom and moving back into my childhood bedroom, I haven't felt that itch needed scratching. Maybe Grainger is just what the doctor ordered.

Later at the library, my mood remains vaguely optimistic. I hum as I shelve books, safe in my cocoon. I haven't been working at Stoneybrook Middle long, but I went to school here. Some of the teachers are still the same ones who taught me over thirteen years ago. And with my posture corrector, complete with the neck brace in eighth grade, I spent a good bit of time in this library alone.

"Morning!" says an overly chipper Lilia, pushing her way through the double doors. "I made pampushky!"

"Yummy," I say, taking two from her outstretched hands. "Take a seat. Do I have a story for you."

Lilia's face lights up. She loves good gossip, and she'll love this info. She knows Grainger McCloskey. Her snooty cousin dated him briefly in high school.

"Oooh... I don't have time. I gotta meet a parent in five. And I still have to grade a test. Tell me at lunch?"

"Sure."

"Gimme a hint?"

"Two words—Grainger McCloskey."

Lilia's eyes bulge comically. "Shoot! How am I gonna wait until lunch?!" But she totters away with a wave.

I take a bite out of the cherry pastry and turn to my email, immediately noticing the third email in my inbox is from Revel Pointe. The subject heading reads: "Archivist Position, request for interview."

After reading the content of the email quickly and not quite believing it, I reread it out loud, under my breath: "*Dear Ms. York, We were impressed with your resume, especially your work and references at the Cleveland Public Library. We would like to conduct a preliminary phone interview with you as soon as possible. Please respond to this email with your availability. We look forward to hearing from you. Best, Jacob Worley, HR Specialist.*"

I read it three more times. I'm not sure how to react. After inhaling the rest of the pampushky, I pace around the library with my coffee. What the heck is happening these days? Is Mercury in retrograde or something? Grainger, now Revel Pointe?

Eventually I find myself in the folklore and fairy tale section, gazing at the spines of books so familiar to me they feel like friends. *Hansel and Gretel. The Snow Queen. Rose Red. Jack and the Beanstalk. Thumbelina.* I pick up the last one, flip through the text, and pause to study the intricate black-and-white drawings by Vilhelm Pedersen. The tiny, delicate girl who could fit in a flower and fly on the back of a swallow, who almost marries a mole, only to escape just in time and find her match—a prince! What luck! Even as a child, I felt the push and pull of the field mouse's advice to marry. Marriage is a major theme in *Thumbelina*. It's a theme in almost all of them. The prince and princess. Concepts of medieval times and ideals. If I land this position, I would be surrounded by these stories every day.

I've never been to Revel Pointe. Honestly, it's never been a dream destination of mine. The real castles, cathedrals, and lighthouses of Europe are the places I've always hoped to see one day. Why spend money on a theme park castle when you can experience an actual French chateau from the 15th century? But this specific opportunity at Revel Pointe is different. It's a job, and maybe even a stepping stone to the next adventure, maybe even the Bodleian at Oxford. And it's temporary, so it's not like I'm committing to something for the rest of my life.

I place my hands on the shelf in front of me and lean in, like I'm waiting for the voices within to tell me what to do. The first bell of the morning nearly stops my heart.

"Just reply to the damn email," I tell myself.

So I do. Short and simple.

They respond within the hour: *How's 4 pm CST today?* That's five my time. Doable, but my stomach somersaults. Without overthinking, I reply with the school number and the library extension.

Lilia returns at 11:45 with her lunch bag, nearly speed-walking in her pregnant condition.

"All right, Grainger McCloskey. Spill the tea," she demands as we head into my office behind the check-out counter.

I had completely forgotten about him. How small that spot of tea now seems in comparison to the morning's turn of events.

"Oh, right. Grainger asked me out. We're having dinner, I think, on Saturday. Or Friday. But Lilia, I suddenly have bigger news."

Lilia stops midway through opening her yogurt. "How? Who? I mean, what?"

I almost want to laugh at her reaction, but I'm bursting with a buzzy feeling in my body.

"I have an interview with Revel Pointe." I pause. "Today."

Lilia puts her spoon and yogurt down, stands, and raises her hands to her head in utter astonishment. Sharing news like this with someone who cherishes Revel Pointe is so much fun.

"How?" she asks, staring down at me with serious dagger eyes, like I better not be joking.

"Remember when we saw that ad, after the *Camp Willow 3* trailer?"

"Yes."

"And you said I should apply?"

"You did?" Lilia drops her heavy body back down into her chair. "You did! Holy shit!" Lilia almost never swears, but this really means something to her. "*Haspyd*, Nito."

"I know. My head is spinning." I show her the email exchange.

She bites into her turkey sandwich, her hazel eyes still popping. "You will physically get to hold all of the original stuff. The animation cels. The books, the scripts, the notes." Her eyes go even wider. "The Reve family documents..." She trails off, chewing, her eyes glazed over. "I'd die."

Lilia tells me about original memos she's only seen scanned replicas of online. The letters between the founder, Mick Reve and his wife, Marie. The original drawings of Mick's first children's book, *A Ragtime Romp*. The blueprints for Revel Pointe, the park.

"I'd be crying every day—screw that, every hour—with all that Revel history in my hands." Lilia stops speaking; her eyes are watery.

"Don't cry. I don't have the gig yet," I say, bringing us back to reality.

"You'll get it." Lilia grabs my forearm, communicating that I *have* to get it. Then, she waves her hands around, excited in a new way. "All right, let's strategize. *Wish upon a moon and awake anew.*" Lilia writes this Revel motto with my purple pen on a legal pad, then proceeds to give me important background information about the Reve family, the studio, the park. I have a lot to learn, and I want to put my best foot forward in this interview. Eventually the fourth-period bell shakes us out of our mini research prep and pep session. After Lilia wishes me good luck and reluctantly leaves, I'm left with five new Revel tabs open on my laptop and a hastily drawn flowchart of the family members, years, and films.

The afternoon drags, worse than usual. I process new books. I supervise a study group on *The Hobbit* with a small group of eighth graders. After 3 p.m., the school is quiet. The teachers stay to grade or leave immediately on holiday errands. I still have two hours to wait, so I pick up *Thumbelina* again, and get lost in the final details. The tiny lady falls in love at first sight. The prince of the flowers asks her to marry him on the spot and her wedding gift is a set of wings. From the bonds of marriage Thumbelina gains a sort of freedom. What mixed messages these tales contain. Finally, at 5 p.m. on the dot, the library phone rings, and I pick it up. "Stoneybrook Middle School Library. This is Summer."

"Hello, Summer. This is Jacob Worley from Revel Pointe HR. How are you today?"

And the interview begins.

I nailed it, I think on my hazy drive home.

The interview lasted almost forty minutes. Jacob from HR was the sweetest man I ever had the pleasure to talk with in my life. His slight Southern accent lulled me into the best version of myself. I could feel the right words flow from my lips. My supervisors at the Cleveland Public had given glowing reviews. They stressed my reliability and professionalism, saying I was "a joy to work with." He told me they called me "the backbone of the archiving project."

Jacob hadn't quizzed me on my knowledge of the studio or the park. Instead, he asked questions like, "What does family mean to you?" and "Have you ever had consequences for doing the right thing?" and "Do others consider you trustworthy?" *How do you prepare for questions like that?*

I simply answered from the heart. He was interviewing me not particularly as an archivist but as a person, and even across hundreds of miles, I felt seen. It seems like Revel is more concerned with integrity than a list of attributes on a resume.

The only strange part of the interview was when Jacob asked if I ever had experience working for a challenging boss. I asked, "Challenging how?"

And he demurred. "Demanding, exacting, a *task*-oriented person?"

"Task-oriented" is code for asshole. "I work with middle-school students. Nothing scares me."

Jacob laughed and sounded relieved.

What was that about? Lilia mentioned something about one of the Reve brothers, James, being the library's architect. Maybe he's the task-oriented boss Jacob referred to on the call.

Chapter Three

James

Seagulls soar above Revel Pointe as the earthy smell of the Mississippi River wafts over the levee, mixing with the scents of popcorn and beignets. It's just past nine in the morning, and sweat already drips down my torso.

I stand fifty yards into the copse of oaks and survey the new Grand Revel Library, my library, the entire façade and outer work complete. I'm waiting for Marcel, our head contractor, to arrive for our daily walk-through meeting, when a mosquito's high buzz coasts near my ear. From my trusty golf cart, I grab the can of bug spray and give myself a healthy dose of the noxious fumes. Curse this fucking swamp. I can't wait to go home.

"James!" Marcel calls to me, rounding the tower wing. I follow him through the weedy gravel to the loading area.

"How's it going?" he asks.

"I'd be better if it actually felt like December." I don't like small talk, so I let the conversation drop here.

As we hit the concrete pad, I see why he's excited. Our shipment of flooring—dark cherry-finished oak planks—has finally arrived.

"Brilliant," I say, borrowing a box cutter from a worker's tool kit and slicing at the cardboard binding. The planks we ordered are twelve-footers. I pull one out with Marcel's help and angle it up and over to the sunlight. The dark stain is so rich it almost reads black. "Bloody brilliant."

I hear "Bloody brilliant" muttered in a shit British accent behind me. I'm well aware of what some of the local workmen think of me—a rich tosser who micromanages. *Screw them.* If I didn't micromanage, we'd be even more behind schedule. I turn and survey the journeymen coming and going, feeling adrenaline course up my spine and burn my ears.

Fuck them. I have work to do.

"Now, hear me out on the rest of the flooring." Marcel pulls me back to the job at hand. "I've got a whole load of Italian Dyna marble ready in Mississippi. It could be here tomorrow."

We have been waiting on flooring, especially the shipment of Mediterranean Pearl marble for the entrance, rotunda gallery, and fireplace. Yesterday we learned that we won't receive our shipment until mid-January at the earliest. There is no substitute, but Marcel, eager to complete this job, wants us to use a subpar product.

"We had this conversation already," I tell him and head toward the back staircase, looking each worker in the eye. I wipe my brow with a handkerchief. I'm in good shape. I run long and hard every morning, but the sun exhausts me. One would think I'd have adapted some, but I've lived elsewhere most of my life, shipped off to boarding school in New England when I was just eight years old. From there, I was off to jolly Old England. The UK feels like home—gray skies, lush green banks of slow-moving canals, hardly anyone recognizing me. Not to mention the gorgeous stone buildings, centuries old, with actual history worth studying.

In the past few years I've only returned for the funeral of my oldest half-brother, Wade, and the wedding of my other half-brother, Ethan. Tilda, my mother and president of our animation studio, Elixir tried to get me home when Ethan was named interim CEO last year, telling me she needed reinforcements.

"Can you believe your grandfather named that scoundrel CEO over me?" Tilda only called when she needed something. I used to care more, wanting her approbation then hating myself for it. She still can get her claws in me sometimes.

When Dad left her for Yasmin, our housekeeper, Tilda was humiliated, but kept up appearances in public. Only my brother and I saw the wreckage behind the scenes.

"What am I going to do now?" she sobbed as Henri and I hugged her. I was eight. Henri was only six. It was the one time we saw her cry. I often think that single moment is why we still answer her calls and respond to her texts. However, we both rejected being a part of the family business—until PawPaw called.

When Mick Reve asked if I would contribute to the family legacy by accepting the role of lead architect on the Grand Revel Library, I could not say no. It's a career-defining opportunity, and it's *PawPaw*.

This stretch of nearly a year at Revel Pointe has been trying. PawPaw has commissioned this library for a park archive. We began excavation last March, but as so often happens with construction in Louisiana, we are behind schedule and will likely not open on Christmas Eve as planned. Very few people here work to my standards or understand my vision.

Our tower and west wing should make the deadline, as I'm finally walking on subflooring. But the extravagant front loggia and gallery will not be done on time. The Grand Revel Library is designed in the Chateauesque style, inspired by the French chateaux of the Renaissance, but with American touches, like the mansions of industry in Detroit, New York, and Newport at the turn of the 20th century. Of course, our library is raised, five feet to be exact, because of flooding. The main two floors are lined with cedar planks, painted a natural stone cream to mimic the stone of Paris' Haussmann buildings. The attics and Flemish dormers are cedar shake, a smoky blue-gray. By far, my favorite element of the entire building is the round clock tower of the east wing, which pierces the oak canopy and will be seen in the skyline from most of the park. *How's that for a legacy?*

Cricket Sugarman, our lead interior designer, is also behind because *we* are behind. She's been purchasing furniture and working with skilled carpenters on the built-in shelving and desks, but she keeps telling us she needs finished walls and floors to get going. Imagine that. Yesterday, she sided with Marcel, actually suggesting faux-marble, as in painting the floor and fireplace, which I thought was a joke.

From the front steps, I text Cricket: *Meet me at the cafe. Dying in heat. Need cold caffeine.*

She responds immediately with a thumbs up emoji.

When it's inconvenient to talk on site, we've been meeting in the air conditioned French Village cafe, La Tortue Bleue—the blue turtle. I run my hands through my longish hair, damp at the neck, and hop in my park golf cart. In London I walk everywhere, but here at Revel the golf cart is my best mate. I speed ten miles an hour down the oak-lined drive and into the early traffic of tourists on the park pathways that circle the signature lighthouse.

I do love the buttery smells that permeate the French Village, which is modeled on one of those picturesque hamlets with the cobblestone walkways and vines blooming everywhere. Though the goal is verisimilitude, the differences are glaring. The bright-green geckos scuttling up the wall, the park signs and paved pathways, the explosive tropical foliage—none of this is authentic French. There are two wide fountains, souvenir shops, an ice cream parlor, a chocolatier, and several boulangeries and cafes. But despite the out-of-place decor, I like La Tortue Bleue for its side garden and delicious coffee.

Cricket and I walk up at the same moment. She's an attractive, curvy woman who has a uniquely American style. Today she's wearing a '50s number, printed with palm trees and sailboats, and chunky orange heels. Her hair is swept up in a twist, and her full-sleeve tattoos are on display.

"Bonjour," I greet her, opening the door.

"Back atcha, Jimmy," she says and heads through.

I like Cricket, though I hate her nickname for me. We've become friends despite my open reluctance to make new ones. Cricket is silly, almost to a fault sometimes. Born and raised in Algiers Point, she now lives here in St. Bernard Parish with her mother and eight-year-old son, Charlie. She's in her mid-thirties but seems younger. She spent a year interning at a design firm in Liverpool, so we share a love of football—real football, not the American version. She's a Reds fan, and my team is Chelsea, but I don't hold it against her.

"You smell like a whole Boy Scout troop," Crickets tells me.

"You don't enjoy my Southern musk?"

"It's a bit much."

At the counter, she makes small talk and asks if I've seen the tea room remodel at the Beau Chêne Resort yet. I haven't.

"Yellow roses," she says, gesturing with a sweeping hand to indicate the idea of "everywhere."

"Sounds positively provincial," I say and order for us both. "Where's the tea room at the resort?" She knows Revel Pointe better than I do, having worked here three years.

"You're useless," she jokes, swatting at my arm. "How could I forget you're essentially a foreigner with that accent?"

"I don't have an accent."

"Oh, no?" She turns her nose up. "Positively provincial. You sound like Cary Grant."

"I sound like a girl?"

"Useless." She rolls her eyes dramatically.

At the table, over iced French roast, we look over the week's schedule. On her tablet, she points to the central rotunda, which has two sets of open interior balconies that wrap almost completely around, with a vaulted, domed ceiling above.

"My ceiling artists are ready, but we need cooler weather. That, or A/C. And we've got to wait for the custom woodworking on the railings to be finished. All that dust needs to settle for at least two days, or so they tell me." Cricket's manicured fingers tap and spread to zoom into the blueprint. "When will that be done?" She points.

"Off the top of my head? Three weeks?" The balusters are all hardwood cypress, hand carved at newel posts. We haven't started the installation phase, and I'm not sure how much they've finished off site, what with sanding, staining, varnishing. I mention the marble again.

Cricket throws out some other real stone options. "Cream Travertine? Polished beige Marfil?" She shows me some photos.

"It's not going to work." I cross my arms, sit back in my seat, and look up at the cafe ceiling, thinking. I cringe at the plastic ceiling fans. Necessary on the bayou. Impossible to find in France. I wish someone else here valued authenticity and history.

"I'm going to do some calling around." I text Lucien, my assistant, to get me phone appointments with two of my contacts as soon as humanly possible.

"There's gotta be other distributors," Cricket suggests. "For expediency."

"Maybe," I say. "But you can start shelf installation in the west and tower wings," I tell her. "The hardwoods will start today."

She claps her hands, then grabs my forearm and bows to me. "Thank you," she whispers, huskily.

I pull away. She's too demonstrative.

"Oh geez," Cricket pokes my bicep. "Are *they* watching?" She mocks again, searching the cafe, referring to the time I pulled away from one of her overly exuberant hugs on-site. I had told her it was inappropriate for work colleagues and that tourists hover and watch us Reves like vultures. There's a fan website devoted to our personal lives, for fuck's sake. Cricket chortled in my face.

"Oh, piss off," I say, embarrassed. She puts a hand on my shoulder, and I have to let her keep it there, to save face. "Come on, then. Back to work," I say, grateful to get out of this uncomfortable corner I've painted myself into.

"Tally ho," she says and follows me.

I give her a look, and she relents. "Sorry, last one."

"I don't believe you," I say, rounding the bend to my cart.

"Pip, pip! Tutt, tutt!" she says, hopping into the passenger seat.

The pathway to the library is not far, and I anticipate the impressive sight on the drive. The way winds gently between the great trees, but the library is visible, bit by bit. Its light façade and filigree flashing hints beyond oak branches that twist and dip, some of them almost to the ground. Cricket is in the middle of describing the new crystal knobs she's picked out for the drawers and how they'll match the chandeliers when I notice another golf cart zooming towards us. Before I realize who's in the driver's seat, the cart veers left, crossing and blocking the path. It's my mother.

"You are just the people I need," Tilda says and steps out from the passenger seat, with Lucien hanging behind the wheel. Even on a casual day, my mother insists on four-inch Louboutins, and today's pair are mauve. The heels put her over six feet. She's lean with almost platinum hair. Today she's more relaxed, in fitted white ankle pants and a black silk tank tucked into a mauve belt that matches the shoes.

To say that she is not maternal is an understatement. She mothers from afar, sending us luxury watches, cars, and trips for birthdays, insisting on short destination holidays, like five nights in Capri for Christmas, or a weekend in New York. Otherwise, we don't see her much—not since she sent us away as children. Just the requisite monthly phone call. My father is vaguely interested in us, which isn't saying much, but he's been more attentive since we lost Wade and he had a stroke. I rarely see him these days as he's busy convalescing on the boat with Yasmin.

"To what do we owe the pleasure?" I ask, parking and stepping out of the golf cart.

"I need a date," Tilda says. Her upright posture doesn't change. She doesn't even squint in the dappled sunlight.

"I'm sure there are many lovely men your age...."

"Hush." She swats at me and then examines the library. "This is a beautiful building, James, but it needs to be finished."

"I know. I'm working on it." I acknowledge Cricket. "We're working on it."

"As I said, I need a date." Tilda pauses, displeased. "The gala is less than a month away."

"We've had a few hiccups," I begin, but she holds up her hand.

"And this section of the park has been closed since May. It's dirty and loud—"

"You can open Mick and Marie's Cabin and the Cajun Log Flume on Friday. We won't need access for big machinery once the landscaping is complete."

Mother looks pleased. "Good. But the Fête Noël gala *will* happen in the library. Christmas Eve." She checks her Cartier watch, encircled in diamonds. "Do what you have to do to get that done, James. It's the 60th anniversary of Revel Pointe and your grandfather's ninety-fifth birthday, not to mention our *Camp Willow Creek 3* premiere." Her voice doesn't rise. She doesn't freak out. It's just a matter-of-fact directive.

"Yes, sir," I tease. Being under someone's thumb doesn't suit me.

She makes a snarling face at me and gets back in her cart.

"Also, it's time you start talking to the press," she says, changing the subject.

"Can't someone else?" I protest.

"No, you're the architect. The man of the hour. Time for you to shine!" Her chipper voice grates, but not as much as knowing she's right. "Oh, and you'll be my date to the Fête. I want to introduce you to some important people." She slides her sunglasses back on to make it final.

"You make me sound like a debutante," I say.

"In a way, you are, darlin," she calls to me as the golf cart speeds away.

Chapter Four

James

The next day, I take a private flight to Quebec City. After making a few calls and scouring the internet, Lucien located a small cache of Mediterranean Pearl marble for our central gallery. Finishing this project on time is paramount. It's a four-hour flight in my father's Gulfstream, *Mona 2*, so I sit back, enjoy a glass of bourbon, and watch a recorded Chelsea match I missed.

Lucien has arranged a car and a fixer to greet me at the airport. Léo is warm and meets me with a firm handshake.

"*Salut*," he says. "Welcome to Quebec."

I thank him and sit up front. As Léo careens onto the highway, I'm happy to be on the move again. Quebec is covered in snow, most of it gray and crusty along the highway, but it's a welcome change of scenery.

"You know the place we're headed?" I ask Léo.

"Yes, a small town west of the city. No more than an hour."

I start to relax when Tilda texts me: *I hear you're in Canada. Hurry back. LA Times journalist will be on site tomorrow.* I can almost hear her tapping her Cartier watch.

When we veer off the highway, the countryside turns into a vintage postcard. White snow covers rolling hills and massive bare trees. Barns and church spires dot the landscape. Restaurants and town halls are decorated with evergreen wreaths and red ribbons. It's what Christmas is supposed to be. The only thing missing is a beautiful woman by my side.

I've always been happy alone. Hell, I was practically trained for solitary life. I've had a few relationships but never felt compelled to commit. The women know who I am, or find out pretty quickly, and I can't trust that their interest is pure. After a few months of trying to discern sincerity, I run, calling them from a hotel room in Istanbul, or on a train to Vienna, to break it off. It's never my intention to be callous, but it's cleaner, less messy. Da Vinci once said, "Life without love is no life at all." Da Vinci, in my humble opinion, was full of shit. A life without love is a less complicated one. Still, I am a man with needs, physical and otherwise.

L&C Granite is a massive yard and warehouse in a town called Petit Ruisseau. Finally, the pearl stone is in front of me, and it's luminous. I sweep my hand alongside the outer slab and note its balanced tone. Up close, there are mushroom-colored veins and tiny flecks of white iridescent pearl.

"I'll take it all," I tell the owner. "When can it be in Louisiana?"

After some fierce negotiation, I emerge from the warehouse with Léo. It's late in the afternoon, dark and snowing. The lights of Petit Ruisseau glow. I'd love to find a quaint restaurant, eat some local food, and enjoy the serenity of this wintry countryside. But as if tethered by an invisible chain, Lucien rings me.

"Your mum's up my arse with this *LA Times* article, mate." Lucien's voice in my ear sounds discordant in this snowy environment. "Get back here ASAP. For my sake."

On the way back to the city, I check my email. Tilda has sent me links to articles by *LA Times* reporter Reya Ghu, with the subject heading "LA Times media prep." I click them for distraction and read the headlines: "Revel Cruise Line to Disrupt Island Ecosystem," "What Revel Is Hiding in The Seven Wonders," "Revel Management Under Scrutiny." Ms. Ghu is not a fan; Tilda must hope the library will woo her. As I tuck into the most recent article, criticizing the studio's recent penchant for cashing in on sequels, my phone buzzes. It's the lead attendant of the flight crew.

"We're grounded for the night, sir. Bad weather."

"Thank you for letting me know," I say, secretly relieved for this perfect chilly respite. Maybe I can find some sexy Québécois to keep me warm overnight.

Chapter Five

Summer

It's Saturday, tree-trimming time with my sister, nieces, and nephew, and I still haven't told Dad that I'm leaving for Revel Pointe tomorrow morning. And that I'll be gone for the rest of the month.

To avoid breakfast with Dad, I sleep in and then go for a long, cold bike ride. My lungs burn in the freezing air at first, but I adjust. My mind is a shiny pinball in an arcade machine. A day after the interview with Mr. Worley, I was offered the position. HR said they needed to "expedite the process due to some staffing issues" and gave me two flight options. I called Lilia, who told me to "ride the destiny wave." Again, without thinking too long or hard, I chose Sunday morning with a Monday morning face-to-face interview, and now I'm starting to panic.

I am taking all of my sick and personal days for this temporary position. The principal was not thrilled, but she understands this was a great opportunity for me. Plus, I found some great parent volunteers to sub the rest of the semester.

I busy myself with methodically packing, as quietly as possible, and preparing a lasagna for dinner, all the while trying to find words for my dad. *I'm leaving you alone for the rest of the month, the month you miss Mom the most.*

My sister Kayla's SUV pulls into the driveway. I'm anticipating a noisy living room when she enters with my loveable nieces and nephew, but all is silent.

"Where are the kids?" I ask Kayla as she takes off her parka.

"Vicky's babysitting. Emma has volleyball." My sister looks up at me with a tired smile. "And Brody's at hockey with Clark. It's just me today." She's eight years older than me, a blonde instead of a brunette, but with the same deep-amber eyes.

"You are more than enough," I tell Kayla. Her girls are tweens, more interested in their friends than us now. Dad looks disappointed as he emerges from the basement with two boxes of ornaments, his thick gray hair sticking up with static electricity.

"It's almost like the old days," Dad says.

No one mentions Mom. To avoid veering into sad reminiscing, I pick a playlist with our favorite Christmas music. Mariah Carey's voice changes the mood.

"What do the girls want for Christmas this year?" I ask Kayla.

"What *don't* they want?" she asks. "Honestly, you can't go wrong with gift cards these days."

"That's no fun," I say. I sometimes long for their cuter, younger, less cool days.

We get straight to the worst job—checking and untangling the string lights. The tree goes up in the corner, but none of us can reach the top without a ladder, as we're all munchkins. Even Dad is a small man at five-foot-six.

Opening the first ornament box and picking up my favorite, an antique bulb with faded script, I think this is actually the perfect time to talk to Dad. Kayla will get him to see the bright side of this Revel Pointe opportunity. She'll spin it into the exciting windfall it is and not me leaving him.

The front doorbell rings as I return from the garage, struggling with the ladder in the hallway. As Dad opens the door, I hear him before I see him. Grainger.

"Mitch! How are ya?"

Shoot! With all the Revel Pointe drama, I'd completely forgotten about him. Now here's Grainger McCloskey, standing in our living room, handsome as a superhero, ready to take me out. I look down at my faded yoga pants, oversized flannel, and mismatched socks. My hair is up in a messy bun, and I'm straining awkwardly with a ladder.

"Here, let me help you with that." Grainger comes to my rescue, easily grabbing the ladder and propping it next to him. He eyes me up and down, clearly confused. "I'm early?" he asks, scratching his perfectly grown out stubble.

"I'm sorry," I tell him. "I meant to call you and switch the night, but something came up this week, and I forgot." I sound like an idiot. "I'm *really* sorry."

Grainger peeks across the living room to the half-decorated tree and gets the picture that he's being rejected for a night in with my dad and sister. Probably a first for him. All four of us stand there, saying nothing.

"It's no big deal," Grainger finally says, slipping out of his boots. "We were just going to The Clean Slate in town. I can help with the tree while you shower."

Kayla sneaks me a look, her eyes wide, her tongue poking and stretching her cheek, so obvious and obscene. I want to pinch her hard.

"But I made lasagna," I say.

Kayla stifles a laugh. Grainger looks even more confused.

"I mean, it's a family tradition." I try to regain my wits, but his eyes search my face, incredulous at this turn of events. I stumble and end up saying, "But, so there's, like, more than enough for you to stay, I mean, if you'd like to." I am an asshole, a bumbling asshole.

Grainger doesn't know what to do with this invite. It's clearly not what he had in mind. He looks to my dad for approval.

"Stay. You can put the angel on without a ladder," Dad says.

"All right then." Grainger shrugs out of his jacket and pushes up his sleeves. A good sport.

"I'll be right back," I say and head toward my bedroom with Kayla not far behind. I look at myself in the mirror above my

Victorian vanity and wince. Kayla flops on my bed, mouth open in shock. It feels like we've gone back in time, except I used to be the one flopping on her bed and watching while she got ready for dances and dates.

"Summer Heather." Kayla sounds like my mom, putting on her Midwestern accent. "Spill the beans, girl. Are you riding the Grainger train?"

"What? Ew, no." I shake my hair loose and try to calm it down. "He asked me out this week. I think Dad put him up to it."

"I doubt that." Kayla says. "Have you seen yourself these days?"

"What are you talking about?" All I see in the mirror is a harried mess.

As I brush my hair and change into a V-neck tee, I fill her in. The bicycle rescue. The poker game. The phone interview with Revel Pointe. The fact that I have a plane ticket to leave in the freaking morning and how I still haven't told Dad.

"Honestly, I don't know how all of this happened in one week. Especially *this*." I point my thumb in the direction of the living room, meaning Grainger McCloskey.

"You're a smoke show, and he noticed. Obviously," Kayla says.

"Smoke show? You're a weirdo." I change my shirt again, not wanting to expose too much skin.

"Here." Kayla hands me a red sweater from my closet. "Put this on."

I apply mascara and lip gloss and step back to assess. Definitely not a smoke show, but presentable.

"One, you will definitely go to Louisiana in the morning. No question. I will be sure to spend more time with Dad. Gran will, too. It'll be fine. You'll get the position, and it's not like it's forever. It's temporary."

I nod at her through the reflection. We have the same heart-shaped face, our chins a touch pointy, except her expression is resolved.

"Second, you should go out tonight with Grainger after this, have a drink, relax, and get boned."

I gasp at her, again in the mirror. "Jesus, Kay."

"Hear me out." She kneels on my bed, loving this. "You're all wound up. Look at you."

I brush my hair into a neat ponytail and glance back at my sister. "I'm not having sex with him."

"Why not? God, he's like sex on a stick."

"Kay!" I whisper-yell at her.

"Think about it. A few glasses of wine, a foot massage. Bing, bam, boom. And you're leaving tomorrow with a pep in your step."

"That's not me," I say. *It's so not me.*

"Damn shame."

"He's slept with half—no, more than half of the women in town."

"So he's probably good at it. All that practice."

"Nope. Not doing it. And stop being so gross." I turn to head back down the hall. "Or I'll pinch you." It's something I used to do as a toddler, pinch with my sharp little nails.

"Don't you dare!" Kayla runs past me as I chase her, pretending my fingers are pincers.

The rest of the evening isn't a complete disaster. Having Grainger around keeps us three from falling into sad nostalgia. We string the lights in record time thanks to Grainger's height. Kayla opens a bottle of Beaujolais and gives me a wink as she passes a generous pour to me. She does the same to Grainger, thinking I haven't noticed. I put the lasagna in the oven, and in the hour that it cooks, we finish trimming the tree with garland, ornaments, and tinsel. I get a snapshot of what life would be like with Grainger around, and it's not terrible. He finds ways to give me attention—touching my arm, telling me I smell nice—and by dinner, I'm calmer around him. I'm also a little tipsy, laughing easily, nearly forgetting the extremely pressing information I have to tell Dad, and also now, Grainger.

We stand back from the tree, admiring our work, the warm, multicolored glow imbuing the living room with Christmas.

"Cheers!" Kayla says and lifts her glass.

We all clink wine glasses, and Grainger slips his arm around my shoulders, squeezing me against him. I let it happen, smelling his woodsy scent, and then twist away, heading for the kitchen.

As we take our first bites of dinner, Kayla can't help herself. She's been making faces, urging me to bring up my Revel Pointe news, but I haven't found the right moment.

"Our little Summer has some amazing news." Kayla takes a huge bite, filling her mouth, handing the conversation over to me.

Dad's eyes brighten, intently searching my face.

Grainger slides a hand on my knee casually, like he did at the poker game, like we're already a couple, and in the middle of chewing asks, "Oh, yeah? What news?"

I pull my long ponytail over my shoulder and stall. "Well," I say, putting down my fork and taking another gulp of wine. "I had a phone interview with Revel Pointe this week...."

"Revel Pointe!?" My dad is excited. He loves their old films, especially that "zany Safari one."

"Yep, Revel Pointe." I use his enthusiasm as a springboard and keep going. "It's a temporary position, only three weeks, and I-I start on Monday."

"*This* Monday?" Grainger asks.

"This is amazing news," Dad says over Grainger. "How? When did this happen? I mean, what's the position?"

I feel like I'm floating inches above my chair as I relay the details. "I have a flight in the morning."

"Tomorrow?" Grainger asks.

I nod, checking my dad's reaction.

"Were you just going to sneak off after breakfast?" Dad asks, frowning.

"I don't know. I was afraid it might upset you?"

"Upset me? I'm thrilled for you! I've been praying for a big opportunity for you, Summer. I never asked for something so impressive, but I'm just so happy for you." Dad gets up from the table and comes around to give me a bear hug.

"It's only temporary," I say, pulling away.

"That's true," Grainger says, sounding far off in his thoughts.

"You'll shine like you always do," Kayla says, beaming.

"You're a hard worker, Summer," Dad says, returning to his seat. "And so smart. They'll see that and want to steal you away. I know it."

Grainger is quiet. He doesn't know me that well, hasn't seen the side of me that's a self starter, the part of me that makes ideas come to life, doesn't know my attention to detail, my meticulous work ethic.

The rest of dinner is filled with talk of Revel Pointe—their movies and characters, the park, the history. My stomach flutters with anticipation as my family's support gives me the boost I needed. I find it hard to eat and get lightheaded as the wine flows. When dinner is over, I stand, grabbing dishes to bring them to the sink, and realize I'm quite tipsy.

"Well, I should get going then," Grainger says "You've got an early morning, unless you want to go out for another drink?" His eyes focus on my lips.

"I really shouldn't."

He looks dejected, but turns to say goodbye. "Well, thanks for dinner and including me in your family tradition." He shakes my dad's hand firmly.

"Anytime," Dad says. "I miss having you around, son."

I stiffen at this language, though I know my dad's just feeling the good vibes and the wine. I've heard him call Grainger 'son' before, as Dad never had one of his own, and they worked so closely together all those years at the boat shop.

"Walk me out?" Grainger turns to me. I'm feeling the vibes too, so I tuck myself into my parka and follow him out into the windy night.

"Feels like another storm," I say.

"They say we're gonna get a foot of snow overnight."

I feel so out of my comfort zone now, indulging Grainger, knowing I'm walking right into a goodbye-kiss scenario. Maybe it's the merry mood, maybe it's my sister's pep talk, but I'm suddenly willing and anxiously anticipating a kiss, standing next to his oversized truck, looking up into his royal blue eyes.

"Thanks for understanding...about the date," I say. "I had so much on my mind, and I was so nervous to tell my dad."

"I get it," he says, slipping a hand into my open jacket and grabbing my waist. "Well, raincheck, for when you get back?"

He leans down to kiss me on the lips, as I tip my head way back. He's a skilled kisser. It's soft and sweet, and it's been so long since I've been kissed by anyone that I feel flustered.

He pulls back and looks at me seriously. "When did you become the hottest girl in Westerville, Summer?"

I'm not sure how I feel about this, but before I can figure it out, his mouth is on mine again. I think it's going to be the same soft touch, but this time his mouth is wide open, prying mine open with his tongue, digging deep and fast. It's too much tongue too fast. After a few moments, I pull away as politely as possible.

I don't know what to say, so I step back, say nothing and wave.

"See you when you get back, gorgeous," Grainger says with a satisfied grin.

"Sure thing." I nod. What just transpired?

With his truck reversing out of the driveway, I race back inside, wiping my face with the back of my hand and ignoring my sister's gaze.

"Well, that was an unusual turn of events," Kayla says, curled up on the sofa, her phone in hand. "I'm staying the night. I've had too much to drink."

"Yeah, thanks for that," I say, slumping down next to her, my head buzzing.

"You're welcome," Kayla says and switches on the TV. "Let's watch an old Revel movie."

Dad loves this idea and searches the streaming services. "Here," he says, clicking on *The Mouse Queen*, Revel's TV special, a rendition of *The Nutcracker* in stop-motion animation. "It's basically research." He gives me a wink.

I love him for this. Even though I have an early morning, I savor this relaxed evening with my dad and sister, knowing they have my back.

Chapter Six

James

My phone stirs me out of a deep sleep. It's the pilot of the *Mona 2*.

"Sorry to wake you, sir, but we've got a short window on weather. If we leave before eight, we could make it back today. Otherwise, we're grounded."

"Thanks," I say, swinging my legs over the side of the bed. I tell him I'll be there as soon as possible, and head to the window for a pre-dawn view of the St. Lawrence River. Everything is covered in snow, which glows blue under the street lamps. Last night, I checked myself into the Chateau Frontenac, a landmark hotel built in 1893 on a two-hundred-foot plateau, in the same Chateauesque style as my library. Instead of searching for companionship, I fell asleep reviewing schematics on my laptop. Turns out working like a beast without a break has its downsides.

The weather is shit, so I arrive at the airport a few minutes late. Once in the air, I stare out the window at the angry gray sky, daydreaming about the next job. If I'm lucky, it will be an art institute and gallery in a county outside Edinburgh–part abbey restoration, part contemporary building. I've been sketching in the little downtime I've had, knowing that the bidding on that project will start next spring. I just have to get through the next month, and then I can go back to my real life.

About an hour into the flight, the plane swings hard to the right. A cracking sound somewhere up front startles all of us. Within minutes, I feel the plane descending and banking right even more, the cabin rattling all the while. Eventually we are below the clouds, in snowfall, and I can faintly see the earth below between gusts.

The pilot breaks over the speakers. "Attention Mr. Reve and crew. This system is getting nasty. We've been cleared to land in roughly 25 minutes at Columbus, Ohio, John Glenn International. Please stay buckled in your seats. Looks like continued gusts and turbulence until we touch down. Hold tight."

What feels like four days later, the ground smashes into us as the *Mona 2* hits the tarmac. We taxi to a gate, and I get the feeling this will be a much longer day than anticipated.

This Midwestern airport is engulfed in snow. It's miserable in the private jet terminal. There's no food, but there is mediocre coffee and a bar cart. I make myself an Irish whiskey and notice my hands shaking as I pour. As if sensing a moment of weakness, my mother calls.

"Good morning." I lean into a corner in an attempt for some privacy.

"When can you make it back?" Tilda asks. So much for motherly concern.

"Ask the weather gods, Tilda."

"Don't be petulant." She pauses, and I can hear keyboard clicks in the background. "Reya Ghu is here now, but she leaves tomorrow evening."

"I don't know what to tell you. I'm sitting in a snowstorm."

"All right, check in with Lucien as soon as you can."

I have nothing else to say to her, so there's a dead moment where I hear her heels clicking wherever she is.

"And James, for the article, don't drone on about the library building itself," she directs. "Sell the personal angle, the family story."

"And you think I'm the best person for this because...?"

"Because you are the architect, and it's time for you to talk to the media."

I say nothing. She knows this is a touchy subject.

She continues, undeterred. "This library project is a money pit, a tax write-off, so play up the goodwill. Revel's scholarships, its contribution to American cinema, its history of shaping culture...." She pauses, clearly in the middle of something, then continues to lecture me. "You have an opportunity here, James, to take a leadership role. It's been almost two years since your father went on medical leave. And despite everything I've done, the sacrifices I've made...." Her voice seethes with bitterness for just a moment, then turns matter-of-fact again. "So if it's to be between Ethan and you, I would prefer that my own flesh and blood step up."

"I'll talk nice to Ms. Ghu, but I'm leaving after the gala. Don't waste your breath on the leadership lecture again."

There's silence, then she says, barely audible, "I need *someone* in my corner, James."

I sigh. I don't want this conversation to continue down the well-worn path of how she's done so much for this company and all she asks in return is our support. She's still sore about losing a second cruise line last year, and she'd rather be developing another money-making sequel with Elixir, the 3D animation studio, than working on PawPaw's legacy library. Maybe this is her way of atoning for last year's debacle.

"Let's touch base later," Tilda says, hanging up before I can reply.

Her sudden interest in my place at Revel Pointe is suspect. In public, she gushed about Henri and me, her "Pride and Joy," but in private, we were meant to be seen, not heard.

Unfortunately for her, I wasn't always this quiet. After the divorce, I began to act out. Getting in fights at school, throwing wicked public tantrums. One terrible day, she took us to an event to promote the opening of Elixir. While Tilda was distracted, an opportunistic reporter asked me some questions about how our "poor mom" was holding up. I reacted...badly. I went after the son of a bitch, screaming. Even though I was a child, the press was bad.

There were op-eds about "children of divorce" and "the consequences of single mothering." Tilda was painted as a wayward parent, a career-driven monster, and it was decided that I was too emotional, too overwrought for public consumption. The very next week I was on a plane to New England. *Lesson learned*, I think, as I take another drink of my Irish coffee.

Nearly three hours later, the snow lets up a little and a mechanic enters our purgatory to chat with the *Mona 2* pilots.

"We've got a cracked propellor blade," the older pilot tells me and the two flight attendants. "This will need repair, probably a new blade. We won't be flying today."

Earlier, I didn't want to get back to Louisiana. Now I'm dying to leave this room. I get Lucien on the phone, asking him to help find me another way back to New Orleans. Eventually, he texts me a ticket: Delta Flight #9620, depart 2:10 pm, 1 stop ATL, depart 6 pm.

This is cutting close–2:10 pm is only an hour from now. As I push out into the still-raging storm to cross the parking lot to the commercial terminal, I realize I may have had one too many drinks.

Chapter Seven

Summer

It's dark again, Sunday evening now, by the time the ticket agent announces we will begin pre-boarding. I've spent the entire day at the airport, feeling exhausted with two flights still ahead of me.

Finally, the snow has subsided, the plane has been de-iced, and all the passengers are lining up in an orderly fashion, which reminds me of school, where I will not be tomorrow.

I'm a little nervous. I haven't flown in four years, since before Mom died, when we set off to visit my aunt and uncle in San Antonio. I'm looking for the seat numbers, excited that my 11A means Economy Comfort, a step between First Class and the rest.

After stowing my luggage, I take my window seat and wait, holding my biography of Queen Isabella in my lap. I close my eyes and take a deep breath, trying to relax after this tedious day. *Soon we'll be in the air*, I tell myself.

I feel my seat jostle and open my eyes to a striking man lifting a bag above my row. With his arms stretched overhead, I get a glimpse of his taut abdomen. He's bearded with longish, wavy, dark hair, and light, inviting eyes.

"Hello," he says. "I'm 11B."

"Hi. I'm 11A."

As he sits, I get a quick whiff of leather and whiskey. I watch from the corner of my eye as he sorts himself out, removing his jacket, sticking his phone in the seat pocket, adjusting the seat belt. His hands are tanned. His thighs stretch his well-worn, faded black jeans, giving the impression of lean muscle underneath. He's elegant, suave even, but with just enough of an untamed quality to make him the absolute sexiest man I've ever laid eyes on.

I can't imagine instigating a conversation with this intimidating person, so I just sit back and take in another breath, smelling hints of amber this time. I'm surprised when he initiates a conversation.

"Queen Isabella of Castille?" he asks, pointing to the book.

"Isabella of France. She was the Queen of England for a short time," I tell him. "In the fourteenth century."

"I live in the UK," he says, and I can hear a bit of British in his accent. He leans in, the perfume of alcohol more evident. "I should know this."

"Well, she was a princess of France and overthrew the king, Edward the Second," I say, and then hand him the book for some reason. "I just started reading it."

"Sounds scandalous," he says, studying the front and back.

"The medieval era was very scandalous. And treacherous."

"Yeah, just a touch of blood and plague," he slurs with a smirk.

"A few betrayals and beheadings."

"Now, just how scandalous are we talking?" Sir Sexy presses his head into the plane chair and rolls his head toward me conspiratorially. "Did she *kill* the King?"

His intense hazel-green eyes flummox me. *Is he flirting? With me?*

"I don't know yet. It says she was betrothed at twelve."

"Criminal." He hands the book back to me. Our fingers touch for a half second.

"It should have been," I say, wondering if I'm killing the light mood.

The flight attendants interrupt us. My seatmate goes quiet and closes his eyes, which is good, because I like to pay attention to the safety instructions. After the oxygen mask demo, I watch him out of the corner of my eye. He fidgets, spreading his legs, but when his knee brushes mine, he tightens up his posture again. He stifles a yawn as the plane maneuvers the taxiways. He looks at ease with his eyes closed and head back, but my nerves are ramping up. Man, I don't like flying.

"Do you like to read?" The question comes flying out of my mouth, a little too loud, and 11B opens his eyes.

"When I have time." He gives me a quick look and brushes something invisible off his pants.

The plane taxis into the runway, and even though I'm sure everything is going to be fine because thousands of people fly safely every day, I grip the armrests. There are exponentially more car accidents daily than there are plane crashes yearly, I remind myself, but tell that to my racing heart. Sweat collects in my armpits. My palms clam up.

As the plane magically lifts off the tarmac, I can't stop myself from asking the hot guy, "Do you like biographies?"

Chapter Eight

James

Oh, Christ, I think. Here we go. Under any other circumstances, I would love to chat up this gorgeous woman, but now I long for silence as I attempt to sober up and quell my nerves.

"Biographies? Yeah, sometimes," I reply out of politeness.

"I live for the Renaissance," she says. "And the medieval period. I'll read anything set before 1700."

A quick image of her in an embroidered corset flashes through my mind. "Hm...the Middle Ages, yeah—"

"Where do you live in England?" the girl breaks in, her voice fluctuating wildly as the plane catches a gust of air.

"London."

"Really? That's cool. Everything in Ohio is less than two hundred years old. Even an older building, like what used to be the train station, has been repurposed over and over again. It was a gift shop for years, then abandoned, and now it's a restaurant."

"Mmm-hmm" is all I manage as I rub my eyes.

"People think that new and modern is best, but that's not always the case. Give me a drafty old castle over a glass skyscraper any day of the week. You know, some people have a fear of old things, or antiques, specifically. I forget what that's called." She smiles, which lights up her eyes, rimmed with long, dark lashes. I now notice they're a deep cognac color.

"I think a modern skyscraper is basically an ant colony for humans," she goes on. "*That* gives me the creeps. You know, the view from a medieval castle might not be as high, but it can be vast, right? Have you been to a castle? I've always wanted to see this 13th century castle in the Scottish Highlands. Eilean Donan Castle. Have you heard of it?"

Here she finally pauses for my answer.

"I haven't."

"Well, it's in the middle of a loch. Stunning in photos. I mean, the ramparts alone. You can't feel the wind whip through your hair in a skyscraper, can you? Give me ramparts for days." She twirls the tassel of her bookmark in her fingers, and finally, in my drunken haze, I get what's happening. She's nervous about flying.

"I completely agree." I smile at her, now feeling like a fellow soldier-at-arms.

"And I love a good turret," she says, as the plane dips on a pocket of air. "A sweeping stone staircase. Long galleries with echoing wood floors."

Part of me wants to listen to this intriguing woman to see what she comes up with next, and another part of me wants to lean in and silence her with a kiss. I decide to exercise contemporary chivalry and distract her with more conversation.

"Sounds like you've been there already," I say, leaning into my seat, nodding toward her, catching her eyes again. "In a drafty old castle."

"In another life, I was." She tugs on her seatbelt. "You know, if I believed in past lives, I'd say I was a favorite lady's maid. Not a princess, or duchess, or someone so elevated. But I can't imagine serfdom, or maybe I just don't want to picture it, toiling away in a field all my life in a cold hut with ten children at my heels." She pauses and breathes deeply through her nose. "Anyway, I'd love to visit the castle in person."

"A lady's maid, huh?" I ask. "Are you good with secrets?"

"I am." She tucks a lock of hair behind her ear, sheepishly. "I'm normally pretty quiet."

"Is that so?" I smile as the plane seems to level off. I don't know if it's the wistfulness in her voice or her waxing poetic about castles that resonates like a church bell in me, but I want to be closer to her. "When this plane lands in Atlanta, we should change our tickets. Get on the next flight to Edinburgh."

My seatmate's smile relaxes her face in a way that showcases her beauty. Her cheekbones round. Slight freckles dapple her nose. Her eyes squint as she almost laughs in reply. She nods toward me, too. "If we must, we must." Now her voice is low and flirty.

"You must see Eilean Donan Castle, good maiden," I tell her, donning my best period drama accent with a touch of Scot. "It would be a crime to keep you from it a day longer." I've never been into role play, but I am willing to play with her.

"Make haste, Sir...." She trails off, not knowing my name.

"James."

"Sir James." In the dim light, I can still see her blush.

"And may I have your name?" I lean in, wanting her more and more.

"Summer," she says. Who sent this intelligent, beautiful woman with an appreciation for the past that rivals my own to this particular seat on this specific plane during a historic snowfall?

"A name fit for royalty," I say, and offer her a lingering handshake in row eleven.

Chapter Nine

Summer

I love a good turret? It's the phrase that repeats in my head as James miraculously keeps chatting with me. *I love a good turret. Real slick, York.*

The beverage service comes through, and despite my better judgment, I order wine. So much for what I had planned for this flight—quiet reading, calm preparation, hydration. It's so unlike me to go off-script, but James' playful smile and deep voice like a purring lion have my full attention.

In the glow of the overhead lights, his green eyes glint at mine. I feel like a snake being charmed to rise out from my basket, out of my personal space. To keep from leaning into him, I plant my shoulders firmly against my seat.

"So, a perfect day for you is touring a castle in Scotland," he says. I try not to focus on his mouth when he raises his water to his lips.

"You've figured me out."

"Yes," James says, shifting in his seat. "And no."

I wonder what the 'no' indicates. What about me—a mid-twenties, white girl with brown hair and brown eyes, in basic clothes—is difficult to read? I probably look like the small-town middle-school librarian that I am. But then I have an idea from an icebreaker I learned in college. I suppose it's the wine, the flying nerves, and his allure that emboldens me.

"Do you like Sherlock Holmes?" I ask.

"Sure."

"His powers of deduction and observation?"

"I've read some Arthur Conan Doyle." James runs a hand across his beard. Grainger's comment about how boring being around books would be flitters to the surface, but I brush it away, consumed with the man before me.

"Sherlock Holmes makes connections between the smallest hints and details to deduce conclusions, or possible conclusions," I explain.

"Go on." He leans closer, placing his fist under his beard.

"For example, there are numerous reasons a man would have short, clean, buffed nails, but let's say this man is otherwise unkempt. What deductions might Holmes make?"

"The unkempt man recently had to clean his nails for some purpose, maybe a special occasion."

"Exactly. A special occasion like cleaning blood from a murder he just committed." I sip to buy myself time. "So, do you think you're good at it? Sizing someone up using your powers of observation?"

James' eyes sparkle. Then he hums, thinking, vibrating the air between us. "I think so."

"Okay, then. This is a perfect opportunity, as I'm a complete stranger."

"I have already deduced that." James quirks his eyebrow.

I laugh then cross my legs, lean back against the window, and motion with my hand along my body, like one of Barker's Beauties. "What do you deduce, good sir?"

His smile curls into his cheeks now. He holds eye contact at first, then scans me head to toe and back again as I had instructed. It's thrilling—what girl wouldn't want those eyes on her? But as James takes his time, pausing in places like my hands or my feet, I start to regret this. I wonder if I need a manicure. Are my sneakers old and shabby? Am I wearing different-colored socks? How's my posture? Wait, I'm not wearing socks. Does he think that's gross? *Who let you out of the house and into the world all awkward and dumb like this, Summer?*

I can't take it anymore and shift back, crossing my legs the opposite direction. "Well? Any guesses?" My stomach seizes tight, waiting.

"A few." James clears his throat, and I hope not to die of embarrassment. "One: you are a hip-hop dancer, on your way to Atlanta to shoot a music video or star in some sort of live dance TV show?"

I bite my lips together, trying not to smile or give anything away.

"Two: you are a college basketball recruiter, returning to Atlanta from Columbus, where you were scouting the next top point guard for the WNBA."

"Really?" I say. "Wow, you're so off."

James smiles and sips. "I had another hypothesis, but I threw it out."

"Why?" I play along.

"Well, I thought maybe you were on your way to meet someone in person for the first time, like a guy you met through your Dungeons and Dragons dating website or something like that. But then I thought, probably not, because she's flirting with me."

I set my wine down, already half finished, and cross my arms. "That's exactly right. I'm a charismatic wood elf named Swanhilde. How the hell did you know?"

James laughs a little loud for an airplane, and I reflexively cup my hand over my mouth.

"So you *do* have an internet boyfriend you've never met in real life. A handsome bard, no doubt. With a castle, obviously." With his smile so wide, I can see he has a chipped tooth on the left side. A detail for my private deduction.

"You read me like a book," I say, patting his knee.

"Me now," James says, raising an eyebrow. He orders a beer from the passing flight attendant.

I enjoy giving him the once-over, taking my time like he did with me. I notice his rough hands, nails clipped almost to the quick. I detect tiny divots in his earlobes that suggest he once wore piercings. Maybe a wild era in college? His clothes–a cream sweater and brown chinos– look vintage but new, the expensive type that comes with that pre-worn style. He's wearing brown suede boots that appear as if they'd been wet and only dried recently. His beard is full, camouflaging a hint of a scar on his cheek. I remember his bare abdomen from when he stowed his carry-on above. No belt. A tingle tickles below my belly.

I finish my wine. "Two guesses," I say.

"Let's hear it."

"Well, you gave me a hint since you said you lived in England. So I assume you're only in the US for a short amount of time."

He nods.

"First thing that popped in my mind was that you're here for an experimental procedure to treat a rare intestinal disease, maybe a parasite. You know, because you're, like, sort of pale and feeble."

Mid-sip, James almost does a spit-take.

"But then, the alcohol killed that idea." I point to his glass. "So I'm thinking maybe you're back for the wedding of your childhood crush, Jenna."

"Jenna?"

"Mm-hm. She kept you in the friend zone until the end, but you had to see it through. You had to give it your last shot. But it didn't work out. In fact, it was sort of pathetic. Publicly humiliating. And that's why you're drowning your sorrows in IPA."

"Not even close," James says, nudging me with his elbow. "But you're fun, Summer."

"Well, you're a total bore," I say. I sip my second wine and feel it going straight to my head. "You know, I kind of want to know what you really do, but playing make-believe is so much more fun than learning you sell insurance or something."

James smiles. "Or finding out my seatmate is a...." He can't come up with something. Or perhaps he's actually an insurance salesman, and I've insulted him.

"Taxidermist?" I offer.

"I might be creeped out a little, but I'd have so many questions."

"My grandad had a stuffed squirrel in his living room." The moment it comes out of my mouth, I wish I possessed the superpower to go back in time three seconds and not say *that*. I sound like a Midwestern hillbilly. No need for power of observation or deduction here.

"A stuffed squirrel." James' eyebrow cocks quizzically.

"Yeah, us Yorks are real classy people."

"York is your last name?" James asks, looking at me again. I nod. "You actually could have aristocratic English ancestry."

"Maybe," I say. "But I think it just means 'from York,' in which case, I could potentially descend from pig farmers."

James laughs and shifts in his seat. His knee brushes my leg again. We both act like we haven't noticed, but neither of us moves.

"How do you feel about a real question," he asks. "And an honest answer?"

"I think I can handle it," I joke.

"Where are you actually from?"

"Westerville, Ohio," I answer. "Ever been?" When James shakes his head, I go on. "Picture any movie ever set in an all-American small town. That's Westerville."

"Sounds nice." His low voice is almost a growl.

"It's fine," I say, hoping not to sound too negative. "And you're living in England, but...."

"I'm originally from Louisiana, but I've been overseas for years," James says, folding his arms across his chest, suddenly seeming guarded or defensive—but I could be reading into that.

"That's where I'm heading," I say. "New Orleans."

James shakes his head, disbelieving. "Connecting in Atlanta?"

I nod and hold my breath when he leans closer.

"Me too," he says, like we're sharing a secret.

James is the snake charmer again, playing his recorder, hypnotizing me with those green eyes. I rest my temple back into the seat, facing him. I want to say something to break the trance, something silly, defensive, but I can't. I'm completely drawn in.

Chapter Ten

James

"How long are you in town for?" I ask because I want to see her again. A natural beauty who is easy to talk to. Easy conversations rarely happen for me. Historically, I don't like anybody, but I really like her. Effortlessly. Though we are confined in a row of a fully booked plane with all the unsexy sounds and smells of a commercial flight, our space feels intimate. I want to kiss her. I angle my face toward her, hoping she'll close the gap.

"Only a few days."

"Have dinner with me." I watch her face register pleasant surprise and continue. "There are no castles in Louisiana, but I know of some pretty great views."

"I think I could make it work," she says, turning to me and placing her hand on the armrest next to mine.

I edge my shoulder over the gap of our seats, even closer now. She tips her face up ever-so-slowly toward mine. I hesitate, but she leans in at the last second, pressing her lips to mine.

My body buzzes from my lips and radiates through my torso. The kiss is close-mouthed and lasts only a moment, but it has a beginning, middle, and end, like the best stories. Soft and patient at first, moving into pressing and savoring, and then sweeping away, leaving a sensation to long for. An echo of the kiss. It's the most turned on I've ever been. This is also ridiculously stupid of me.

I don't do public displays of affection, or public displays of any emotion really. My college mates used to tease me about my reserved exterior, calling me "the Statue." They'd joke, "The Statue strikes again," or "Did the Statue go home with Kate or Lindy?" This reluctance to be demonstrative was a problem with the handful of women I dated longer than a few months. Every last one of them wanted me to hold hands in the park or kiss them on the street or at an event, but it never made sense to me. What purpose did it serve? Why advertise your private life? I'm sure a therapist would have a field day with this, but given the scrutiny my family is under, it works for me. Stiff upper lip, as they say.

But this feels different. Maybe it's the near-privacy created in these cramped rows that provided just enough shelter to disarm me. The long day and the alcohol and the long dating drought at the park are definite excuses. In combination with Summer's bookish sexiness and her alluring eyes. The perfect conditions to break down my usual defenses. *For Summer, practically a stranger, I'll risk it.*

Turbulence ruins the moment. We pull away and shift self-consciously.

"So dinner?" I find her amber-brown eyes.

"Yes," she whispers, meeting mine. "If it's possible. I don't know my schedule just yet."

"Let's exchange numbers." I pull out my phone, and we share numbers.

"I'm starting a temporary job tomorrow morning," Summer volunteers.

"Oh yeah? What's the position?" I finish typing her contact info into my phone, excited by the prospect of kissing Summer properly, in private, starting with her lips and moving to her neck, and then—

"It's a position at Revel Pointe. Have you ever been?"

Shit.

Chapter Eleven

Summer

With all the delays yesterday, I didn't arrive in New Orleans until almost 10 pm. And my luggage was rerouted to the wrong airport, so I only have my carry-on. Luckily, a driver stood near the baggage-claim carousels holding a sign with my name on it. I was whisked away in a black sedan down a dark freeway. After a forty-five-minute drive, the carnival lights of Revel Pointe appeared in the distant sky, and I could see the Mona Moon lighthouse beaming into the clouds, high above the rides. I'd seen the animated Revel Moon production company logo countless times, and there it was, right in front of me now. A salve after the night's strange twists and turns.

Now, cozy in my hotel bed, I force myself up and grab my phone. There's a text message from Grainger sent late last night: *Still thinking of that kiss.*

Grainger's sloppy kiss from Saturday feels like ages ago, but part of me is flattered to know he's thinking about me. Unfortunately, the word *kiss* reminds me of James in row eleven. Remembering his low voice, the way he said "good maiden," sends a shiver up my spine.

After a life of enjoying romance from the sidelines and in books, I've now had *two* whirlwind meet-cutes—seriously adorable stories that people tell their grandkids—within one week. It seems like a dream, a dream that went sideways somehow.

After I mentioned my new job, James went quiet and cold. *Did I say something wrong? Was he just looking for a one-night stand? Did James worry that I might be clingy if I got the job and moved to his city?* I didn't share details.

All I know is he shut down, and the rest of the flight was so awkward it hurt.

I accidentally brushed his elbow on our shared armrest and felt tingles rise up my neck. I wondered if he felt it too, if these sparks that crackled with each word, each look, were happening only to me. I wondered if he had a girlfriend. Sitting next to James for the rest of that flight, very aware of his movements, I tried hard not to look at him, but it was impossible. The heat we'd spun between us lingered in my body, on my skin, between my legs. It took landing and parting to release the sensitivity that had been building in my body ever since he'd used the word *scandalous*.

Thank god we lost track of each other for a while at ATL. He got a phone call and walked away to take it. It must have been a doozy because the next time I saw him, we were boarding the flight to New Orleans. He was in First Class, and my resentment for "Sir" James simmered.

Who does that? I repeat in my head as I brush my teeth in my hotel bathroom. Maybe he's a sociopath. Maybe I dodged becoming a gruesome, true-crime headline. I gather my hair into a high ponytail and change into my running shorts, T-shirt, and shoes. I decide to go for a half-hour jog to clear out these last bewildering thoughts.

Two hours later, I'm ready and sweating on the edge of the bed in my first-day outfit—a thrifted short-sleeved, gray tweed dress and black tights. It's really my only appropriate work outfit. I have yoga pants, jeans, two tees, and a pair of blue shorts. I tried the dress without the tights, but it was a tad too short, and I didn't want to show so much bare leg. So I turned down the A/C, and now sit as still as possible, going through Lilia's dossier of Revel Pointe research.

With thirty minutes to cross the park to the headquarters in the French Palace, I pull the lanyard with the words "Production Personnel" over my head and leave my hotel room. The Beau Chêne

Resort is grand. Everything is white and gray with accents of gold and fuchsia. Hanging in the lobby is a breathtaking chandelier in the shape of an enormous upside-down magnolia tree. The bar beneath it is mirrored and circular, reflecting the giant white blossoms, the yellow flickering bulbs with broad, patina-green leaves from below.

Outside is warm, but there's a breeze, maybe a front sweeping in. Hopefully. All of my clothes are for an actual winter, not this subtropical oasis. I approach the gates for the Revel Pointe personnel and show my pass to the ticket clerk. Finally, I'm in the Revel Pointe amusement park, its popcorn and fried dough scent wafting on the wind. Families already swarm at the *Around and Far and Upside Down* steampunk roller coaster entrance. I weave around strollers shaped like pelicans and through an enormous group of young people wearing T-shirts with the words "Michigan State All-Star Marching Band." I have to remind myself not to get too distracted, passing the path to the San Francisco Safari Ride, a massive cage of tropical birds, and the quaint French Village. The palace looms between attractions, my North Star. I check my mom's tiny gold watch that I only wear on special occasions. It's my good luck charm, used sparingly for moments I needed a little extra support, a way of carrying her with me. I almost didn't pack it for fear of losing it, but I'm glad I have her with me this morning.

Finally, the palace employee entrance is before me, and directed by the security guard, I find my way up to the fourth floor in a room with tall ceilings and windows facing the cobblestone entrance to the park. I sit and sip the water in front of me on a long, cherrywood table. I hear my sister's final words to me yesterday morning. "I believe in you, little sis." Was that just yesterday morning? It feels like last year.

"Hello!" A sing-song voice enters the room before a short and busty woman with a large top bun does. "I'm Frances Maceta,

Director of Production & Operations. You must be Summer! It's such a pleasure to meet you."

I shake her hand. "Pleased to meet you as well."

A pretty white top shows off her olive skin tone. "I always beat HR to meetings, but that doesn't matter. I'm more important than they are." She winks and motions for me to take my seat. I like her immediately.

A stiff, tall man in a crisp white shirt and blue bowtie makes a brisk entrance. "Hi, welcome. I'm Jacob." He offers a friendly, no-nonsense handshake. "I hope your travel was uneventful." It's more of a statement than a question, so I just nod and don't mention the storm or the luggage.

"All right, then," Frances says. "Let's get started, shall we?"

"First." Jacob opens a large binder, whips out a document, and then slides it over to me. He clicks a pen and places it next to a non-disclosure agreement. "It's standard." He goes on to recite, much too quickly, the basics of what I can and cannot say about Revel Pointe moving forward. After quickly reading the three full pages of legal jargon, I sign.

"Good," Frances sighs. She opens the folder on the desk in front of her, revealing spreadsheets and blueprints, and then focuses on me with smiling eyes. "Revel Pointe, all of it—animation, production, park, merchandising, resort, everything—has never had a proper archive. Long story short, when the late Wade Reve was positioned to take over, it was his idea to consolidate the growing archives from Elixir, Revel Pointe Studios, RP Cruises, and the park into one. We've been leasing an off-site warehouse just a mile down the road. Some material is here in storage." Frances motions down, presumably to indicate the floors below us.

"This archiving project will combine and classify the materials into a master catalogue in two main facilities. One will remain off-site, moved to the official archive warehouse and closed to the public. The other, what we're calling the Grand Revel Library for now, is currently under construction here in the park. This library will be open to select public visits. We envision academic passes, and in some cases, passes for journalists or writers. In special, exclusive circumstances, passes for fan experiences."

I am experiencing imposter syndrome the longer she talks, but I nod along. Frances explains how Mick Reve, the founder of Revel Pointe, wants this project to begin with a small, extraordinary team of archivists, but he also wants some of them to continue as resident archivists who would oversee guest appointments and extended research.

"There have been some delays with the library's construction, which has pushed back our schedule, so this whole process has been less organized than we'd like," Frances admits, a little smirk playing on her raspberry lips.

"I understand," I say, my voice cracking.

"Tilda Olsen-Reve has designated the library as the venue for our anniversary Christmas Eve gala this year. So, not only does the interior construction need to be finished in the next month, but select memorabilia will need to be located and displayed safely before we open the doors."

"It's a nightmare schedule," Jacob chimes in. "I mean, just between us..." He taps the NDA.

Frances purses her lips. "I'm going to level with you. It's going to be a mad dash to Christmas."

My heart skips beats in my chest as I meet their eyes—one, then the other, and back again.

"So let's finish this HR formality quickly," Frances says, smiling warmly again. "Then we'll grab a cafe au lait at The Blue Turtle and give you the tour."

They explain to me in detail how the positions will work. There will be three teams of library specialists working until Christmas, then one lead archivist and supervisor will be chosen to continue on at the library full-time. There will also be other full-time positions available both on-site and at the larger off-site archive. Everyone will start full-time on the gala prep.

"So if you are interested in staying on full-time, think of the next three weeks as a training and evaluation period," Frances explains.

The task at hand, the job itself, morphs from something vague into a concrete assignment in my mind. I see the ways I will tackle this job, the flowchart branching out from a real and weighted center. My voice takes on conviction, my diction becomes more precise.

There's a pause between my last answer and their next question. Frances presses her fingers against the edge of the table, cracking her knuckles. She throws an almost imperceptible glance at Jacob, and then sweeps her hair back gently.

"Well, that's all my questions for today," Frances says. "Do you have any questions for us?"

I hesitate. I did not know this position could be permanent, but I want it. This means having a difficult conversation with my principal at the middle school, but I don't want to put the cart before the horse. I touch Mom's gold watch to muster gumption.

"What are the hours and compensation?" I ask Frances and Jacob. It takes effort to ignore my meek instincts and imbue my voice with the same confidence I've managed throughout this meeting.

"For this crunch time, we're asking for six days a week, Monday to Saturday, mostly ten to six with some evenings, potentially." Jacob rifles through documents in his folder. He slides one over to me, pointing. "Because this is a special expedited situation between now and Christmas, and there will probably be quite a bit of overtime, we're offering two grand per week. For the perm position, the yearly salary is seventy-five to start."

I freeze, staring down at the little black numbers and letters on the white sheet. They blur and jumble. I make just over half that now. At $75,000 a year, I could fly home often, fly my family here for visits, and pay off my student loans faster. It's a dream.

"That number is obviously flexible for the head librarian position," Frances chimes in. "These are new positions, new buildings, new everything. So it's all a starting point."

Jacob snaps back into a tight-lipped HR specialist then, gathering up his stuff and holding it against his chest. "Any more questions, Summer? Before we show you around?"

I shake my head and thank them for the opportunity. My stomach cartwheels as we stand. I feel like I'm walking on marshmallows as I follow them out of the palace.

Chapter Twelve

Summer

The park is jumping by the time we emerge from the palace. Kids race around two massive oval ponds where lemon-chiffon water lilies sprout from waxy lily pads. At the center of both ponds are gray stone statues. On the left, *The Secret Quest Book* is poised high on a swirling staircase with sheets of waterfalls on either side, as if the stories within are continuously spilling out for all to enjoy. On the right, Thumbelina, holding a deep arch in her spine, her arms and wings delicately aloft, floats above a fountain of butterflies, birds, and fish, where water spouts and trickles to the flowers below. I know these references well. They were part of my childhood, part of practically everyone's childhood in America, and the reverence they've been given here, just inside the entrance, gives me chills I didn't expect.

"They're beautiful, aren't they?" Frances says, her face turned up to the fairy pixie girl. "Is this your first time in the park?"

"Yes, it is." I tuck my hair behind my ears and feel the waterfall spray on the wind. "These fountains are stunning. I could spend all morning here."

"My favorite part is the little gator on the bottom stair." Jacob points to the opposite fountain as we stride down the center path.

I spot it and laugh. A gator, no bigger than a skateboard, is attempting to climb the massive, swirling staircase. I would have never spotted it.

"So cute," I say. "I hope he makes it someday." The attention to detail and quality is astounding. Up ahead, the Mona Moon lighthouse beams into a sky filling with metal-blue storm clouds.

"The humidity is dropping," Frances says.

"God, I hope that's the last time we flip-flop back to hot weather," Jacob complains. "December is too late for eighty degrees."

On my face and bare arms, I can feel the air shifting from warm and wet to dry and cool. *Change coming*, my mom would say, when the autumn weather would set in.

"Perfect for coffee," I say, and they both agree, as we make our way into the charming French Village, complete with bakeries, ice cream parlors, souvenir shops, and cafes decorated with flower boxes overflowing with color. We veer to the left, and there's a perfect Parisian corner cafe, La Bleu Tortue, like the kind in vintage postcards. Character actors dressed like Rose Red and Prince Roland from the famous '80s animated film are posted at the opposite corner. The park is busy with tourists now, with a line for princess photos and another for the cafe.

"This place is adorable," I say as we duck inside and line up.

Jacob agrees and checks his phone. "I'm gonna have to take mine back to the office. Duty calls."

The cafe smells amazing. I picture myself here on Sunday mornings with my Queen Isabella book and several *pains au chocolat*. We get our large cafe au laits to-go and part ways with Jacob. As Frances and I wind our way back through the wide outdoor fan of tables and emerge on the busy path, we run smack into a stunningly handsome man with a face I recognize immediately.

"Oh, hello, James," Frances says, laughing. "Excuse us."

"My fault," he says, a hand on his chest.

I feel a rollercoaster whoosh through my chest into my stomach.

"James, this is Summer York," Frances says. "Summer, James Reve."

James holds his hand out. "Hello." His shake is brief and stiff, his voice cold.

My mind screams. *"Sir" James is James Reve!* I try to remember the family tree from Lilia's coaching.

"Hi" is all I can manage to squeak out.

"James is the architect leading the project," Frances says to me. James raises his eyebrows, communicating what I don't know. He's so hard to read. All I can do is keep nodding.

"And Summer is going to be a part of our archive team," Frances thankfully continues. If she senses an awkwardness between James and me, she doesn't let on.

James steps aside to let park guests enter the cafe. "Hmm," he says, his eyes cool and detached. "That's an important job."

"It certainly is," Frances says, as a pretty Asian-American woman with a lanyard walks up beside James and hovers. She's stylish and beautiful in an out-of-place way here in the park, in wide jeans, chunky ankle boots, and a heavy-looking shoulder bag.

"James?" she asks. "I'm Reya."

There's another jumbling of handshakes and introductions while tourists enter and exit the cafe. Awkwardly, I step aside and watch as Reya and James walk away. He doesn't spare me another glance. As he turns his head to speak to Reya, I briefly catch a glimpse of his reserved grin and notice the chip in his canine again. *A handsome beast.*

"Sorry about that. He's a bit abrupt, such a busy guy." Frances guides me away from the cafe. "As I mentioned, construction has had some hiccups. James and I, and our site manager, Marcel, are carrying the weight of it. But we're making strides. Wait until you see the library."

Frances keeps explaining the ins and outs of the process to conceptualize and build this library, which I'm learning is a sort of a last grand wish of the founder and creator, Mick Reve. James' grandfather. As interested as I am in the full story of the project, my mind keeps skipping back, like a scratched record, to what just happened. My hand closed in the warmth of James' hand. His deep growl of hello. *Did he even recognize me?* His face gave nothing away. Then I rewind back to last night, his eyes half-closing, leaning into me. His lips. *James Reve's lips!* I can't possibly work here now.

I don't know how to break it to this lovely woman that I can't take the position. I rehearse my speech as Frances leads me away from the cafe, through a locked gate, and down a gravel path in a copse of the largest trees I've ever seen in my life. Some have branches that twist and bend to the ground, where the bushy tips reach back up toward the sky, a puzzle of fuzzy green octopi. Up ahead the dramatic clock tower peeks through. How is every angle of this place stunning? *Enchanting.* By the time we reach the cobblestone drive and another fountain, understated and empty, a friggin' castle stands before us. This is the *library*?!

"Here it is." Frances sighs dreamily. "The Grand Revel library. I love it. I can't wait for it to be finished."

My eyes trace the double stone staircases, the Juliet balcony, the romantic clock in the tower, the *goddamn turrets*. Jesus Murphy, this guy knows how to build a turret. Despite the hubbub of painters, carpenters, and gardeners hard at work all around us, I'm feeling suddenly hot all over. Turned on by a turret? *Get a grip, York.*

"Obviously, I'm speechless," I finally say.

"This is the main place you'd work, if you take the permanent position."

"It's gorgeous." I am genuinely overwhelmed by its beauty. *Screw James.* I want to work here, and I won't let some privileged a-hole deter me. I turn to Frances. "I just want to say, for the record, I'm very interested in the permanent job."

"Wonderful!" Frances squeals. "Well, enough chitchat. Let's get to work. *Pronto.*"

I nod and follow Frances into the library castle, and as she gives me a tour of the interior, I use my imagination to fill in her descriptions.

"There's Cricket," Frances says, calling over a tall woman with liberty rolls pinned in her hair, wearing an army green jumper and chunky jewelry. When we're introduced, Cricket shakes my hand firmly.

"Welcome to the funhouse." Cricket gestures like a game-show host to the construction chaos. "I've been waiting as patiently as a toddler for some help with organizing this mess. I hope you're here to help?"

I laugh at her simile. "I'll do my best."

"It'll be nice to have another lady around here." Cricket gives a knowing look to Frances, who only smirks. "Most days I feel like I'm a cat in that 'dogs playing poker' painting."

"I've always thought cats were smarter," I say, "At least more self-sufficient."

"I like her," Cricket grins at Frances, who agrees.

I have an immediate friend crush. I imagine drinking cocktails with this woman and getting all the tea about the job, the crews, and maybe even a sugar cube about James Reve.

I meet more people on the project and feel completely welcome. But two major issues are never far from my mind: my dad is alone for the first time, and I will have to see the unattainable, mega-wealthy son of a magical entertainment dynasty whom I've already kissed. And it's clear he's not interested in doing so again.

Chapter Thirteen

James

Reya Ghu is easy to talk to in that breezy California way, but I keep myself in check. After all, this is the person who wrote, "*In an ever-more-progressive world, Revel is two-faced—one minute supporting Save Our Oceans, and the next, docking a polluting cruise ship on a delicate Caribbean reef.*"

We take our drinks out to the last table at La Bleu Tortue, tucked away without a view. I expect her to set a phone on the table and ask to record our conversation, but she doesn't. Reya doesn't even pull out a pen and paper to take notes.

She just crosses her legs and asks, "So, you just got back from Canada?" She sips her coffee. "Tilda said something about an emergency landing?"

"Well, that's a bit dramatic," I say. "But I suppose technically it was."

"Stiff upper lip, right?" Reya smiles. "Nothing much ruffles your feathers?"

I grunt noncommittally. Boarding the commercial plane, shuffling to row eleven, and finding adorable Summer there flashes before my eyes. Summer definitely ruffled my feathers this morning.

"What was in Canada?" Reya asks.

"Marble," I begin, getting down to business. "Mediterranean Pearl for the entrance and fireplace. Have you been in the building yet?"

"Yes, briefly, but I'd like another tour with your commentary."

"Of course." I sip my coffee and wonder if she's actually secretly recording me. How is she going to remember details like Mediterranean Pearl?

"So, the trip was a success?" she continues. Her shoulder-length hair is parted severely down the middle, but it suits her. Her white sweater droops to one side, showing a black bra strap and more shoulder than is professional, in my opinion. Perhaps this is her tactic, to get comfortable and entice people to leak information.

"It was," I say. "Should be here in three days. Quebec is beautiful. Have you been?"

"Yes, to Montreal. It's charming."

"I agree." Tilda told me to seem relatable, but I hate talking about myself, so I tell Reya about the trip to the Christmas-card perfect Petit Ruisseau. I impart these details because they seem innocuous—the rolling snow-covered hills, the quaint winter town, the Chateau Frontenac. I even tell Reya about the driver, Léo, smoking his pipe and the tortière I had for dinner.

"So that's something you're into?" Reya asks.

"What's that?" I ask, searching her eyes, wondering what she's leading me to say.

Reya pauses and sips. *She's good*, I think. Disarming. Giving me space to impart something odious.

"French Canadian architecture?" I finally respond, ready to elaborate. "I guess I—"

"No," she cuts me off. "Romance."

I guffaw, surprising a table of park guests close by. The inelegant sound of it surprises me as well. She smiles and waits.

"Sure," I concede. "I like romantic landscapes. The library is revival Renaissance. Gothic, in ways. Chateauesque asymmetry is inviting, its textures," I explain.

"Yeah, but, come on. A castle is the ultimate symbol of romantic stories," Reya challenges. "Legends? Fairy tales? Every fairy tale has a castle."

"Is that true?" I wonder aloud, changing tack. "Fairy tales and castles are embedded in the classics. Arthurian myths. Shakespeare. They're imbued in our Western storytelling DNA."

"And specifically, in your *family* DNA."

She has me there. "Right." I say no more, hoping to steer the conversation away from romance. "Let's go see the library." I shove back from the table and stand, pushing my shoulders back.

On the way, I parrot Tilda's prompts, minus the PR jargon. I blabber about the Fête Noël gala and the 60th anniversary on Christmas Eve. I talk up the cultural importance of our family business.

This is for PawPaw, I remind myself.

"It's truly an honor for the library to host this annual fundraiser," I say, which is not lip service. "I'm thrilled to contribute to the tradition and legacy of this place. It's something I don't take lightly."

"It's quite the responsibility," Reya says. "*Legacy*. Do you feel equal to the task?" I glance over at her and say nothing for a while. Has she seen the library? It speaks for itself.

But I hear Tilda's voice in my mind and continue to feed her the boilerplate line—scholarship, American cinematic contributions, etc., etc....

"My PawPaw always said that Revel Pointe—this place, the studio, everything—comes not only from his imagination but from the imagination of the people who love stories."

"*Gaze upon the moon and find somebody true*," Reya says. It's from the first Revel movie, *A Ragtime Romp*.

"You're a fan," I say dryly.

"Sure." It's her turn to sound noncommittal.

We've reached the locked gate, so I busy myself with unlatching it, ignoring her. I haven't figured out her angle yet, but it's clear she's flirting.

"So let's see..." I wrack my mind for details. "The main floor will display memorabilia highlights from—"

"I know. I read the press release." Reya shifts her bag from one shoulder to the other. I offer to hold it, and surprisingly she lets me.

I run my free hand over my beard. "What more do you need to know?"

"It's your grandfather's ninety-fifth birthday this year?" Reya asks. "How is he?"

"Well, he's ninety-five," I say, laughing a little. "A little slower, but he's all there"—I tap my temple—"up here."

"You see him often?" Reya asks.

"Not as often as I'd like."

"Are you close?"

I stop at the edge of the cobblestone before the empty fountain and the best view of the library. "What are you getting at here?" I ask. I'm being mined. "I was under the impression you wanted information about the building, the project."

"And it's your grandfather's project."

"Actually, it's *all* my grandfather's project, Ms. Ghu." I gesture to the park behind us.

She grins, nodding in agreement, and then circumnavigates the fountain, leaving me to follow. I watch Reya as she bends to smell a bright pink camellia blossom. Then she stands, gazing up at the clock tower. "Is there a view from up there?"

"There is." Scanning the roof, I recall Summer's babbling. *I love a good turret*, she'd said, and I can't help smiling to myself. A girl after my own heart.

"Can I see it?" Reya asks, interrupting thoughts of Summer smiling, which is definitely a good thing.

"Not today," I say. "It would be a safety hazard." I cross my arms and sigh. I've got actual work to do.

She nods. "You grew up in England, right? I detect an accent."

"I'm sure you know the answers to this, Ms. Ghu, but yes, I have lived in England for about a dozen years."

"And now you're back." It's both a statement and a question. "For good?"

"No comment." I glare at her.

She points to the second-floor balcony above the entrance. "Could we see the view from up there?" I swear she bats her lashes. "I'd like to get a visual on the rest of the park from up there. How connected it feels to the rest of Revel Pointe."

I shuffle some pebbles into the cobblestone grooves with my boot.

"It would help me picture the gala," she continues.

Checking my watch, I agree to take her up via the elevator, as the staircase is still without a railing. "You'll have to wear a hard hat," I say and head for the main entrance.

I'm happy to see the hardwood floors are going in fast, as I lead Reya to the elevator doors and tell her we'd be standing atop the marble here in a week if all goes well. I describe its color and luminescence as the elevator rises to the second floor, which is a dramatic thirty-five feet up.

"Wow," she says, without enthusiasm. I think about how Summer would appreciate these details, and then shake my head like that will help me forget her. We exit onto the round balcony encircling the interior rotunda. Only a temporary railing is fashioned, and I hold out a protective arm to keep Reya from accidentally tumbling to a serious injury below. She adjusts her hard hat and gazes around the wide-open spaces. Now she's interested.

"It's really impressive," Reya says. "Almost too much."

"Ostentatious?" I try not to sound prickly.

"I mean too much to behold," Reya says and backs away. "Is the outside balcony this way?" She's grabbing a door handle and pulling before I can answer.

"You can see Thumbelina's Ferris wheel," Reya says, her face lighting up. She points, and her childlike wonder relaxes me.

Then she attacks. "What do you think about the gossip about your family?"

"Not much. I don't read trash," I parry.

"Not even The Secret Reveler?" she asks. "They seem to have the inside scoop."

"I wouldn't know."

"Some say that particular blog is a plant, written by a Revel employee to drum up cheap publicity." Ah, here's an angle.

"Again, if it was, I wouldn't know," I respond flatly. I look over at Ms. Ghu and meet her eyes to show I have nothing to hide. She gives a minuscule shrug and leans against the railing, as the wind sweeps up again.

I lean against it as well and watch the tree canopy sway. We're perched directly in line with the highest leaf tips here, a quivering lake of green before us. The lighthouse looms above in the center of everything, its rotating bulb 165 feet high in the sky. Reya is quiet, taking it all in with me—the coasters, the Ferris wheel, the Revel Pointe sign on the palace roof. In the distance beyond the levee, the mast of a cargo ship drifts on the Mississippi River. *She's right*, I think. It's almost too much to behold.

Movement from below on the cobblestone catches my eye. It's Frances, Cricket, and Summer leaving the library. Summer York, right there. Long braid, gray dress, black stockings. I picture the faint freckles on her nose one could only see from as close as I've been. Summer York is a good name, I think, and just then she turns and looks up over her shoulder our way before disappearing beneath the oaks.

"It's funny," Reya says, right next to me now.

"I suppose this is the part where I say, 'What?'"

"Yes, it is." She pauses for effect. "This is one of the most beautiful, dare I say *romantic* places I've ever seen, but you reject being called a romantic."

"Humor is subjective, I suppose."

"I just find it hard to believe that the man who made this and talks about marble and cornices and legacy with such devotion is not a romantic." Reya leans closer, resting her hand on my bicep. I motion her back to the stairwell.

"Are you dating anyone?" Reya pulls her hand away slowly.

"We're done, Ms. Ghu. I have to get back to work."

After playing catch-up all afternoon, I remember I haven't eaten since breakfast. I call Cricket to invite her to a work dinner but get her voicemail. The rain has come and gone, leaving a cloudy December chill in its wake. It reminds me of London and makes me long for a real pub.

Cricket texts me: *Can't tonight. Charlie has a recital. Rain check for tomorrow?*

I return: *Deal. Let's head into the city.*

I feel claustrophobic again. It's as if the trip, Reya Ghu, and Summer York shook something up inside of me.

Cricket replies with a bright yellow thumbs up.

The next best thing to a pub around here is the RP Lounge. I'd call Ethan, but he's up to his ears in work and Marin. I'm the only other Reve sibling in the park, with my brother Henri off somewhere in Australia, and the "Little Angels" a.k.a. Dominic and Elsie—my half brother and sister—away at school. And the next best thing after my siblings or Cricket is my assistant, Lucien Musgrove. For the past few months, Lucien's been annexed by Tilda's team, working on the top floor of the palace, but we often meet at the lounge for an end-of-day pint. I message that I'm on my way to The RPL, and he texts that he's only fifteen minutes behind me.

The RPL is hardly a cozy pub, with its luxury banquettes and sparkling chandeliers, but I like it because at its core is Bobby LaFleur, bartender extraordinaire. I've known the man since I was a boy, and when he heard I would be around a while, Bobby brought in a new tap of my favorite British lager. That alone has been a comfort in this tumultuous dive back into my family's business. I'm feeling the weight of it today, especially after that shit show of an interview. I pull up a stool to the bar.

"Hey, Bobby. How'd you weather the storm yesterday?" I ask as he places a pint in front of me.

"On my toes as usual," Bobby says, adding that several tourists purchased the premium lounge membership when they saw that much of the day would be rained out. "We got a surprise slam midday." He fiddles with a remote and turns on the one television in the bar, a smallish one nestled inconspicuously in the corner.

I look around the bar and dining room to note it's mostly full now as well. This is another of Tilda's wins. What was once a lazy, old boys' club is now a major moneymaker. I read somewhere that this exclusive dining membership goes for eight grand a year.

After a pint, I pull out my phone and spend five minutes trying to think of something to say to Summer that would make up for my behavior on the plane and earlier today. I shouldn't even contact her. I should let her think the worst of me—but I can't.

"That work or pleasure?" Bobby asks.

"Both," I grumble. Thankfully, Lucien arrives bounding in like a husky before I tell Bobby anything too revealing.

"Whaaaat's up?" Lucien tries this with a comically bad American accent. "How was Reya Ghu? A right battle-ax?"

Bobby is there with Lucien's pint, timing it perfectly, and they shake hands.

"I don't really want to talk about it," I say.

"She hot?" Lucien asks, pulling out his mobile to google her. His floppy haircut falls over his eyes.

"She's attractive, yes," I concede.

"The ol' Statue charm not working, then?" Lucien sips, but his eyes are laughing.

"Fuck off."

"No, you fuck off," he slaps me on the shoulder again. "Literally, go get shagged, you gloomy git. You've been wearing this look for too long."

Lucien was my friend before he was my assistant. Though it's extremely casual, it's always worked for us. He gets that I'm a moody bastard. Sharing him with Tilda has been a new development, changing the dynamic a little.

"You talk to my mother like that?"

"Definitely," Lucien says and laughs like a monkey. "She likes when I dom."

I punch his shoulder hard, fake-defending my mother's honor.

"Ow, seriously, though. I've got, whadda-they-call-it, cabin fever." Lucien rubs his arm. "We need to get out of this circus, mate."

I'm familiar with the feeling, but I don't say so. There are more grueling weeks ahead of us, and we have to buckle down. I tell him to join Cricket and me for dinner in the city tomorrow.

"Maybe I should arrange a date," Lucien says, a little too enthused. "There's this cute yoga chick at the resort I've been chatting up–"

"No way." I can't hang out with the staff. I can't trust them not to film me or post the world's most unflattering photo on The Secret Reveler.

"Fine," Lucien huffs. "You're a drag, you know?"

"Three and a half more weeks." I hold my pint up.

"Three and a half more weeks." Lucien clinks his glass to mine. "And then what?"

Good question. The idea of getting out of here lifts my mood.

"I don't know. Christmas in London? New Year's in Barcelona?" I offer.

"What about Christmas *and* the New Year in Miami?" His eyebrows lift to his hairline. "Let's mess about America a little longer? My accent is like a superpower here."

I screw up my face with distaste.

"You're no fun," he says and then turns to Bobby, asking him to change the channel to SkySports. "Well, maybe I'll go on a solo vacay if that's cool with you, boss."

"Be my guest," I tell him, and then we both lock onto the replay of the Arsenal v. Fulham match.

Zoning out, I think about my options. I'll be thirty-one in February, and that Scottish art institute job will be right around the corner, *if* I win the bid. I know Tilda wants me here, but there's nothing for me here after the gala. It clicks with me suddenly. This funk I've been in is not just about being restless, stuck on the same project and place. And, it's not just about getting laid. It's deeper than that.

Sent away as a boy, I feel like a tourist in my own home. But it's worse than that, because tourists visit enthusiastically, and I feel trapped.

After another pint, I head to the Reve compound, our family home on-site. My mind is so cluttered that I don't even realize I'm standing in front of the duck pond, staring at egrets stalking minnows in the tall grasses. It's not dark yet. The park is about to close.

I find a bench and watch the Spanish moss sway. The cool breeze helps clear my head. I wonder where Henri is right now. Last time

I saw him was in London last summer, right before he headed to Australia. My little brother is perhaps the only person I miss intensely. It always catches me off guard. Though younger than me, Henri's always just known who he was from a small boy, off collecting beetles or spending hours watching a bald eagle nest through a pair of binoculars. I've always envied his uncluttered view of life.

"Excuse me." I hear a female voice close by and look up. Two teenage girls wearing matching *Island of Sirens* T-shirts, polka dot skirts, and similar sneakers stand at the end of my bench, eyeing me strangely.

"Me?" I point to my chest.

They nod. The slightly shorter one asks, "Are you James Reve?"

There's no use denying it, so I nod back.

"Hi," they say together.

I stand, about to excuse myself, when the shorter one steps forward, holding a phone.

"Could we get a selfie?"

"What?" I say gruffly, then take off in the direction of the compound.

"What a jerk," says one of the girls, loud enough for me to hear.

"A hot jerk," says the other, equally loud.

This park is my fish bowl, my dungeon, my curse.

Chapter Fourteen

Summer

My first day on the job is more of a cyclone than a whirlwind, with all the markers of professional initiation—signing documents, being issued keys and a laptop, following different personnel around, learning the hierarchies, etc. On top of that, it began in a fashion panic. After my morning shower, I faced a fashion conundrum. My work clothes are currently lost in airport purgatory. Recalling what Frances, Jacob, and Cricket were wearing yesterday, I knew that nothing I brought was going to cut it. I pulled on my jeans and top and headed to the clothing store off the lobby that I remembered seeing the day before. Unfortunately, it was closed until 9 a.m. Of course.

After trying on multiple outfit combinations back in the hotel room, I settled on tights and the oversized cardigan I wore on the plane. I attempt to dress it up, donning all the jewelry I brought—simple hoop earrings, a daisy pendant necklace, and my mom's gold watch again. It's the best I can do, which did nothing for my confidence, my figure, or my fears of running into James Reve again.

I race back to the palace offices and meet my new co-workers, Gemma and Horace, in a boardroom. There are two other sets of teams, but it's too overwhelming to commit all their names to memory right now. Gemma, a super-tan fortyish librarian from Gainesville, Florida, rubs me the wrong way immediately. She combs her long, pink fingernails through her bouncy blonde hair constantly, and one of the first things she says to me is, "Can you believe they're not making a decision about the permanent positions until after we've busted our asses for a month?"

Horace, on the other hand, is a bit harder to read, keeping comments to himself and his gestures to a minimum. He's a well-dressed Black man in his fifties who exudes competence.

To begin, Frances emails us a list of desired memorabilia that Cricket and her team are planning to display on the main floor of the library. We've also been given a binder with maps of the park, resort, warehouses, and Reve family compound, the last of which is off-limits without upper management. The maps identify storage spaces to navigate and explore.

"Eventually, you're going to catalogue it all," Frances explains. "But the priority is the list."

The A-List, as we would begin calling it as early as lunch time, came straight from the family—Tilda Olsen-Reve, current CEO Ethan Reve, and the elusive, out-on-extended medical leave, Gaspard Reve, Mick's only son and James' father.

It's probably the most exciting list a Reveler could imagine: animation cels and merchandise from all of the films, including the original *Ragtime Romp* (and a first-edition copy of the book), a replica of Theo Tomcat's lantern jar of fireflies, Kara's ballet slippers and tutu from *The Red Shoes*, Prudence Pleasant's crazy compass necklace and mood ring, *Rose Red* toys from the '80s, the spell book from *San Francisco Safari*, a bound original script of *Thumbelina*, and so much more.

My head buzzes with executive-level information. My body is tired and wired simultaneously. Frances, in her casual elegance, her chambray shirt tucked into a bright purple pencil skirt, her wide gold hoop earrings, makes me shrink in my sad outfit. I feel like a kid dressed in a hobo costume at Halloween when she hands me the box of white gloves to use for old documents and textiles.

"You need to communicate with Cricket Sugarman daily," Frances says, opening her phone. "Only one of you should message her. Summer, you met Cricket yesterday, right?"

"Yes." I nod, feeling sweat dampen my bra.

"Here, why don't you take that role," Frances suggests and motions for me to save Cricket's number in my phone. "My guess is she'll want to see what you find on the list as soon as possible."

"Right," I say, remembering the cool woman I met with the '50s hairdo and colorful arm tattoos.

"One more thing," Frances says, addressing Horace, Gemma, and me as she fished a set of car keys from her pocket. "You've got access to one golf cart. To share. This one has an ad for *Camp Willow Creek 3* on it." It's parked outside the front gate, she tells us, and we may not drive it through the park during operating hours. We are to use the access road only until the park is closed.

As soon as Frances leaves the room with a chipper "Good luck!" Gemma opens her laptop and takes the lead for our team. She tries to delegate Horace and me to find scripts in the warehouse offsite, but it's clear to us that we should work together first to familiarize ourselves with all the spaces in order to make an efficient plan. Gemma's way would send us scattered. It's apparent that she wants control over finding the highest-value items on the list, which is beside the point. Horace suggests that we should start with finding the four storage rooms in the palace and the vault. This way we'll start on the same footing tomorrow and maybe even find an item or two in the palace today. Gemma clicks her manicure on her laptop and hesitates. She doesn't want to be on equal footing with us.

We adopt Horace's strategy and finally start the massive task I've been visualizing since that first phone interview. In some ways, it's like any other job—heaps of files, copiers, cubicles, hallways, employee kitchenettes—but as we begin to open boxes in storage spaces, the surrealism factor dials up. Much of what we're searching through at first is promotional material, going back to the mid-'60s. By 2 p.m., I find our first A-list item—a small box of opening-day tickets to the Revel Pointe theme park.

"I think I got one," I say cautiously, eyeing the short stack of faded blue tickets the size of baseball cards.

I stand, holding the three-by-five-inch red box, and I move it carefully to the table. Our breathing turns shallow as I don my white gloves and lift one ticket, as if guiding a feather, off the stack and onto the table top.

Horace takes out his magnifying glass and reads it out loud. "Admit One Guest to REVEL POINTE Theme Park. Good for any age and every attraction. Three dollars. May 19th, 1961. Welcome all dreamers!"

"Wow, three bucks!" Gemma says. "What's it now? A hundred fifty?"

"Something like that," Horace says.

"It reads like a poem." I take the magnifying glass Horace offers to look closer. The font is whimsical with a mid-century flare, sleek and dramatic at once. "*Welcome all dreamers.* I love that."

During our break, we celebrate our big find by grabbing a cafe au lait from La Bleue Tortue. At a table, we learn that Horace had served in the military in the late '80s, and lived all over the world until finding himself back in Louisiana, his home state, after Hurricane Katrina. I imagine Horace has a wealth of stories, but he's a natural introvert. When he opens up a bit more, I can't wait to hear them.

Gemma is not shy about sharing details. She was married for six years but got divorced after her ex-husband gambled and lost all their savings. She went back to school in her early thirties and currently works at the University of Florida library, but is looking for a change. There's little time left in our break for me to share much, which is fine by me.

Before leaving, I text Cricket pictures of the tickets. I figure if she's been waiting this long to unearth these items, she'd want to know immediately.

As we pass between the two massive fountains, the air feels heavy with moisture, and I remember I have a sartorial problem to solve. I need clean underwear for tomorrow. I also could use some socks, at least one other outfit, and sunscreen. My suitcase is supposed to arrive tomorrow, but who knows.

"I need to make some phone calls," I tell my new co-workers. "Meet you up there." I point to the third floor of the palace.

I find myself a quiet corner in the courtyard, take out my phone, and hesitate. This feels really unprofessional, but I'm desperate. I dial Cricket.

"Hey, Summer!" Cricket chimes, picking up after one ring. "Great news about the tickets."

"I know. They're kind of beautiful," I say. "Look. I need some... advice."

"Shoot." Cricket is somehow both sunshine and business.

As quickly as I can, I explain my situation, my lost luggage, no clothes, yada yada. "Basically, I need to get to Target."

"I hear you, but we're in the-middle-of-nowhere parish out here," she says. "Let me think..." She trails off, and I almost tell her not to worry about it when she yelps. "I just had a great idea! I'm heading into the city tonight. Come with me. We'll coast through the West Bank and get you some supplies. I could use a trip to Target myself."

"Are you sure?" I ask. "I absolutely hate to impose."

"Yeah, I'm just having dinner with a friend. You can totally join us."

After a few rounds of me trying not to be a burden and Cricket assuring me that I'm not, we make plans for her to pick me up in front of the Beau Chêne Hotel after work.

After a fun and productive trip to Target with Cricket, I'm all set with a capsule work wardrobe plus a little black dress that currently hugs my figure comfortably. As we cross a massive bridge high over the Mississippi into the moody lights of New Orleans, Cricket fills me in on where we're having dinner.

"And don't worry. Jimmy's a gem." Cricket careens her car around a sharp corner, expertly dodging three drunk guys crossing the road with glowing green cups, and finds a parking spot. "This is it."

I follow Cricket down a cobblestone sidewalk, attempting not to break my ankles in my new espadrilles. I nearly trip on a broken waterworks cover and stop fussing around enough to appreciate where I am. Music drifts from an alleyway. Laughing voices echo off old brick buildings. The streets are narrow and dark, lined with flickering gas lamps in archways and under balconies draped with blooming vines. Hand-painted signs hang in ancient-looking doorways. I'm taking in the Old World charm when a familiar voice calls my name.

"Summer?" There he is, James Reve, leaning against a shiny black town car. He crosses the street, and his movie-star good looks make me freeze on the spot.

I catch him taking in my fitted black dress, which sends heat coursing through my limbs. I have no words.

Cricket fills the silence by introducing us.

"We've met," James says, taking the lead and offering a hand for me to shake. His demeanor is warmer this time. "That's Lucien." He points to a tall man in a bomber jacket and highlighted hair. Lucien waves, and I awkwardly wave back.

We float through the restaurant and arrive at a cozy corner table set with glowing tea lights and shiny wine glasses. Cricket and I take the bench facing the dining room. Suddenly, I'm sitting across from James Reve. I grab my menu; my heart is vibrating. I study the entrees intently, not sure how I'm going to get through the evening. I flip my braid over my shoulder and try not to fidget. Is my body tricking me, or is his mere presence going to my head like whiskey? I peek at him above my tiny menu, and he looks up, too. We lock eyes for a second and then he smirks, looking away. *Is this funny to him?* Stuck at a dinner with co-workers, pretending like the row eleven kiss never happened?

I take a sip of water as soon as our server has poured my glass. *Be cool*, I tell myself. As James removes his suit jacket, leans back in a forest green button-down, and folds his strong arms over his chest, I know I have my work cut out for me.

Chapter Fifteen

James

Dinner is absolute torture. With Summer across from me in a sexy black dress, her eyes sparkling in the low light, I'm roasting on a stake. It's literal hell trying not to look at her. Each time her voice joins the conversation, my body betrays me. Every time she laughs at some stupid joke Lucien tells, my temperature rises. Not only is Lucien flirting with her, which instinctively pisses me off, but the adorable way her laugh goes high at the end makes me want to grab her and drag her away like a caveman.

"I don't mean to talk shop," Cricket says. "But Summer and her team found some cool artifacts today." Cricket tells us about the first-day park tickets.

Summer grabs her phone, pulls up a photo, and then looks up at me through her lashes, handing it over. My fingers graze hers for just a moment. Instead of grabbing her hand and sucking on each delicate finger, I busy myself with reading the mint-green ticket.

"I don't think I've ever seen one of these before," I tell her, letting Lucien check out the photo. My own phone buzzes in my pocket, but I ignore it.

"I love the font," Cricket and Summer say together and smile at each other.

"It's giving me some ideas." Cricket says, sipping her Sancerre.

"Like what?" Summer asks. I watch her from my peripherals as she takes a bite of her redfish. She's a classic stunner, seemingly oblivious to how her beauty and presence affects those around her. How is that possible?

"I'm not sure yet," Cricket says. "A custom print, maybe? For wallpaper?"

"Your brain is always churning," I say.

"And yours isn't, Jimmy?" Cricket shoots back at me.

"She's got you there." Lucien elbows me.

"Well, Revel Pointe is lucky to have me." Cricket leans away as the server takes her empty plate. She tosses her napkin on the table and leans into Summer. "Make yourself invaluable to them, Summer Girl." Cricket nods her head at me. "They've got the big bucks."

"I don't know why you're looking at me. As if I have any influence in the corporation," I say, wishing to talk about anything but the family business.

"Oh, come off it, mate," Lucien says. "Your mum has *big* plans for you."

"Big plans?" I balk. My phone buzzes in my pocket again, and I pull it out as a distraction to find it's a text from the devil herself, Tilda: *The article is absolute perfection. XO.*

"What are you on about?" I'm dying to change the subject, but I hate nothing more than being caught off guard. My phone buzzes yet again.

Tilda: *Check your email.*

I pull up my email and see the *LA Times* article. The headline reads, "Romance in the Time of Cash Cows: The Third Reve Son Returns."

"What is it?" Summer asks, a concerned frown on her face.

"The *LA Times* article already posted," I say. I place my phone face down on the table, not wanting to ruin the evening. However, I notice Lucien and Cricket are already typing on their phones. Only Summer resists the temptation to read.

"Oh my," Cricket says under her breath. "You've got to hear this: *'From certain angles, Revel Pointe is a Russian doll. Nestled in an oak grove, within a meticulous, carnivalesque playground, deep in the wispy bayous of Louisiana, a library grows. This isn't just any library. It's a symbol, a homecoming, a beautillion—'"*

"What's a beautillion?" Lucien asks.

"A coming-of-age party for a young man," Summer whispers matter-of-factly. Every time she drops a fact, I find myself wanting her more.

"Let me finish." Cricket lowers her voice and affects a posh accent. *"'Inside this building is the last doll, the first child of Gaspard Reve and his second wife, current Vice President of Operations Tilda Olsen-Reve: James Reve. He's also the lead architect of this prestige project and may be the company's first true romantic since its founder, Mick Reve.'"*

I say nothing. *What the hell is this?*

Lucien picks up where Cricket left off, with the same accent. His is somehow worse than hers. *"'With his rough exterior, James Reve feigns a desire for privacy and anonymity, a trapped royal distancing himself from the harsh, glittering fandom.'* You're royalty now, mate!" Lucien says cheerfully. He continues, unaware that my ire is building with each overwritten word. *"But at his core, a romantic lies in wait. The library is his pronouncement, his not-so-subtle call to be acknowledged, albeit by his own personal manifestation. The clock tower is his raised hand, communicating that he's ready. But ready for the heat lamp of the American media or ready to fight for a bigger share of the Revel pie? The world waits to see. Surely, behind the beard and brooding, behind the prep-school posture and British manners, is a theme-park prince about to emerge. And what a show that will be."*

"Ooh la la." Cricket fans herself.

Summer's eyebrows are raised, a quizzical pull at her mouth. She looks away, pulling her hands into her lap.

"Wow, mate. Sounds like you're the next contestant on *The Bachelor.*" Lucien nudges me.

I barely manage a curt nod, then excuse myself to the bathroom, bumping the table noisily. As I walk away, I hear Cricket say, "Shit, I don't think he's taking that well."

Lucien replies, "Nah, he's all right." *But I'm not all right,* I think as I throw open the bathroom door.

I lean against the sink and peruse the rest of the article only to discover the focus is me—my history and my involvement, or lack thereof, in all things Revel Pointe. There's even a quick survey of my romantic past. Somewhere near the end of the article, Ghu sets me up to be this gothic character, à la the Hunchback of Notre Dame, building himself a replica castle in the midst of animation land "*perhaps in order to entice his ultimate princess.*"

Tilda thinks this is perfect? It's barely about the library! Based on some of her past work, I thought Reya Ghu was going to write a hit piece. I'd have preferred it to this fluff. Why this angle?

Tilda's behind this. Somehow this is a ploy to secure her power, and I'm just a fucking pawn. Her flesh and blood, an extension of her narcissistic dreams. I step back, feeling like a bear in a trap. Maybe she's trying to drum up social cachet for me so she can pit me against Ethan and have me perform as her puppet CEO. She hasn't listened to a damn word I've said to her.

PawPaw would never allow it, but he's ninety-five and not as influential as he once was. And there is no way my father would transfer the reins to Tilda after the debacle she pulled with Ethan last year. No, it'll skip her for sure. I vote Ethan, but I remember something she said recently: "*My own flesh and blood.*"

Until a few years ago, it would have been Wade, my oldest half brother, but something in him snapped. Maybe it was the pressure Dad put on him, but Wade joined the Marines, and just over a year later, died in Afghanistan. He was the heir apparent at Revel Pointe, but he wanted to serve his country first. Wade was the best of us. I wish I knew him better, but I spent more time with my boarding-school soccer coach than my own brothers.

Now Ethan is in the lead, having cleaned up his life and married Marin, who actually wants to live and breathe Revel Pointe.

Let them have it.

I splash my face with water and watch it drip from my beard to the countertop. Up until now, I have controlled my narrative and image. I don't give the press, those parasitic vultures, anything they can use against me, and haven't since I was eight.

Fury swirls inward, with an ache in my chest like a hundred bee stings. Under the anger and frustration, there's another feeling, but I don't want to go there. Anger is better.

My pecs twitch and my vision blurs as I punch the wall. Plaster crumbles to the floor; my hand comes away dusty and wet with blood. I've probably busted a knuckle or two. *Fuck it.* I've done this before, on the rugby pitch, into punching bags. At least this mess is minimal, though I feel like an instant twat for the damages.

A high-pitched noise buzzes in my ear as I run water over my sore right hand. I'm not sure what I want to do now. Leave Louisiana immediately? Stay, finish the library, and then leave?

I take a deep breath. Right this minute, I have to return to my company, which includes a beautiful young woman whose brown eyes just witnessed my personal nightmare. I clean up my hand, tuck in my shirt, and put the mask back on.

I return to the table, contrite. "I'm sorry. Just needed a minute. Let me make it up to you all with a drink somewhere."

Summer looks flummoxed. "The check?" she asks, holding her purse and scooting along the banquet.

"Taken care of," I say.

"Thanks." Cricket reaches for her bag, clearly flustered. "The sitter called, Charlie's a mess. I've got to get home."

Cricket asks if we would mind taking Summer back to the park, so she can head straight home.

"Fine," I say, and chance a look at Summer, who doesn't meet my eye.

On the cobblestones in front of the restaurant, Cricket pulls me in for a quick hug before taking off. In my ear, she whispers, "So sorry, hon. Let's chat tomorrow."

I nod, and as we watch Cricket cross the busy street, my body senses Summer standing next to me, all sporty curves, a full foot shorter. Lucien says we should still pop out somewhere for a nightcap or two when Cricket calls back to us from the open door of her car.

"Summer! Your supplies!" In her hand she holds a bunch of plastic shopping bags.

Chapter Sixteen

Summer

James and Lucien gallantly retrieve my Target bags full of cheap underwear, sensible work clothes, and toiletries from Cricket's sports car. To say I am uncomfortable would be an understatement. The air has been prickly since James first left the table. As we stand waiting for the Revel Pointe town car, I stare at my new thirty-dollar black wedges on the cracked slate, where glitter has pooled, sparkling in the grout.

The town car appears, shiny in the lamplight, and I give James a quiet "thanks," ducking into the back seat when he opens the door for me. Lucien puts my shopping bags in the trunk and takes the passenger seat. James slips in beside me on the soft leather bench. As the driver navigates the old narrow streets, I people watch. Groups of tourists wander and dance, wearing multi-colored beads, sequins, and silly hats, laughing on the sidewalk.

With James so close in the quiet back seat, my body is confused. I want to follow his lead and remain quiet, but I also feel helpless against his strong magnetic pull—his pheromones, his energy, his very being. There's something confusingly dangerous and alluring beneath his fit exterior. He does not want to be in this car with me; that much is clear.

I sneak a look at him. In the dark, with the changing lights of the city passing by, James' dark, wavy hair catches the gas-lamp glow.

"I'm sorry. About...everything." His voice is so deep, he practically purrs. His eyes find mine, but I can't read his expression.

I almost laugh out of nervousness, and I wonder if he can read my thoughts on my face. "Well, who could've guessed I'd be working and dining with you today?"

"Hmm," he says, turning away again. "I could've." He sighs deeply. "My life is complicated lately."

There's a flicker of an opening here to return to the intimacy of row eleven, when we were strangers sizing each other up across an armrest. I hesitate to engage, though, as now the boundaries between us are clear. I'm a Revel Pointe employee. He is my boss's boss. The boss of everyone in this car we're sitting in, where two people are listening in the front seat.

There's a long stretch of silence as we wind onto the freeway. On the elevated I-10, the city flashes below. It's a clear night, and the moon is a chunky crescent in a milky sky. In the space between us, I sense movement. Without turning my head, I note that James is methodically stretching his fingers and then balling them into a fist. Slow and measured. I mask my interest, looking down into my own lap and shifting my eyes for a better look. His right knuckles are swollen, and a bloody cut slices across the meaty part of his index and middle fingers.

"You're hurt." The whispery words fall out of my mouth. Instinctively, I reach my hand out, but stop just short of touching his.

"Yeah." His voice catches. He pulls his hand back and tucks it away from me.

What happened when he left the table? A fight? An accident?

"Let me see," I say, though I don't know why. I'm no nurse, and the last time I did a first-aid course was when I was hired at Westerville Middle.

"I'm fine." James won't look at me.

"Come on," I insist. "Let me see." A desire to take care of him surfaces. Whatever is going on with his family, and this article, it goes deeper than he lets on. I rest my hand on his elbow, and he relaxes.

He lets me guide his arm towards me. His palm is hot in my hands, which feel small in comparison. There's not enough light in the back seat to really see the full damage, but his knuckles have ballooned and purpled.

"This needs ice."

"I'm fine," James mutters. His tone is dismissive, but I don't let it go. His fingers could be broken.

I raise my voice and tilt toward the front seat. "We need some ice," I say. "James' hand is injured. Could we pull off for some ice? Maybe a gas station? A pharmacy?"

"I'm fine, Mr. Danny," James tells the driver, but I insist, stating my case to Lucien, who nods. We take the next exit into a dimly lit neighborhood.

"This is a lot of fuss for nothing," James growls at me as Lucien pops into a 24-hour market.

"Put it this way," I say. "We're saving you some grief and pain in the morning."

"*You're* saving me," James corrects.

"Without icing it, your hand might be a black and blue catcher's mitt tomorrow." I cross my legs. "And you'd lose a precious day or more of work just recovering from this."

James lays his head against the seat rest. "I shouldn't even be here. I need every hour at this point."

"It's really beautiful," I say. "The library. I saw it yesterday."

"Thank you," he whispers.

A moment passes. I read the restrained bulk of his body and countenance like the power of a crouching lion. He doesn't need more praise. He knows it's beautiful.

Lucien returns to the car with a small ziplock bag of ice.

James places the ice bag on his hand and winces.

"See?" I tease.

"Maybe." His eyes communicate gratitude.

"Summer's your heroine!" Lucien chimes from the front seat. "Well done."

After that, the ride home is filled with Lucien asking me questions about my life in Ohio. I do my best to offer the most exotic tidbits, but it's hard to spice up my small-town, middle-school-librarian life. James is quiet, looking out the window. Occasionally, I catch a hint of a smile. I shoot back questions about London, favorite places—coffee shops, pubs, restaurants. The conversation is buoyant until Lucien asks about my family and the fact of my mother's death surfaces.

"She passed away two years ago. Unexpectedly."

James turns to face me. "I'm sorry, Summer," he says with such gravity that it makes my eyes well.

If Mom could see me now. It's a thought that comes to mind often, but this time is truly unique—in a fancy car with a fancy man who built a fancy place. She'd tell me not to take it too seriously, giving me some homespun saying about how everyone bleeds red and pisses yellow. God, I miss her.

Perhaps James senses the emotion in my silent nod because he reaches over with his swollen hand to cup my shoulder. Even through my jacket, I feel the current between us. His subtle acts of affection make me want to sweep across the bench and cuddle close. *Slow down, Summer.*

I distract myself by taking his hand to survey the puffiness, which is already subsiding.

"This looks better already," I say, cradling his hand in mine.

James nods, but he leaves his hand there in my lap longer than he needs to, our palms touching in a gesture beyond care, wading into a quiet intimacy.

The next morning, as I'm leaving La Tortue Bleue with my cafe au lait (I'm addicted), I see James crossing through the French Village because of course I do. He's making a beeline for me. I notice his hand is wrapped in a type of high-tech splint.

"Good morning," he says, slightly out of breath.

"How's the hand?" I ask. "Did you see a doctor?"

He holds it up sheepishly. "I've broken many a knuckle in my day. Rugby, boxing, the odd tree. I'll be fine."

"Yikes," I say, but James looks so good in his navy blue sweater, his dark hair casting almost silver in the bright sun that the thought of him engaged in any physical activity is intoxicating.

"It'll be fine in a few days," James says. "Thanks to you." His eyes briefly go warm before icing. "It seems we'll be seeing each other quite a bit." He glances around, as if he's making sure no one is watching.

"Okay," I say, then motion toward the palace. "Well, I'm on my way—"

"Of course," James says. "Look, honestly, I want to explain... I was thinking about it last night in the car..."

If he's about to bring up row eleven, I don't want to hear it. I can't bear to hear him say something trite or even worse, apologize for it. I cut him off.

"Let me guess. You wanted to explain that the real reason you were on that plane was because you were hired as an undercover air marshal to escort a criminal mastermind somewhere back overseas, but you were thwarted by the blizzard?"

James' smile lights up his face. "Something like that, yeah."

"Well, I'm glad that's cleared up then."

"Me too." James takes a step toward me. Even though it's still chilly out, heat flushes my face. I pull my braid forward, wondering why he's pushing this issue. He's too close now, and I don't want people to see us together.

"I'd still like the opportunity to explain—"

I hold up my hand. "No need. It makes sense. You found out I work *here*." I take a step closer to *The Secret Quest* fountain and feel the cool mist on the back of my neck.

"But, on the plane, I feel—"

"Don't worry about it. You don't have to explain. Let's just keep it professional." My feelings are so jumbled that I can't think straight. Between starting a new job and leaving my dad and maybe starting something with Grainger and finding out James is a Reve and kind of my boss and dying to feel the press of his lips on mine, I just want to flee.

"Okay," James says, scratching at his beard, a bemused expression in his eyes.

"So, until the next time we accidentally meet," I say, toasting him with my cup, turning around, and walking the hell away.

As I pass the striving gator statue in the fountain, I congratulate myself on a benign, if slightly awkward, exchange with James Reve. What happened on the plane was happenstance. If we'd acted like regular passengers, we would have exchanged pleasantries and that would have been it. Having dinner with him last night was also a fluke. I can limit how much we interact from now on. I need to because if I keep spending time with him, my crush will only grow, and in the end that's going to be more of a problem for me. Not for him.

There's an unbalanced power dynamic between us, plus my colleagues cannot catch us hanging out, not even for a friendly coffee. I want to earn the head archivist position through my own merit, not from appearing to flirt with the boss. There's just too much on the line to screw up this opportunity.

Chapter Seventeen

James

As I turn back to the cafe and my busy schedule, I tell myself that I'm glad Summer rebuffed me. After my behavior on the plane and that goddamn article, I don't blame her. My brain understands, my body does not. It wants to find her and show her the best time of her life.

When I reach the oak wood next to the San Francisco Safari, juggling my coffee in my good hand and hugging my work folder under my armpit, I get a notification on my phone and then another, and then the deluge begins. I'm flooded with texts, phone calls, and emails about the article. Mates from Cambridge sending memes. An ex-girlfriend rings. I don't pick up. Revel Publicity emails looking for follow-ups. One request asks me to make an appearance on *Good Morning America*. No fucking way.

The anger returns. I can't walk into the library with all this pent-up rage. My head is too fuzzy, so I head down the dirt drive. It leads to one of the first rides in the park—a swamp log flume with a replica of PawPaw's childhood Cajun cabin. It's a chilly day for Louisiana, but tourists are still willing to get wet. Through the trees, I can see the tallest peak where awkward log carts carry a full load of shrieking riders over the top. A flash of a memory, of Henri and me riding the flume over and over one hot summer day in our hazy youth. What I would give to just take off to wherever Henri is right now and have an adventure, far away from this annoying game of family chess.

I sit down on a bench. The "Little Angels"—Dad's youngest kids, Dominic and Elsie—send me texts. Dom texts me a *New Yorker*-style cartoon that he drew of me with a crown and gold chains, arms raised and sitting in a kiddie ride cart with the caption "The Fresh Prince of Reve-Air." *Cute.*

Elsie, the youngest, texts: *They need to develop a reality show around you. Call it 'Romance Castle' or 'To Catch a Prince.'*

Me: *I will murder you and frame your best friend if you so much as breathe a hint of this idea to anyone.*

Elsie: *Too late. I've pitched all the networks.*

She's always been hilarious and precocious. Then I notice Henri calling.

"Hey bro."

He launches in. "She's all over that piece. She's trying to sell an image whether you like it or not."

"It's customary to respond back with small talk, 'Hi, how are you?' and whatnot," I say.

"Hi, how are you? What the hell is this article?" Henri's anger on my behalf is strangely comforting.

"I should have never agreed to talk to that reporter," I say. "When am I going to learn that everything with Tilda is transactional?"

"Something we can pay therapists a lot of money to help us figure out, no doubt. But for now, big bro, grab a pint and avoid Tilda."

It's good to hear his voice. It makes me feel like the person I was before I came back here. This good feeling is interrupted by a service gate opening fifty yards down the path. A golf cart enters the dirt drive. Not too many people have that kind of access, and it doesn't take me long to identify my older brother Ethan chauffeuring PawPaw this way.

"Gotta run, talk soon." I end the call, not waiting for a reply.

I would know their shapes anywhere, even though I haven't seen them much in the last ten years. Ethan and I are roughly the same height, and PawPaw is almost as tall. Though his stature has shrunk with age and his shoulders are thin and pointy now, he's still an impressive man at almost ninety-five. Wearing a smart, soft blue button-down under a black cardigan, he carries the formality of the mid-century, when men wore suits and hats. I know I'd prefer that to this age of pajamas on airplanes and slippers in the supermarket.

"James! Just the man we were hoping to find." Ethan's smile is his mother's, a woman I've only seen in photos. It's big and generous, and he has her dimples. "We've come to see your masterpiece. I've been hearing good things."

"Hop in, kiddo," PawPaw says. "It's good to see you." He pats my hand as I give his arm a squeeze and climb aboard behind them. The quiver in his voice makes me feel ashamed that I haven't gone to visit him more since I've been back in the States.

I run my hands through my hair and beard, trying to conceal my ire from these two men I respect.

"How's it going?" Ethan asks, giving me a backwards glance, probably noticing my frustrated face. "Are you feeling that Reve pressure yet?"

I laugh a little too loud. A knee-jerk reaction to his vast understatement.

"Pressure? What pressure?" I feign nonchalance.

"Want my advice?" Ethan asks. "Don't read your own press."

"What's the fun in that?" PawPaw adds and gives Ethan an elbow.

Of course they've seen the article. But it suddenly matters less to me. I haven't experienced even a tenth of the media spotlight they have. And the article just painted me as a lovesick twat, a fairy-tale prince. These familiar faces and voices are exactly what I need at this moment. *Perspective.*

As Ethan pulls the cart to a stop near the still-empty courtyard fountain, I feel my blood pressure finally drop. I jump out and offer PawPaw my arm to grasp, and he stands with a little wobble.

"Now, this"—PawPaw gestures to the library—"is spectacular, James. Even more than I envisioned." His eyes go glassy with sentiment.

This is all the motivation I need to ignore all the extraneous bullshit and stay focused on the work. This library is for him. I've taken all of his stories, all of his journeys—from World War II to meeting my grandmother to their years of living in Paris, where he sketched the first two children's books that would inspire the Revel universe—and infused them into every detail. Without this man's imagination, none of this exists.

"It really is stunning," Ethan says. "Reminds me of Parisian streets, but with a little touch of home. What are those tiles called?"

"Cedar shake."

"I feel like I'm in the..." PawPaw trails off thinking. "That neighborhood, arrondissement..." He sputters a second, trying to recall, not giving in.

"The Left Bank?" Ethan asks.

"Yes." PawPaw holds up a hand, telling us he's going to get it. "Saint Germain-des-Pres."

"Come on. Let me show you around." I lead them up the path.

I find hard hats for us and lead PawPaw to the ramp, hidden behind the front staircase. In the main foyer, I find the subfloor waiting for the marble, but the rest of the hardwood flooring has been laid throughout. It's gleaming in the morning sun and perfect. From the west wing, Cricket approaches with concern on her face, but I give her a look that says *Not now*. I see her register my grandfather, and she gives me a wink. I guide PawPaw to the east wing, giving a running commentary on the pedestals for special artifacts being crafted out of cherry wood.

"These should be a little lower," PawPaw says, pointing to a corner where glass has been inlaid and is awaiting a nostalgic item to be displayed.

"We've been working with museum designers..." I begin, but then I defer to him. "Have they made a mistake?"

"They should be at a ten-year-old's eyeline." The old man crosses his arms, and I can see the inner workings of his creative brain. "Between nine and ten. That's when they want to see behind the curtain. How things work. Before that, children can look up, or be held. A ten-year-old wants to discover for themselves."

He's still putting a child's dream first.

"You're right," I say, risking a glance at my brother, current CEO of Revel.

"He's always right," Ethan says, and he grasps PawPaw's shoulder again, smiling. They've grown closer. I envy him.

"The scarlet slippers should go here," PawPaw says, pointing to an alcove in the foyer that will soon be lit by a large crystal chandelier.

"That's a great idea," I say. "We've got a whole team working on locating and prepping the items for this space. I'm sure they'd love your input on the displays. You know best how to create a sense of wonder."

"Oh, I'll leave that up to you," PawPaw says, still surveying the place with his clear blue eyes. "Looks like you know what you're doing. It's not my time anymore."

Ethan folds his arms and defers to PawPaw again. "Who knows better than you?" Then he directs his attention to me. "Don't screw it up, Pride."

"Wouldn't dream of it, Bambino." I punch his arm playfully.

"Actually..." PawPaw clears his throat. "James, if you could get with one of the archivists, I'm looking for some documents and photographs from '79 or '80."

"I could ask one of them." I picture Summer again in the cool winter sun. "Could you be more specific?"

PawPaw smoothes his close shave. "They're of a sensitive nature. They might be at the compound in your dad's archive."

"I'm sure they've all signed NDAs," Ethan chimes in.

"Of course," I say. "The person I'm thinking of is trustworthy."

"Good." PawPaw seems to shrink a bit. "This is important to me. They'll be unmarked or stamped 'From the City of New Orleans.'"

"I hope everything's okay." This sounds heavy. "Maybe I should just look for this stuff myself?"

"No, no..." PawPaw surveys the building again, looking wistful. "You've got a lot on your plate."

"Yeah, Romeo has a lot to live up to," Ethan teases, but stops short when I shoot him a "don't go there" look.

"I'll talk to Summer York, PawPaw," I say, giving him my arm as we turn to head back outside. "She's reliable."

"Good, good." My grandfather notices my finger splint. "I hope that's not serious. Still hitting the heavy bags?"

"Always."

After we part ways at their golf cart, I want to reach out to Summer immediately about my PawPaw's secret task, but pushing to see her again after she insisted on keeping things professional may look pathetic. Instead, I put my frustrations into a long day of work.

Chapter Eighteen

Summer

With the cooler temperature, in my new business-casual outfit, and back at work, I feel more like myself than I have in days. It's hard for me to believe it's only been three days since I left Ohio, but here I am in the Revel warehouses for the first time, just over a mile off site.

"OMG," Gemma says, literally smacking her hands on her bronzed cheeks.

We've been told the warehouse is 80,000 square feet of secure, climate-controlled storage, but it's really something to behold. We wander together into the first of thirty-plus rows of shelving, not unlike Home Depot stores, but I quickly notice what I assume my colleagues have noticed as well—there's no specific labeling system. A librarian's nightmare. To my left, I find an odd-shaped box scribbled in red marker with "Mermaid Pins," next to three bankers boxes with printed labels that read "2017 flyers."

"It's like trying to find the Ark of the Covenant," Horace says, his voice grave and muted in this cardboard cave.

"Thankfully, without the Nazis," I joke, and I'm glad he gets my Indiana Jones reference. If Gemma gets it, she doesn't let on.

We waste no time. After walking each full row, which takes a half hour and adds three thousand steps to our daily count, we identify a general year-by-year order, starting in the 1990s. Most of the boxes and containers from before 1997 are lumped together haphazardly throughout the building, which is a massive headache. Many of the items on the list are pre-1980s, the heavy, childhood nostalgia era of Revel, so we'll be digging through a lot of extraneous storage.

Once again, Gemma wants to take the lead and target the high-ticket items herself, and once again Horace and I join together with a better idea.

"Since management has identified their top artifacts," Horace says, "let's work together at first. We can find two or three faster that way, and then we'll start to understand whether Revel has some sort of hidden filing system we can't identify just by looking at this..." He's searching for a polite word for *mess* but can't come up with one.

By lunchtime, we've found what seems to be all of the hand-painted cels for the animated segments of *San Francisco Safari* and all of the cels for *Portia's Power*. I dutifully text Cricket to let her know, and she tells me she'll send someone to collect them soon. My mind wanders through the history of Revel Pointe with each box and file we discover. It's thrilling.

On the chilly cart ride back to the Beau Chêne hotel, I feel satisfied. It's not exactly the Bodleian Library, but spending the day in this warehouse, steeped in pop culture history, getting my hands dirty, has reignited my excitement at the prospect of a long-term job here in Louisiana.

My phone buzzes with more texts in the elevator. Another from Lilia, one from Grainger, and one from James Reve.

Lilia: *Have you done the Island of Sirens experience yet? I am GREEN with envy. Send details. I need to live vicariously through you.*

Grainger: *What's up, Summer. Did you get my email?*

James Reve: *I need to ask a favor. A professional favor. When would be a good time for a call?*

My mind spins. A favor for James? An email from Grainger? The left turns just keep on coming.

In my room, I realize that I'm covered in dust and bits of frayed cardboard. Before I respond to any of these texts, I take a hot shower, and as I scrub the black ink from underneath my nails, I remember holding James' hand in the car last night. *Snap out of it!*

In a daze with a fresh towel around my hair, I finally have some time to relax. I open my laptop. First, I check my work email and find that Frances wants me at the palace tomorrow, while my colleagues will be back at the warehouse. Next, I check my personal email and find the one from Grainger McCloskey.

Hello, Beautiful, it starts. *I got your address from your dad. I was able to score balcony box tickets to the Cleveland Ballet. Small, private side balcony.*

I roll my eyes and continue.

The tickets are for New Year's Eve. Your dad said you'd be home by then and that you love live performances. Anyway, I'm stoked for you to get back so we can actually have a first date. Take care down south. Grainger. PS. I have attached a fun list of questions below. A friend said it made him and his girlfriend fall in love.

Spending New Year's with Grainger McCloskey at the Cleveland Ballet? A questionnaire to make us fall in love? I burst out laughing because I have no idea how to respond. It's too much. He's coming on so strong. I decide to ignore it for now and decide what to do about James' request.

My phone pings with another message from Lilia: *Have you seen this?*

She's also sent me a link to the *LA Times* article.

I reread James' text and my mind swirls. *Little does she know,* I think. I click on the link, even though I've read it a few times already. There's a beautiful photo of the library, but there are also three of James—one of him from high school in a rugby uniform, his face smudged with mud, a publicity shot of him in front of the palace, and a photo of him at ten years old with his little brother Henri, posed in front of the new *Portia's Power* ride with their grandfather, Mick Reve.

The writer has painted the library as a "prestige project," but what's most interesting to me is how she's profiled James, this purposely mysterious character who is poised to save Revel with "romance." The journalist, Reya Ghu, clearly has an angle, with sentences like *"James' own handsome prince stature fits his vision for the Grand Revel Library, which stands in for his noble castle."* James created a beautiful building and this Ghu chick reduces him to a stock character in a fairy tale.

The short paragraph about his childhood makes me a little sad. Private school in New Orleans, raised by nannies in the city. Shipped off to Exeter at eight, then leaving America for college at seventeen. There's hardly a word about a solid connection with his parents or his many siblings.

I scroll back to the rugby photo of James. His eyes seem far away. Even though he's looking at the camera, little is revealed in his expression. But he looks rugged and too damn hot. I exhale a breath I've been holding. A ping wakes me from my reverie.

Lilia: *Have you met James Reve yet? He seems dreamy.*

I flip back to the picture of him in front of the palace.

He's very dreamy. Sexy as sin, I type and hit send. But when the text reads "delivered," I glance up at the top of the screen and panic.

No, no, no! This text went directly to James. I stand and pace.

Do I ignore it?

Course correct with a lie?

Come clean?

I need to make a move before he does, so I quickly tap out: *Sorry, wrong chat. That wasn't for you.*

But damn it! I need to respond to his "favor" text now.

What's the favor? I'm happy to help. I hit send before I reconsider.

I want to tell Lilia what happened and get her opinion on how I should proceed, but James' number lights up on my phone. He's CALLING. I throw the phone on the bed, but then my frazzled brain lunges for it. He knows I just texted, so not answering isn't an option.

"Hello?" I say, sounding as if I don't know who could be calling. So awkward!

"Summer." James sounds calm and collected. "How are you?" His deep voice on the line gives me goosebumps.

"Good, tired. We had a big day in the warehouse. It's not really organized, but we found some stuff. Anyway. You?" I am talking too fast.

"I'm fine," he says. I detect a smile in his voice. "Look, my grandfather has asked me for a favor, and I'd like your help."

"Okay." I take a deep breath. "What can I help with?"

"Do you have time to meet me in the park?" James asks, his voice lower like it's a secret.

"Now?" I ask. "Isn't it closing soon?"

"I have a skeleton key," James jokes.

"Of course you do." I stall. I'm sitting here in a T-shirt with a towel still wrapped around my hair. "Give me a half hour."

"Great," James says. The *grrr* of the word vibrating low in my ear. "Meet me at Maisy's Dance Hall. I want to show you something."

"Got it," I say with the tone of an employee being as enthusiastically agreeable as possible. "See you soon."

After we say goodbye, I text Lilia, double-checking that it's her name at the top of the phone screen. "*Can I call you later?*" When she doesn't respond immediately, I throw my phone on the bed again and race around, readying myself to see James again. In my head, I start a mantra.

You cannot have a crush on James Reve. You cannot have a crush on James Reve.

I let my hair down to air dry; it'll go all wavy and wild, but I don't have time to style it. I settle on a pair of black jeans and a pale blue sweater from my Target haul. I don't have time for full makeup, but I brush on some mascara and my tinted lip gloss.

As I breeze through the park gates and wind my way toward Miss Maisy's Dance Hall, the center of my body gets warmer. *You cannot have a crush on James Reve.*

I check my mom's watch; only thirty minutes until the park officially closes. Tourists are heading toward the front gates. As I round the path past the Princess and the Pea ride, I spot James waiting on the steps of a large old building with a vintage sign in pink lights—Miss Maisy's Dance Hall.

"Evening," James says.

"Good evening," I say, as professionally as I can manage, but my insides are a gooey mess.

Chapter Nineteen

James

This is a professional meeting for my dear PawPaw. I have no ulterior motive, nor do I particularly care that Summer, climbing the wide staircase to the old dance hall, catches me off guard. She looks less buttoned up than usual, a more comfortable version of herself, her long hair falling loose down her back, in a baggy sweater, dark jeans, and sneakers. Up close she smells like lavender.

"Come on, let me show you around." I almost grab her hand, but that wouldn't be professional. Over her shoulder, I note a group of Revelers spotting us as we enter the rarely used Miss Maisy's Dance Hall, and I'm glad we're getting away from the fishbowl of both the park and our workplaces.

"Is that your skeleton key?" Summer asks. "I've always wanted one."

I hold up the very normal, boring key to the old hall. "I swiped it from the security office."

"Oh, right." Summer smiles as we duck into the dim, empty building, our footsteps echoing. "Is there something for the archives here? I don't think this location is on any of our lists." We round a corner, and I wait for Summer's reaction, but she's suddenly quiet.

I lead her across the creaky wooden floor to the center for a better view through the two-story windows. The view is spectacular from here. It's something I remember from when I was a kid. The 1940s style dance hall was my favorite building in the park—that is, before we built the library. The terraced galleries that flank the sides are a unique touch, allowing for breezes to sweep through when opened. Broad, square columns hold up the balconies.

I finally break the silence, unable to gauge her reaction. "Pretty, isn't it?"

"Just...wow." She glances over at me and her skin glows almost pink in this light.

We walk toward the windows. "The park was built in '61, but my PawPaw's era was the '40s. The dance hall was one of the first constructions after the lighthouse, Ferris wheel, and palace."

"Is it still used for dancing?" Summer asks.

"Not really." I'd never been to one of the grand old dances, but I've seen photos. "They used to have events here every weekend. Big bands, touring musicians. Louis Armstrong played here several times."

"Really?"

"I heard they turned it into a disco for a short time in the mid-'70s."

Summer's eyes dart around the place, and I enjoy watching her take it all in. "I'd love to go back in time to see it all."

"Do you dance?" I ask her.

"If you count the Macarena, then yes."

She's so bloody cute that I can't help but close the gap between us.

"So what's it used for now?" She walks away from me, moving in a semicircle, eyeing the balconies and the ceiling above.

"Nothing anymore." I shove my hands in my pockets. "We had the annual holiday gala here, but otherwise, it sits empty. I've heard grumblings about tearing it down. More square footage for another ride or shop, but PawPaw won't have it." By grumblings, I mean my mother's gripes specifically.

"What a shame," Summer says. "I'd love to see it all lit up."

"I could turn the fixtures on, but that would alert security."

"We wouldn't want that," Summer says, and there's a playful tone in her voice. She takes a step toward me.

"No, we wouldn't."

"Do you dance?" Summer asks, looking up at me. She sweeps her hair back. Her sweater has drooped, revealing a pink bra strap and a bare shoulder that I'd like to bend down and kiss. Maybe bite.

I nod. "The waltz."

"Fancy." She actually nudges my arm like we're two kids flirting on a playground.

I take her touch as a cue. In one swift move, I grab her hand, sweep it up and around her head, releasing her out and pull her back against my side. The lavender in Summer's hair mixes with a light undertone. Maybe vanilla. I'd like to nuzzle my nose into her neck, but I hold back.

"You've got moves," she says.

"A few." I keep her tucked along my ribs.

"Seems like your hand is better."

"It is." I gaze down into her maple syrup eyes and nearly move to brush my lips against hers, but she pulls away slightly.

"James."

I want her to say my name again, so I say nothing and wait.

"So, what's this favor about?" Summer clears her throat, letting go of my hand and putting space between us again.

I want to pick her up and kiss her hard against one of these columns and feel her thighs wrap around my waist. I want her to tell me to screw propriety. Speaking of propriety, I remember her misdirected text.

"That text," I say, lifting an eyebrow. "Whose sexiness were you talking about?" My gaze drops down to her bare clavicle. I want to slip my finger under that bra strap and nudge it off her shoulder. I want her to whisper my name.

The look on her face turns to panic. Shit, I've killed the vibe.

"Oh, that was..." she stammers. "About this guy I started, uh, seeing right before I came here." Summer reaches for her hair, twisting and pulling it forward over her shoulder.

"You have a boyfriend." Of course she does. She's gorgeous and smart.

"He's not exactly...my boyfriend, I mean..." Summer keeps twisting a strand of her hair. "I'm not sure what is going on, honestly."

"Ah." Disappointment rises like bile in my throat.

"He asked me out a few times... I've known him since I was in high school."

I want to punch this "dreamy" person until he's black and blue. So, on top of her wanting to keep things professional, there's someone back home.

"There's no need to explain anything to me," I tell her. "I understand. You kissed a total stranger on a plane while dating someone else."

"No, it's not—" She steps towards me.

"True?"

"Well, sort of. I—"

"Don't concern yourself, Summer. I get it." I take a step back. This is good. It makes it easier to walk away.

I cross my arms over my chest and shift us back to business. "My PawPaw asked me to connect with an archivist working on the project in order to find some sensitive documents and photos."

"Oh." Summer lets go of her wavy locks, and I can't help but appreciate how they frame her face. "Okay. I can help with that," she says earnestly.

"Can you come by the compound tomorrow afternoon? It's that ugly, faux medieval-looking castle on the riverside." I've always hated the oddity that is our "family" home, the place my dad built in the early '80s, when he was coked out and full of *ideas*.

"I'll have to check. We work late tomorrow."

"What about Friday? Why don't you come after work?" I suggest without a trace of flirtation in my tone. "I'll feed you for your trouble. A *professional* dinner. Then we can search my father's study together if you don't mind putting in a few late hours."

"I can do that," she says.

"Good." I look her square in the eyes. When she smiles at me, I forget my ire. "Now I do have one more thing, potentially, for the archive. Come with me."

I lead her up onto the wide stage and into the wings. I stop short to reach for a switch behind some dusty curtains, and Summer bumps into my back.

"Careful," I tell her, grasping her arm behind me. "It's this way."

Down another hallway, we find the Green Room where musicians and bands would congregate and warm up before shows. When I flick the switch, the overhead fluorescents blink to life, humming and giving everything a sepia tinge.

"Good, it's still here," I say, crossing the room to a side table with a large lamp.

"What is this?" Summer says, hovering next to me, leaning over to see the glass lamp base that's filled with signatures in various colors of ink.

There's a layer of dust covering everything. I run a finger through it to reveal a vibrant orange script.

"*Luck Always, Fats Domino*," Summer reads aloud.

"A bunch of the greats who played here signed this lamp," I explain.

"Who would know about it?" she asks.

I shrug. "Do you think it would be a contender for display in the library?" I ask her.

"I'm not sure," she says, leaning in to read another signature. "Wait, does that say Sonny Bono and Cher?"

"I think so." This is fun, listening to Summer get all worked up. Even in this awful harsh overhead light, she's stunning.

She tucks her long hair behind her ears to get a better look at another signature. "Gladys Knight? My Gran would flip."

When Summer looks back at me, excitement lighting up her features, I'm glad I asked her to Miss Maisy's. It's so easy to get swept up in her wholesome charm, but now I'm trying not to look forward to dinner Friday night, especially knowing there's a sexy man waiting for her back home. The fucker.

Chapter Twenty

Summer

Despite my best efforts, my crush has fully formed, a troublesome sidekick to keep in check. Recalling the way he took control on the dance floor, gracefully spinning then pulling me into him so that I could smell the cedar musk of his skin and hear his breath in my ear makes me shiver. All over.

I report for duty to Frances at the palace to find I'm back in the storage rooms, searching for documents and photos. I'm alone with my thoughts in these stuffy, confined spaces, searching for the least sexy sounding items, like the blueprints for the Hansel and Gretel ride, a photo of Mick Reve on the set of *Around and Far and Upside Down*, and Mick's contract with his first publisher for a four-book deal that resulted in *Mona's Christmas Party, Theo's Haunted Forest, Maisy's Treasure Hunt, Lucky's Surprise*—foundational children's books and cartoons. I keep telling myself it doesn't matter who finds what, but I'm a little jealous, wondering if Gemma has been tasked with finding the magic staff from *Portia's Power* or Bianca's nightgown from the *Princess and the Pea*.

And even when I find the blueprints, my elation over a job well done is closely followed by a jittery wave of nerves and mortification. I'm meeting James for dinner tomorrow, and I told him I have a boyfriend, sort of, to cover my slip-up text. Would it have been better to just admit I was referring to him?

Another thing that keeps bothering me is my dad relentlessly texting today. I'm concerned. With each meme and joke and question that pops up on my phone, I can tell that he's lonely. After all, it's the holiday season and none of his kids are close by to do all of the Christmasy things. I picture him watching sports and doing his crosswords every night in the glow of the tree lights, alone. I text Kayla. She assures me that they're taking him to Brody's hockey game later.

Needing sunshine, I decide to head out for lunch. As I flick the light switch and swing out from the storage room, I physically bump right into the most fashionable person I've ever seen. The stunning woman, over six feet in her uber-expensive stilettos, drops her file as I drop mine.

"I'm so sorry," I stammer. I crouch and pick up both files, which have scattered on the hardwood floor.

"Next time, maybe look before you leap?" The woman wears a sleek, ice blue dress with a whip of platinum blonde hair on her head.

"Of course," I say, scrambling to make sense of what is hers and what's mine. When I grab a portion of the blueprint, the one with a large mock-up of the Wood Witch's candy house, the woman leans toward me.

"What do you have there?" she asks. When I hand it to her, I get a better look at her angular face. Her eyes and hairstyle seem familiar.

"They're *Hansel and Gretel* ride blueprints," I tell her. "I'm an archivist on the library project." I straighten my black Target skirt and smooth my cardigan, feeling like a pauper next to this woman.

"Ah. How is that going?" she asks, her impeccable, sharp eyebrows raised on her smooth forehead.

"It's going well," I say, trying to imbue my voice with confidence. "We've found quite a few items already."

"Good." She draws out the *o*'s, and I detect a slight Southern accent. When she opens the blueprint to scan it, I take the opportunity to gather up the rest of the scattered files. One folder has lodged itself under the corner of a cubicle. Pages spill out with images of the library in its contents. The heading, "Grand Revel Couture" jumps out at me. I flip the page quickly, noticing a rendering of a high-end store. I reach for another page and see a color-coded graph with the title "Bridal Wear Market Share: The Revel Romance Collection." Before the woman can look at me, I place the pages in her folder and hand it to her.

"Oh, thank you," she says and hands me the blueprint. "This is important work." She points to my old manilla folder with a light pink, manicured fingernail. "Preserving Revel history."

"I think so too," I say. I don't want to keep her, and I'm trying to decipher what my brain just saw. "Again, I'm sorry." I stand aside.

She only nods to me and continues down the hall, her steel-gray heels echoing until they reach the carpet of a boardroom.

"You're lucky," says a deep voice behind me.

I turn to see an extremely handsome man in a navy wool suit towering above me. I recognize him immediately from Lilia's debriefing. He's far more exposed than James, especially on The Secret Reveler blog. It's Ethan Reve, James' older half brother.

"She's in a good mood if she didn't bite your head off," he says with a wink and continues to the boardroom himself.

Holy mackerel. I just literally ran into James' mother, Tilda Olsen-Reve. As I drop off the old blueprint file down to Frances' desk, my mind does somersaults. What exactly was I looking at in her files? Was that market research for Revel bridal wear? *Who would buy a wedding dress from a theme park?* I think as I make my way through hordes of tourists and past the fountains to the French Village. *Duh, all of these women.* It looked like the proposed couture boutique was set up in the library.

When I reach the cafe, I grab food to go and eat while wandering the park, past the boarded and fenced off library site, wondering if James is hard at work inside. I round the path to the lighthouse moat and notice a long line for an observation tower high above.

Finding a bench, I turn my face up to the sun and listen to visitors passing. Some argue about what to do next. A child begs for an ice cream cone and his parents say it's too cold out. Teenage girls hum a familiar song from *Island of Sirens*. This really is some people's happy place, but I can also understand how James feels. He was born into an obligation he can't escape even though none of this, however nice, seems like him.

The Revel complex is so clean and particular, almost nothing out of place. Everything is planned meticulously. It can't be a coincidence that an illustration of the library building was filled with information about Grand Revel Couture and Revel Bridal Wear.

Whatever that was, it's above my pay grade, but I wonder if James knows about this. My thoughts are interrupted by my phone buzzing.

"My favorite youngest daughter!" Dad bellows through the speakerphone, at an ear-splitting tone from a thousand miles away.

"Hi Dad," I begin. Hearing his voice triggers tears out of nowhere. I'm not homesick, but after these whirlwind days, his voice makes me feel like me. "How's it going at home?"

"Good, good." He sounds busy with something on the other end. "You picked a good time to leave. We're in a deep freeze. Nineteen degrees..." And he drops his phone.

"Dad? What are you up to?"

"Oh, well, Grainger asked me to help him out at work," he says, still shuffling with something. "These deck chairs are really something. Simple design. It feels good to give my hands something to do."

I love this image of my dad, back at work, with purpose. It's sweet of Grainger to hire his mentor after all these years. Dad turns the conversation back to me, asking about the job.

"This place is wonderful." I tell him about the tickets I found on the first day and the blueprints I found this morning. "You raised a nerd. It's nerd heaven."

"Like a pig in shit," he says, using my mom's old saying. This makes my heart ache.

"You know I am," I say, surprised when a tear falls onto my lap. "I gotta get back to work, Dad, but you need to visit."

"Sounds good, kid." Something loud in the background obscures his voice. "Go find the Hope Diamond! Love you."

"Love you too."

Buoyed with the knowledge that my dad is keeping himself busy, at least for now, I head back to the palace to look for more priceless objects, feeling a tug of guilt because I haven't thought about Grainger much since sitting in row eleven.

Chapter Twenty-One

James

Tilda asked me to have lunch with her in her penthouse suite at the Resort, where she stays when she's working on park projects. She also has a home in uptown New Orleans, an apartment just north of Lincoln Square in Manhattan, and a flat in Paris in the 7th arrondissement. She never stops working, so her other homes are empty or lent to potential business partners.

The private penthouse elevator opens directly into her apartment foyer where a striking painting, a Mondrian Chrysanthemum, hangs in shades of purple and gray. Tilda's personal chef passes me on his way out of the suite. I wind my way through the large, empty kitchen that my mother never uses and find her seated at the dining room table, looking at her phone. There are two plates on the table, each covered with a sterling silver dome.

"What's for lunch?" I ask, giving her a light kiss on the cheek.

"Seared tuna Niçoise." She puts her phone down, screen up, on the glass table. "Bon appétit."

I sit opposite her at the square table. I place my napkin in my lap and spear my first green bean. "So, the article." I dive right in, but it doesn't catch her off guard. She only raises an eyebrow as she slices into half of a hard-boiled egg.

"Must you always be so blunt?" she asks.

"I don't have time to be coy," I reply. She usually prefers direct.

"Neither do I, frankly." She gives me a look and chews. "You need a haircut, darlin.'"

I run my hand over my beard, which definitely could use a trim. "I know."

"Have Lucien make you an appointment at The Wright on Carondelet," Tilda says without looking up. "Go see Bill's barber. He's excellent."

Bill Symons, the Chief Financial Officer? That fortysomething CrossFit douche? How would she know where he gets his haircuts? Their familiarity points me to the obvious. She's sleeping with him.

"Do it before the gala," she commands. "You need to look the part for the photos."

"What part? What is this about?" I try to control myself. Emotions have no effect on her. Never show your cards to Tilda Olsen-Reve.

"I'm trying to do my job." She looks up at me, a halved cherry tomato on her fork. "We need you to sell this library concept to the average woman. The wives bring the husbands, and the husbands bring the wallets."

"That's a pretty mid-century view of Revel fans."

"Don't be naïve," Tilda says, taking a sip of her sparkling water. "We've done the market research."

"I don't doubt it."

We eat in silence. For a second, I can hear the distant screams of park guests on the Steampunk Coaster.

"You know," I begin, clearing my throat. "I don't appreciate being a pawn."

"What do you mean?"

"This sham *LA Times* article that was pitched to me as library publicity," I continue. "If it was going to be a bullshit piece about me, then I needed to know."

"You wouldn't have gone along with it." She's right, but so wrong.

"Regardless," I go on. "You're interfering with my life." I look her in the eyes.

She leans forward, her voice sweeter. "I'm just pushing you a little 'in the direction of your dreams.'"

My mouth drops, shocked she remembers a line from my favorite movie, *The Secret Quest Book*. Who is this woman and what has she done with my mother?

"I have my own dreams, Mother."

She stabs a rare piece of tuna and gives me a pointed look, as if to say, *Sure you do*.

"Listen," I say, and Tilda's eye twitches. Her look suddenly turns into one that says, *Don't fuck with me today*. "We have the script for this conversation, and we could perform it, but let me do it quickly for the both of us. I say, 'My dream is to build my own architecture firm,' then you say, "But you're a Reve,' and I say, 'But I'm not interested in working here,' and you say, 'One day you will be CEO of this company,' then I flip a table and tell you I don't want it. Then you breathe fire and tell me I'm giving up my birthright. Am I far off?"

Tilda puts her fork down and threads her fingers together on the table. "Why fight it? You belong here."

"No, I don't. You sent me away from here, and I've built a life elsewhere. A profession. And frankly, I don't have any connection to any of this." I gesture to the park, and though it does have some sentimental value to me, I don't want to spend my life pleasing the shareholders in a swamp.

"Don't punish me for giving you the best education money can buy. And you *do* have a connection to this place." My mother smiles. She knows I'd do anything for PawPaw, for Henri and my half siblings. "You can't run from who you are. You're a Reve. *You* can have it all. Ethan is bound to fuck up, and you—"

Tilda's phone screen lights up, interrupting her flow.

"I'm finishing this job, and then I'm leaving," I tell her.

"Speaking of the job, the gala is fast approaching." Although Tilda has changed the subject, I know she hasn't given up.

I sigh, then bring her up to speed on the marble, plumbing, design, and chandeliers.

"Sounds like it's under control," Tilda says as she throws her napkin on her plate.

"It's going to be tight, but we will finish for the gala."

"Good." The tone in her voice signals that this lunch is over even though I haven't touched more than a quarter of my plate.

"But there's a little snafu you need to work around. The gala team will need to get in there by December 20th. Can you make that happen?"

"You just cut three days off our schedule." I feel my stomach drop. "This is unrealistic."

"But you can make it happen, yes?" Tilda sits back in her seat, leveling an all-business stare at me. This is the shark look that helped make her the success she is today. It's gone in a flash and replaced by a softer look and a smile. "It *is* PawPaw's big evening, and it has to be perfect."

I scan the project plans and schedule in my head. The main job left is finishing all of the woodwork—the railings, spindles, moldings, and ornate banisters that are being made at a shop off site. I'll have to go there today for a status check. The install should be fairly quick if we have the manpower.

"I'll let you know by end of day." I stand and once again feel ambushed on my way out. "No promises."

"Ta, darlin'. I know you'll figure it all out." Tilda waves and immediately answers a call. "Ciao, Luca!"

In the Beau Chêne Resort lobby, I run into Cricket, who launches into an explanation for why she's here.

"After the library's done, we're going to remodel the old *Hansel and Gretel* suites into *Island of Sirens* suites." She matches my stride as we leave together. "Out with the old and in with the new," she chimes. "Hey, that reminds me, Summer contacted me today. She said you brought her to Miss Maisy's, and there's a priceless lamp to collect for the library? Fill me in, James. What's this lamp and why'd you call her and not me, huh?"

Ambushed again. I have no real response except that I wanted to see Summer again because I'm not sure I should mention PawPaw's request to find those sensitive documents.

"It's her job," I say. "To handle the archival items... and I figured you'd be gone for the day..."

"I'm teasing, James." Cricket elbows me. "It's okay to have a thing for a co-worker."

"I don't have a 'thing' for Summer." I run a hand through my hair and try to recover my composure. The search for the documents is tonight. The professional, not-a-date dinner is too. I can feel Cricket's smug gaze.

"Yes, you do," Cricket says. "You were a mess at dinner, and it's kind of adorable."

"Oh, bugger off," I say. "Don't you start with all the romance shit. That sodding article."

"I won't, but you should at least ask her to the gala. You need a date."

"She has a boyfriend," I tell her. The thought of Summer's blushing cheeks as she flustered over the mistaken text and told me about the hometown boyfriend flashes through my mind. My jaw clenches.

"Perfect. That makes it strictly a professional outing," Cricket says. "You know, if you go alone, especially after that article, the vultures will be circling. You will be the belle—excuse me, the *beau* of the ball, and the ladies will be on you like Cajun spice on rice."

"Fuck." A scene of what the gala could be—a maze of reporters, dolled-up single women, and photographers—flashes through my brain, and I recoil.

"Yeah." Cricket looks at me, her expressive eyebrows raised, her tangerine lips smirking.

She's right, but I don't concede. We have a different issue to contend with—one that is sure to put an end to the romance talk.

"Tilda's moved up the project completion date by three days," I tell Cricket, who grabs my arm and stops me in my tracks.

"You're lying," she gasps.

"I'm not."

"You need to finish the damn woodwork," Cricket complains. "We can't hang wallpaper or any of the artwork until that dust has settled."

I know this. I've heard it before. We've already employed every last available skilled carpenter in the Gulf region. I'm going to have to work some magic somehow. Call in favors. I cannot let PawPaw down. The clock is ticking.

Chapter Twenty-Two

Summer

By our end-of-day meeting, my muscles ache. I'll need to soak in an Epsom salt bath before I meet James. Spending days in the warehouse lifting and lowering boxes of all shapes and sizes, sometimes sitting on the floor, not to mention walking close to twenty thousand steps a day—that will do it to a body.

Frances and Cricket are excited by our finds. Horace, Gemma, and I have gathered twenty-eight of the fifty-five pieces on our A-List and laid them all out in a palace conference room on the second floor. The other teams have already met with them. Among the items are some truly magnificent objects: early sketches of the Nautilus, Atlantis, and Captain Nemo from *20,000 Leagues Under the Sea*, delicate figurine prototypes from *Thumbelina*, helmets and storyboards from the space film *Mission: Tranquility*, props like the flower pot and umbrella from *Around and Far and Upside Down*, and Technicolor animation cels from *Rose Red* and *The Snow Queen*.

Frances keeps cupping her hands over her mouth in awe. She's like a kid, though a reserved one, each time she lingers over another piece of Revel history. Cricket is more tactile and calculating, touching each one at the corners, gingerly with her index finger and thumb. Her eyes narrow as she thinks out loud about where each one might be placed in the library.

"I'm going to call the curators today," Frances says. "They've been on standby."

Cricket grabs a copy of the A-List from the table and scans it. "I'm still waiting for these. She pulls out a blue highlighter and circles six items.

Frances leans over to see what she's prioritizing and nods. "Well, we've got one set of the red shoes in the offices here. In the boardroom." She points up, in the general direction of the room where Tilda Olsen-Reve and Ethan Reve met yesterday. "But we have more than one set. I can't believe the others are buried in the warehouse." She shoots a look at each one of us—Horace, then Gemma, then me.

"And *The Secret Quest Book*, too." Cricket sets the list back down and places her hands on her hips. "We should have more than one first-print copy. There's one in the lobby here, but where are the rest?"

"Maybe Gaspard or Mick knows?" Frances says. "Hm... Maybe I'll approach James..."

"You'll approach me with what?"

My body goes warm all over at his voice behind me. I haven't seen him since our rendezvous at Miss Maisy's, and I'm suddenly very aware of the dirty patches on my khaki pants, my messy bun that I did without a mirror hours before, and my faded and likely smudged makeup.

"Perfect timing," Cricket says, smiling wide.

James notices the Nautilus sketches and moves to that side of the table. "This is brilliant." He looks back at us, and the light in his green eyes shows his playful side, even though his expression is muted.

Frances lists the items we're still looking for. "Would your father know where might be?"

"I doubt Gaspard knows," James says. "But I could check with my grandfather." He moves around the table, examining items from his family legacy, and then he lingers closest to where I stand. He picks up a photograph of his grandparents standing under a movie marquee, each the hand of a child, one boy and one girl.

"I've never seen this," James says and reflexively leans toward me. "This is my dad and my aunt Alice."

"They're so cute," I say. Gaspard can't be much older than eight and his little sister even younger. They're dressed like tiny adults, surrounded by photographers and 1960s paparazzi.

He puts the photo back down and ends the sidebar to address everyone else. "I'll do what I can, but frankly I'm strapped. I'm bringing the horologists in tomorrow to make sure the clock is ship-shape, and I need more carpenters. Yesterday." He runs a hand through his unruly, walnut-colored hair, which merely flops back over one eye. A thrill warms the center of my body when his eyes meet mine again for a half-second. "Anyone know where I can find a crew of woodworkers?" He scans each of our faces with a sheepish look. "I wouldn't ask, but we've hired everyone in the Gulf region and it's the holidays, so desperate times..."

It takes me five seconds to snap out of my dreamy daze to realize that I *do* know woodworkers. I know at least two—my Dad and Grainger. But Grainger has his own business, and he'll also be busy with holiday orders.

"Actually, my dad is a skilled craftsman," I say. "He made custom, luxury wooden boats his whole life." I start to feel stupid for mentioning it. The skills for building wooden motor boats probably has nothing to do with crafting whatever James needs in the library. "It's probably not the type of carpenter you need."

James' posture straightens, his chest puffing out, shoulders back. "Depends. But I'm thinking he's exactly the type of craftsman I'm looking for."

James asks for my dad's number, handing me his phone. I copy it into his contacts with his name—Mitch York—and hand it back to him, our hands grazing for a half-second.

"That is serendipitous," Cricket says, winking at me.

Frances nods along, and our meeting comes to a quick end. "If you want to earn some overtime," Frances offers, "I can approve Sunday hours tomorrow." She grabs her phone and makes a note when Horace and I agree. Gemma, looking as if she ate a lemon, says she can't as her sister is flying her son in tomorrow for the weekend.

As we file out of the conference room, James motions for me to linger. My body is on alert, his familiar scent of soap and lumber tightening my chest, but he's all business.

"Do you want to give your dad a heads-up that I'll be calling?"

"Sure," I say and text Dad as we saunter down the hall.

"Nice work in there," he says, holding the elevator door for me. "I wish I had time to really take it in, but I'm under the wire." He pushes his shoulders back and seems even taller than usual.

A random employee rushes in behind James, and we all ride down one floor in silence. Tense silence.

My dad's return text dings the second we cross into the reception area.

Dad: *Sure thing! Free in 30 min.*

I tell James, and my head spins at the possibility that my dad could be on site at the library soon.

"Brilliant," James says and cups my shoulder in his big palm.

Outside, Revel Pointe is in full-swing madness. Crowds of families and friends fill the walkways around the two massive fountains at the entrance that I've come to love. As we wind our way up the center path, heading straight for the lighthouse, James and I are pushed together in the chaos. He dons his sunglasses, and as I brush past his chest, I become almost dizzy on contact.

In a small clearing near a French Village crepe cart, we stop to part ways.

"We're still on for tonight?" James asks. "Around seven?"

"Uh, sure," I say, not meaning to sound so hesitant. With Dad potentially coming to Louisiana and James' attention making me dizzy, I'm a little lost for words. "I mean yes. Where should I meet you?" I rub my aching shoulders. I feel like I've pinched a nerve. My body needs a break; I haven't pushed it this hard since physical therapy.

"I'm not sure, but I'll text you," James says. His eyes narrow. "Are you okay?"

"What?"

"Your neck." He points to where I'm pinching my shoulder. "Did you hurt yourself?"

"Oh, no, I'm just sore," I say, laughing it off. "It's been a long, physical week, using muscles I rarely use, I guess."

"Take a bath with Epsom salt," James says, frowning at me with authoritative concern.

"That's the plan," I return, almost melting at the way James' slight accent gives the word 'bath' a sensual feeling.

"Okay, well, I'll let you know what happens with your dad."

"Yes, okay." This is all happening so fast.

"All right."

"All right."

But neither of us moves to go. We hold each other's gaze, and I wonder what he's thinking. A nearby child screeching at full blast breaks our moment.

"Text you later," James finally says and turns, disappearing into the crowd.

Forty-five minutes later, when I've already been in my bath for ten minutes, my dad calls. His voice is full of pure joy. James Reve has hired him to come work on the library, and Lucien, James' assistant, is setting up travel plans for Dad this weekend.

I'm beyond thrilled. One, my dad will be here at Revel Pointe during the holidays and not alone missing Mom. And two, this job gives him purpose, a team to work with, and maybe new ideas for a part-time retirement gig. At sixty-two, he's still full of energy, and it would be a shame to see him grow more sedentary in the coming years. The pay is outstanding, too.

"I've always wanted to see the park," Dad says, sounding like a little kid. "And now I'll get to see it at Christmas!"

"It's so beautiful lit up with twinkle lights at night," I tell him. "You'll see."

A knock at my hotel door startles me. At first I think it can't be for me, so I listen and wait.

"I think there's a knock at my door," I tell Dad. "Can I call you back?"

"Go, go..." he says. "We'll see you soon!"

There's another knock on the door, louder this time.

"Coming!" I call, stepping out of the tub and pulling on the fluffy white hotel robe.

When I open the door, expecting maybe Horace or Gemma, I'm surprised by a blonde woman in a spa uniform carrying a large folded table.

"Are you Summer York?"

"Yes," I reply, confused.

"You have a massage booked."

"I do?" I ask. "No, it must be a mistake."

"It's not a mistake. Mr. Reve's assistant called. If you're free...?" The woman shifts in the hall, resting the table on the carpet.

Goosebumps rise from my ankles to my neck. "Yes, I'm absolutely free," I say as I realize that James has sent this massage therapist angel to me. My body floods with gratitude. After I tell her what to expect, specifically the scarring on my back, she's all business.

During the soothing but deep-tissue massage, I think of James' generosity, but also his mixed messages, how one minute he's grabbing my hand for a twirl on a dance floor and the next his eyes are stony, his body rigid. He's an enigma that I want to unravel, but maybe part of his allure is his total off-limits position in my life.

Luckily it starts to pour outside, and the sound of rain pelting the hotel balcony signals my entire being to shut down and give in to complete relaxation.

After my heavenly massage, the therapist packs up the table and sheets, and I check my phone. James has texted.

"Thank you so much," I tell the RMT as she ducks back out into the hallway.

I flop onto my bed in the plush robe, my muscles all relaxed and gooey, and eagerly read James' text..

I hired your father. He should be here Saturday by noon. Thanks for the tip, Summer.

Part of me wants to dance and squeal, but my body is now mush.

I text back: *So happy I could help.*

I wait a second while the tingles below my tummy pulse excitement into my hips. I can't believe he can turn me on like this from far away. No one has ever excited me the way he does, not even Grainger.

I can't wait for his reply, and text again: *Btw, thank you for the massage fairy.*

The three pulsing dots send more ripples of anticipation into my core. Finally, his response comes.

James: *My pleasure.*

Goosebumps rise again on my flesh at the thought of his voice saying, "pleasure." Arrows of heat shoot through my limbs, down my torso, and between my legs. The white noise of the rain dripping lulls me, and I instinctively reach for the steady pulsing at the center of me. My hand finds its way down, cupping over my panties, first massaging, and then finally slipping under. I close my eyes and groan when I recall his kiss in row eleven, how he indulged my fantasies by suggesting we board a plane to Europe. My imagination finds us making out on an ancient rampart, overlooking a rugged highland landscape.

I tuck a finger inside and moan with visions of his green eyes looking down at me in the dance hall last night. Instead of him pulling away, I imagine he leaned in, giving me another of his firm and lingering kisses. The idea of his lips against mine, his arms wrapped around my back, his tongue finding its way down my neck, sets me off easily in surprising waves.

My chest heaves, and I almost laugh out loud in the quiet room. This is so unlike me. Self-pleasuring rarely does the trick, but just the idea of James sends me over the top. Afterward, I stare at the rain streaming along the window pane, letting it put me in a meditative space. I can't be *this* into a guy, can I? I definitely can't be this into James Reve, my superior, a man so off-limits and out of my league it's a joke.

After a quick shower, I get ready for our "professional" dinner. As I apply mascara, my phone buzzes. I check my screen eagerly.

It's Grainger: *Guess what, gorgeous? I'm coming to Revel Pointe. Saturday. With your dad to work on that library. They're paying us a crapload of $$. Funny coincidence, right?*

Another text springs up. Grainger, again: *Can't wait to see you! (Kiss emoji)*

Shit, I think, as I realize my dad said, "*We'll* see you soon."

Chapter Twenty-Three

James

It's too cold to pick Summer up in a golf cart, so I head to my father's garage and choose his least ostentatious vehicle, a charcoal gray 1980 Porsche. I arrive at 6:45 on the dot. Summer's waiting in the lobby, and I jump out quickly to meet her. I'm well aware of how many eyes could be on me, so speed is my strategy. She looks edible in a cream-colored sweater dress, black tights and boots, and her long winter coat.

"Hello."

"Hi," she says, pulling her long braid forward.

I open the passenger door for her, and she says, "Cool car," as she ducks inside.

I feel desire tighten my body. This is going to be a long night.

Summer's eyes fill with wonder when we pull up to the Reve compound.

"It's my father's home. We call it the compound." I go on to detail how Gaspard built this place in the '80s when he started to take over more responsibility in the company. "It's his fortress," I tell her, opening the side entrance door and smelling her gorgeous floral scent as she walks past me. "I think of it as ugly-beautiful," I continue, explaining how it's a faux 12th century Anglo-Saxon castle that's completely mismatched with the signature French Palais at the front entrance. There's a stretch of rampart that hides the hillside levee. "It's actually an architectural windfall. It could act like a second levee if the river should ever flood here."

In the first-floor sitting room, decorated in soothing sage with an Andy Warhol—a pastel Queen Elizabeth II—on one wall and a Monet landscape on another, Summer gasps and slows her pace, taking everything in. I take her coat and fold it in my arms.

"I'll give you the tour after dinner," I tell her, keeping my distance so I can watch her. "Are you hungry?"

She nods as we pass through the downstairs hall into the open turret, where a circular staircase rises past a three-tiered gas-lamp medieval chandelier that makes the space bounce with delicate orange shadows. Summer gasps again.

"Oh my goodness," she says, her head back, exposing her slender neck. "I've been wondering what was inside this building. I can see it from my room on the sixth floor. This is where you've been staying?"

I nod, but she doesn't look back at me. "Yes. I'm alone here right now," I say. "With the staff," I add, trying not to sound creepy. "My father and his wife, Yasmin, are staying on his boat on the North Shore."

"So this is where you grew up?" Summer takes each step slowly in front of me, giving me a perfect view of her curves as they shift beneath her fitted sweater dress. *Damn*, she's killing me. I avert my eyes and focus on the three suits of armor rising into view on the landing. I imagine a knight's bloody guts filling the lower breastplate as he lay dying on a Scottish battlefield, to keep from imaging Summer beneath that dress.

"Not really." I clear my throat. "I left for boarding school at eight."

"This is..." She spots the suits of armor and speeds to them. "Are these real?"

I nod, smirking, holding back my delight at her enthusiasm.

"Late 15th century." She's hovering over them closely, examining the etching on the shoulders. "You can touch them. I know you're going to say they belong in a museum, but this is basically a museum." I slide the helmet visor up and down, letting her know my father has experts who maintain them properly.

"Oh my gosh," she says, running her fingers lightly over detail on the breastplate. Her Midwest accent drifting in the vowels is so fucking cute.

We pass through the turret study, where Summer lingers again. And why shouldn't she? The room has floor-to-ceiling bookshelves, a massive brick fireplace, and inviting dark decor. I want to grab her hand and pull her by the fire, but I don't because I'm being professional.

In the dining room, the staff has set the table for two at one end of the twelve-seat set. Thankfully, they've got us facing each other. Lots of space between us.

As soon as we sit, the server, Rene, pours a light Beaujolais, and Summer's eyes meet mine. She holds her glass out to toast and simply says, "Thank you for bringing my dad here. He's so happy to be working on such a prestigious project."

"Of course," I say, reminding myself this is a "work" dinner.

"He's really good at what he does. You should see his boats. Anyway, cheers."

"Cheers." I raise my glass, and we have to reach to clink them.

"How's the hand?" Summer asks.

My body goes rigid. I don't want to think about it or what caused me to punch a wall. "It's fine."

"Oh, good." Her features go blank, but her cheeks flush.

I know I must appear rude, having dropped the small-talk ball she's just lobbed to me. "I apologize. I'd just rather not talk about it," I explain. "I've had enough drama for the week. For a lifetime, actually."

Rene returns with small plates, a fried green tomato Caprese salad.

"I can only imagine what it's like," Summer offers.

"What?"

She gestures around the room. "All of this..."

"Ah, well. It's constant drama, spitting at us like a Gatling gun. I used to worry about how every feeling I expressed or didn't expressed would look. Every word I utter or don't utter, every action I take or don't take to this day will be analyzed and pilloried in the press. If I never read another story about Revel family scandal again, real or imagined, I'd be happy—" I stop myself. My candor surprises me. I focus on cutting the tomatoes into little pieces.

"Shitballs," Summer whispers and I look up.

Her face is fucking priceless. I burst out laughing.

"What?" she says indignantly.

"Your face... It's just... You look so sad and earnest—" I try to stifle my laughter, but I can't stop now that I've started. "Shitballs!?"

"So sorry that I'm— I'm empathetic!" She crosses her arms.

This causes another peal of laughter to erupt from me, but then something magical happens: Summer's laughing with me. Her provincial ease is so foreign in this place, it's completely disarming. She doesn't take my laughing as an offense. In fact, she's beaming at me, and I can't remember the last time I've laughed this hard.

When Rene comes in to remove the salad dishes, he's clearly confused, which prompts another outburst. Eventually we settle down into amiable silence, both of us catching our breath. I take the moment as a cue to bring up the reason for this dinner.

"I spoke to my grandfather about the documents again," I tell her. "If we don't find anything tonight, I'm going to head over to his cottage sometime tomorrow." Then I get an idea. "Would you like to come?"

"Come where?"

"To my grandfather's house. It's much easier for us to go to him." I explain how he doesn't live far, in a modest home with a nurse who checks in on him.

"I mean, I'd love to." Summer blinks at me, her eyes slightly glassy, reflecting the warm glow of a votive between us. "If it fits in with my schedule."

"It's technically work," I tell her. "I approve it." I smile, but she frowns back.

"All right," she says. "I'll just check in with Frances first."

"I'm sure she'll be fine with it if we're returning with the red shoes or a copy of *The Secret Quest Book*."

"You mean the scarlet slippers..." Summer starts and then stops herself. "Never mind. I'll go with you tomorrow."

"Great," I say. "You'll love my grandfather. Everyone does."

Summer grins and nods, and I wonder if the idea of meeting *the* Mick Reve is too overwhelming, so I change the subject.

"The clock is finally keeping time," I tell her, and when she gives me a quizzical look, I clarify. "The clock tower? These large clocks apparently still only work analogue. There are so few people left who are skilled enough to keep them working."

"That's sort of depressing." She glances at me through her eyelashes. "A dying craft. Digital clocks wiping out a whole profession."

I nod. "Well, I found a small network of horologists who are keeping the torch lit."

This makes her smile again. "Thank heavens."

"You should meet them," I say, raising a saucy eyebrow to keep her smiling. "The horologists. They'll be back in a few days. I'll introduce you."

"Okay, I guess..." She appears confused.

"The view from the clock tower is extraordinary," I offer, trying to get the beaming Summer back.

"I'm sure it is," she says, seemingly retreating into herself more.

She takes a sip of wine, so I do as well, filling the space. We remain silent until the server returns with our entrees, fresh crawfish ravioli in a light lemon-cream sauce. I know I'm staring, but her lips on the glass are mesmerizing.

I wait for Summer to take the first bite, and she makes an adorable "mmm" sound.

"This is too good." She moans with satisfaction.

The need to touch her is overpowering.

"I'm sorry," Summer says, and I look up, concerned that I've telegraphed my thoughts out loud, but her gaze is fixed on something over my left shoulder. I glance over toward that side of the room, where a statue sits on a maple table between two dark windows. "I've been distracted by that piece over there." She points. "What is it?"

"That is actually my favorite thing in the whole house." I stand without finishing my plate. I'm too excited. This intricate work of art was my favorite as a child. I cross the dining room, telling her I'll bring it over.

"It's called *The Little Warrior*," I tell her, picking up the metal automaton of Joan of Arc on horseback under a tree. There's a hound on the metal ground next to the horse and a crow on a branch of the tree.

I'm remembering my father winding up the delicate toy for the first time with a coin, when my shoe hits the edge of the massive carpet and I trip forward, stumbling down hard to one knee, but saving the precious 18th century automaton in the process. I land like I'm genuflecting to Summer, holding out a gift to her in my hand.

Summer gasps, and at first I'm mortified. Her already large, expressive eyes go comically wide. *This night just couldn't go worse,* I think. But then a genuine laugh ripples up from my gut. This whole night is absurd. Her, me, working together, attracted to each other, wanting to cross the romantic line but deliberately *not* crossing the line because of the circumstances.

I'm laughing again, which triggers Summer's giggling.

"Milady." I gesture for her to take the piece from my hand. I'm relieved when her laughter grows.

"I'm sorry," she snorts. "For a second, I thought you were going to land right on top of me."

I can only imagine what that clumsy trip must have looked like, paired with my obvious relief at not smashing this priceless piece. It has me laughing so hard it brings tears to my eyes.

I ham it up as I rise. "How quickly you have me on one knee, Princess Summer of York."

"Stop," Summer giggles, holding her middle. "Are you okay?"

"'Tis but a flesh wound," I say, standing and straightening my shirt. I want to keep her laughing, that little, high trill at the end of every chuckle sending extra beats to my heart. I breathe, shaking out the jitters of the whole evening so far.

I sit down next to Summer. "Now that I've lost my dignity entirely, check this out." I pull a coin from my pocket and carefully crank the little groove in the base of the automaton.

We both go quiet as the gears whir in the mechanism. Joan of Arc raises her sword as the horse rears back, lifting its front hooves off the base. Next, the hound bows, and the crow opens its beak as if cawing.

"It's so beautiful," she says. I chance a peek at her gorgeous amber eyes.

"Wait..."

As the horse lowers, the whole base moves along the table twelve inches, then turns ninety degrees and advances six inches, then again and again until it makes a rectangle and comes to a stop.

"Extraordinary," she whispers.

"Isn't it?" I say, very aware that our knees are now touching. "My dad brought it home from his travels when I was six or seven. My brother Henri and I weren't allowed to touch it. We had our own toys, but this thing fascinated us."

"I can see why." Summer leans her elbow on the table and searches my face. The sparks from row eleven return. "Do it again."

I oblige, and we watch the automaton make its elegant gestures and full rectangle. When the horse lands again, I search her relaxed face, her full lips so close.

Just then, Rene returns to the dining room to check on us. I return to my seat, clearing my throat. We've barely touched our cooled ravioli.

"It sort of reminds me of my Gran's cuckoo clock," Summer says, still examining the intricate piece on the table between us. "She could reset it so that it went off every five minutes, so my sister and I would watch it over and over. The little dancers circled and the little bird popped out of the window at the top."

"I've seen those." I nod and tuck back into my pasta.

"My mom always wanted one of her own," she says, moving her fork through the sauce and focusing her gaze on her plate. "She always said she wanted to get one in Germany. She dreamed of a big anniversary trip to Europe, and my dad would always say he'd get her an authentic cuckoo clock from the Black Forest region."

Summer's deep brown eyes go misty, darting from her plate to the automaton to me, but I give her space and keep listening.

A tear drips from the inner corner of her eye when she looks up at me quickly.

I reach my hand across the table, and she allows me to hold hers.

"I'm sorry," I say and caress her knuckles with my thumb.

"It's okay," she says. "It's still hard, especially during the holidays."

"I can imagine." Strangely, I *can* imagine missing a parent even though mine are both living. "Was she sick?" I tread as lightly as I can. I've been told I'm terrible at emotions, erring on the side of stoic. I never know what to say, so I say nothing, but I always feel them. And right now, I feel for Summer. I want to make her feel better.

"No." Another tear escapes down her cheek over her tawny freckles. "It was a freak accident, at home. She was alone in the garden at the back of our lot. My dad found her. She cracked her skull on a rock." She stops, sucking in a breath to keep from breaking down. "Head trauma. They say she probably died instantly, but we'll never know."

"I'm so sorry, Summer." I don't know what else to say. The image of a woman dying alone in her garden is so tragic. I ask, "What was her name?"

She looks up at me then, directly into my eyes. Tears have wet her long, dark lashes, and another drips down the crease of her nose. "Isabelle."

"Like your book," I say.

"Yes." The smile that spreads onto Summer's face is so lovely it physically hurts. "You remembered."

My throat feels tight. "Who could forget the scandalous Queen Isabella?" I attempt a lighter tone, and the look in Summer's eyes tells me it's the right move.

Her gaze lingers on me, and it makes me want to hold her in my arms, stroke her long, soft hair, keep her safe from more heartache.

She takes a few more bites, and then finally breaks the moment by dabbing her eyes, asking, "Um, which way is the bathroom?"

I give her the directions and tell her I'll meet her back in the turret study.

As Summer stands and walks away, brushing her long braid over her shoulder, I realize I'm in trouble. I like her, in a way I haven't liked a woman in...well, ever. But with her father arriving tomorrow, she'll be dealing with her home life clashing with her work life. And then there's the boyfriend-slash-guy-she's-seeing issue, which usually wouldn't deter me, mostly because my romantic relationships are basically flings. But seeing how raw her feelings are still about her mother, I know I can't risk a fling with Summer. And I know I can't give her what she needs either. I'm out of this place, this country, as soon as possible.

I shake my head, refill our wine glasses, and make my way to the study, vowing to respect her boundaries and really keep it professional from here on out.

Chapter Twenty-Four

Summer

In the beautiful hall bathroom, looking into a stunning gold mirror etched with birds, I dab the smudged mascara under my eyes and take stock of the roller coaster of emotions I'm dealing with.

When will talking about my mother get easier? My grief feels like a never-ending pit that keeps opening up just when I thought I'd grabbed a foothold. Though it's been two years, it feels like it just happened. But James asked *her name.* That tore me apart inside. And when he remembered the book and made the connection, it felt like he could see a part of me that no one else has. The moment was so intimate that I wanted to live in it with him. This is such an impossible situation. *James Reve? Who am I kidding?*

And then there's the other issue at hand that is so much bigger than James knows. My dad and Grainger will be in town tomorrow. I am still trying to figure out the Grainger McCloskey situation. In the first place, why is he suddenly so interested in me? All evening, Grainger has been blowing up my phone, insisting we have our rescheduled date here in Louisiana. I tap my phone screen in the bathroom, and there's two more texts:

Grainger: *We could take a riverboat cruise. There's a sunset jazz dinner we could do. Sounds fun, right?*

Grainger: *Just let me know when you're available. Can't wait to see ya.*

And then there's the minefield that is James himself. *Why did I tell him I have a boyfriend?* When he pulled up in that sports car, I was immediately off-balance. I've never been a car girl, but in that moment he was such a movie star guy, opening my car door and setting such an overtly sexy tone that it was all just too much for me. My reality tipped again, learning that the odd, castle-like building is actually the Reve family home? The opulence. The original works of art. Everything so over-the-top, it's like Technicolor come to life.

Dinner was *interesting*. True, there is no clarity as to what this friendship/working relationship/attraction is between James and me, but when he took control of my work schedule, after he insisted he's not my boss the other day, that irritated me. After that, he kept throwing gas on that fire, whether he realized it or not. It still irks me, knowing that tomorrow I have to ask, or tell, Frances—my actual supervisor—that James Reve requests my presence at his grandfather's house. It looks like some kind of flirty favoritism, which it is. He's put me in a shitty position, but he doesn't even know it. I should go out there and tell him.

Then again, part of me wants to meet the famous Mick Reve, one of the most important innovators of American culture. And part of me, my elemental desire, just reacts to James' pheromones when he's close to me. That's what it is, I tell myself. *Biological chemistry*. I can't help it. Hormones want what they want. I picture the goofy look on James' face when he fell, and my inner thighs melt.

I wash my hands and tell myself to keep it all business for the next few days at least. Juggle my dad, Grainger, and my own yearning to sit in James' lap until this project is done. Maybe I could give in to these innate desires after that, but for now, James is a mistake that I can't make. Not now when the stakes are so high.

In the study, James stands before another priceless painting with a glass of wine in his hand and turns when a plank creaks under my foot.

"More wine?" he asks, but I shake my head.

"Let's get to work."

He nods, his expression mute. He leads me past the incredible suits of armor again and through a door on the left. It's completely dark except for three narrow windows with views of the sparkly lights in the park. It's nearing closing time, but the twinkling Thumbelina Ferris wheel still circles slowly in the distance. I can't help but hold my breath while James searches for the light switch.

When he finds it, dim wall sconces come to life, casting a warm glow across two brown leather sofas and two matching armchairs. At the far end is a chunky, wide desk fit for the likes of kings. The walls and ceiling are a pretty wintergreen between thick wooden beams, giving the room a sense of the outdoors; it's like finding myself enclosed in a lush forest with a dense canopy. I want to just drop into a sofa and read a book.

But James wanders over to the coffee table where six large lidded boxes await us. Two are marked "Revel Channel," referring to the Revel Pointe TV Channel that was popular in the late '80s to mid '90s. Two are marked "Family Merch." One says "Originals" and the other is unmarked.

"This is juicy," I say, hovering over them.

"Go ahead," James says. "You signed the NDA, right?"

I nod and he opens the box marked "Originals."

In the first envelope, there's an item we've been looking for—color storyboards for *San Francisco Safari*. In another box, we find a proposal with blueprints for the actual Mona Moon lighthouse. I take it out carefully and spread it onto the desk.

"I take it you were looking for both of those?" James asks.

I nod and also shake my head, taking in the wonder of this beautiful original illustration, leaning over the desk to examine the intricate detail.

"This is the coolest job I've ever had," I tell James, getting carried away by the whimsy of these items.

James' wide smile is so sexy that a knot pulses beneath my belly button. He perches on the arm of a sofa and folds his arms. I swear he must see the lust rising like steam off my body. To distract myself, I turn back to the boxes.

I uncover a stack of black and white photos of famous people in the early days of the theme park—Elizabeth Taylor, Doris Day, Louis Armstrong, and several of Elvis Presley. The Elvis photos are my favorite of the bunch. The others merely pose with Mick Reve, but Elvis is having a blast, riding the rides and eating a hot dog. These aren't on the list, but I think Cricket would be interested in them. James inches toward me on the sofa.

"We need to show these to Cricket," I tell him.

"I totally agree," he says. "I'll send her a few shots." He leans over them with his phone, trying not to cast shadows, and takes a few quick photos.

There's so much more, including an envelope of contracts with actors and voice actors over the years, framed papal blessings from Pope Paul VI and Pope John Paul II, and a script written by Billy Wilder called *The Popsicle Stand Man*, a film that was never made. None of the items seem like the sensitive photos and documents that Mick Reve is looking for, and I say so.

"There's more where those came from," James says.

I'm exhilarated, wanting more, but I'm starting to feel the long day.

"Want some water?" James asks, and when I nod, he says, "Be right back."

Stupidly, I watch him leave, letting my eyes drift to his fit behind. I need to actually shake my head to turn back to the boxes. I choose the unmarked one and look through what mostly seems like documents in file folders. These could be what his grandfather is looking for. In the final file, there are three small Revel-blue envelopes. My first thought is jewelry. We've definitely been looking for Princess Marie's diamond necklace and Prudence Pleasant's ruby flower earrings. Of course, there have been dozens of real versions made, but the originals would be costume jewels. When I grab the envelopes, though, I feel only paper.

The first appears to be a financial document. I notice the word "Trust" along with a name and date: Aurora Marie Mallory-Reve, June 4, 1979. I wonder if this is a stepsister or cousin I haven't heard about yet, and though it doesn't matter to my work, I keep digging, opening the other envelope. It's another trust, this one for Simon Edward Mallory-Reve, also dated June 4, 1979. Another sibling? I close it and open the third, having a strong hunch this is exactly what Mick Reve is looking for. In this envelope are photocopies of Louisiana State birth certificates for Simon Edward Mallory-Reve and Aurora Marie Mallory-Reve, born twins, April 30, 1979. Father: Gaspard Michael Reve. Mother: Celeste Ann Mallory. Place of birth: Charity Hospital, New Orleans. There's a single photo of a woman with a blonde bob holding a baby in her arms with an older woman standing alongside her hospital bed holding the other.

I'm no Revel expert, but I know for a fact that these babies are not a part of the official family tree. *Oh, shit.* This is too much. James' words at dinner echo in my head: *"If I never read another story about Revel family intrigue again, real or imagined, I'd be happy."* Before I've had enough time to think too much, I stuff the sensitive envelopes into the box I've earmarked to take with me to the office tomorrow. If there's a way to put these directly into Mick Reve's hands and spare James some family drama that he wants no part of, then I feel like I should try to make that happen. Someone closer to him should share this information. A big part of me feels protective of James in a way that is risky for me, but I don't have time to examine that. When I hear James' returning footsteps, I put the lid back on the box and stand in front of it.

"Find any other valuables?" James asks, handing me a glass of water. He has the red wine bottle in his other hand and pours himself another. This time he sits comfortably closer, looking up at me where I stand awkwardly, probably wondering what I was just looking at.

"Not really," I say, knowing I do not have a convincing poker face, especially when I'm not playing poker.

"That sounds like something," he says, sipping, not taking his eyes off of me.

A wave of heat ripples through me. God, he's hot. It takes everything in me not to straddle him on this sofa and run my fingers through his wavy hair.

I clear a space on the coffee table and take a seat across from him. "No, it's just that everything is valuable," I say. "And my eyes are getting tired."

"It's been a long week," James says, his body sunk back into the sofa as if there's nowhere else he'd rather be.

"It really has," I say, hands on my knees so I won't put them anywhere else. For a second, I think maybe I made the wrong move, that I should tell him and show him exactly what I found. But he looks so at ease finally, the stress lines gone from his forehead.

"I'm glad you came tonight," James says. "It seems like it was fruitful."

"And thank you for dinner. Best meal I've had in years. I'd love the recipe. I... uh..." I'm rambling, and I know it's because I'm terrified that he will kiss me and at the same time praying for it.

James takes a sip, looking so laid-back and in control that I want to scream, "Just take me!" but he scoots forward and tells me, "You'll have to come back."

I nod and look at the boxes, wanting to want to keep my distance.

"One more before I take you back?" James stands next to me, leaning closer to open a lid.

I turn toward him and his cedar scent mixed with the bouquet of red wine is enough to intoxicate me. I peer into the box but focus on his hand, his strong wrist. My hand involuntarily brushes his forearm, and we turn toward each other, my breast lightly brushing his bicep. There's a half-second I hesitate before looking up at him.

His head tilts down, and just as I'm convinced he's going to kiss me, a loud mechanical noise drifts into the office from the hallway. James jerks his head away and looks over his shoulder. An elevator bell chimes softly, and then there's the clear sound of shoes on hardwood floors.

"Who the hell...?" James turns completely away from me.

We wait for a second, then another, my heart beating so hard it pulses in my ears.

"James?" A man's voice floats into the room.

"PawPaw?" James calls, now heading for the open door as *the* Mick Reve enters the frame, pushing a walker to the side and stepping unaided into Gaspard Reve's office with a tote bag over his shoulder. "What are you doing here?"

"I got your message," Mick says, grabbing his grandson's arm and pulling him in for a hug. He's about to go on when he sees me, standing amid a mess of work in his son's house. "Oh, dang... I hope I'm not interrupting..."

"Of course not," James says. "This is Summer York. She's an archivist working on the library project."

"Yes, Summer," he says. "I know who you are. It's a pleasure to meet you in person."

I try to take in what he just said, but it doesn't compute. Mick Reve knows who *I am*?

"The pleasure is all mine," I say, hopping over to his side to shake his hand. "But how do you know me?"

"I was at your interview. Over the phone?" he cues me. "I didn't say a word, but I was listening."

"You were?"

"I was." His dark blue eyes almost twinkle in the lamplight. "I wanted to know who would be sorting through our mess to find our rare gems. Some of this stuff is so precious to me. I couldn't have just anyone digging through it."

My mind immediately jumps to the trusts and birth certificates. I can't help but think those are precisely what he's referring to. And now I feel like I should hand them over. I just don't want to involve James if I can avoid it.

"It's my honor," I tell him.

"Have a seat with us, PawPaw?" James offers. "A glass of wine?"

Mick says no to the wine but takes a seat in the closest armchair. Then he holds out the canvas bag for me to take. "I think your team is looking for these?"

James crosses to the opposite side of his grandfather and together they watch me remove a small shadow box with a set of the scarlet slippers from the film mounted inside. They're much smaller than I anticipated and more worn, too. I imagine they were actually worn by the actress, Audrina Petrov, for at least some of the filming of Revel's famous musical. The satin is still shiny in places. The black suede soles are brushed. The square toes of the ballet slippers have tears and a shade of dust.

"Wow." I'm sure my face says it all. "Just wow."

Mick Reve is nodding along with me, his smile wistful, perhaps for those days on set, promoting the film, his life when it was still unfolding. He holds his index finger up. "Oh, and this as well..." From the bag he pulls an old copy of *The Secret Quest Book*, wrapped in plastic. It's the original square printing in French. He hands it to me, and I'm bombarded again by the weight of this almost sacred object. "And this one, too."

This time, he hands me the first American edition, the fancy one with the gold filigree.

"I had a copy of this when I was a kid," I tell Mick and James. "It was my mother's." I can't help it. My eyes water. There's too much wholesome goodness in these books I'm holding, in my memories, and in the eyes of the two sweet men watching me react in awe. "I'm sorry," I say, overcome.

"Don't be," Mick says, leaning over and grabbing my hand. "These stories are powerful. Not to be toyed with." He sighs and then releases my hand. "My Marie loved them, too."

"Are you sure I can't get you a nightcap, PawPaw?" James asks. "Join us?"

"No, no..." Mick says, pressing himself back up, as James comes to his side.

"Do you want your walker?" James asks, rising to fetch it.

"Nah, don't need it." The Revel giant waves him off. "It's just for show. Insurance and all."

And it's obvious Mick doesn't need it, moving slow but sturdy and standing almost as tall as his grandson. I want to run after him, but I can't think of an excuse. I feel stuck, glued to the floor.

"Can I drive you home?" James asks, holding the door frame as Mick leaves the office.

"Got a car waiting downstairs." He winks at me. "I was never gonna stay long. Good night, Summer. *James.*" He claps his grandson on the arm, gives him a wink, and then he's off down the hall again. When the elevator chimes again, I meet James' green eyes across the room.

"Wow," I say, sounding like a broken record. "That was something else."

"He always is." James scratches at his beard.

A tender feeling passes between us, and I break it to look down at the shoes and books again. Suddenly overwhelmed and exhausted, I sigh with my whole body. I don't want to leave James, but I must for so many reasons.

"Shall I drive you home?" James asks, reading me correctly.

"If you don't mind?"

"Of course," he says, telling me to leave everything as is, motioning to the boxes, files, blueprints, documents, photos, and truly precious objects. "I'll have Cricket send someone to gather these up in the morning."

"I'm going to take this one," I say, pointing to the lidded box I set aside. "These *San Francisco Safari* storyboards will complete the set we found at the warehouse." I picture the three blue envelopes I tucked under those illustrations and hope James doesn't want to double check the contents. "You might want to hand deliver these to Frances." I point to what Mick has hand delivered to us.

"I will," he says.

The short drive back is quiet but relaxed. The evening has been a carnival ride. I need a minute to gather all that I've felt and witnessed tonight. As we pull up to the lobby, under the bright lights of the Revel blue awning, the jitters enter my belly again. *Is James going to kiss me goodnight?*

But he places the car in park, and the valet opens my passenger door. A chilly wind whips into the cramped space. James places his warm hand over mine.

"Thanks again for tonight," he says. "I had a great time."

"Me too." I blink back at him, sure he's not going to make a move in front of this valet. Appreciation for him swells in my chest. "Thank you. I guess I'll see you..."

"See you, Summer," he says, his voice so low it sounds like a growl.

Chapter Twenty-Five

James

I've driven myself out to meet Summer's dad and his two helpers—a round man with a handlebar mustache named Derek and an all-American type with a rower's chest called Grainger about my age. All three have arrived at the shop bright-eyed and crisply Midwestern in their flannels and Cleveland Browns apparel. Summer's father, Mitch, is almost exactly as I had pictured him, with a bit of a potbelly but polite and handsomely gray in his early senior years.

His handshake is firm. "I can't thank you enough for the opportunity, Mr. Reve," Mitch says. "For me and Summer. She just loves it here."

"Please, just James," I say. "And I should be thanking you. This job is massive, and we're running out of time."

"We've worked with tight deadlines before," Mitch says, his eyes already searching the shop.

I shake hands with the other two. I don't really need to meet them all, but they're Summer's people and I'm curious. Grainger gives me his full name and attempts to crush my hand. I don't dignify this with a comment.

"Well, I trust you've been taken care of?" I ask.

"Oh sure." Mitch's hand rests on his tool belt like he's itching to stop talking and start mitering or sanding something.

Derek pipes up. "They've got us at the Holiday Inn Express. Seems new."

"Great, well..." I turn to survey the spindles on a bench close by.

"I thought we'd be staying at the resort, where Summer's staying," Grainger says, his chest puffed like a high-school jock. So he's been in touch with Summer.

"No, no..." Mitch says. "We're fine. Better than fine. Just down the street from the shop."

"Perfect," Derek says.

"But we'd like to see her." Grainger gives Mitch a leading look and then gives me a stern one that pisses me off.

"I'm sure she's busy too," Mitch says. "We're all working with the same schedule, right?"

I nod, but I want to oblige her father and please Summer, whose face lit up just at the thought of showing her dad Revel Pointe. I speak to Mitch directly, ignoring Grainger, who uses too much product in his slick blond hair. *Keep him away from the blowtorches*, I think.

"I'll see her later today," I tell Mitch, enjoying this flex. "I'll ask what works for her."

This seemed to satisfy Mitch, but not Grainger.

"I'll just text her," he says, pulling out his phone. "And send her an Uber or something."

Mitch tries to quiet him, an embarrassed look crossing his face. "Let's just get to work."

"She's expecting me to get in touch." Grainger folds his sleeves back, and I note two of those rubber bracelets people sell to fundraise noble causes. Another type of flex.

The workshop foreman brings over two guys he's poached from a crew in Biloxi.

"We're heading to the site and need more guys for the banister install," the foreman tells me.

"Good." We discuss logistics for a second, then we're ready to move forward, which is excellent news.

"I'll go," Grainger volunteers and before I can intervene to choose another guy, the foreman nods in the affirmative. "Sweet."

I leave, but all the way back to the library site, I wonder if this Grainger is the guy Summer said she's "kind of" dating. I remind myself it doesn't matter; I'll be leaving for London soon.

As I drive the winding river roads back to the park and it starts to rain, images of last night flicker through my thoughts. Summer's laughter. Her easy vulnerability when she shared about her mother. Her eyes full of wonder, examining the *Little Warrior* automaton. Her intensity as she uncovered the memorabilia from my dad's study.

The rain subsides as I reach the library, and the sun opens up the cold sky. Revel has rain contingencies for the die-hard tourists, but the crowds are usually thinner on days like this. I've beat the carpenters here, and as I cross the gravel parking lot, a hawk swoops low, landing briefly in the grass right in front of me. When it flaps its wings to lift from the ground, I see a small rodent in his talons. *Ominous*, I think, as I duck inside the building.

Cricket and her team have performed miracles. The painting and wallpapering are done in the east and west wings, mostly in understated navy blues, grays, and a surprising, muted honey-mustard color that makes the Revel blue pop in subtle ways. Some furniture is in place. I linger in a space between the foyer, hall, and west wing and notice how she's already hung some black and white photos here, mostly of Mick and my grandmother, Marie, at premieres. Three lamp fixtures hang low above the library tables and carrels, providing a soft but clear light, making the wood and brass glow.

My first thought is that I can't wait to show Summer around this building when it's complete. I picture her in a gown at the gala, taking in all the sights, getting excited with each detail as she did last night in my father's home office. And now I think I probably shouldn't ask her because of how excited I'm getting.

I spend an hour inspecting workmanship and job status. I'm distracted by the sound of a van pulling up. I take out my phone and snap a few photos of the temporary railing that follows the length of the sweeping staircase and circles the gallery around the grand foyer above.

Marcel enters ahead of the team, not surprised to find me here. He brings me up to speed on the banister team. There's going to be a lot of sawdust from the sanding today, but he assures me that most of the spindles are pre-lacquered and ready to install.

Behind Marcel, Grainger practically bounds through the door carrying two heavy-looking containers and sets them down on our newly laid and grouted marble.

"Hey," Grainger says to me. "We're here to save the day." He gives me a toothy smile that probably wins most people over, but not me.

"Indeed," I say, backing away.

Summer's father and Derek are not far behind with the rest of the hefty team, just as the sky breaks with rain again. We all hear it pound the roof.

"Sounds like a hurricane," Grainger says in his obnoxiously booming voice.

"Then you've never heard a real one," I say, trying not to sneer.

"You're right, I haven't," he says, reaching into a canvas bag and yanking out his tool belt. "We're safe from natural disasters back in Ohio. Who'd want to live in a place with hurricanes? Doesn't make sense to me."

I ball my fists and need to walk away, but I hate when people who don't know what they're talking about run their mouths.

"Because it isn't a suburban hellscape with no history," I say.

Grainger opens his mouth, but he's cut off by Marcel who directs the crews to hang drop cloths and plastic sheets across the west wing.

"Well, I'd love to hang and chat, but there's work to do, chief," Grainger says to me, grabbing his hammer and actually making a clicking sound with his tongue. He gives me the once over. "You might want to stand back. Things are about to get intense."

I'm wearing black jeans, a cream Henley, and my dark green wool jacket, but this bro scoffs at me like I'm sporting a tuxedo. I run a hand over my beard and then step away, taking off my coat, setting it on an empty pedestal. Nothing seems as important in this moment than showing this dickbag who's actually the boss. I ask Marcel if I can borrow some of his tools today and get my hands dirty.

Fuck him, I think, ready to put my back into this big install. I know my way around a site. Guys are setting up saws and tables on drop cloths laid over the marble.

"I'm here to be an extra set of hands," I tell Marcel and the carpentry team leader. "Anything you need, I'm here."

Marcel slaps me on the back, guiding me to a container of pre-cut sections of banister to bring up to the second floor. It's heavier than I anticipate, but I lift with my legs. As I take the stairs instead of the elevator, I feel my body strain in a satisfying way. I glance down at Grainger and Derek, determining which box of spindles to start with, and they glance back up at me. When I reach the top, I can feel my abs fire. Already my mind is clearer with my body hard at work.

Chapter Twenty-Six

Summer

All night I tossed and turned, nightmares disrupting my sleep.

I couldn't fall asleep because of James. I almost made the move to kiss him again, leaning toward him in his father's study. *What the hell am I doing?*

And speaking of complicated, there's Grainger. Oh, he's handsome, but he flaunts it, and I don't feel a fraction of the attraction I feel for James. Grainger also sees us having a relationship as a foregone conclusion. It's too much. He sent me fourteen texts yesterday. *Fourteen.* Some were in conversation with me, but the final eight were just narration of what he was doing at the shop, suggestions for where to go on a date, memes, and photos. Is this what other girls like? Even if I don't get the permanent position and I go back to Ohio, to my job at Westerville High and living with my dad, I don't think I'll be dating Grainger. I feel that certainty to my core. Farewell, teenage dream.

And then there was Mick Reve and the documents I found. I need to give those to him somehow. Why the hell didn't I just give them to James? After getting back to my hotel room last night, I did some internet sleuthing. The twins would be in their mid-thirties now, older than James' older brother, Ethan. I found a Simon Mallory, a family counselor in Baton Rouge, but I couldn't find anything on an Aurora Mallory or Aurora Reve anywhere, not even on social media sites. I looked up their mother, Celeste Mallory, but there was only a high school yearbook thumbnail that popped up on an ancestry website. When I clicked on it, the photo was behind a paywall, but the high school listed was Ursuline Academy, an all-girls

Catholic school in uptown New Orleans. I got nowhere, but I didn't really know what I was looking for. And again, it is none of my business. *How do I get this to Mick Reve without upsetting James?*

The whole morning was a blur at the warehouse as I kept caffeinating myself, rereading labels, and finding nothing, alone in my row of late 1970s storage.

At midday, the lights flicker as thunder passes overhead. I check my phone from time to time, hoping to hear from James, expecting to hear from Grainger, but they are both absent, which is fine by me. I have enough in my head without them invading again. My sister Kayla sent holiday photos of my nieces. She wants updates on Dad and Grainger and the job, which includes intel on James Reve, as she's also read the *LA Times* article.

I haven't found a single item on my A-List today, but I've started to come up with cataloguing ideas for after this temp job ends. Gemma and Horace have both scored today, and I'm thrilled. It keeps the spotlight away from me. They still don't know about the scarlet slippers, *The Secret Quest Book*, or any of the other items that James was supposed to deliver today to Frances. Maybe I'm just tired, but I'm a little annoyed that Frances hasn't shared that news yet because this secrecy is troubling me. I don't want my co-workers or Frances to learn I've been hanging out with James Reve in the evening at his family home. Even though nothing has actually happened between us, at least since row eleven, that's exactly where their minds will go.

Finally, just before we call it quits for the day, I find two boxes with *Tail of the Dragon* figurines and play sets. Cricket has asked after these several times, and I immediately text her. They are cool little action-figure dolls with a tree fort set, a mountain lair, and a dungeon.

"The '70s got trippy," Gemma says, holding a purple boar-like creature with daisies growing on its back.

"Yes, they were," Horace replies, opening the warehouse door to a blustery wind that blows it shut with a scary thwack.

"Damn." Gemma looks concerned.

I get a return text from Cricket regarding our finds of the day: *Can you bring me the Dragon stuff? I'm at the library for another twenty.*

"I'll drop you guys off," I tell my colleagues. "I gotta make a special delivery."

Neither of them argues as thunder rumbles in the distance.

On our way back to the resort, wind sweeps over the levee. My long skirt billows, and I have to tuck it under me as I drive so it doesn't get caught in the wheels. The golf cart provides no shelter from the weather, but the library isn't far on the service road. Despite the impending rain, I'm thrilled to be visiting the library again, as I haven't seen my dad yet and he'd texted me a photo of himself on site.

As I arrive just past six, the crews are loading the construction vans, and I see him exit the building with a duffel over his shoulder.

"Dad!" I call as I jog as well as I can with two awkward boxes. "Dad!"

As he reaches the van, he looks over, finally sees me, and waves. "Summer!"

I set my boxes down, and his familiar warmth and deodorant scent envelope me in a giant embrace. "I'm so glad you're here," I tell him. "How was your day?" My laughter is filled with giddy wonder.

"Busy," he says. "But we accomplished so much. You need to go see."

"I will," I say and hug him again. "It's so good to see you. It feels like I've been gone two years, not two weeks—"

I'm cut off by massive arms wrapping around me from behind, which sends a cold panic through my body. I stiffen and then hear the sound of Grainger in my ear.

"Surprise!" he says, spinning me around and picking me up in a bear hug. "You look amazing as usual."

"Careful! I have collectibles!" I try to sound playful and forceful simultaneously.

My dad chuckles awkwardly when Grainger finally puts me down.

"What did you find today, Summer?" Dad asks. I pull out just one troll from *Tail of the Dragon*, still in its original package.

"Originals from the '70s." I hand the troll to Dad, then Grainger swiftly grabs it.

"My brother used to have these," he says, and the plastic packaging crinkles in his large, dirty hands.

"Careful," my dad and I say at the same time.

The crew behind us continues loading the van.

"Well, we're off," Dad says "Getting something called 'oyster po-boys,' and then we've got a couple more hours back at the shop." My dad looks tired but thrilled. Happy to be useful.

"We'll be done next Friday," Grainger interjects. "And I'd like—"

"I'd like to show my dad around the park," I tell him and turn to Dad. "As soon as you have time." I hope my tone and lack of texting communicates to Grainger that I'm not interested in going on a date with him anymore, whether here or back at home.

Someone bangs on the van and shouts, "Let's go! I need a brewski."

"We need to talk," Grainger says, clearly annoyed.

"I gotta go, too," I say, picking up my boxes.

"See you later," Dad says and gives me a quick peck on the cheek.

I wave to them as the van pulls onto the service road and disappears.

Returning to my mission, I skip up the back stairs to the library. The wind whips open the door, slamming it against an iron railing.

My hair loosens and falls in my face as I enter a wing of the library covered in drop cloths. Cricket peeks her head around a plastic sheet.

"You know how to make an entrance," she says with a smile.

The place is empty, smelling of lacquer, sawdust, and male body odor, but the railing and banister on the grand staircase and gallery are almost complete. It has a stunning effect. So much has changed since I was here a week ago.

"Wow," I say. "Nice job."

Cricket and one of the curators smile wide.

"Thanks," she says, motioning me to spread the toys on the table.

They're both clearly excited, holding each toy up to admire. They murmur ideas and point to areas of the first floor, deciding on where to place these dynamic pieces.

"People will love these," Cricket says. "Even though this film wasn't a smash hit."

"It has niche fans," the curator says.

Cricket moves to an alcove where a sticky note that reads 'Lighthouse Blueprint' is stuck to the wall. "Maybe here? In plexi?"

If they have the Lighthouse Blueprint, then James delivered the stuff we found from his dad's office. So far, no one has mentioned my part in finding it. I hope it stays that way.

Lightning flashes. All three of us jump.

"I'm taking these to the studio," the curator says, leaving through the draped plastic.

"All good?" Cricket asks, glancing over at me as she picks up her many bags.

"Oh yeah," I say. "Just a bit exhausted. But I'll power through. I think there's only about eight A-List items left to find."

"That's incredible," she says. "Seriously, needles in haystacks." Thunder rumbles closer now. "Shit, I'm parked on the opposite side of the park."

We cross the foyer, and I open the front door for her. "You should run before you get caught in this," I say.

"You too," she says. "See ya! And thanks for bringing the toys!" She trots off down the front steps and away down the oak path.

Alone, I wonder who is going to shut off the lights and lock up. Fortunately, two painters arrive at the top of the stairs, trying to leave before the storm hits as well. I follow them out the back way, racing out to where I parked the golf cart, but it isn't there. *What the hell.* Some worker must have commandeered it. The first drops of rain plink the gravel, and I'm stuck without a ride back to the resort.

I duck back into the library. Intense and impressive, the rain pours down loud on the roof. Everyone has gone now; I suppose I could just wait out the storm. I take the tie out of my dampened hair to let it dry. In the open foyer, I stand dead center and do a full rotation, taking it all in. This could be where I work full-time. It's too big of a thought to really comprehend, so I wander away to where containers of books wait to be shelved. I scan the titles. So many classics. Revel reference books. Biographies. I don't want to snoop too much, but I wonder if this is the next part of my job anyway.

Without warning, the rain lightens. I wait, thinking maybe I should make a move before the storm lets loose again. The quickest way back to the resort is through the oak glen, past the Safari ride, and around the Steampunk Coaster, so I race out the front doors, down the steps and into a light rain. As my boots crunch on the pebble path, I notice a man coming from the opposite way. I'd know his figure anywhere. It's James, drenched, his strong chest and abs defined in a clinging white shirt. Dear god, he's heading straight for me.

Chapter Twenty-Seven

James

A day of hard labor was just what I needed. To feel my hands callous, my shoulders strain, and my patience tested on the banister install was a kind of meditation. I channeled all my tension and angst about where my life is headed into the job, putting my sweat into the library.

The only downside was dealing with that complete wanker, Grainger. I tried to keep my distance, but the meathead was hard to ignore with his loud, obnoxious voice dropping hints about his romantic intentions for Summer.

I left work in a daze. Halfway home, I reached for my phone, but it wasn't in my pocket. Fuck. I'd left it with my green jacket at the library. Just as I turn back, the sky lets loose, forcing me to duck under the awning of a souvenir shop in the French Village. The storm pushed in closer to the park, and the few tourists and employees huddled at the edges to watch the downpour.

When the rain tapers off again, I decide to book it back to the library. Entering the oak glen, I see a woman exit the library and race down the front staircase. I only catch a glimpse, but I know it's Summer. She appears on the path, obscured by foliage, and then she's walking right toward me in a long, full burgundy skirt and gray winter coat. A classic beauty. Her breath plumes in the cold air and light rain.

I say nothing. What is there to say? I'm not expecting to see her here, but here she is.

"James, hi," Summer says, only steps away now.

Her voice is breathy and so damn sexy that I break. I reach out and grab her hand. I pull her to me and cup her chin in my hands, and then I kiss her, as I've been imagining since our lips last touched on that damn plane. She gives in to me, and her mouth tastes like cinnamon candy, so sweet I want to devour her. My lips move across her jaw, down her neck, and the sound that comes from her throat hardens every muscle in my body. Eventually, I pull back. Out of breath, she searches my eyes. A smile curls her pink lips, and only then do I realize it's pouring again.

Grabbing her hand again, I lead her in a dash toward the library just as lightning strobes across the rooftop. In less than two seconds, thunder cracks close. Summer lets out a squeal. I want to sweep her into my arms and keep her safe.

Inside the foyer, I pace quickly, like a wolf sniffing its territory, checking to see if any crew still lingers. When I turn back to Summer, she is standing at the newel post at the bottom of the stairs.

"We're alone," Summer says, her voice meek but assured, her signal to me. She wants this, too.

I bound across the foyer, taking her in my arms again, diving my hands into her coat and pushing it off her tight body. Our mouths move on each other again, and we stumble back onto the stairs. My hands explore over her thin sweater, feeling the firmness of her breasts pressing into my touch. Her nipples are so taut, and I need to taste them.

"Wait," she says, pulling back. "What if..." Her eyes shift to the front doors. If anyone were to return, they would get quite an immediate view.

I pull myself off her, clasp my hand around her hip, and sweep her to her feet in one motion. Without thinking, I bound up the stairs, pulling her behind me. At the top of the staircase, I pause for another kiss. My head swims with possibilities. Visions of Summer, naked, in every nook and cranny of this library.

"This way." I hold Summer's hand and lead her to the east wing, across the dim room where white lightning flashes through the wide windows.

Summer says nothing, but her grip is firm in my hand. She keeps up with me as I weave us to a door at the far end. Inside is another staircase, this one with narrow, enclosed corners.

"James," she pleads. She wants me to touch her, and I'm overcome with lust. I sit on the stairs and pull her onto me. Her body, on mine, is heaven. I lift her sweater to feel her skin, and she helps me take it off. In the dim storm light, I get a peek of her black lace bra and can't help myself. My mouth is on her neck, my hands are on her, cupping, squeezing, over and under the delicate lace. My mouth moves along her collarbone, moving down with an intensity I've been holding back since we met. She moans, and it's what I've been desperate to hear. She hikes her skirt so that she can straddle me on the stairs. Through our clothes, we press ourselves together. My hands find her hips, pulling her as close to me as possible.

Thunder shakes the building. I lean back as lightning from the open door flickers over her body. Her hair cascades away from her face as she arches her back.

"You are so damn beautiful," I tell her, tracing my hand from her jaw, down her neck, over her breast, along her waist and then her hip. I need to see more of her.

"You are too," she whispers. I can sense her blush in the darkness, but she follows my lead, sneaking her hand up my wet shirt, and caressing my skin underneath.

Just as I'm about to unhook her bra, we hear a door open and slam below.

"Come on," I say. We get up, and I pull the tower door shut behind us.

Chapter Twenty-Eight

Summer

"Come on." James' deep voice vibrates into my body, and when he closes the door, we're left in almost total darkness. I cling to him at first, then slowly work my hands under his wet shirt and help him peel it from his hard body. His strong scent alone, of wood and sweat and amber, amplifies my desire.

My center throbs at his every touch. We hear more movement and voices below, but James kisses me anyway, softly, like he's enjoying dessert instead of devouring a meal. I worry someone will hear us, but I can't stop my hands from exploring James as I wrap my arms around his wide back. The chance of getting caught makes this even more delicious. Every time the lightning flickers, I get flashes of him, his eyelashes, his broad shoulders, his dark beard.

"I want to see you better," James growls. As he stands, he lifts me up with him. I grip my legs around his waist and wrap myself around him. As he climbs the rounded stairs, I think we must be in the clock tower. I kiss his neck, and his groan is almost a whimper of pain. We go up and around steadily and slowly as the rain pounding the roof gets louder. The anticipation of feeling more of James and what is yet to come sends pulses of heat between my legs.

Just above us, light from the sky filters in through the frosted glass of the clock face. I can see the clock hands and Roman numerals clearly now as the storm continues to illuminate the sky. James sets me down on a landing and runs his hands through my hair as he kisses me deep.

"Summer," he whispers, slipping off my bra. His hands wander down again, one finding its way up my skirt, pushing the fabric aside, and gripping my thigh, as his mouth finally finds my unencumbered breasts. When his hand hesitates, massaging near my ass, it makes me ache.

"More," I tell him, hearing the sexy pleading in my voice that I've never experienced before in my life. Goosebumps cover my skin. I might pass out if he doesn't keep going.

James' hand finally reaches between my legs, shooting ripples of euphoria through my body. Thunder rumbles further away, and I moan into his mouth as his tongue sweeps across mine.

"Tell me what you want," James purrs like a panther.

"Keep going," I whimper.

His fingers tuck inside my panties, then inside of my wetness, and I bite back a guttural sound.

"Don't hold back," he says. "We're safe in the tower, Summer."

I release the breath I was holding in a dreamy sigh, and James continues to move his fingers and palm between my legs, anticipating the exact motion my body is aching for. I reach for his face, but he's busy inhaling my breasts, teasing my nipples, biting my neck and shoulder. The tickle of his full beard on my delicate skin starts a reaction of tingles down my arms. My whole body explodes from the center in wave after wave of overwhelming bliss.

When I'm reduced to calm twitches, James kisses my lips again, gently.

"I've imagined you like this." His voice is almost as deep as the thunder. He backs away, straddling my leg, and I get a beautiful view of him, his strong chest and his sculpted abs, all with a spray of dark hair. "Do you want to...?"

"Do you have a— you know."

He nods and grabs his wallet from his back pocket. He gives me a sexy grin as he unbuttons his damp jeans, unzips, and then pulls at the wet denim. I sit up and kiss his abs, helping him scrape the pants down his legs. God, he's beautiful. When he's naked and ready, I pull him back down on me.

"I need you," I demand.

He lifts my skirt up around my waist and moans as he enters me. He's slow at first, and the sensation is almost enough to set me off right away, surprising me. I've never had two orgasms back-to-back. I squeeze my thighs against his ass, taking a little pressure off, even though James tells me not to hold back.

"Are you comfortable?" His beard brushes my ear.

"You feel incredible," I tell him. "Almost too incredible."

James groans again, then he moves harder against me, edging on rough, reduced to his animal nature. I lick the rain and sweat up the front of his neck. He tastes of minerals and sex. We finally buck together on the stairs, and James presses his face into my shoulder. The only sounds he makes are deep in his throat. Alone in my hotel room, I've fantasized about James like this, but with the real man on top of me, in this clock tower, with the thunder masking our groans, I can't hold back any longer. I shatter again and again, crashing against his hard body.

After, when we're damp with sweat and holding each other, James snuggles into my neck and goes so quiet I think he must have fallen asleep. I stroke his damp wavy hair and watch the clouds pass in the corner of the clock glass. I almost giggle, playing it all back in my mind, turning myself on again with images of us.

James stirs, looks up at me, and kisses my lips. I want to do it all again, but I'm happy just to lie here for now, his body like a heater in this cold space. My body involuntarily shivers, and he shifts to envelope me in his arms.

"Are you good?" he asks, and I feel his breath on my neck.

"Mm-hm." Inside, my thoughts stretch. *What happens now?*

"That's what I would call serendipity," James says.

"Meaning?"

"Meeting you in the rain, alone, wanting exactly what I wanted." His toned arms squeeze me affectionately. The cocoon of him has a relaxing effect.

"I was starting to think I'd dreamt that kiss on the plane," I chance telling him.

James kisses my forehead. "That wasn't a dream."

"The last few weeks have sort of felt like one," I admit. "Two weeks ago, I was leading an eighth-grade reading group through *The Hobbit*."

"Do you like working with kids?" he asks, kissing the crest of my ear.

"Yes, and no," I say. "It's not exactly my dream."

"What is?" James shifts again, so that I can rest my head on his broad, hairy chest. He tucks me into him closer as I savor his woodsy smell.

"The Bodleian."

"Oxford?" he says. "Really?"

"Yes," I admit shyly. "Have you been there?"

"Not to the library."

James pauses for a long time, and when a slow breath escapes his mouth, I swear I can see it in the chill. "You'd leave your hometown and move to England?"

"There's this graduate program in library science..." I begin, but think better of continuing. "But it would be hard to leave, yes..." My voice catches and tears fill my eyes, so I deflect. "Are you living your dream?"

"Sort of," James says, his voice dipping into a whisper.

"What would be the ideal for you?" I ask. "Best job and city?"

"I'd like to start my own firm. Ideally in London, but I'm open to a lot of places. Mostly in the UK."

"You don't see yourself at Revel?"

"Not really. I'm proud of this place and my family's legacy, but it's just not..." He rubs my arm to keep me warm. "My mother wants me here now, but I was sent away years ago. I don't feel a strong attachment to the place."

"What about your PawPaw?" I ask. "Does he want you to work for Revel?"

"He'd probably like all of us here, but there's a lot of us." James laughs, and it shakes me with him. "And not a lot of room at the top."

"You like doing your own thing."

"I do," James says. He kisses my neck, sending shivers down my body. "You get me."

I think I do and look up at him to confirm. His green eyes search my face for a second before he leans down to kiss me soft and slow. This feels intensely intimate, and the sensation makes me feel tipsy. Dim evening light streams into the clock tower then, reminding me of the world that exists beyond this building. Suddenly, this is all too much. I feel exposed. What does this all mean now? How are we going to move forward? Work together? I cover my chest and sit up, looking for my bra.

"Whoa, Summer," James says, lightly touching my back. "Is something wrong?"

In the heat of the moment, I completely forgot about my scoliosis scar, which is crazy because I usually give a rehearsed speech about the multiple surgeries before showing the wicked scar that traces my spine. I slightly twist to see James eyeing my back. More intrigued than horrified.

"I had scoliosis," I explain matter-of-factly. "When I grew, it got worse. My first surgery at fourteen was botched, so I had to have another. Scoliosis is the curvature of the spine—"

"I know what it is," he says. "Are you okay now?" Despite his gruff voice, concern emanates from it. "Did I hurt you?"

"No, it's better now." I smile at him. "Don't worry about it. Really. I just need to be sure to stay active and stretch to avoid stiffness and pain."

James says nothing. Despite feeling no shame about my scars, I start to feel uncomfortable. Maybe he doesn't like them. Maybe they're a turn-off. The need to run away overwhelms me. I start to move away again, but then I feel the lightest touch on my back.

"What are you doing?" I ask.

"Kissing you," James says, leaving a trail of kisses down my spine. Each brush of his lips is firmer than the last. By the time he is at the base of my spine, I want him again. So bad it hurts.

"Summer," James growls. "I need to be inside you again."

"Yes" is all I can manage before he kneels behind me and enters me slowly. When we finish this time, we both collapse and sleep.

Later, I spread my long skirt down over my waist. I find my panties and realize my sweater is at the base of the stairs.

James pulls himself together as well, slipping on his damp jeans again. He notices me shiver and pulls me into his bare chest again. "Come here." Somehow his body is like a fire, radiating heat. "Come see the view," he says and guides me up the final length of stairs.

He holds me from behind, and through the clear windows that frame the iron clock numbers, we watch the night sky lit with pastel hues beyond the dark storm clouds over Revel Pointe and the river beyond. In the center of the park, the lighthouse lamp shines bright, a beacon lighting the way, but inside I'm more confused now. The reality of my situation—that I've just slept with my boss's boss, and I'm supposed to want to work here, in this library that he built, more than anything—comes crashing down over my head.

Chapter Twenty-Nine

James

Summer is quiet. As we descend the stairs—which I will never look at the same way again—and make our way out of the building, I feel revitalized, calm and alert at once, as though I've climbed a mountain and now I can enjoy the view.

"Let me walk you back," I say, reaching for her hand. She lets me fold her into me before we exit the library back into the open theme park. I kiss her deep and soft, knowing I could go for round three if she wanted. I cup her ass in my hands, and even through the fabric of her skirt, I enjoy the firmness, remembering how her skin felt. And I'm ready again.

"I should go," she says, pulling back, making me ache.

I groan, louder than I expect. "I was just about to invite you back to my place."

"It's a school night," she says, even as she wraps her arms tighter around me, digging her fingernails into my shoulder blades.

We kiss again, and it turns fierce fast. I'm at her neck again. My hand finds its way up and under her bra, trying hard not to squeeze with all my strength. Her fingers are in my hair, and her body yields to me, asking for more. Just as I'm picking her up again, thinking of where I'll lay her down next, a loud crack in the library startles us both. We're panting, eyes wide, wondering if someone has opened the back door.

"Fuuuck" escapes from my mouth, and I adjust myself, pulling her with me out the front door.

The quick interruption and sharp cold wakes me a little from the yearning that keeps clouding my brain. Night has fallen, and the street lamps that light the oak path glow a pale shade of yellow. We take the steps slowly, one by one, not touching any longer. It feels off. I still want to be entwined with her. I want as much of her as I can get.

"Go to the gala with me," I say, smiling over at her as we reach the fountain.

A wide smile spreads across her face before fading just as quickly. "I'm not sure how that would look." Something is holding her back, and I recall the guy she's "known forever" and "sort of dating." A flash of that ultimate dude-bro, Grainger, comes to mind, and I have to know the truth.

"Is Grainger the guy you were texting about?" I ask point-blank.

"No," Summer blurts a bit too quickly, and her cheeks redden. "I mean, I was into him, sort of, well... He's into me now. I had a massive crush on him in high school."

"So, he's not the sexy guy from the text?"

"No." She looks away, and I notice her neck is flushed. "You were."

Relief rushes through me. I take another step toward her, wanting to do a victory dance. "Good. I'm glad it was me."

"It was a mistake. A mortifying mistake."

"So you don't think I'm sexier in person?" I stop and pout dramatically.

Rolling her eyes, she pushes me flirtatiously and keeps walking.

"So you'll go with me?" I ask, catching up with her.

"I need to think about it," she says warily.

We've reached the gate. I want to sweep Summer back into my arms and carry her all the way back to my suite at the compound, but it's too late. Before I can kiss her again, she creaks open the enclosure gate and steps onto a Revel Pointe walkway across from a building that's designed like a fairytale cottage but is actually the cast members' staging area.

"Let me walk you to the resort?"

She sighs. "I don't want my colleagues to see me with you."

I nod, trying to swallow my hurt. So this is how it feels to be with a statue.

"Before you go..." I reach for her hand and feel how cold it is in mine. "Please, just think about it." I'm genuinely confused by my own need to stake such a public claim, but I can't envision the gala night without her now.

"Okay." Her full, pink lips turn upward in a reluctant grin.

"I'd love for you to be my date, but we can keep it as prof—"

"I'll go, James," she says, holding back a full smile and gazing up at me through her long brown lashes like she's daring me not to kiss her.

Even though we're still in public, I can't help myself and lean down for one last tender kiss, before she spins around and heads back to her hotel, her long skirt swishing with every step.

Chapter Thirty

Summer

Today is our last day of working on the A-List. Gemma, Horace, and I are back in the warehouse, which is a shame for many reasons. First, the weather is glorious today. A cool fifty-five degrees with bright sunshine. For a girl from Ohio, this is a treat just three days to Christmas. Second, I'm still playing images of a naked James a day later in my head. I'm also asking the big questions that sex with a boss brings, especially when that boss is an heir to billions, who plans to go back to London in a week.

Why did I agree to go to the gala with James? What will it look like to my colleagues? What happens now that we've had sex? Does it mean to him what it meant to me?

Ultimately, these questions boil down to a big one: What do I want—a relationship with James? The job? Both?

Another nagging, far-fetched question is: If James and I start dating, will I get a permanent position at the library because of favoritism? I would never feel on solid ground then.

By lunch, I have to admit to myself that it's genuine, straight-up passion that I'm dealing with. It's the first time I've ever felt it, and I'm twenty-six. James has me twisted in knots. A song lyric echoes in my mind: *When you're close I feel like coming undone.* My college boyfriend, Pete, never once incited this intense feeling of longing and frenzy in me, and we were together for four years. Every time I think of James, blood drains from my extremities, rushes between my legs, and I feel lightheaded. This morning, I had to take care of myself in the shower to clear my head. That has *never* happened to me before.

And there's one last looming question: Should I tell James about his half-siblings? I need to get these documents in the hands of Mick Reve, but the only person I know well enough to ask for his information is James. If I think about it too long, I practically break out in hives.

By the end of the day, Gemma, Horace, and I each find another important item for the library project, but when we deliver these to the palace offices, we find that we're too late. The curators and design team have filled the rest of the spots in the library with the fruits of other teams.

"You're finished," Frances chimes. "At least this part of the job. This calls for champagne!" She opens her schedule on her tablet and confirms. "Y'all head up to the RP Lounge, and I'll meet you there in thirty."

She tells us how to find it, by exiting the building and re-entering from a "secret door" exclusive to Revel Pointe membership holders and top-tier employees only. I'm not really in the mood to celebrate, but I do feel a sense of accomplishment. Once we find the not-so-secret door, marked with a discreet silver "RP Lounge" sign, I relax. This part of the job is over, which is a set of nerves I'm happy to set aside.

We take a small elevator to the fourth floor and step out into a room with wide corner windows overlooking the Mississippi River, the Reve compound castle, and Thumbelina's Ferris wheel. The lush, raspberry-colored room is accented with unique light fixtures and lamps, high-backed teal chairs, and a bar the length of one wall.

"This place just keeps on surprising me," Gemma says. "What a cool space." She drops down on an empty green sofa in the bar area and crosses her long legs.

"I'm really looking forward to seeing the finished library now," Horace says. "I want to see our hard work on display." He eyes me like I know something he doesn't know.

"Me too," I say, trying to hide my insider Revel knowledge with brevity.

"But you've been there," Gemma says. "The other day. How does it look?"

"Oh, right." I try not to stammer when flashes of "the other day" obscure my thoughts. "It was still sort of a mess, but the west wing was completely finished. The opening-day tickets are there in frames, and three of Portia's Power cels too. I didn't really get a chance to look around."

"Awesome," Gemma says. "I wonder if they'd let us go see it tomorrow. I changed my flight to the 23rd. I have Christmas morning with my kid, you know?"

"Are you going to the gala?" I ask Horace, who nods.

"A bunch of over-injected, mega-wealthy ninnyhammers drooling over our work? Champagne and Chef Tim's hors d'oeuvres?" Horace raises an eyebrow for effect. "Of course. It gives me a reason to pull my aubergine tux out of storage. Wouldn't miss it."

"I suppose you're going?" Gemma asks, and I'm grateful that I'm interrupted by a cocktail server coming over with a tray of pink champagne flutes.

"Cheers," I say, raising my glass and clinking with each of them, thinking that I've actually become quite fond of my co-workers, even if Gemma rubs me the wrong way at least twice a day.

"Are you going to bring your dad?" Gemma's still on me about the gala.

"That would be perfect if he wasn't also flying back the day after tomorrow." I sip again. "He doesn't want to miss Christmas with the grandkids."

"But you're going," Gemma persists. "To the gala."

"Yes, I plan on it," I say. "But I have no clue what I'm going to wear. I didn't exactly pack a gown." That little detail has not even been added to the things-I'm-worried-about list, but I can't show up on the arm of James Reve in a Target dress.

"Order something online, girl," Gemma says. "Overnight express it. That's what I'd do."

I'm kind of surprised that Gemma feels comfortable enough in her position here to leave and not attend the gala at all. A bit more respect for her grows in me, for her choice of putting her kid first. I'm so distracted by the champagne and Horace's questions about what's next for all of us that I don't register that James has been at the bar with two gray-haired men and is now walking over to us. When my eyes land on him, he looks so good my body freezes.

"Hello," James says to the group, not holding my gaze even a half-second longer than the others. "Nice to see you again. Celebrating?"

Gemma sits up straighter on the sofa. "We've completed the A-List."

"For now," Horace says. "There's more to uncover, but the curators have all they need for the gala displays."

"Well, cheers to that," James says, lifting his glass of amber liquor. He looks insanely hot in his dark jeans, blue shirt, and a perfectly weathered khaki jacket. "We're doing a little celebrating as well. Tell them..." James points to the shorter man.

"Our chime works," the man says, his cheeks flushing pink.

Horace, Gemma, and I blink, waiting for more information.

"On the clock tower," the other man says in a thick Irish accent.

My body stiffens and flushes at the words, and I can't help but glance at James, who's grinning at both men. The clockmakers. James formally introduces them.

"We've been working on getting it right, the chime, that is," the Irish man goes on. "And see, it's both an exact science and not. But we got it."

"Installed today," the short one adds.

"We'll start testing it when the park closes at eight," James says, giving a nod to the men and scanning our faces, not once acknowledging me specifically, which makes me shrink a little.

"That's wonderful," Horace says. "Cheers to you as well."

We all raise glasses again and drink. Only then does James steal a glance at me across his Scotch. An image of him on top of me, naked and breathing heavily, flashes through my mind. My temperature rises.

"Well, congratulations again," James says to all of us. "Thank you so much for your hard work. The library looks stunning."

Gemma starts to ask if they can go see it, but he's already moved off with the clockmakers. She leans forward conspiratorially. "A bit too hoity-toity for my taste," she whispers. "But I'd still screw him into next Tuesday."

Horace only raises his eyebrows, and I feign shock.

"What?" Gemma asks, a little too loud. "You wouldn't?"

I give her the cut-it-out gesture, and Horace smirks. There's no way I'm confiding in these two about anything. Not even acknowledging that I think James is handsome. No way I'm falling for that.

I'm so in my head that I wander the park aimlessly. I find myself at the railing of the lighthouse moat, staring down into it, watching the reflections kaleidoscope. It's soothing, but I still don't know what I'm going to do. I should just keep it cool until everything calms down. Enjoy the gala. Find out the position. Handle one thing at a time.

I think to call my dad, who should be finishing his day soon, but there's no way I'm heading back to the library to chance seeing James, or Grainger for that matter, whose texts are starting to get concerning:

8:30am: *I know you're busy, but why won't you answer my calls?*

10:45am: *Did I say something to upset you?*

12:04pm: *We need to talk. Can I come by your room later?*

I know what I need to do. It's finally time to call him and end whatever he thinks is happening between us. Even though he's all I thought I ever wanted once upon a time, I can't actually see myself living in Westerville and seriously dating Grainger. Not after this whole experience at Revel. He picks up on the second ring.

"Hi, how are you? Just a minute." Muffled talking in the background fills my ears and then it's quiet again. "We're just getting back to the shop. How are you?"

"I'm good. Exhausted." I don't know how to start this so out of the blue.

"I bet..." he says. "Take a long bath, and I'll head over in an hour." It's a command, not a question.

"I don't think that's a good idea," I begin, but he cuts me off.

"We'll grab some food—"

"No, that's not..." I just have to rip the Band-Aid. "I don't think you coming to my hotel is a good idea."

"We need to talk, Summer."

This *is* the talk, I tell myself. "Grainger, I'm really flattered by your attention and gestures, but I don't think this, uh..." I can't think of what to call this. He kissed me once. It was weird. "I don't think this thing between us is going to work."

"Of course it will work," he says. "We're into each other. You're talking nonsense, Summer."

"Grainger, listen to me."

"We should talk in person. You're exhausted. I'll order some room service, and we'll talk it out."

I let him ramble because it's no use interrupting. I wait until he stops.

"Please do not come to my hotel," I say firmly. "I don't want to meet and talk. There is nothing to talk about. I'm not interested in dating you."

The silence on the other end scares me.

"You were interested a few weeks ago," he says. "What happened?"

"Nothing happened," I say, knowing that's not going to suffice. "Actually, that's not true. I got this job and my world flipped upside down. I might stay here at Revel Pointe. I've applied for a permanent position."

"We could do long distance," Grainger says. "My job is flexible. It could work."

"No, Grainger, I'm just not interested. We're too different; we want different things." Now my voice is pleading. I'm trying to be gracious, remembering that he's probably never been rejected in his entire life.

"Is it because I ignored you for so long?" Grainger asks, throwing me off so completely that I need to sit down. I find a bench and listen to him ramble. "I've been wanting to apologize for that. I mean, I was an idiot, and you wore that complicated back thing and were just this kid who worshiped me, and that was cute, but then I saw you after college. You became this different person. The most beautiful girl in Westerville, and suddenly it clicked. You're the girl for me. Someone beautiful and good, without a past, you know. Someone you can settle down with, have a family with—"

I stop listening. I was right. I'm the last girl in Westerville he hasn't slept with. My gut folds on itself painfully as feelings of inadequacy and loneliness ripple through me. I was wife material because I was a dork in high school. It's been a long time since I've thought about the specific bullying I experienced in school. My mind involuntarily scans the years of being an outcast, the quiet girl who walked funny and read alone at lunch, the strange girl no one even bothered to call names after a while. There's no fun in name-calling when the person doesn't so much as blink at cruelty. I don't remember Grainger ever specifically making fun of me. Outside of seeing him at my father's shop, I don't remember him ever addressing me directly. Yet he knew I had a crush. He must've thought his attention was a dream come true for me.

"Summer?" Grainger's voice pleads on the line.

I snap back to Revel Pointe and this awkward conversation.

When I don't answer, Grainger continues. "You met someone." It sounds like he's both pouting and seething on the other end. "It's that rich asshole, Reve."

"What? No!" I protest too quickly and forcefully, and it couldn't sound more like a lie if I'd tried. "Grainger, I—"

"I fucking knew it," he continues. "He was being such a tool."

"Look, James has...is... a work colleague," I say, trying to lessen the blow, grasping at what is actually true. "But even if it were romantic, he doesn't live here. He lives in England, and he's going back after Christmas."

"Whatever, Summer. You're lying."

What can I say to that? He's not wrong, but I'm not about to tell Grainger that James can make my whole being vibrate, over and over again, whether he's inside of me or across the park. I imagine he could make me climax from across the Atlantic.

"Grainger, I'm sorry. I don't know what else to say."

He's silent again for a while, his breathing audible.

"You're going to regret this," he says and then hangs up on me.

I silent scream in my head, anger and desperation building. I look up at the lighthouse in the cloudless sunset sky, then run my hands along my scalp and untie my braid. I'm equal parts relieved and horrified. I'm not quite sure how this spun so out of control with Grainger, but I search my mind. I didn't do anything to deserve this.

Could I have communicated more? Definitely. Could I have shut down his gestures, like the ballet, immediately? Yes. But I'm certain he made a bunch of leaps in his head, connecting us in a more solid way than I had ever intended, even from the very beginning of this weird flirtation, before I ever thought I had a chance of coming to Revel Pointe. It's like he chose me, and I needed to get on board.

I wander the perimeter of the moat and eventually find a seat at the entrance fountains where tourists are taking sunset selfies of the lighthouse and buying souvenirs before exiting the park for the day. I've landed near the baby alligator that Jacob pointed out after my interview. I feel like I'm such a different person than I was that day. But why?

I watch a couple kissing and having their photo taken by a park photographer. They look so in love. I have no doubt this is what Grainger had in mind for us, but as I zone out on this couple posing together in front of the lighthouse, I realize I could be making similar assumptions about James. I know how quickly my crush on James is transforming into real feelings. All this flirting and longing and and the mindblowing sex has been magic, but that's probably all it is for him. A puff of smoke, and he'll be gone back to England without a thought about me.

It's just lust. Our pheromones want each other. I mean, my body has never felt this way. It can't be sustainable.

A huge sense of relief rests in my muscles as I reach this conclusion. If I'm just experiencing a sexual awakening with James, and he's leaving in less than a week anyway, then why not enjoy it while I can? No real harm in that. And this way, I can compartmentalize the permanent job at the Grand Revel Library.

When I'm back in my room, cozy in my pj's, reading my Queen Isabella biography in bed, I hear rich, low chimes sing from somewhere close by. *The clock tower.* Tossing my book on the bed, I open the curtains and slide the glass balcony door wide. Even though it's chilly and dark out, my body goes warm, tingling between my legs, at the sight of the chiming clock tower. It's such a pretty, innocent song. Familiar, too. But now it signals everything we did, everything I saw and felt with James inside that tower. When the chimes end, goosebumps rise all over my body, and I throw myself on the bed.

My phone pings, and it's James: *Did you hear them?*

I respond immediately: *I did.*

James: *And... your response?*

It takes me a while to think of a way to communicate how the clock chime affected me. Reminding myself it's just fun and lust, a sexual awakening, I finally settle on something naughty.

I felt the notes inside me.

The three dots pulse and vanish, pulse and vanish. Finally, he responds: *The notes remind me of you.*

Chapter Thirty-One

James

"Fancy finding you here, mate." Lucien pokes his head into the office that Revel set me up with back in May. It's just down the hall from my mother, but since I've never been an office guy, I've hardly used it.

I wave him in. It's been a while since we've caught up. Of course, we've been in touch, mostly him sending me options for obnoxious-looking parties and obscenely modern houses to rent in Miami Beach for New Year's Eve. I don't want to go but I said I would, and I keep my word.

"Tell me," I ask him. "Did you book the giant white one with the fleet of jet skis? Or the one with all the glass?"

"Jet skis, mate." He makes a face at me, flopping into a square leather chair. "Do you take me for a fool?"

"Never," I tell him. Maybe we will have fun. Maybe I need a change of scenery after so much time at this place, but instead of South Beach, all I see is amber eyes.

He looks at his watch. "What've you got on for today?"

"Nothing but micromanaging at this point," I say, wanting desperately to be on site and knowing my mere presence slows everything down.

"Wanna beg off into town? Do one of them swanky martini lunches?"

I scratch my beard. It's all just paperwork, and I wouldn't mind getting off the property. And every time that damn clock tower chimes the main theme from *Portia's Power*, I get hard. I feel like

Pavlov's sodding dog, my little brain immediately wondering where Summer is.

"You know what, yes." I stand and grab my heavy coat. "Let's see if we can't get into that posh barbershop on Carondelet, too."

Lucien is on it before I even have to ask. "Brilliant. A proper gentlemen's day."

Instead of hiring a car, I take my dad's Porsche again. I feel more like myself at the wheel. Lucien fills me in on the state of Premiership League football all the way into the city. I've missed most of the matches, except of course Chelsea's against Sheff United. A sense of normalcy permeates the car, and my mood lifts.

I've been in such a post-coitus fog since the encounter with Summer that I haven't known up from down, left from right. It's always been second nature to keep my distance, living up to my idiot nickname. But this time, I have this deep, visceral desire to be next to Summer, which is so unlike me that I'm disoriented.

We find a table at a restaurant in the CBD, just blocks away from the barbershop.

We order Old Fashioneds, and Lucien goes on and on about how he loves the city, that he's been out on the town a lot lately and can't see why I don't want to live here.

"It's not that I hate it," I tell him. "But the parties and parades and heat. It's just not me. It's an extroverts' city. Not to mention there are eyes everywhere."

"I want to stay for Mardi Gras," Lucien says and then ventures further. "I feel like I'm just getting settled in."

I feel for him because I do see it. New Orleans enchants the masses that visit. Tourists return over and over again. Sometimes people move here purely for the living, breathing culture of Louisiana. It's unique. And Lucien's the ultimate man about town. He makes instant friends everywhere he lands. The lovable, good-looking goof. I can see him at Mardi Gras balls. He'd thrive during carnival season.

"You should come back in February," I tell him and go on to explain how I've missed every Mardi Gras since I was seventeen, and it doesn't even matter to me.

"Shame," Lucien says.

"How is Tilda?" She hasn't texted, emailed, or called in a few days.

"She's all about this new proposal. Revel Couture."

"As in runway, ready-to-wear?"

"As in bridal."

I scoff. My mother is a money-making machine. If it was just about the bottom line, she *should* be CEO. Of course, she'd turn it into a corporation devoid of ethical accountability, hell-bent on making every last cent possible.

"Damn, she's good," I admit.

"The board seems to love the idea so far."

I shake my head. The board. She wants me on it so badly, but would I even vote for Revel princess bridal wear? Even if it's haute couture, I can't make myself care.

"Well, more power to them, I guess," I say, deciding it's not my battle.

Lucien scratches his neck and looks like he wants to say something.

"Out with it, mate," I nudge.

"To be frank, mate, I don't get why you don't want a piece of that pie."

"I make my own money," I say. "And I also have a trust and I invest wisely."

"Yeah, but this is your family legacy. And it's a good one." Lucien drops back in his seat like he's defeated. "People fight all their lives to be in your position, and you're just walking away."

"For now," I say. "What is there for me to do at Revel right now anyway? Ethan's the acting CEO, and let's face it, my dad isn't in the best of shape, and Tilda showed her ass last year. Ethan's a shoe-in."

"But you could be part of it." Lucien leans forward. "A *big* part of it if Tilda has anything to do with it."

"Not my bag."

Lucien just shakes his head. "Only knobs shirk their royal duties," he says, affecting the Windsor accent.

"Don't compare me to Willie or Harry. I have all my hair."

Lucien laughs, shaking his head like he can't believe what I'm saying, but he lets it go.

Our lunch is on the house, as someone on staff recognizes me and invites us to return. I leave a generous tip, and we head to the uber-masculine barbershop that smells sharply of pine needles and soap.

When it's our turn, the stylist offers his chair and runs his hands through my mop.

"Looks like it's been a while," he says and then asks if I want to keep the length and the beard.

"You're the expert, mate," I laugh, finally seeing how beastly my locks have become. When he combs the length of my hair straight, it reaches my shoulders.

Lucien and I ask for the full treatment—haircut and style, beard treatment and trim, and a botanical steam facial—and it feels bloody great. We emerge an hour later like new men, ready for a red carpet event.

"You look like Cillian Murphy's ugly cousin," Lucien jokes.

I run my hand over the back of my head, razored and faded to perfection, and feel like a new man. The stylist has left plenty of dark waves on the top of my head and has trimmed my beard down tremendously, so the actual shape of my face comes through. Not half bad.

"We'll be killing it at the gala," Lucien says, excited by his reflection in a passing window. "Too bad your mum's your date."

"Actually, I asked Summer," I tell him.

"No way." He hesitates, then continues. "Oi, mate. You need to tell Tilda. She's fully expecting to be at your side, introducing you to the big wigs. She'll be fuming."

"I'm not playing the game, bro," I tell him, fully aware she wants to show me off like a million-dollar racehorse.

Lucien whistles. "Be careful, mate. You're poking a bear."

"I don't care," I say as we pass a gorgeous white and silver gown in the window of a high-fashion shop. "Wait."

Next to this gown is a stunning gold dress that I know Summer would look incredible in.

"Can we pop in there?" I ask Lucien, and his eyebrows raise higher than I've ever seen.

"You need a gown for the ball?" He runs a hand over his new haircut.

"Summer probably doesn't have a gown," I say. "I didn't even think of that. I'm such an asshole."

"Wait, did something *happen* with her?" Lucien eyes me, but I give nothing away.

"It was Cricket's idea," I tell him because it was. "She said I'll be swarmed by Tilda's goons and the paparazzi if I'm alone. More nonsense like the *LA Times*."

"All right, the statue is back," Lucien jokes.

Without deliberating too long, I text Cricket, asking what size she thinks Summer would be. I'll send Summer three dresses in her size. That way, it's her choice.

Twenty minutes later, Lucien and I are in the Porsche with three large boxes in the backseat. I'll send them over via courier to her hotel room today. I wish I could be there to see her face light up, to watch her try each one on, but I'll just have to imagine it. I don't think I've ever been so excited to see a woman again in my entire life.

Chapter Thirty-Two

Summer

"So, what do you want to see first?" I ask my dad when I greet him with a giant hug at the Revel Pointe Park entrance. It's another beautiful day, and I'm thrilled to spend the rest of the afternoon and evening with my dad in the magical place he's always wanted to see. Dad says he wants the full tourist experience, so we grab a glossy map and take a seat near the burbling Scarlet Slippers fountain to make a plan.

"Let's get a view from Thumbelina's Ferris wheel first," he says, pointing to the brightly colored drawings when he could just point at the sky as the real thing is in plain view.

"I've been dying to see the view from there."

Dad stands and offers me his elbow, and accompanied by music from *The Snow Queen* pumping through the speakers, we set off toward the French Village before hanging a right down the busy path.

"So tell me," Dad begins. "What's your favorite thing about this place so far?"

My heart speeds against my ribcage as I recall James Reve striding toward me in the oak copse, his wet shirt cleaved to his chest, reaching me and grabbing my face for the kiss I'd been fantasizing about since I landed here.

"Probably when I met Mick Reve," I say, kind of surprising myself. I feel so safe with Dad that I don't think twice about explaining the off-duty work I'd been up to with James that night at the Reve compound.

"You met him?" Dad asks excitedly. "Isn't he like a hundred?"

I swat my dad's arm. "He'll be ninety-five tomorrow, but he doesn't look it. He's more mobile than most seventy-year-olds we know. He lives alone and walks without a cane." I go on, telling Dad about how he hand-delivered a pair of the red ballet slippers from *The Scarlet Slippers* and an original printing of *The Secret Quest Book*.

"Okay, now that's something to brag about," Dad says, joining a line at a mint green concession stand selling hot chocolate and beignets covered in powdered sugar.

An all-too familiar voice bombs our conversation from behind. "What's something to brag about?"

My stomach drops.

Dad turns to Grainger, easygoing, as if he expected to see him here in the park. "She met Mick Reve, and he handed her a copy of the original *Secret Quest Book*."

From behind Grainger, a young woman with a long pink ponytail bounces into view when I turn around in line. Her lips are bubblegum pink; she's wearing a tight pink *Island of Sirens* T-shirt and white yoga pants that leave nothing to the imagination.

"Like, the actual book?" she asks.

"I mean, there are several," I explain, but I suppose it's written on my face. *Who is this stranger?*

"This is Lottie," Grainger says, draping an arm around her.

Lottie shakes our hands heartily. Her energy is like a puppy let out of its pen.

"It's short for Charlotte," she says. "But wouldn't you know there were three Charlottes on my street when I was growing up, and well, we all got nicknames that stuck."

My brain is still thinking, *What is happening?* as Grainger continues, explaining how he met Lottie at a bar near their hotel, and how he plans to treat her to a fancy dinner in the French Quarter tonight. I'm still wondering what the hell Grainger is doing here.

This is finally my time with my dad, who looks sheepish, like he knows something I don't.

"Mind if we join you?" Lottie asks my dad, who of course isn't going to say "No, fuck right off" like I want him to.

In the long snaking line to board Thumbelina's Ferris wheel, we learn more about Lottie than I care to know, including the fact that she's the youngest daughter of some big-shot real estate developer and that her family has always had the exclusive RP membership.

Grainger wraps an arm around her waist and gloats at me. "Lottie's asked me to be her plus one at the gala. So I guess I'll see you there." Somehow, he's showing me all of his teeth at once with the size of his grin.

"This will be my third year going," Lottie brags. "What are you wearing?"

"A black formal dress," I tell her joylessly. I ordered it last night; it's boring but not embarrassing.

"Mine is light pink this year to match my hair," Lottie says, gazing up at Grainger. There's a familiarity in the way their bodies angle toward each other that leads me to believe they've already been intimate. It's good to confirm so quickly that I've dodged a bullet.

"Leave a little to the imagination," Grainger tells her. "I want to be surprised."

Thankfully, when we reach the front of the line, Dad separates us. "Let's go two and two instead of squishing."

"Fine by me," Grainger says, hooking an elbow around Lottie's neck as she takes six hundred selfies in line. Dad and I board our round passenger car, and the park employee locks us in. Up close, the Ferris wheel is intricately painted with birds, butterflies, frogs, and fairies. Tiny white and blue light bulbs line the car and the spokes, ready to light up at night.

"Meet you back down here," Grainger calls as the wheel mechanism sweeps us away.

"Thank you for that," I tell my dad, somewhat under my breath in case Grainger has X-ray ears. "Did you invite him?"

"Not exactly. I didn't know he'd bring someone." Dad looks perplexed again, as if he wants to say or ask something.

"I wasn't going to mention it, but now I feel I have to," I say. "Grainger has been kind of stalking me."

"What?!"

"Shhh," I say, though the calliope notes of Thumbelina's musical themes are loud enough to drown out our voices. "Maybe *stalking's* an extreme word. He's been, like, love bombing me."

"What the heck is love bombing?"

"Like, when a guy, or a girl, goes overboard to show how much they're into you."

"Isn't that a good thing?" Now Dad is super confused. Our pretty cornflower-blue car sweeps forward and up again as new cars are filled.

"Not if the recipient doesn't want that kind of attention," I explain. "It's annoying and kind of threatening."

"In my day, that was called courting," Dad says, frowning.

"Courting, Dad?" I give him a funny look. "In the 1870s?"

Dad elbows me. "Come on! You'd shower a girl with notes or flowers until she gave in because your effort and gestures are so sweet."

"You mean, you wear her down?" My tone is incredulous. "Like, you bug her with 'nice' things, even when she says she's not interested, until she 'gives in.' That's just not acceptable anymore. No wonder dating is so messed up these days."

"I just never thought of it that way," Dad says. The ride swishes forward again, this time continuing in fluid motion. "So Grainger's been bugging you? I thought you liked him?"

"When I was a teenager, but now we have nothing in common... Listen, can we change the subject?" I turn my head as we swiftly approach the top. "Look at this view!"

And just like that, we're finally enjoying the time I hoped we'd have together at Revel Pointe. Our car swivels and faces the Mississippi River, which catches the sunlight at a wide bend even though it's a murky steel blue. Far beyond the lush banks, teeming swamps, and tilled farmland of Louisiana, a tiny cluster of towers shines. New Orleans. And there's water everywhere. Dad and I marvel at just how little land makes up this part of the state.

"I guess we're closer to the coast here than I thought," I say the next time we crest the summit.

"It's such a unique place," Dad says.

"I know. It's wild." And he doesn't even know the half of it.

As the wheel slows to unload park guests, Grainger calls out to Dad and me, reminding us to wait at the exit for them. Why the heck would he want to spend all his time with us when he clearly has a sure thing lined up? Heading down the shrub-lined path toward the exit, we hear the chime of the library clock tower. My pelvis floods with warmth, and my pulse quickens. This now happens every time I hear those whimsical notes from *Portia's Power.* It's thrilling but merciless. My body reacts automatically, and my mind follows those notes drifting across the park, connecting me again and again with James.

"That's coming from the library?" Dad asks.

I nod, pulling myself from the lust daze, and explain the dying art of clockmaking to him. It doesn't take long to completely wash away the pulsing below my belly, especially when Grainger returns, bounding down the path, leaving Lottie trotting behind in her platform sneakers.

Unfortunately, Dad and I suffer through another hour with Grainger and Lottie purely out of Midwestern manners. Standing in lines and wandering the park, Grainger spends half of this time showering Lottie with PDA and the other half glowering at me.

Finally, we part ways when they leave to ride the Steampunk Coaster. Dad and I decide to experience the San Francisco Safari before heading back to my hotel room to order burgers and chill.

It's so comforting to be with my dad. I'm no longer competing for a high-profile job, on my guard around new colleagues, or navigating myself around intimidating, media-giant family members. I'm just my goofy self. Dad whistles when we enter my hotel suite.

"Far cry from the one we're at," he says, checking out the view from the balcony window where the sky is turning grapefruit pink.

I kick off my sneakers as he scans the menu. I'm about to call in our room service order when there's a knock at the door. I shrug at my dad and then answer it.

"Delivery for Summer York?" the resort porter asks.

"That's me," I reply, and the porter hands me an envelope and three large boxes from a store called Satine. "Thank you." I turn to Dad, wide-eyed.

"What is it?" he asks.

I lift the lid of one box, find light blue tissue paper, and set it down to open the envelope tucked inside. It's a simple notecard with black ink scrawl: *I thought you might like a few options for the gala. No pressure if you're already set. James*

I hand the card to my dad and cover my mouth.

"James Reve?" Dad asks and I nod. I'm still speechless, anticipating what I will find in these chic boxes. "Well, open them!"

In the first one, I peel back the tissue paper and find a silky fabric of rich peacock green. I lift it from the box and a floor-length gown unfurls.

"Oh my gosh!" I can't stop the excitement from flooding out of me. It's like I've been holding back a wall of emotions like the levees along the river. I lay the beautiful dress over one of the armchairs in my room and turn to the second box. From this one I pull a tea length, strapless white and silver gown.

"Whoa!" my dad says, clearly dazzled by this one.

I hold it up against me and look at myself in the mirror. Holy mackerel, I can't believe James sent me ball gowns.

"There's one more." My dad sounds like a seven-year-old on Christmas morning.

From the last box, I pull a glittering gold dress with a satin belt.

"Wow." I sway and the light fabric dances.

"Are you going to the gala with James?"

All I can do is nod at this point.

"Try them on!" Dad directs, shooing me toward the bathroom. "Go!"

I pull all three of them into the bathroom and shimmy out of my clothes, practically bursting with giddiness. One by one, I try them on and model them for my dad. Having raised daughters, Dad is totally used to this ritual, though I haven't given him the opportunity to fulfill this role in a long time—not since I was a little girl showing off Easter outfits.

"The gold is the winner," Dad says, lounging on the bed with an ESPN football recap show on in the background.

With its simple cap sleeves and neckline, plus the satin belt that makes my waist appear tinier than it is, the gold *is* the one. I feel most comfortable in it, and the sunrise shade sets off the copper tones in my brown hair. It's not like me to get this wrapped up in my looks, but this dress even has a medieval shape to it, with a slight drop waist and full pleats in the skirt.

"I'm in love with this dress," I say to my reflection.

"It looks fantastic on you," my dad says. "But what's going on with James Reve?"

I hide my face from my dad, making for the bathroom again to change out of the dress.

"Yeah, he asked me to the gala," I say, closing the door behind me. In the bathroom light, the golden hue glows, doing wonders for my complexion, but I wince. *Can I really accept this expensive dress from James?*

"He's really a nice guy. You'd like him," I tell Dad through the bathroom door.

"I've met him," he calls back. "But isn't this what you called, uh, love blasting?"

I laugh. "Love bombing?"

"Yeah."

"No," I reply, too quickly perhaps. I change out of the dress, put on my joggers and T-shirt, and exit the bathroom. "James is being thoughtful," I explain. "He needs a date, and I need a proper dress to be that date."

I'm pretty sure my dad can tell I'm holding back an avalanche of information, but he doesn't press. I cross the room to gather up the dresses and fold them one by one back into the boxes.

"Okay," Dad says. "As long as he's a gentleman."

I toss a stray sock at him in an attempt to deflate and avoid the awkward turn in the conversation.

"He is," I say, and then a vision of James, shirtless, standing over me, unbuttoning his jeans, zooms through my mind. "And it's just a work thing. Harmless."

"Doesn't look harmless," Dad says, moving to the edge of the bed. "Looks romantic as hell." He sweeps his arm at the boxes and the space where I twirled girlishly just moments before.

My face warms as I realize what he's just witnessed—me, going all gooey about these exquisite dresses and the guy who sent them.

"I guess galas and ball gowns and stuff are kinda romantic," I say. "Fundamentally."

"Fundamentally, my butt," Dad says. "Just be careful there, sweetheart."

"I always am."

"He's a powerful fellow." Dad reaches for the phone to finally put in our cheeseburger order. "And he's one of them rugged hunks, too."

I burst out laughing. "One of them rugged hunks?!" Leave it to my dad to turn a fatherly advice conversation into a goofy sound bite.

After my dad left in a cab for the night, I take out the gold dress again and put it on. I turn the lights low and imagine myself at the gala with James. I put my hair up and enjoy the view of my unencumbered neck. For so many awkward years, I wore it down, long and shaggy, trying to camouflage my brace. When you spend so much time hiding, it's hard to step into the spotlight.

It's all fun and games, I try to convince myself. James just upped the romance of it all by sending this, and why not revel in it—pun intended. Why not bathe in the absolute sex of these next few days?

Slightly turned on, I reach for my phone and text him: *You up?*

Then I immediately regret it. It's only nine o'clock. Of course he's up, and I'm not about to invite him over for a cheesy hookup, am I?

James texts back right away: (laugh/crying emoji*) Yup.*

I don't know what I'm even going to follow that up with. As I begin to type out a thank-you for sending the dresses, my phone rings.

"Good evening." James' deep voice tickles my eardrum. "How are you?"

"I'm good." Somehow, I don't know how to talk, let alone know what to say. "I mean, better than good because someone sent me the loveliest gifts today."

"Oh really?" I can hear the grin in his voice. "Care to elaborate?"

"Well, there's a gorgeous dark green one that makes me feel all old Hollywood. Like, Elizabeth Taylor in her glory days."

"Mmm. How does it fit?"

"They all fit beautifully, like this mysterious person really understands the shape of my body." I let my voice get whispery.

"How advantageous. Do you like the others?"

"I love them."

"Tell me what they look like on you." James' voice drops a register and it sends heat down my lower spine.

"There's a flirty and sparkly white dress." I add a little Marilyn Monroe sweetness to my delivery. "It's strapless, and when I zip it up, it's a perfect fit. Maybe it was made especially for me?"

"That would be a feat," James chuckles slightly. "And what about the gold one?"

"Well, isn't that funny. How did *you* know it's gold?" I move to the bed, still in the gold gown, and drape my body carefully on the duvet. The slippery fabric against my skin feels luxurious and sexy. I already know this is the one.

James murmurs something so low that I don't understand him.

"Excuse me, sir," I tease. "Did you say something?"

"I said, you caught me."

"Well, well, well..." I draw out the words, letting the sound complete to silence. I can hear my heartbeat in my ears. My core clenches as heat builds below. I reach down on top of the dress, kneading slowly between my legs.

"How does the gold one look on you?" James finally asks with a crack in his low voice.

I breathe into the phone and trace my body from neck to breast to abdomen and down. "The gold one follows the exact curves of my bust, my waist, and over my hips and the drapes to the floor."

"I'd like to see it on you."

"Perhaps you will."

There's silence for a moment. Then James asks, "Where are you right now?"

"Lying on my bed." I whisper. "In the gold gown."

James groans and my lady parts swell with heat. "I can picture you sprawled across the white duvet. What are you wearing underneath?"

"White panties." The words feel awkward and silly. I've literally never had phone sex.

"Mmm, nice," he says.

"White lace panties." I have no game.

"No bra?"

"No," I say, and sigh. "The dress wouldn't look right with one."

"So you were trying them on, one by one, alone in your dim hotel room, right before I called?"

"Yes."

"And would you undress for me?" James nearly growls. "Slowly, just for me."

"Yes, I would." His command fills by body with desire to please him. I stand in the low lit room and narrate. "I'm standing next to the bed. Now I'm unzipping the side and sliding the little cap sleeves off my shoulders.

"Summer, I need to know how it feels on your bare skin." James' breathing is more pronounced now.

"So soft." I breathe deeply.

"As it slides across your nipples?" James' tone dips impossibly deeper, and I swear I'm already close to climaxing.

"Yes." I shiver as I shimmy the top half of the dress to my hips, completely bare from the waist up now.

"And if I slide my thumb across your hard nipple, how would that feel?"

"Warm," I whisper. "And sensual."

"Mmm," James groans. "Tell me."

This time I slow it down, spreading honey into my voice. "When you move your thumb across my nipple it gets so much harder. And it feels so warm and sensual." I touch my breast, mirroring the movement and imagine his hand there.

"I want to feel every part of you. I want to be the fabric of that dress."

A sound escapes my throat that I don't anticipate. I let the dress fall to the ground and stand there, naked.

"The dress just slipped of me onto the ground."

"Good. Are you standing there in your panties in the center of it?"

"Yes."

"Are you sliding your fingers into the lace?"

"Yes." I do as he asks and massage myself as James continues, describing what he wants to do to me and how he will do it until I'm biting my lip to hold back my release.

"I wish you were with me here." I say between panting. "Watching and touching..."

"Summer, I... I need to hear you come now," he insists.

That's all I need. I moan as the tension throughout my body releases in waves of pleasure, imagining him here, sitting on the edge of the bed, watching me touch myself.

James goes quiet.

"Are you still there?" I ask meekly between breathes.

"I am."

"Did you... you know."

"I did."

"That was a surprise." I flop onto the bed, pulling the duvet over my body that still vibrates with shivers.

"It certainly was." James clears his throat. "Now I really can't wait to see which dress you wear, although I'm partial to the gold one after listening to you describe it." His voice is filling with dreamy sleep.

"Well, you'll have to wait and see," I say, sated and relaxed. The whole day has washed away and I'm gloriously spent. "And thank you, mysterious admirer."

"Good night, Summer."

Chapter Thirty-Three

James

My phone playing Henri's ringtone interrupts my morning run.

"I'm flying back today for the holidays. I should be there late afternoon." My brother's voice is bright and loud.

"Brilliant," I say, huffing into the phone. "Want me to send a car or something?"

"Mum's already got that sorted. I just wanted to let you know."

"You could... have sent me a text... at a normal time." I'm breathing hard.

"What's the fun in that, loser?" Henri signs off after we make loose plans to have dinner together.

I return from the run and stretch my entire body, remembering the early night I had after that hot phone sex with Summer. God, her words, her release, they sent me over the edge.

Later that morning, when I'm heading out the door to work, Tilda rings.

"Morning, Mum."

"Ugh, Henri got to you already?"

"Yes, why? What?" Why does the tone in her voice irk me so much?

"Nothing urgent, it's just that we're very close to sealing a partnership, and they want to meet you and Henri."

"What's this about?" I dare to ask. "Who are we meeting exactly?"

"It's extremely hush-hush at the moment, but I've arranged a relaxed meeting at my flat tonight around seven." Tilda isn't asking.

"I'm having dinner with Henri." I exit the building and linger in the courtyard a moment before entering the park.

"Henri is coming too," she tells me. "By the way, I approve of the makeover. Very dashing, James. But who in the world are you shopping for?"

"Excuse me?" I ask. She does this—bombards me with too much information all at once that I'm flabbergasted and don't know what to respond to first.

"Google yourself," Tilda says. "See you later, dear." She hangs up before I get a chance to respond. What possible deal could she be arranging a few days to Christmas? Why does she need Henri and me? And how the hell did she even know I cut my hair?

I scroll through social media on my way across the park and find The Secret Reveler's Instagram page. There I am with Lucien, sporting our fresh haircuts in the CBD, holding the large dress boxes in front of the boutique waiting for the car. The caption: *Check him out... Second in line to the Revel Pointe throne, James Reve, finally gave up the weathered outdoorsman look for a coiffed makeover - #JamesReve #beastnomore - but who is he shopping for at @satineboutique in New Orleans? What's in the boxes, James? Something pretty?*

Posted yesterday evening. I wish I knew who this Secret Reveler is so I can find them and wring their neck. I search my name and see this "news" has been shared over two thousand times already. Why would anyone give a shit about my hair? Reya Ghu has shared it with the caption: *Told you romance reigns supreme with this dreamy Reve. #JamesReve #beastnomore Can't wait to see who wears the dress. #RPgala #RP60thanniversary.*

Fuck my public life. I don my sunglasses, hoping to stay incognito this morning. No sooner do I round the corner into the French Village than a park guest unabashedly takes a photo of me.

"Come on," I tell the twenty-something dude in the *Mission: Tranquility* sweatshirt. "Common decency, eh?"

"Free country, man!" the douchey fan calls after me.

I almost double back to spend the entire day in the compound, but I persevere to the library, feeling a pang of empathy for all Ethan and Marin had to endure last year. Cricket and the curators have finished the memorabilia install, and they're waiting to show me. I want to see it all before the gala decorators descend today after lunch. It might be the last time I see my library unadorned before taking off to Miami and then home. Perhaps Summer would be willing to join us in Florida.

When I enter the enclosure gate, I note that a large white gala tent is already constructed, and the fountain has been filled. Sunlight glints off the water, cascading over three elegant tiers. As my boots crush the tiny pebbles along the path, I feel a quick rush of pride. This building in this landscape is breathtaking, something I accomplished with a lot of help, but it's my first solo project and it will stay with me forever. The fact that it's for my PawPaw is a bonus.

I take the steps two at a time, registering that the last time I was here was with Summer during the storm. But that's pushed out of my head the moment I open the door and find the team of curators and a handful of crew members finishing jobs, among them Summer's father and the dickhead, Greg or Grant or whatever.

Cricket sees me and waves, meeting me in the center of the foyer. "Nice haircut. You good?"

"Ask me another time." I run my hand through my shorter hair and try not to notice people watching me.

"So, you sent her the dresses," Cricket comments.

"Yes. And the world knows."

"And they fit? She likes at least one?"

"I think so, yes." I hear Summer's voice in my head telling me how they felt slipping over her bare, hard nipples.

"Good, put it out of your mind until tomorrow." Easier said than done. I feel Summer's father in the room and wonder if he knows she'll be my date or if she told him about the gifts. I follow Cricket upstairs, where the scarlet ballet slippers are prominently displayed in a glass case so they are visible both from below and close up.

"We thought it would bring traffic through the building to have these signature pieces up here." Cricket rests her hands on her hips. "At least for the gala."

"Perfect choice," I say.

Cricket beams and takes me on a tour of the rest of the interior that is, honestly, pitch perfect. From the rich textiles to the furniture, from the colors to the placement of the nostalgic works of art, the Grand Revel Library is complete.

She leads me back down to the foyer. "There's talk of commissioning a painting of Mick, but—"

"Of him now? At ninety-five?"

Cricket shrugs.

"You could ask him, but I'll tell you what he's going to say." I cross my arms and gaze up at the massive chandelier. "He'll want to hang the last portrait they had done with my grandmother. Unless he wants to keep that at home."

"Thanks for the input," Cricket says. "Anyway, we're hanging a six-foot holiday wreath up there today filled with Revel-blue baubles."

"Perfect."

"You keep saying that. What's gotten into you? Has someone tamed the beast?" Cricket elbows me and wiggles her eyebrows.

I glower at her, which only makes her smile widen. A presence hovers behind me. I turn to find that nutsack carpenter lurking. "Can I help you, Gary?"

"It's Grainger." The blond oaf pulls his shoulder back and clenches his fists as if he's actually about to throw a punch.

"What's up, mate?" I check my watch, lacking the patience for this today.

"Are you dating Summer?" The guy strains his neck as if trying to gain an inch on me.

"Don't see how that's relevant."

"Seems unprofessional to date an employee," Grainger says and sniffs dramatically.

I would love to haul back and brawl with this dickbag, but I need his last few hours of skilled labor. More importantly, over his shoulder I see Summer's father taking note.

"Excuse me, but we're not having this conversation," I say, then step away before I make headlines again for the second time in twenty-four hours. As I reach for the front door, calling over my shoulder to Cricket that I'll talk to her later, Summer rushes in, nearly bumping into me.

"Oh, hello," she says, her cheeks instantly pink. "I'm looking for my dad."

It takes everything I've got not to sweep her upstairs, but I say hello cordially for public appearances and step aside, pointing in his direction.

"Thanks," she says, her bright eyes melting the anger in me.

Chapter Thirty-Four

Summer

It's the morning before Christmas Eve, and my first official day off since I arrived in Louisiana. I wake up to a Secret Reveler link from my friend Lilia. "CHECK THIS OUT!"

When I click it, a photo of James and Lucien pops onto my screen. James cut his hair off, but he's still a "rugged hunk" (according to my dad). He and Lucien are carrying the Satine dress boxes. My body goes cold as I read through the write-up:

Uh oh, Revelers... Christmas has come early for us devoted masses! Could our RP prince have found his princess? James Reve, currently second in line to the Revel Pointe throne, was spotted only three days before the 60th anniversary gala carrying dress boxes from Satine. If you weren't aware, good Reveler, Satine is a high-end dress boutique and does not carry menswear. So... Does this mean Mr. James Reve has a date to the gala? And is this date someone who's become close enough to shop for? If you read the LA Times piece, you'll know all about this handsome third son of Gaspard Reve and his penchant for privacy. Has he been hiding his one true love from the world? And will we learn who she is on Christmas Eve? Personally, I can't wait to reveal this holiday gift to you, dear Revelers!

I sink down onto the bed and look over at the Satine boxes on my credenza. What am I supposed to do? I knew that going to the gala with James would affect my life in general, namely, potentially getting in the way of earning the head archive librarian job. But I was naïve to think this wouldn't be gossip-worthy. *Could our RP prince have found his princess?* This is *way* too much for me to handle. I need to talk to someone, but I can't tell Lilia. Not yet. I text her a simple: *Wow, yeah. Catch up soon!*

I start pacing. Should I call off the gala date? My mind is so scattered that I can only come up with two pros—my job and my sanity—and two cons—doing James the favor he asked and enjoying the most exciting thing that has ever happened to me. I want to wear that dress. I want to be with James, in public, all evening. But I also want that job, a simple and secure life out of the spotlight.

Who could help me sort this out and make this decision? Would it be inappropriate to ask Cricket? She knows him and me, the situation, the brand. Hell, she's definitely signed an NDA. I decide to go for broke and text her: *Got time for a quick call?*

Cricket is likely busy at work, but her name lights up my phone only five minutes later.

"What's up?" Cricket is no nonsense per usual.

"I'm so sorry to take up your time with personal issues, but well, James asked me to the gala. I said yes. And then he sent me this dress, and it's so beautiful. I'm just worried. There's this article, or like, blog post. I mean, I don't know if..."

"You're concerned with how it will look regarding your position at Revel?"

I release the breath I've been holding. "Yes, exactly."

"Look, he needs you at that gala. If he's alone, he's going to be swarmed by the media after that *Times* article. And his mother, as I think you know, will be pimping him around that party. It's going to be a minefield for James."

"Right," I say. My guts churn. Perhaps this is just a strategy to James, and he's a better actor than I imagined.

"Don't worry about social media. It's relentless, but it's part of the Revel fandom."

"Right."

"And, don't worry about the job. That's a separate thing. Frances understands."

"She does?" I can't imagine what that means exactly.

"Of course. It's kind of romantic if you think about it— a sweet Midwestern librarian goes to the ball with the sexy library architect? It's a fairy tale. Frances will eat this up. It's free publicity."

"Okay..."

Maybe the tone in my voice forces Cricket to go on. "Listen, I know James is fond of you. I can tell. But he's a pretty closed-off guy. Given the article and the posts, I think you can see why. I would have trust issues, too."

"Right." I'm on autopilot. I feel like now I have so much information that I can't keep it all straight.

"What's the dress look like?" Cricket switches tones so fast that I'm confused for a second.

"Oh, gold and flowy..." I trail off.

"Amazing," she says. "Just take a breath. I'll be there. It'll be fun."

I thank her, and she signs off.

Her words swirl in my head like a gathering tornado. The words "trust issues" hit me like a sucker punch. Suddenly, the information I've been sitting on about the twins seems more significant. Maybe I should bring it up. But when is a good time to bring *that* up? I can just imagine how that'll go: "*Hi, I stole important family secrets in an effort to protect your feelings.*" We never went to visit Mick Reve because he visited us. Between finishing work and whatever we've been doing since the clock tower, the documents are still waiting to be delivered to Mick Reve.

Overwhelmed, I click on the television, which I haven't done since I arrived, and flip on the Revel Channel. *Portia's Power* is playing, the animated hit from Revel's glory days. I haven't seen this one since I was a pre-teen, but I remember most of it. I wander around the room, pull the shades closed, then flop down on the bed.

To prevent an anxiety spiral, I give myself this brief break. I need to shut my brain off.

Portia is a young maiden, born with powers to control the natural elements and held captive by a cruel giant. Portia needs a "true heart" to help her escape bondage, and when Prince Kasen of Winterbriar comes along, they fall instantly in love. But that's only where the story begins. Their love is tested over and over again by curses and adventure all over the kingdom. I've heard it's a Revel-ized version of a Scandinavian folktale called "The Master Maid" that I've never read. The librarian in me wonders what Revel Pointe has changed and what the source material contains. For now, I just veg out and enjoy the animation. *Portia's Power* is the first liberated princess who saves herself and the prince in the end, finding happiness on her own terms despite impossible circumstances.

As the final credits roll with the familiar theme music, I realize it's the chime from the clock tower. All of my issues are still right in front of me to deal with, and it's not even ten in the morning. Taking a cue from Portia, I seek a little perspective from a trusted source.

My dad said he'd be back at the library this morning but the job would be done by noon. Maybe I can catch him there before he heads back to his hotel. I shower, change, and brush on some blush and mascara because I'm still "at work" even if I'm not on duty. Just the thought of spending more time with my dad brings my anxiety down a few notches. He already knows a lot, and now I can fill him in all the way.

I speed walk through the park and take off at a jog when I reach the library. Today the fountain is flowing, and the place looks more alive than ever with personnel setting up tents for the gala. I bound up the front steps, and without thinking, push the wide wooden doors open, stopping just short of barreling into James himself. His now-familiar scent triggers a heightened feeling all over.

"Oh, hello," I say, feeling my face flush. "I'm looking for my dad."

James returns the greeting before stepping aside and motioning to the staircase. He looks like he wants to say more, but I cut him off.

"Thanks," I tell him, holding back a sea of questions and facts I want to share. But not yet. I'm not ready. "Dad!"

Trying not to make a scene, I calmly take the sweeping stairs to the second floor. Out of the corner of my eye, I notice Cricket, Grainger, and the curators down below. My father is gluing a slender strip of wood along one of the impressive banisters.

Dad looks up from his work. "Summer! What's up?"

I tell him I need to talk and ask when we can get together before he leaves. I'm praying he'll take lunch soon, but he suggests an early dinner because of his pre-dawn flight tomorrow morning. We agree on a time, but this means I have to sit with my own thoughts for the entire afternoon. I have nothing to do but pace my hotel room or circle the park by myself, stewing in my own anxieties.

Before descending the staircase, I scan the second floor and note the boxes and tote containers of books waiting to be shelved. It gives me an idea. Leaning carefully over the new railing, still slightly sticky with new varnish, I wait to catch Cricket's eye. When she looks up, I ask, "Got a minute?" from above. She waves and scoots into the elevator.

"Do you know how many times I've climbed those stairs?" she asks, when the elevator doors open on the second-floor landing. "What's up?"

It's the second time she's asked me that this morning, and I'm grateful I'm coming to her with work this time.

"When are those going to be shelved?" I point to the far end of the west wing.

"That's a last-minute oversight," she says. "I was going to call in some park assistants this afternoon, why?"

"Let me do it," I plead. "I need something to do, and books will make me feel normal."

Cricket embraces me in a side hug and walks me toward the jumble of boxes. "I totally get it, girl," she says, lowering her voice. "The whole thing with James is a lot. But the frenzy will pass, and those obsessive fans will be onto the next Revel thing the day after Christmas. Believe me, it'll be all about reviewing *Camp Willow Creek III* soon."

"I hope so," I say, keeping the rest of my complicated worries to myself.

"Have at it." Cricket sweeps a hand over the maze of boxes. "You'd be doing me a huge favor, and you're the expert anyway, right?"

I nod, and she doesn't waste another moment heading back to the elevator. Alone in the massive west wing, surrounded by books, with my father only a room away, I take a cleansing breath. Even though the door to the clock tower is within view and I know that chime is about to sing above us any minute, I'm in a place where I can lose myself for a while. As soon as I unlatch the plastic lid from a tote and smell the specific scent of covers, bindings, and pages, I'm at home. The first novel I lift from the bunch is *Ragtime Romp*, a classic. It's a beautiful edition, with an embossed title and faded gold filigree.

I bring the book to my nose, sniff, and feel my pulse slow.

Chapter Thirty-Five

James

Henri shuffles into the living room where I'm finishing up some paperwork and half-watching an Everton vs. Arsenal match. He's as tan as I've ever seen him, laden with a heavy-looking backpack and a rolling carry-on. When I get up to hug him, the goof still smells a touch like tropical sunscreen.

"Hey, welcome back." I slap him on the shoulder, and he drops his luggage right where he stands.

"Look at you."

"Not bad, right? Not such a caveman after all." I run my hand across the shaved fade at the back. "How was the trip and all that?"

Henri waves his hand, not one to complain, and flops himself down on the nearest sofa. "Just a long day. I need a shower."

"Yeah, you do." I offer to grab him a beer, and he nods.

"So, are you having a meltdown about all this romance shit?" Henri asks.

"I was, but it's almost over." I explain that Lucien and I are leaving for Miami and then home to England.

"You know they have cameras in Miami, right?" Henri's blue eyes twinkle. "And London?"

"Whatever." I train my attention back on the match as Arsenal almost scores again. "I won't be *here*, and that's a world of difference to me."

"Has it been that terrible?" he presses.

"No, it's just... claustrophobic," I say. "And devoid of culture."

"But you've been keeping yourself busy, I see." When he pauses, forcing me to look over at him, he's holding up his phone with the photo of Lucien and me with the boutique boxes.

"Not you fucking too."

"But there is a girl?"

"Yes, I have a date for the gala. Her name is Summer, and she's an archivist on the library project."

"An employee? How very Ethan of you." Henri knows that will get under my skin. Ethan was always so careless, the antithesis of the life and image I've cultivated. He just got lucky with Marin, his sweet wife, marrying her within the year. When I see them together, it just makes sense.

"Summer is not a Revel fan." I know I sound defensive, but it's the truth. "It's a different situation."

"Huh." Henri turns back to the match and takes a long swig. "So, it's a sort of platonic, professional thing?"

"I wouldn't call it platonic."

"Niiice." Henri sits up and unlaces his leather sneakers. "So she's hot."

I give him a look as if to say *You have no idea*, and then return to watching the match as Arsenal's striker gets a breakaway and scores in the lower left corner of the goal. "Ah, shite!" I turn it off. It's now 2-nil, and I'm not about to sit and watch Arsenal take the win.

"You ready for Mum?" I ask Henri.

"Is one ever ready for Tilda?"

I shrug as both of our phones light up. It's our sibling group text.

Elsie: *I'm coming home, bitches! Who's gonna be there besides the most eligible Reve prince-of-the-moment, James?*

I roll my eyes.

Henri texts: *I'm already here.*

Elsie: *Oh, goody! How about my other big brothers?*

Henri and I wait to see if Ethan or Dom will weigh in, but there's no immediate response.

"Well, I'm gonna go shower and shave before this ambush— I mean, meeting," Henri says.

Alone again, I flop back onto the sofa in the quiet and text Summer. This morning she looked a little distracted when she came in looking for her dad. I feel like I should prepare her for the media storm tomorrow. As the heat has never been so fixed on me, I'm no expert, but I've got a bit of practice.

I'm not sure where to begin so I float out a neutral *How are you? Ready for tomorrow?*

I pace around, waiting for a response, but it doesn't come before we have to leave for Tilda's eleventh-hour meeting.

It's bloody cold and damp out, but Henri and I still decide to walk the stone rampart along the river and around the grassy levee to the resort instead of crossing through the still-open park. I'm not in the mood for selfies, and with my brother, it'll be twice as enticing to get a photo of us.

Along the way, we catch up, and he tells me how much the last few hurricanes devastated Puerto Rico. Henri's always been a naturalist who turned into a full-fledged environmental scientist over the past five years. He's been traveling the world on grants, and sometimes on his own dime, working special projects.

"It's the most simple work in the world, just planting mangroves and tending the habitat, but it takes manpower and, frankly, luck at this point," Henri explains. "If they get another storm like the ones they just had, our work will be washed away again."

I love listening to him talk about work, feeling a sense of pride in my little brother for doing the hard and necessary work of keeping the planet alive. I ask him questions about the mangrove site, and as he elaborates on the ecosystem with passion, about the sea turtles and bird species, it finally feels like the Christmas season. Funny, I've been surrounded by holiday promotions for weeks, talking about this Christmas Eve gala for months, and not once did it actually feel like the holidays to me. It took Henri's physical presence for me to realize the library is done. Suddenly, I feel celebratory and less annoyed by this meeting with our mother.

When the elevator doors open, there's faint jazzy background music playing in Tilda's penthouse. It's vaguely festive. For as much as she's on about family values, she hates religious carols and despises the catchy pop songs that invade this time of year. The place smells like basil and pine, but not overwhelmingly so. When we round the corner to the large, minimalist sitting room, we find Tilda holding court from a high-backed chair. There's Bill Symons, CFO of Revel Pointe–Park Division, Shirleen Watson, longtime board member, and Frances Maceta, who I've been working closely with on the library project. But among them are two very striking people, an Asian man and woman, dressed severely in black and white.

A server notices Henri and me and asks for our drink order. I shrug out of my heavy coat and ask for a Scotch. This night has taken a turn I wasn't prepared for.

"Do you know who they are?" I whisper, nudging my brother.

Henri shakes his head no, and we're interrupted by Frances and Shirleen before we can confer.

"It's good to see you two together," Shirleen says, offering both of us a hug. As one of my grandfather's first protégées, she's known us since we were in diapers. Shirleen was the first Black woman on the board and still one of the most powerful members outside the family, according to Ethan.

Our drinks arrive as we exchange catch-up pleasantries. Both Shirleen and Frances congratulate me on the library. Frances is noticeably distant. *Weird*. Tilda beckons us over. Wearing a simple but stylish gray dress with a large black belt, our mother towers over her guests in her Manolo Blahniks. She actually hugs Henri, likely because she hasn't seen him in about a year, and then squeezes my arm hello.

"These are my fashionably late sons, James and Henri," Tilda tells the guests. "And these are our honored visitors from Japan, Ami and Noa Kimura."

Ami and Noa shake our hands.

"Noa and Ami are the owners and designers of Kimura Fantasy, a top fashion house in Japan, which is growing around the world." Tilda nods to them. "They're a father/daughter team, and I just thought it would be fitting for all of us to meet since we're also a family company."

It finally all clicks together like a simple Lego set. The bridal-wear couture that Lucien mentioned. Henri and I being trotted out like show ponies for another family-structured company. This is why we're here.

"The library is ethereal," Ami says to me, explaining how Tilda brought them through this afternoon. "A sublime setting. So, so perfect."

I'm not exactly sure what she's talking about, so I just nod and take the compliment. But Noa continues speaking in elaborate diction about the library as if he's going to purchase it or hire me.

"It's as if you spent a year in my head, looking through my eyes and working with my hands, in order to weave such a flattering space," Noa says enthusiastically.

I ignore their flowery language, chalking it up to fashionable people being pretentious, and take another sip of my drink. I let Tilda take over, and the conversation drifts to Henri's work around the world, how he spent a month with the Fukushima tsunami cleanup in college. Tilda beams with parental pride: "Look at my altruistic, talented boys!" She's never more maternal than when she's trying to impress. *God bless her "Pride and Joy."*

On a side table, there's a small spread of hors d'oeuvres and caviar, so I move off for a bite to get my bearings. The room isn't exactly cozy, but there's a light feeling in the air. Bill catches my eye and raises his glass slightly. He's looking a little tipsy, but if he's sleeping with my mother, he'll need it.

Frances joins me at the appetizers, and she doesn't waste time getting to the point, her mouth turned down like she ate a lemon.

"I have to say, I'm surprised by this turn of events," she says. "And I'm sort of shocked that you're fine with the library being repurposed."

I nearly choke on the olive in my mouth. "Repurposed? Says who? For what?" My voice is gruff. "I'm not fine with that."

Frances stares at me, mouth agape. "You don't know?" Frances' defiant posture deflates. "Oh shoot. Shoot. I thought because of all that romantic *LA Times* stuff about you, you were in on it."

"What's 'it,' Frances?" I eye my mother, still with Henri, Noa, and Ami, smiling and performing. "I need to know."

Frances leans closer, whispering, "She's turning the library into an elite bridal salon."

I fume as I listen to Frances explain the five-year deal with Kimura Fantasy to create princess-worthy bridal couture for Revel Pointe, and the current plan to transform the library into a high-fashion retail space at the end of the 60th anniversary year. The eternal smoldering in my ribcage ignites, burning hot and overheating my limbs. My chest feels tight. I want to punch something. Hard.

"That will crush my PawPaw," I seethe.

Frances gives me a knowing look. It dawns on me.

"She doesn't plan on him being around much longer to care." I motion to Tilda and temper my words and voice in front of Frances.

"I would never speak ill of your mother," Frances says. "But this feels like the wrong move with the library. Sure, bridal will do phenomenal business, but the library is legacy. *You* get that."

"Frances," I say. "Tilda doesn't care. She's going to break my grandfather's heart for a buck." My pulse pounds in my ears.

"I'm so sorry, James," Frances says, her eyes full of trepidation.

I feel eight years old again. Once more, Tilda has put profit above family, and I want to tear a hole through this utterly revolting party. I down the last of my drink and carry the empty glass with me to where Tilda is still licking the shoes of these oblivious fashion designers.

"I bet you're excited to get started in the library," I say to the Kimuras.

"Very much so," Ami says. "In my mind, it's like the inside of a cloud."

"A cloud? Really?" I can't contain my derision.

"Yes, we'll need more baby seashell."

"Baby seashell?" Now I'm just repeating her, completely bulldozed by this turn.

"Soft pink." Ami blinks at me, finally noticing my deteriorating state.

All of my painstaking work to make something beautiful for PawPaw melts into a corporate puddle before my eyes.

"So, where do you envision the cash register will go?" I ask the little group, including Tilda. "Next to the mantel where you can't miss it? Or maybe something more discreet, like a giant ATM in the west wing? Oh, how about right next to PawPaw's broken fucking heart?"

"James, darlin'..." Tilda begins, but I cut her off.

"So fill me in. What's the timeline on this venture? Are you going to wait until after PawPaw dies or just until he doesn't have the energy left to fight you anymore? If you thought for one second that I would be okay with this... Maybe that's why you failed to tell me until now, hoping I'd be too polite, too well-behaved to make a scene. Well, mother dearest, I'm fucking not." I smash my crystal lowball down on the glass side table, and it shatters with a startling pop. Tilda's guests gasp as shards of glass spray across the Persian carpet and hardwood floors.

"My apologies," I say to the Kimuras and Shirleen, who stand frozen nearby, and I keep moving toward the elevator.

Henri jogs up to me as I'm putting on my coat. "What was that?" Genuine concern emanates from him.

"I'll explain later," I tell him, thinking I might just head back to the compound, pack up all my shit, and take the private jet back to London tonight. "I can't be here anymore."

The elevator closes, and I'm numbed by rage. When my pocket buzzes with an incoming call, I cross onto the freezing rampart, staring across the Mississippi.

My phone screen flashes with the name *Summer York*.

"I need to talk to you," she says, sounding breathy and anxious. Something's wrong. Suddenly, all of my energy focuses on her.

"Where are you? Are you okay?"

"I'm in a cab heading back to the park," she says. I picture a worried look on her face, and all I want to do is hold her, be held by her.

"Come to the compound," I tell her. "I'll meet you there."

Chapter Thirty-Six

Summer

My dad answers the door of his budget hotel room with a wet head, wearing his sweats and slippers. His luggage is spread neatly across a queen-size bed.

"Ready to head home?" I ask, holding out the Popeye's take-out he requested.

"Just about." He sets the bags on the small table in the corner of the room, and we begin unwrapping our chicken fingers and fries.

Dad cuts right to the chase. "So, what's on your mind, sweetheart?"

I sigh with my whole body before starting. While I was organizing and shelving books this afternoon, I rehearsed what I'd tell my dad about James and me, the information I've learned, and the state of my job. I know I can confide in Dad, as I've done more and more since Mom passed, but there are some delicate details—like the make-out session on the flight and the mind-blowing clock tower sex—that I'll definitely leave out. I've also signed an NDA, and legally I can't tell anyone about the confidential information I've seen anyway. So I can't tell the whole story, but I tip-toe to the very edge.

"That's when James left his father's study," I continue, "and I found the documents Mick Reve wanted me to find. I never gave them to James. He was just so upset about his mother and family drama that I didn't want to pile on this new information."

"Okay."

"Yes, but..." And here I pause, scanning the room, treading carefully. "But these documents contained really sensitive

229

information. Like top secret. Like, I don't think even James, or his siblings, know about this stuff."

"I see. And why do you have this hunch?"

"Because of the way everyone talks about their family within the business." I struggle to find the words. "Like royal succession. Who's next to take over as CEO? If it's not Ethan, will it be James? If not James, back to Gaspard, his father? Stuff like that."

"Gotcha." Dad takes a second to mull this over. "And this information would change the succession?"

"It might," I continue. "And I don't think James even cares about all that, but it'll definitely cause more family drama. It's really none of my business, but I would hate to, I don't know..."

"You don't want to keep secrets from him if this, uh, interest you have in one another becomes a relationship?" Dad asks.

Hearing my dad put it so plainly this way makes me feel dumb. How would a relationship even work? James is going back to London. It sounds like a ridiculous fantasy I've made up in my head.

"I don't know. He's, like, pop culture royalty, for Pete's sake. And I'm just me."

"Don't sell yourself short, Summer." Dad's voice changes, taking on more conviction. "Any young man would be lucky to have you. Don't let all that fancy malarky intimidate you."

"Not to mention our jobs," I blurt. "His is in the UK, and today in the library I overheard Frances tell Cricket that the head librarian position was between me and Horace."

"Of course, you'll get it! But is this really your dream job?" Dad asks, digging deeper.

"Well, yes, and no..." I trail off, thinking about Oxford and the Bodleian.

In the quiet pause, Dad and I hear a door slam and a voice close by ask, "Dude, what're you doing?"

I freeze. It sounds like Derek is in Dad's bathroom. Derek's voice is followed by the sound of shuffling. I shoot Dad a look that asks, *What's going on?*

"Thin walls..." Dad starts to explain, but not three seconds later, there's a knock, and the door next to my Dad's bathroom opens to reveal Grainger, and then Derek, entering from the adjoining room.

My body goes cold with panic. *How much have they heard? Were they listening?*

"Hey, Summer," Grainger says, pushing my dad's luggage aside and flopping on the bed. "Come to say goodbye?"

Grainger was one hundred percent eavesdropping on Dad and me through the suite door, which I didn't even think to check.

"Yep. She came to visit her old pop before I ship out tomorrow." Dad saves me as I'm still speechless with dread, shock, and anger.

"That's sweet," Derek says and begins telling us about how he won fifty bucks hustling some locals at pool at the bar down the street. He seems totally oblivious, but Grainger looks guilty as hell.

"What were *you* up to?" I ask Grainger.

"Working out," he says. "The hotel gym was getting busy, so I finished my push-ups and sit-ups in the room." He runs a hand through his hair and asks me and Dad if we want to go have a beer in the lobby bar.

It's literally the last thing I want to do in the world.

"No, thanks," Dad says as he gets up to clear our fast food trash "I've got that early flight." His tone is cooler than usual.

"I've got to get back to the park," I say. "Huge day tomorrow." I stand too, hoping they get the hint to leave.

"I know, right?" Grainger says and starts blabbing on about Lottie and the Christmas Eve gala.

What I wouldn't give to ensure that Grainger couldn't go to the gala. The guys don't take the cue to leave Dad's room, so I hug him and say goodbye with the two of them watching and listening.

I'm silently fuming that Dad and I can't finish our much-needed conversation.

Luckily, Dad walks me to the elevator, clutching my shoulder and speaking low by my ear.

"Be there for James as a friend," he begins. "Tell him or don't tell him, you'll know when it's the right time. You're a good judge of character, Summer. Trust that it'll work out."

"But how? I'm so confused."

"I think you need to talk to him. Clear the air. Get a little clarity on what's happening between you two first."

"Argh. Okay."

"And give those documents to Mick Reve ASAP," he says sternly. "That's *your* job."

The pained expression on my face turns him to mush as he hugs me again. "It's all going to be fine. Come on, enjoy yourself. You're going to a ball tomorrow with a handsome prince!"

I laugh, blinking back tears.

"And you've got that beautiful dress to wear, too."

He's right. I need to enjoy this, but I also need to talk to James.

"Love you, Dad," I say, stepping into the elevator car. "See you in a few days."

Nervous as hell, I pull out my phone and call the handsome prince.

Later, when my cab pulls up to the compound, outlined by the twinkling lights of the park and the moon slice projected into the sky from the lighthouse, I experience a strange mix of emotions. The familiar sights have a settling effect, as I've been here nearly three weeks now, but the jitters in my stomach activate as James comes into view, standing on the front doorstep of his family's home.

"You're a sight for sore eyes," he says, and after I enter the house, he pulls me in for a long hug.

"I could say the same about you," I say into the soft cotton of his shirt, inhaling his scent like healing vapors.

He releases his grasp to kiss me. It's light at first, but the sparks fly fast, and soon our mouths are hungrily searching, devouring each other. Before I realize what's happening, James has picked me up, my legs wrapping around his waist. We're still in the front foyer, but he's backed me up against the wall next to a large painting, and his face is at my neck, licking and playfully biting. His hands squeeze my ass, and I suddenly remember why I'm here.

"Wait, we need to talk. I—"

"Yes, but first, I need this. I need you." He pulls back for a moment, searching my face, looking for consent. This close to him, our bodies pressed together, gazing deep into the forest of his eyes, all I can do is bite my lip and nod.

Slowly he lowers me, then takes my hand and guides me up the stairs. My brain floods with lust. As we reach the landing, he pulls me to him again, his mouth traveling down to my clavicle, his hand reaching up my sweater, cupping my breast.

"God, Summer," James growls, and then leads me up the next flight. Finally, down a short hallway in this maze of a castle home, he pushes us into a luxurious bedroom suite. We crash into each other again, all of my worries forgotten. I just want to be naked with him. I shiver as he lifts my sweater over my head. I reach for his shirt buttons, but he's already dropped down to his knees, kissing my belly, unzipping my jeans.

"Is this okay?" he asks, looking up at me with wild eyes.

"Yes." It comes out like a whimper.

Suddenly, my jeans are pulled down to the floor, and he walks me backward until I'm falling onto a plush sofa. For a second, I feel sort of self-conscious in my pink flower-print panties and blue T-shirt bra, but the moan that comes from James' throat as he unbuttons his shirt and inches closer shows his rapt anticipation.

I want his mouth on me so badly it makes my knees shake. James notices and plants fervent kisses on the inside of my knees, traveling up and up.

He looks up at me, his hands wrapped around my waist, his mouth so close to my delicate flesh that I can feel his hot breath. In reply, I slouch into the sofa, pressing myself closer to his lips. James takes his time, and my desire is so hot that I nearly lose it all before he's even really started.

"Damn, I've been looking forward to this," James says between caresses as he pulls my panties off.

"Me too." I reach down and tangle my fingers into his now shorter hair.

My whole body gasps and tightens as his mouth finally meets me, but as James works deliberately, I relax into the plush sofa beneath my naked skin. I unhook and remove my bra, grazing my nipples with my fingertips. My breath hitches again. Goosebumps rise all over and warmth pours through me as he takes me up to a crest and back again with wave after wave of pleasure.

Finally, James kisses his way up my torso and drops onto the sofa beside me, gripping my waist and flipping me onto him. I straddle him and unbuckle his belt as our mouths meet again. His lips feel swollen and soft, but his beard is still a bit rough against my cheeks. Suddenly, he's lifting us both off the sofa and over to the bed, where he sits on the edge. Leaning over, he grabs a condom from the side table, and I help him out of his pants and boxer briefs while he tends to the protection. But before he can slip it on, I slip to the floor on my knees, reach up, and bring my mouth to the length of him, licking as slowly and attentively as he did to me.

"Fuck, Summer"—the words escape his mouth. Making James hum like a semi-truck motor turns me on in a way I've never felt before.

James grabs my shoulders and pulls me up, a little rough, then secures the condom. I can't wait anymore and climb onto him, gripping his hips with my thighs. Finally, we're together again. I've never felt so sexy in my life, undulating on top of him as he licks the sweat beading between my breasts. He watches me, and I watch him too, as we move into each other, bracing and swelling, over and over, pounding and panting with the deepest pleasure until we both release in moans and wails.

We both lay back on the cool comforter, breathing hard. I curl into his side and place my hand on his heaving chest, my body and mind calm. After a while, James turns his head to kiss my forehead and brings me in for a cuddle.

"Your body is just..." James trails off, looking for a word. "Sublime."

I can't handle the compliment, though it makes me want to mount him again. "Pot, meet kettle."

He trails his hand down the length of my bare side, pulling me to him by the hip. "I can't wait to see you in one of those dresses." He pauses and sighs. "And then take it off you after."

My body involuntarily shivers, and we both laugh.

As James reaches over to kiss me deeply again, my mind starts to betray my body and wanders. Why can't I just let this be what it is? The sexist fling I've ever had. The word "after" echoes in my head, and my insecurities come flooding back. What happens after the gala? Do we never see each other again? Do we try some kind of long-distance dating?

"Will you stay the night?" James asks, and this ruffles the butterflies in my chest. I find a clock on the nightstand, and it's still so early.

"All right," I say and snuggle into him tighter. I'm really not sure if I *should* stay, but this gives me more time to actually talk to him, the whole point of coming here.

As if he's reading my mind, he asks, "Want a glass of wine?" He lifts up to his elbow, yawning. "You said you wanted to talk."

"Yes, I did." I feel too naked to have this kind of conversation. "And yes to wine," I add, looking for my clothes, which are on the sofa at the other end of the room.

I catch James watching me, lust clouding his features. "I don't want you to put clothes on."

The idea of spending an entire naked evening sipping wine with James at the table sounds really hot. Another jolt of pleasure ripples down my spine, but I'm interrupted by a loud crash somewhere in the house. I jump and reflexively cover my breasts. I shoot James a what-was-that look as he slips back into his black boxer briefs, shaking his head.

"My brother's home," he says. "Henri. Come on, we'll go down to hang with him. You'll love him. Everybody loves him."

So now I'm going to meet his brother? This water I'm treading keeps getting deeper and rougher.

"Okay," I say, completely unsure of myself. "Just let me freshen up first. I don't wanna look like—"

"Like you just rode me like a cowgirl?"

I blush, and he comes to me, still in his underwear, and pulls me into a massive hug. "You're fucking adorable when you blush."

When he lets me go with a pat on the bottom, I pull my clothes together and head for the bathroom. He's treating me like a girlfriend. What the heck am I supposed to do with that? And how the heck am I going to keep it cool around another Reve?

Chapter Thirty-Seven

James

In the kitchen, we find Henri filling a bucket with water. He looks up at us as if caught in the middle of some crime, and I note that beyond the large island, a clear red liquid has pooled.

"What's the ruckus? Burying a body?" I ask him, noticing the change in his expression as Summer follows me into the scene.

"Grab a broom. You're my accomplices now." Henri gives Summer his winning smile. "Hi, I'm Henri."

Summer introduces herself. She closes the gap between us and the kitchen island and leans over. "Was it self-defense?" she asks, continuing the gag.

"Yes." Henri straightens. "Yes, it was. This damn bowl of fruit launched itself off the top shelf, aiming for my face, but I deflected and hit the wine bottle. It got me in the gut." He points to the large stain on the lower half of his gray shirt.

"Tilda didn't serve dinner?" I ask, a bit curious to learn what happened after I left.

"You know her," Henri says, then turns to Summer. "Our mother thinks a meal is two bites of tuna crudo on an endive leaf. I'm still starving. I need, like, a turkey leg at this point."

"Well, Christmas is only a day away," Summer says. "Want some help?"

"I got it," Henri says, swabbing the mop back and forth. "You're a guest. Have a seat."

"Yes, let me open another bottle," I say, giving Summer a rub on the back before leaving her side to survey the bottles I'd brought up from the cellar. I open the French grenache and listen to her answer my brother's questions about her time working at the park. A warm, cozy feeling floods my veins. There's a natural ease between Summer and Henri that makes me realize it's been years since I've introduced a woman to anyone in my family. In fact, it was so long ago that I wouldn't have called her a woman. Freshman year at uni.

I pour out two glasses and deliver them before pouring my own.

"Cheers," Henri says. "Hope I didn't interrupt your evening."

"Oh, no." Summer nearly jumps off her stool. "I just needed to talk to James about—"

"You totally ruined the night, mate," I joke, saving her. "But I wouldn't have anybody else crash the party." We all clink glasses and drink the dry, earthy wine.

As if on some divine cue, both Henri's and my phones buzz. His lights up on the island, and I don't even have to crane my neck to know it's our mother.

"Oooh, you released the kraken," Henri says, reading through the short text.

"Ignore her," I say.

"You know it only gets worse if you don't kiss the ring."

"She's not the queen or a mob boss," I say, gulping down more wine. "I'm done. With her. She's gone too far this time. I'm out of here the day after tomorrow."

Henri's raises his eyebrows. I haven't had much time to think about what happened earlier tonight. I just masked my rage with sex, and I feel guilty for turning all that energy onto Summer without her knowing. Not that we've declared any intentions beyond the gala. The fact that I'm even feeling some shame reminds me there are deeper feelings than physical desire with Summer. *She's probably leaving too*, I remind myself.

"Were you actually thinking about joining the board?" Henri asks.

"Absolutely not."

"My mind is blown," Henri says, then to Summer: "Sorry for all the shop talk, but he told you what happened tonight, right?"

Summer's wide eyes give her innocence away.

"Not yet, no." My stomach growls, and I realize I haven't had anything but a few olives at Tilda's. I circle the island and open the fridge, nudging my brother out of the way. "It's not exactly news we can share." I hate leaving her in the dark, especially since what Tilda's planning affects Summer directly. I hadn't really processed that fact until now, and this heats my chest again with anger.

"Yeah, but you must have signed an NDA, right?" Henri asks Summer, and I wish I could kick him under the island, but we're exposed here in the light of the kitchen.

Summer affirms his question. "But I don't need to know. It's none of my business."

But it is, I think. "I was going to tell you," I say, but I want to pull her in and protect her if I can. "First, do you want something to eat? I'm starving."

Summer shakes her head and sips her wine, looking nervous. This is going to suck. As Henri finishes with the mop and paper towels, I reach into the fridge to find leftover roast beef, sharp cheddar, and some spicy mustard. While I begin to whip up some sandwiches, I attempt to explain what happened at our mother's weird soiree tonight with as much sensitivity to Summer's position in all this as I can manage.

"Basically, our mother is so business-minded that having a space in the park just to preserve the culture our family created is unacceptable. In other words, the library is not profitable. Every inch of this park needs to be a cash cow, and our library might be collateral damage." I'm surprised at my own words, *our library*, Summer's and mine—but this is how I've come to think of it.

"But-but how can she do that to your grandfather?" Summer shakes her head, confused.

Bless her for thinking of my PawPaw before herself and her job.

"She's a Mammon," Henri says between large sips of wine. "A money-hungry demon."

"We should start calling her that," I say. "She'll think we're using the French, *maman*."

"Yikes. You two don't hold back," Summer says.

I guess my mommy issues are out of the bag. "Trust me, we're being generous." I butter the bread and place the sandwiches in the pan. "But I can't let her do this to PawPaw. Or to you."

"Well, yes, that would be awful for him, especially at this stage of his life when I'm sure he wants to see his hard work live on through his grandchildren." Summer looks lost in thought when I glance at her. I wonder what she wanted to talk about earlier.

"Sounds like you've got a plan," Henri says to me. "Other than getting the hell outta Dodge."

"I really don't." I sip my wine and think. "I'm sorry," I say to Summer. "You can't tell anyone about this. Whatever deal she's trying to set up with the Fimuras still has to be voted on. I don't know where my dad stands on this, but we'll be seeing him tomorrow night."

"And your mom, she keeps things from him?" Summer asks.

"All the time," Henri says. "They're business partners, but since his stroke, she's been power hungry, making all sorts of moves without his knowledge."

"And then there's Ethan," I remind them both. "I wonder if he knows anything about this."

Summer sits up straight. "I think he does," she says.

Henri and I exchange looks, waiting for her to elaborate.

"Last week I met him, and your mother, actually." Summer takes a long sip of wine, and the sizzle of butter in the pan fills the silence in the kitchen. "I was in the palace offices working alone, and when

I turned a corner, I bumped right into your mom. Documents went flying."

Henri raises his eyebrows again. "She must have loved that."

I flip the sandwiches and listen to the rest of Summer's story.

"I didn't know what I was looking at then, but when I picked up her files, there was a Bridal Wear Market Share chart and a document called Grand Revel Couture. I thought it was smart, actually. Business-wise."

"It is smart, but not in the library." I don't hear the harshness in my voice until it's too late.

"Right, well, I agree," Summer says meekly. "But anyway, she went into a meeting right after that, and your brother Ethan followed her in."

Henri and I share another knowing glance.

"Those two are like oil and water," Henri explains. "No way he would agree to anything she's plotting."

"I gave Ethan and PawPaw a tour of the library last week. E was thrilled with it," I share.

"He'll be at the gala, right?" Summer asks.

Henri nods. "Of course."

I plate the sandwiches and cut them in half. "Dad will be hard to pin down. I might be able to get a moment with Ethan." I take my first bites and think. I could just text my older brother, but I don't know where to begin. Plus, this is the sort of conversation one has face-to-face. "Anyway, thanks for telling me about that." I smile at Summer and feel instantly closer to her. "I'm sorry about what this might mean for your position here."

"That's all right," she says, finishing her wine. "I prepared myself for that possibility." When I motion to refill her glass, she slides off her stool and shakes her head. "I think I should get going. Tomorrow's a big day."

At this moment, she looks so small and lost in our giant kitchen. I want to sweep her back into my arms and carry her all the way up the stairs to my suite again. My family shit continues to mess up everything.

"Are you sure?" I ask, and when she nods, I offer to drive her home to the resort.

"No, thanks," she says. "I'd actually like to walk. Clear my head a little before bed."

I set down my sandwich and wipe my hands on a towel before rounding the island to her. "Let me walk you out."

I lead Summer through the house and outside to the side exit where she can safely cut through the park to the resort.

"Tonight was fun," I say, reaching down to hold her against me. With my face against her voluminous hair, I take in her clean, floral scent. I want her to stay and talk more, to figure things out together. A new feeling for me.

"Yes, it was," she says into my chest.

"We can do it again tomorrow," I say, hoping she can stay the night then.

Summer laughs. "Yes, please." She looks up at me and I lean into her, kissing her softly on the mouth, and then trail kisses from her cheek to her neck. "Whoa," she says, giggling.

"All right, I'll stop." I pull back but keep hold of her waist and kiss her lips lightly again. "But you just taste so good. I'm addicted."

She laughs again, a little out of breath. "You taste like spicy mustard."

I lick my lips and grin. "Well, good night then, Summer," I say, still holding her and making no effort to let go.

"Good night, James." She blinks up at me. With our bodies still pressed together, for a second I think she's going to change her mind, but then she crosses her arms over her chest. "You're going to have to let me go."

"I don't want to." I don't. This should scare the shit out of me, but I'm too exhausted to pretend otherwise.

I reluctantly release her body and feel a frigid breeze rush in as she takes a step away. She doesn't say another word as I hold the gate open for her and she heads off into the park, in the shadows of the motionless rides. In the chaos of the evening, I realize we never had that talk she wanted to have.

Chapter Thirty-Eight

Summer

My brain has been doing back handsprings all day long, and in an effort to distract myself, I turn to self-care. I start with an extra-long spin session in the hotel's fitness center. Over breakfast, I watch another Revel movie on the park channel—*Princess and the Pea*, which is funnier than I remember. I paint my toenails and fingernails a shiny nude shade. I pluck my eyebrows and give myself a sheet mask. I do a little yoga. I take a bath and finally finish my Queen Isabella biography.

I fill the day as best I can to push away worries about being a good date in front of, you know, the whole freaking Revel universe, not to mention thoughts about the confusing conversation James, Henri, and I had last night. Oh, and then there's the fact that I never told him about the twins. The silver lining is now I don't have to worry about how going to the gala may affect my position in the future. There will be no position, only bridal couture. The thought enrages me, but I try to put it out of my mind, for tonight only.

I'm ready way too early, sitting alone on the edge of my bed in my dress, full makeup and flowing, half up, roller set hair. Outside, the clouds are low, and the setting sun beyond dyes them with stunning raspberry and plum hues. Starting to sweat inside, I take myself out to the balcony, where the surprising chill gives me an energy boost. It's the same temperature here as it is in Ohio. It even smells like snow in the air. To fill time, I video call my dad.

His round face is too close to the phone when he answers. "Kiddo! Aren't you at the ball yet?"

I can hear people talking in the background, and it's surreal to me that my family is all together, having a normal Christmas Eve.

"I'm about to go," I say, when my six-year old nephew, Brody, climbs onto my dad's lap and enters the view.

"Hi Auntie Summie!" Brody says. "Why aren't you here?"

It breaks my heart. "I'll be there tomorrow, buddy." When it comes out of my mouth, it's hard to actually imagine that I'm leaving Revel Pointe tomorrow, Christmas Day.

"We miss you," Dad says. "Right, stinker?" Dad tickles Brody, and the phone shakes with the boy's squirmy giggles. The screen goes all swishy and suddenly I'm looking at my sister Kayla's face.

"Dad said you're James Reve's date tonight?!" Kayla walks away from the group. "You better bring back details on that hottie, if you know what I'm saying. Make it a night to remember." She wiggles her eyebrows.

"Kayla, you're so mature." I roll my eyes dramatically.

"I mean it. Make me jealous."

"Oh, don't worry about me," I say and point to my nose, noting I've got tales to tell.

Kayla squeals. "Okay, you look stunning! Now go have fun. Love you!"

"Love you, too!" I laugh. "I miss you guys!" I yell to everyone else.

"We miss you too!" A chorus of voices meets me and fills my chest with love. I hear Gran, my nieces, and my brother-in-law in the background.

I sign off, smiling. That was exactly what I needed: a reminder that I have a big, goofy, loving family waiting for me at home back in Ohio, no matter what happens tonight. My jitters have subsided into happy anticipation. I can't wait to see James all dressed up. I can't wait to see how the library looks all decorated for Christmas, even if it's only a library for a year. The whole thing is bittersweet, but I shore myself up with the echoes of my family. Tonight I'm just going to soak it all in. I cross the room to grab Mom's little gold watch from the nightstand. I wasn't going to wear it for fear it would clash with this fancy ensemble, but I want her with me.

My phone chimes. It's James: *On my way.*

The bumblebees in my ribcage start buzzing again. It's all happening now. I step into my navy blue kitten heels that I bought online, recommended by Cricket—*Who knew the color combination would look so chic?*—and head out the door.

I feel eyes on me already in the lobby. Of course, the resort is still filled with tourists catching dinner after a long day at the park, and no one is dressed for the gala in the gift shops or the lobby bar. Since it's cold out, I wait in the entrance before the revolving doors, keeping my eye out for the same car he picked me up in last week. I take deep breaths and pray that my makeup looks okay. I don't have to wait long. The car pulls up and James pops out, looking amazing.

I meet him outside. His eyes soften; his lips curve in an adoring smile.

"You look beautiful," he says, offering his hand and leading me to the passenger side.

"Thank you," I say. "You too." He does. He's wearing a classic black tuxedo, complete with a bow tie and a white pocket square. It fits him perfectly. His new haircut and trimmed beard show off his dark green eyes and his smile, and the words *rugged hunk* flash through my mind again.

Someone's phone camera flashes our way as I duck into the sports car, tucking the layers of fabric in carefully before James closes the door. When he rounds the front of the car, I notice people filming him from the sidewalk.

"Ready?" he asks, behind the wheel again.

"It's too late to turn back now," I say, and when he gives me a hesitant look, I correct myself. "I mean, I was nervous, I am nervous, but I'm excited, I mean, I'm ready."

James grabs my hand and grins. "It's going to be fine. Crazy, but fine. Just stick with me." He winks, and then puts the car in gear, leaving the lights of the resort behind.

We don't have far to go, and there's a line of cars on the service road for the valet at the gala. In the minutes we wait, James leans over and kisses my neck with the lightest touch, sending shivers down my bare arms.

"I don't want to mess up your lipstick," he says. "But you're so gorgeous it hurts not to kiss you."

"Part of me wants you to just keep driving me away, so you can mess it all up," I tell him, and he groans.

"You're killing me." He takes my hand again and kisses the back of it just once, sending pulses to the nerve endings between my legs. A whimper escapes my mouth.

He groans and straightens himself in the driver's seat. "We're up next," he says, coasting to a stop at the valet stand and the red carpet that has been rolled out alongside the library. Waiting behind the rope is a collection of reporters with photographers and videographers. After the first one spots James, the chaos begins. Each one calls his name with the urgency of a kid begging for candy at checkout, as if he'll wander right past without posing for a photo or answering one question.

James grabs my hand and leans into my ear. "Just smile. You don't have to answer any questions. It's awkward, but we're going to just keep walking."

I nod and squeeze his hand. We walk slowly along the paparazzi setup, and I notice that spotlights have been installed, pointing up at the library, showing off the architectural details against the evening sky. Photographers snap our picture. They shout, "Together, get closer!" to both of us. Someone yells, "James, over here!" And we both turn toward the voice, but I'm almost blind from all the flashes.

James leans his face into my ear again and says, "You're doing great. It's just a big, dumb game I have to play sometimes. Keep smiling."

I laugh reflexively, nervously, and then someone yells, "Who's the girl?" A woman in a short red dress shouts, "Miss, miss, tell us your name!" I look at James, and he winks.

"Summer York," I tell the woman.

"Are you dating?" someone else asks. "How long have you been dating?" And this has more questions of that sort thrown our way. "Did James buy you that dress, Summer?" And now people are also yelling my name. I give James a quick glance. We can't answer most of these questions because we don't even know the answers. Instead of looking as flustered as I feel, he just keeps grinning and nodding and slowly leading me toward the front courtyard.

James waves at the paparazzi and turns to me. "I think that's about enough," he says, holding an elbow out for me to take. After the red carpet gauntlet, we arrive at the big tents among the oak trees. Tasteful white strings of lights illuminate the edges, and large chandeliers hang inside. The fountain also has new light features, casting moving shadows on the well-dressed guests as they make their way to the library steps. Outside the library entrance, I note James' mother, Tilda, standing with some familiar faces. As we make our way toward them, James notices where my gaze has landed.

"Let me fill you in. You know my mother." He nods toward her. "Next to her is my dad, Gaspard. And next to him is his wife, Yasmin." He adds that this has been his longest marriage, twenty years next year.

I note the tall, barrel-chested man in the black suit, with a thick head of graying hair. His younger wife is stunning in a full-length, strapless burgundy dress and a spray of diamonds around her neck.

Her dark, sleek hair is parted down the middle, flowing over toned shoulders.

"They're quite a striking couple," I say.

"I agree," James says. "Yasmin's good for Dad. She dotes on him, and that's what he needs."

"Are you close with your dad?" Summer asks quietly.

"No. Dad cheated on Mum with Yasmin when I was just four, so I never really knew my folks together. It always felt like I was betraying my mother to get too close." Under my hand, I feel James' bicep flex. *Ah*, I think, that's how Tilda has kept James and Henri close when it's clear she's not winning a mother-of-the-year award anytime soon. Now is not the time or place to go deeper, so I keep it light.

"And they have two kids, too?"

"Yep." James leads us toward the steps now. "Dominic and Elsie. She should be around here somewhere..." He cranes his head to have a look around. "I think Dom skipped again."

"And that's Ethan, right?" I point as discreetly as I can at the handsome guy across the fountain. He's full of life, laughing with an older couple. On his arm is a curvaceous redhead wearing a form-fitting, raspberry-colored mermaid gown, and she's also laughing and dabbing at happy tears.

"Yep, and his wife, Marin," James says. "You'll love her. She's a total Reveler. I'll introduce you later."

James leads me around the fountain, nodding to the guests we pass, and up the steps directly toward his father, who is in the middle of greeting another older couple. Yasmin notices James first and reaches out to grab his hand.

When the couple has shuffled inside, Yasmin kisses James on the cheek, telling him how beautiful the library turned out. "It's truly beyond anything I was imagining. Like going back to another time."

"It's good to see you," Gaspard says, shaking James' hand and grabbing his shoulder.

Not a hugging family, I see.

"Excellent work here, James," his dad continues. "Very impressive. You've really proven yourself with this one." He gestures to the building above.

"Well, thank you." James gives his father a measured smile.

"And you must be the girl causing all the buzz?" Yasmin says, smiling with her eyes. "It's a pleasure to meet you." She gives me a dainty handshake.

"This is Summer York." As James presents me to his dad and stepmom, I feel like I'm in one of those fairy tales meeting the king and queen. I manage not to curtsy. "We met working on this project. She's on the archiving team..." James goes on to explain what I've been doing for the last few weeks while my mind wanders, watching Gaspard's hard-to-read reactions.

This is the man who is hiding the fact that he has children out in the world that very few people know about, I think. Does his current wife know about them? Aurora and Simon?

"It's really been an honor to find and hold Revel Pointe history in my hands," I say, sounding like a press release.

"Isn't it all so wonderful?" Yasmin asks me. "Like, in the real sense of the word?" I decide right there that she's a genuine person. She may be married to an intimidating mogul, maybe a dishonest one, but Yasmin seems relatable.

Next, we say hello to Tilda. It's a far cry from Yasmin's warm smiles.

"Mother, this is Summer York," James says, not making even one motion of affection toward her.

"Yes, I know," Tilda says, nodding her head toward me, leaving my outstretched hand awkwardly waiting between us as she holds a clutch with both hands. "Hello again. Are you having a nice time?" Her tone is patronizing.

"It's so rewarding to see James' hard work come to life tonight," I say, maybe a touch too defensively.

"It really is," she says, then turns her attention back to James. "You should be greeting guests up here with *us*. Why don't you escort Miss York to her team and come back and join me." She gestures inside, where Horace, Cricket, and Frances are probably gathered.

James screws up his lips, biting back something he'd like to say, and then for the sake of decorum, simply turns away and holds out his elbow for me to take again.

"I'm so sorry about that," James whispers to me when we're inside the grand foyer, but it's already rolled off my back at the sight of the library all decorated for Christmas. All of the Revel Pointe nostalgic paraphernalia are in place. A garland with twinkle lights winds up the newly completed banister, the one my father helped make. A massive evergreen tree is lit up and hung with crystalline ornaments, reflecting prisms of light around the west wing. And beautiful people everywhere in suits and gowns mill about with champagne flutes, bringing an added holiday shimmer to the library.

"It's so pretty it hurts," I say with a hand at my heart.

"I could say the same about you," James says, and I nearly turn to him for an appreciative kiss before I remember where we are.

"Hey, you two." Cricket's voice arrives before she does, but I quickly spot her in a stylish, asymmetrical green gown. "Oh, you look amazing," she says to me, motioning with a finger in the air for me to twirl. I can't help but laugh as I indulge her.

"Thank you," I say. "So do you. You always look so chic."

"It's a job," she says. "But girl, you look vintage Hollywood. Like a sexy, fairy bombshell."

"Stop," I say. "Seriously."

"No, keep going," James says. "She's adorable when she blushes."

Cricket gives him a look. "I like this," she says. "This looks good on you." It's obvious that she means me and him together. "The tux is a nice touch, too."

"Is my PawPaw here yet?" James asks, and my gut clenches, remembering what I have to give him. We all crane our necks looking for Mick Reve.

"He's planned a late arrival and an early exit," Crickets informs us.

The look on James' face is difficult to read, and now I know where he gets this from—both of his parents—but I can tell there's a lot of unsettled feelings in his tight features. He's holding back anger toward his mother and what this library might become. He's probably juggling whether or not to tell his grandfather, and whether or not to bring it up to Ethan tonight as well. As I blink at a bright flash, a cell-phone photo from across the foyer, I'm also reminded of the scrutiny he is under—actually, *we* are under—just by arriving with me tonight.

Frances joins us then with her husband, Eduardo, a handsome man with a round face and salt-and-pepper hair.

"Well, hello there." The tone in her voice is more subdued than I've heard in the last three weeks. She hugs me and Cricket, introduces us to Eduardo, and then attempts to usher us onto the dance floor outside. "Come on," she says, grabbing James by the arm. "One dance to celebrate this long project being over, just in the nick of time." She tells us that she and Eduardo have agreed to one dance, one drink, quick hellos, and an Irish goodbye so they can get home to their twins, Mia and Max.

"I didn't know you had kids," I say.

"They're nine and full of mischief," Frances says, winking. "Don't know where they get it."

Eduardo looks uncomfortable in his navy suit, like he'd rather be back home with the twins.

"Well, come on," Cricket says. "Let's complete this mission and get you on the road."

She raises her eyebrows conspiratorially at me, motioning for me to coax James outside to join the festivities.

"Whaddaya say?" I ask him, hooking my hand into his elbow and tugging. "Better than meet-and-greet duty?" James relents, and we follow the crew out the west wing side door into the cold night air again.

I'm following Cricket's rich green dress through the crowd, feeling eyes on me, on James, as we cross into a white tent and pass one of the busy bars. But just as my kitten heels hit the dance floor, where maybe a hundred people are shuffling to a jazzy, big-band holiday song, I lose my grip on James. When I turn back, prepared to nudge him onto the floor, I find him wrapped up in a swinging hug with a tall, slender woman. Her long, espresso-colored ponytail bounces and her red tulle dress poofs wide like a long tutu. Before my heart does a full roller-coaster drop of jealousy, she pulls back and I immediately see her resemblance to Yasmin. This must be Elsie.

James motions to me and introduces us when I return to his side.

"Hiiii!" Elsie nearly screams over the music and pulls me in for a hug. "I'm so excited to meet you. I've never met a single girlfriend of James'!"

I try to match her enthusiasm, but I'm choking on the word *girlfriend*. I avoid James' eyes and focus on Elsie, complimenting her on a very cool outfit, which is, on closer inspection, not a dress but a red tulle skirt paired with a form-fitting black boatneck tee.

"My bestie is a fashionista," she says, waving it off. "About to blow up in New York."

"Don't be modest," James says. "You have style, Else."

Elsie just shrugs and elbows her older half brother. Side by side, the only resemblance between the two of them is the dark hair and height. Even without her heels, Elsie has to be at least five-foot-nine. I feel like a shrimp next to them.

"Come on." Cricket and Frances wave the three of us over, and Elsie leads us to them, side-bumping James in the hips on the way.

"James doesn't dance," Elsie tells me as she shimmies with her shoulders.

"Of course, I do," James retorts, grabbing my waist and pulling me towards him in a sort of partner swing move I don't immediately know how to follow.

Elsie's eyes go wide and she claps, laughing. I glance at Cricket, who winks at me, and then I'm spinning in James' arms as the upbeat song dies down.

"Saved by the band," James says, but he keeps me close, swaying us into the slower Christmas waltz.

"One more," I hear Frances telling Eduardo, and I see that her husband has obliged by the time James and I circle back around.

A side flash of light, and then another and another, puts me on alert that James and I are not only being watched but recorded. I stiffen.

"Don't worry about them," James says into my ear. "I am so glad you came with me tonight."

My chest seizes with his sincere tone, and in this romantic setting, where we're now the spectacle, it's too much for me to take. "Well, I expect to again later," I joke.

James laughs, and I suppress the urge to kiss him for the seventieth time this evening. He holds my gaze a moment, and my anxiety softens. He twirls me and brings me back into his arms. When he smiles, I see his chipped canine. I look into his soulful green eyes, and that's when it happens—my heart combusts. In this moment, I know—this isn't just lust, it's respect and admiration and friendship and, oh god, I'm certifiably crazy about this man.

James spins me again and I look away, trying to hide what I know is clear now. The dance floor has cleared to allow us freedom to move about, and I'm just glad James is able to guide me so well, so I don't look silly or fall on my face. I should be soaking in this fairy tale, like my sister urged me to. I suddenly realize that this waltz is the melody of a Christmas carol and the theme from *The Scarlet Slippers*.

As the song comes to a close, James dips me and whispers, "Merry Christmas, Summer." When he pulls me up, some guests in the crowd clap, and I don't know how to react. James only smiles at me, keeping my hand in his and leading us out of the spotlight to the bar. My heartbeat sounds like a bass drum in my ears, flooding my veins with what feels like hot chocolate, an overwhelmingly warm and sweet rush of emotions toward James. I'm so screwed now, falling for him with the world watching. And me in this fairy-tale dress, I can't see how the whole fantasy will last. How any of it can be real. But when he reaches for another glass of champagne for both of us, slips an arm comfortably around my waist, and looks deeply into my eyes, I know it's too late.

"Did you know that was going to happen?" I ask timidly, still feeling eyes and phones trained on us.

"That we'd dance at a ball?" James teases. "Are you having a good time?"

"Too good," I say, and he gives me a quizzical look. I want to explain how the magic of all of this—the setting, the dress, the passion between us—is overwhelmingly beautiful, but I hold back.

There's a murmur around the tent, and for a moment with my head buzzing, I have a flash of panic that I've said all this out loud and that everyone in the tent heard me. A woman's voice exclaims, "It's snowing!"

People head for the exits, and the band fades.

"What's the big deal?" I ask James.

"It never snows in Louisiana," he says, grabbing my hand and leading us toward the main exit.

Chapter Thirty-Nine

James

If I believed in magic, I'd say some Christmas wizard had enchanted this evening at our library gala. For a second, I even wonder if Cricket or someone on the Anniversary Gala team had rigged a hidden snow machine in the oaks beyond the party lights. But when we emerge into the fountain courtyard, it is, in fact, snowing. Real, cold, feathery snow.

The oohs and ahs in the crowd add to the wonder of the moment as people of all ages reach their hands out to touch the tiny flakes.

"This is hilarious," Summer says. "It's like the first day of snow at my school."

"I've never seen it snow here," I tell her.

An older gentlemen leans into our conversation. "It snowed here in '08" he tells us. "People lost their minds. Everything closed for a measly half an inch."

I spot Henri on the library steps, and we cross over to him through the crowd.

"Would you look at this?" Henri says, and the scene from this vantage is quite beautiful. The snow is light and shimmery, giving the oaks, park rides, and lighthouse the aura of a sparkling winter fantasy scene. It reminds me of Montreal and the quaint Canadian village I visited almost a month ago. I glance over at Summer, and my stomach somersaults. *How quickly life can change*, I think. I just waltzed with Summer in front of a slew of cameras, and I didn't care. I only wanted to see her smile.

Summer shivers, her arms and neck bare in this freezing, fluke weather. I remove my jacket and place it around her shoulders, thinking that I've never seen anything more beautiful than Summer in the snowfall.

"Now, that's a sight." Cricket arrives at my other side. "Better get on the merchandising division to start manufacturing Grand Revel Library snow globes."

"Mammon would love that," Henri says, sharing our new nickname for her.

"Is PawPaw here yet?" I ask him.

"He's inside." Henri jerks a thumb toward the foyer. "They're going to cut the cake soon."

"I'm going to freshen up," Summer says, handing me back my suit jacket. I want to kiss her before she leaves my side, but there's no way I'd chance it. Not up here where the crowd can see. Not even in a shadowy corner. The place is crawling with press. In a second she's gone with Cricket, and I'm left with Henri. I feel her absence immediately, and I don't like it.

"Well, I guess this is your night to shine, huh?" a grating voice says from behind, and the hair stands on the back of my neck. A hand clamps down on my shoulder, and I shrug it off a little too brusquely. "This must be another Reve. Am I right?"

That wanker Grainger circles to the front of us, pointing squarely at my brother. He's with a woman, head-to-toe in pink, but even her tipsy exclamations over the snow can't distract me from the annoyance that boils up in this dickhead's presence. When I don't answer and Henri introduces himself, Grainger straightens his back so we're eye-to-eye on the edge of the steps.

"I saw your stunt with Summer," he says, moving to fill my vision. "On the dance floor?"

I say nothing, meeting his stupid showdown with feigned nonchalance.

"You don't know her like I do," Grainger continues. I can smell he's been hitting the open bar.

At this I grin, knowing all the ways I've known her this week. Still, I keep it restrained. "Well, mate. I beg to differ."

"You beg to differ?" Grainger mocks. "I'm serious... *mate*. We go way back. You've known her for like three days."

"Who's this asshat, James?" Henri smiles menacingly. God love him.

"No one I'm worried about." I turn back to Grainger. "Why don't you grab another drink and enjoy the party?" Magnanimity is my middle name.

"You should worry because I know Summer's hiding something from you."

I put my hands in my pockets to keep from balling them into fists, then I think better of it and remove them, prepared for anything. Again, I don't dignify this dick with a response. He's not worth it, especially in this setting. I back away, thinking it might be wiser just to go inside and find Summer or PawPaw. But the idiot grabs my arm.

"I'm serious," Grainger says.

I can't help myself any longer. I rip my arm away from him. "Back off."

He comes right back at me, chest first. "Summer shared some pretty serious stuff with me, facts about your family that you don't know, and I'm just warning you..."

"You're warning me?" I ask, my voice rising above the others around me. Steam rises from my feet, filling my chest with rage. I take a deep breath. Keep it cool, no outbursts, not here of all places. Not with the world watching. The edges of my sight blur like a blizzard as I square off to him again.

The asshat smiles wide. "You have no idea... What she told *me* could bring all of this crashing down. Family secrets. Total embarrassment..."

As if in an attempt to pull me aside conspiratorially, Grainger tries to grab my shoulder again. I pull away aggressively, and he loses his balance on the top stair. Instinctively, he grabs my tuxedo lapel, and with nothing stable to brace myself, I get pulled down with the fool. His body turns sideways, trying to stop the fall, pushing his date out of the way. My knees buckle, falling clumsily beside him, face down. But we keep rolling with the momentum of our large bodies and nothing to break the snowball of our limbs, flailing for a foothold until we land at the feet of shocked party guests.

I'm about to get up and walk away. "Call security. Mr. Grainger is clearly intoxicated." I stand up.

"You're just going to hook up with her and ghost," Grainger says, loud enough for the crowd to hear. "But don't worry, I'll be there to pick up the pieces."

His stupid smug smile makes me see red. I coil my arm back for the first punch. But I'm stopped mid-swing by my name being shouted.

"James!" Summer stands on the landing, looking down at us.

"Ask her, man," Grainger says, getting to his feet and climbing the stairs to his date, who was tossed aside in our epic tumble.

From below, I find Summer's wide, confused eyes.

"Tell him, Summer! What you know!" Grainger calls, slurring.

For a second, time slows. I look up and see her face register Grainger's demand. As the phones and cameras flash around me, Summer eyes drop, *guilty. What the fuck?*

"James, it's not what you think..." she stammers, trying to negotiate her dress to descend the stairs.

"See, man, I told you. She's been playing you and me—" Grainger gestures to Summer who's now frozen mid-step.

"Enough!" I roar. I climb a few steps towards Summer, but the percussive flashes bring me back to reality. I have no idea how much of this disaster they have captured. As if some divine, sadistic entity is directing this farce, my mother exits the front doors to stand beside Summer. Tilda gives me a head shake of disapproval, and I'm eight years old all over again. I barely register Henri by my side, asking if I'm okay. I replay my childhood nightmare, but Summer's betrayal is so much worse.

"Fuck this," I mutter and compose myself, trying to blink away all of the people watching me. Then I turn my back on the whole scene, heading for the darkness beyond the tent lights. My ears ring as my shoes hit the soft path through the snowy oaks.

I need to be alone to try to make sense of what just happened. Instead, every problem collides in my brain like bumper cars. My mother's constant control undermining my agency in life; Grainger's insistence on some hidden agenda against me and my family; the library, my first solo building that's doomed to become yet another symbol of Tilda's greed; and even Summer, who I let in, betrays me. Part of me is ashamed for dragging her into this at all. Revel Pointe is simply too much. All of it. An undertow that even the strongest swimmer can't escape.

My phone buzzes; it's Henri.

You okay? What should I tell Summer?

What *should* he tell Summer? Even though Grainger is a miscreant, his words linger in my head. *She's hiding something from you. She knows something about your family you don't know.* As much as I don't trust him, her guilty expression combined with my own misgivings flood in. How well do I actually know her? It's been less than a month. God, I'm an idiot.

What did she actually tell him? My first thought is that she shared the future plans for the library, which I do know, but that would be a total breach of her NDA—more importantly, of my trust in her. But Grainger had said she knows something about my family. The doubts and rage build within me. Why was she talking to him in the first place? Are they truly closer than I thought? Was she just playing me like every other fake fucker grasping at a bit of fame and money? I'd wanted to ask her to come to Miami later tonight, knowing I was going to ask her to visit in London, wanting to keep her near. God, I was so blind. I was actually falling for her. Turns out I was falling for a fucking act.

I breathe out a thick plume of air into a snowy sky as I wander past the lighthouse moat on my way to the compound. Things with Summer had been so achingly good. I should have known it couldn't last. The fantasy of us left me open for this blind side. The whole thing is obvious to me now. Time to wake up. It's over.

I pull out my phone again and text Henri: *Tell her I'm sorry and goodbye. I'm leaving tonight.*

Chapter Forty

Summer

I feel like Alice on the other side of the looking glass, watching my regular life through a murky prism. I'm back in my childhood home, but I'm not here mentally. Everything is exactly as I left it, but so much has changed. I can't reconcile the before-Revel me with the after-Revel me. When I left, I was a middle school librarian embarking on an experience of a lifetime, full of optimism. Now, I am a shaky, world-weary shadow of my former self.

The first thing I did when I stumbled into my hotel room after the gala was change my flight. I missed Christmas Eve and Christmas morning with my family in Westerville, but I made it back late afternoon to warm hugs from Dad and Gran at the airport. Neither pressed me to explain why I'm home early, unable to recount how the fairy tale turned to disaster.

But we weren't in the car for five minutes when my phone started blowing up with texts from Lilia. The paparazzi photos went live last night, but since it's Christmas, it's taken everyone a minute for the gossip of the day to filter into their newsfeeds. I lived it. I know what happened, so why on Earth would I want to replay images of James almost beating up Grainger and publicly ditching me? He left me standing next to his heartless mother, no less.

I'll never forget what she said to me: "James is ruining everything."

I looked up at Tilda, her gorgeous platinum hair and silver-blue eyes. I shouldn't have been shocked by her cruelty, but I guess there's no end to my naivety. When I moved to run after James, she grabbed my wrist, forcefully.

"Let him go," Tilda said. "He's destined for a bigger life."

And with that dagger to the heart that spoke to every insecurity I had about our burgeoning relationship, my hope for more with James dissipated. Poof. Gone. Camera flashes startled me back to the moment—the pathetic center of attention at the top of the library entrance stairs, facing the who's who of Revel. Abandoned, facing the illustrious crowd, I have no doubt that my look of total shock and dejection is what's splashed all over the Internet today.

As I enter the house, full of familiar Christmas smells and sounds, Brody, the youngest of the family, races at me full steam, knocking me back into my rolling suitcase with his weight.

"You missed Santa!" Brody says.

I can't help the tears from flooding my eyes again. This is the homecoming I needed. "Well, I missed you!" I say, hugging him to me.

"Did you bring back Revel presents?" Emma asks, coming in for a quick hug. Though she's eleven, she's always been a little behind on social cues.

I feign that I've forgotten, but she doesn't buy it, her gaze suspicious.

I relent. "Of course I brought presents."

This is enough to bring us all into the living room. Kayla gives me a pity smile. Thank god her husband is oblivious to what's going on in my life. He takes a break from putting together an elaborate plastic racetrack to hug me, treating me like he always does.

The rest of the evening is a blur of the usual Christmas customs, with my mind mostly back in Revel Pointe, images of James flitting in and out of my consciousness as I go through the motions. My sister repeatedly asks how I'm doing, and my response is always that I don't want to talk about it. Gran hangs back, knowing I'll come to her when I'm ready.

When we raise a glass to Mom at dinner, I completely lose it. All I want to do is curl up on the living-room sofa and tell my mom all about it, but I can't. I dab my eyes with my fancy linen napkin from the set we only take out at special occasions, and I'm again reminded of Mom, ironing and folding them at holidays. My oldest niece, Vicky, tears up when she sees my emotion, and our quick toast turns into a longer moment of remembrance.

"All right," Gran says. "Food's getting cold." She's not being callous. It's something my mom would say. We all laugh and dig in.

When everyone has gone home, it's just me and Dad. He asks how I'm doing.

"Did you tell him?" he adds, plopping down in his recliner.

I shake my head and begin to cry again, shrugging a blanket around my shoulders and sinking into the couch. "I didn't even get a chance. It all happened so fast."

The whole story of the gala spills out of me now—the spectacle of the red carpet and how James coached me and made me feel secure, meeting his father and sweet stepmother, and his bubbly sister, Elsie, too, dancing with my colleagues, and how James led me in a waltz while everyone on the dance floor watched, and finally, my shock at finding him at the bottom of the stairs about to punch Grainger.

"Grainger told James that I'd been hiding something from him and, Dad, James gave me this look," I recall through sniffles. "He looked shocked, betrayed, and worse, he looked like he'd expected me to betray him. And the thing is, I did. I should have told him. I wanted to tell him then, but he just turned and walked away from the party."

"You haven't heard from him at all?" Dad asks cautiously.

I shake my head and bury my face in the blanket hugging my knees. I feel like such an idiot. I only sent James one text: *Please call me.*

I figured that was the only one I needed to send, and his non-response spoke volumes.

"Well, he's not the man I thought he was then." Dad folds his arms and scowls. James is now on his list.

I lift my head, and the multicolored lights on our Christmas tree blur in my vision. I'm such a fool for falling so hard. I knew all along what a dangerous game I was playing. Now I just have to accept that it was a shimmering moment in time and move on. Be the pragmatic Summer my friends and family know me to be, pick up the pieces of my life with as much grace as I can muster.

"He's carrying a lot," I say, still feeling the weight the Reves put on James' shoulders, the way the media twists his life into something unmanageable.

"Well, he was also carrying your heart," Dad says. "And that's more important than everything else."

This wakes me up. A part of me is angry with James, but I'm mostly mad at myself. James didn't know he was carrying my heart. Hell, I only realized it minutes before while we were floating around the dance floor. It's not like we had made each other any promises. But I wanted to. I wanted him.

"Thanks, Dad." I give him a weak smile and tell him I'm going to bed. "It's been a long few weeks."

When I'm curled up under the covers, in the same room and bed I slept in as a teenager, I decide I need to move out. Living back at home, grieving with Dad for so long, was necessary at first, but now it's time to stand on my own. I've been trapped on a merry-go-round, heading right back to the beginning with every full rotation.

My time at Revel Pointe shook me up, showed me that I do want more than this small-town life. It proved that I'm capable of bigger things. I'll take it easy next week, but in the new year, I'm going to find an apartment of my own to rent. I'm going to look for other jobs. A new city at a new library or university archive should help me put this very public crash-and-burn behind me.

A fresh start, I think. That will get me through this heartache. Though I don't entirely believe it, this lie helps me finally fall asleep.

Chapter Forty-One

James

Miami is miserable. It was always going to be. I'm not a beach person. I can't stand the constant stream of sports cars blaring hip-hop and the extremely tanned, fake bodies. But it's not the company I'm keeping—Lucien, Henri, and Elsie—or the ridiculously lux house we're renting, complete with a fifty-foot Sea Ray boat at the end of the dock. It's not even the fact that I blew up my life while the world watched. It's Summer. Her face when that clown told her to tell me what she knew.

After I left the gala, when Lucien and Henri met me back at the compound, I arranged to leave as soon as humanly possible for Florida on our Gulfstream, *Mona 2.* There was no use in waiting around to face Tilda, and I'm done with the library project. Am I still pissed that my mother sold the soul of that building right out from under me? Of course. But at this point, I'm not sure what I can do. Plus, I never want to hear that clock tower chime again. No, I'm better off on my own, completely separate from Revel Pointe and the spotlight that comes with it.

It's been three days in Miami now, and my skin feels tight and itchy. It's not just from the sun. I'd gotten used to hearing from Summer daily, used to seeing her both deliberately and randomly, a light relieving me from my brooding work mode. And now I have no work to focus on either. I haven't heard from her since that last text, only minutes after I stormed off. I haven't seen her beautiful face since.

In the quiet moments here on the beach, when the rest are off jet-skiing or shopping, I've nearly phoned Summer to hear what she has to say, but recalling her downcast eyes, guilt radiating from her, reminds me that I don't really know Summer. I thought she was real, that her feelings were real.

This afternoon I have the mansion to myself, and I'm planning to spend it reading with a green smoothie out by the pool. But as I'm feeding spinach and green apples into the blender, the cryptic thing Grainger had planted in my brain slides forward again. Summer knows *something about my family that could bring the whole thing crashing down*. I turn that sentence over and over in my head as the blades whir the green produce to a pulp.

I find it extremely hard to believe Summer would confide anything in that dude, but how would he know she was hiding something? Why would he make up such a specific lie? Summer definitely could have uncovered something about the Reves in her digging. It was likely that her team would find delicate information, business documents and such, that would not be for public consumption. Summer seemed like an ethical person. She seemed into me before finding out who I was. She'd understood my frustration over Tilda's intention to repurpose the library into retail space. Never once did I feel like she was the type of person to insert herself in order to capitalize. The type to sell stories to the press. Of course, I couldn't know for sure. Hell, she could be the bloody Secret Reveler. In truth, I had less than a month to get to know her. How could I possibly know her? And I've been burned before.

I only get a few pages into the first chapter of my book when Cricket calls.

"How you holding up?" she asks. No hello, no small talk. Just straight to the point, and I love her for it.

"Oh, you know me," I say, getting up to pace the pool in the shade of tropical foliage. "Fucking sunshine and rainbows. How are you? How was Christmas with Charlie?"

"It was fine." Cricket swats away my attempt at shifting the conversation, but it's the first time we've chatted since I left in a dramatic huff. I know why she's calling. "Have you heard from her?"

I appreciate that Cricket has avoided using Summer's name. It helps to downplay what I now know is heartache.

"I haven't," I say, picking a waxy leaf off an outstretched branch.

"And I guess you haven't reached out?"

"It's over," I say. "No need."

"God, how can two smart people be so dumb?" she says. "You clearly had real feelings for each other."

"Maybe," I say. "But it doesn't matter now."

"I assume you're avoiding the internet?"

"Like the sodding plague." I turn to pace back the other way along the pool.

"So you haven't seen any of the fallout?"

"No," I say, hesitating. The way she's leading worries me. How can it be worse than what I'm imagining? "Why?"

"Not the *LA Times* piece? Or *Variety*?"

"*Variety*?" I lose my breath for a second. While I don't love the press, I can handle the scrutiny; plus, I'm getting the hell out of the country. It's my concern for Summer that overwhelms me. I can't help it.

"Yes—stop avoiding, and read what's online," Cricket says, snapping me out of my spiral.

"I get it," I tell her. "For damage control."

"It's more than that," she says. "Trust me. It's too much to tell you over the phone. You need to read it."

I exhale and stare down at my wavy reflection in the clear blue water.

"I promise," Cricket says encouragingly. "You won't regret it."

After we say goodbye, I head back into the house to find my tablet and mentally psych myself up to read the worst. I'm sure they've painted me as the most impetuous man-child, a poster boy for trust-fund lads. But fuck it.

I take a deep breath and search my name and "LA Times." I might as well start there since Reya Ghu was the first to thrust me into the spotlight last week. There it is. The first result in over fifty thousand links is the one I'm looking for, but I'm shocked by the headline: "Revel Misleads Public on Mick Reve's Legacy Project." The date is from this morning, and again, Ms. Ghu has the byline.

"Alternate plans and motives for the vanity project, the Grand Revel Library at Revel Pointe theme park in south Louisiana, were uncovered after a physical altercation at the annual Christmas Eve gala. Two sources confirmed the impending deal with Japanese bridal house Fimura to launch a Revel bridal couture line and repurpose the library building for retail space. New acting-CEO Ethan Reve, second son of Gaspard Reve, did not deny the possible deal, stating, 'I have no comment at this time.'"

Motherfucker. I nearly toss my tablet across the room. I didn't spend almost two years of my life designing and building an overblown bridal boutique. I need to call Ethan to hear just what he really thinks about this proposal, but for now I read on.

"Revel fans have expressed shock at the disclosure after 18 months of hype leading to the opening of the library, which was touted as a hall of archival material to preserve Revel Pointe history in the name of its 95-year-old founder, Mick Reve. 'It feels like a money grab,' said Celia Brown of Sweetwater, Tenn., president of the southeast chapter of Revel Moms, a group devoted to monitoring the content of Revel films for children 12 and under. 'We were all looking forward to a chance to see the actual items of our favorite movies in person. A museum made just for us.'

"Not all Revel followers are opposed to the bridal-wear plans, however. The fans currently storming social media appear to be divided into two camps—#preserveRevelhistory and

#teamRevelbridal. "Who doesn't want the chance to be a Revel princess for the day?' @briannarules posted. She's reinforced by an army of future Revel bridezillas-to-be. 'Thumbelina Bride is my dream!' posted @yay_huang. 'Just got engaged. Now waiting for Revel bridal to launch,' proclaimed @jamila_ajg."

I roll my eyes, but I'm rapt. Thank the gods for Cricket. This isn't all about me or Summer.

"But for every pro-Revel bridal couture fan, there's a pro-Revel legacy advocate. 'Bring the Revel memorabilia to light for all to see and enjoy as Mick intended,' posted @grantgood98, garnering over three hundred thousand likes and shares in only 24 hours. The hashtag #asmickintended has started trending, as well as #Revelmagic4eva. Marissa Gomes, a Revel fan who chronicles new Revel merch, park food and drink, and special events on her blog, Reveler Leveler, posted on her socials, 'Why can't we have both? Save the library. Build the bridal brand off-site.'"

Smart girl, I think.

"But where did this all begin? It's time to shine a light on The Secret Reveler, a mystery blogger now proven to be so close to the Revel company action that they must be an insider. On the evening of December 25th, *The Secret Reveler* leaked this scoop first, turning Revel fandom upside down and kick-starting the debate. Quoted from that blog article: Little Revel bluebirds are singing about something borrowed and something new pushing out the something old from the Grand Revel Library that James Reve worked so hard to build. And with all the work his lovely date, Summer York, put into preserving the archival Revel items in question, could this be what pushed James to his boiling point?'"

I set my tablet down and try to remember who was in attendance at the Fimura cocktail party in Tilda's condo. Mom, Bill, Frances, Shirleen, Noa and Ami Fimura, then Henri and myself. That was it. Summer knew, but it would be strange for her to write about herself in the third person? It feels so unlike her. Of course Ethan knows, maybe Marin, and definitely the board. It's enough people that if any trickle of detail got out, it could turn into this information flood fast. But Reya Ghu is right—this Secret Reveler person has to be close. I read on.

"The Secret Reveler blogger must have had front row seats at the ball for the very particular details of the waltz James and Summer danced before the night turned nasty. Directing readers to 'zoom in' on the photos, the Reveler writes: 'The look of love is clearly in Summer's eyes. A smitten kitten if I've ever seen one.'"

I stare at the picture. Summer, in her shimmery ball gown, looks up at me, her brown eyes gazing intently into mine, a soft smile playing on her lips. I screenshot it and keep reading.

"With the hot spotlight Revel has on this project and annual holiday gala, fan speculation about manufactured publicity is already reaching conspiracy-level. To some critics, it seems obvious and advantageous that Revel has created it's own controversy machine in The Secret Reveler blogger. During this holiday season covering James Reve's succession in the company and his love life, the Camp Willow III Christmas Day release, and the library project, The Secret Reveler has almost tripled subscribers from 35,000 to 91,000. From here, the spread of information is near impossible to calculate. It's free advertising"

It's true, and I wouldn't put it past my own mother to feed our personal details and insider secrets to independent media. I'd consider it brilliant if it didn't involve me.

"Whether or not The Secret Reveler is in fact part of the Revel publicity platform, what they didn't bargain for is what Revelers are calling The Fall at the Ball. Even those only mildly interested in Revel Pointe would be enchanted by the scene. It was shaping up to be the ball of the decade. The entertainment darling of America hosted its biggest night of the year at its newest attraction—The Grand

Revel Library—to celebrate the 95th birthday of its beloved founder, Mick Reve. The champagne was flowing, and the who's who of the industry were dancing under glowing chandeliers. Revel gods even managed to conjure actual snow from the heavens, in a spectacular, sparkling display of Revel magic. But the winds changed when the nearly crowned prince of the gala abruptly left the party."

Here I almost quit reading. Why relive this night? But I hear Cricket's voice in my head—*Trust me. You need to read it.*

"James Reve, the architect of the library, exchanged heated words with a guest, Grainger McCloskey, a small-business owner from Westerville, Ohio. The two men took an unfortunate tumble down the steps to the main entrance, nearly wiping out Miles Fisher, director of Revel's critical darling, *Island of Sirens*, and his wife, Tanya."

Ghu's getting name-droppy here, but I keep going. I know this part and skim through the details until I land on something new.

"'I just want what's best for Summer,' Mr. McCloskey told the *Times* in a phone interview yesterday. When asked what that meant exactly, he replied: 'That guy [James Reve] *isn't* the best.'"

Now I wish I had stuck around to knock out Grainger's oversized teeth.

The article continues. "Though it seems to be a classic case of romantic competition, McCloskey alludes to something deeper. 'She's a good girl. There's something shady going on at Revel, and I just want her to be safe.' Whether McCloskey's fishing for a tabloid payout or whether he's sincere is not clear at this time."

The next sentence guts me. "Summer York has been unavailable to comment and is no longer working at Revel Pointe, which raises more questions. Did she play a pivotal role in the library/bridal scandal? Or did she unearth secrets about the seemingly unstoppable Reve family? Perhaps The Secret Reveler will reveal the answers soon."

My chest burns just seeing her name in print. I go back to the picture of us dancing and zoom in on her lovely face. She's beaming, her eyes warm chocolate. She does, in fact, look smitten. I look like I want to devour her right there on the floor. Is it possible I am all wrong? *Shit.*

I imagine she's probably been hounded by phone calls from the press. I get up and pace around this stupid South Beach monstrosity of granite and glass. I need to talk to her, but maybe I should text first? Will she even answer? I wouldn't blame her if she blocked me forever.

"We're baaaack!" Elsie's voice sings from the front foyer. "With treeeeats!" Seconds later, she appears in the living room, holding aloft two fistfuls of bags from designer shops.

Lucien's voice follows: "You gotta try these brown-butter chocolate chip biscuits!" He flops himself over the back of a modular sofa and lands with a bounce. "Here, mate!" Lucien holds up a greasy paper bag.

Henri arrives behind them, empty-handed and scanning my face. "What happened?" he asks, and the other two stop their frivolity to notice I'm not well.

"You have to read this," I tell them, grabbing my tablet again and showing the screen to the trio. "I need advice. I think I royally fucked up."

"Oh, thank god," Elsie says. "We've been waiting for you to say that the entire trip!"

Chapter Forty-Two

Summer

In that lull between Christmas and New Year's Eve, I'm experiencing a bad case of the doldrums. I don't want to label this depression or heartbreak because I fear naming it would give it power. I'm perfectly happy to stay in denial, in my sweats and unwashed hair, cutting a new pattern for another Renaissance Fair gown to keep my mind counting stitches and not lingering on James Reve. It's not working.

I tell myself that even if things hadn't completely blown up at the gala (and then online), I would have ended up here anyway. Maybe I would still have a job to look forward to at Revel Pointe, but the whirlwind holiday romance would be over and I'd still be nursing disappointment.

With every unknown caller, every email, every message on my dad's landline from journalists wanting a statement from me, I'm reminded that what happened between me and James, and all the controversy at Revel, was much bigger than I understood. Even two Columbus news affiliates knocked on the door, and when my dad refused to comment or admit that I was home, they each taped a story from the street. I watched a few local segments and saw some of my neighbors and colleagues comment on my character. "Summer's a nice young woman from a good family. I'm sorry to see her get wrapped up in all that mess."

Mrs. Multree, the crotchety math teacher at my school, yelled at a local reporter, "Leave her alone, the girl's been through enough already!" When asked if she cared to elaborate, she said, "No!" and continued shoveling her walk. I plan to bake that woman a pie.

Sensing a story, the news dug up the basic details of my life and my unfortunate high-school yearbook photo and splattered it on the screen. "Summer York, having undergone a major transformation after multiple surgeries and physical therapy, lost her mother recently, and now this—being publicly rejected by James Reve."

Within just one news cycle, I'm the victim and he's the villain. The predator and prey; beauty and the beast. That local news clip went viral.

The day after Christmas, both Frances and Cricket had called; Cricket to check in on my well-being, and Frances to break the news that I didn't get the job (no surprise there) and to suss out what "information" I had found. The news says I'm hiding something, and they aren't wrong, which is giving me hives. I told Frances the information I learned was the Fimura bridal news, that I'd learned about it organically that day I bumped into Tilda in the hall. But I still kept the information about Aurora and Simon Mallory-Reve secret because I feel loyal to Mick Reve—and James, if I'm being honest.

Horace was named the head archivist, even though the position is now temporary. Revel Pointe, likely through Tilda's team, has been strategically dropping dress designs on social media. It seems the witch will win the day.

"We're in a holding pattern right now, but we really appreciate all the hard work you've done," Frances said diplomatically.

"It was my pleasure," I responded, surprising myself with more tears. I had thought the job really didn't matter to me, but not getting it is icing on this shit cake. I completely understand, though; I'm a PR nightmare now, and Horace is brilliant.

Now I'm measuring eyelet trim for the pinafore of my dress and ignoring the world outside this bedroom. Then Lilia's name lights up my phone. I've ignored her, unwilling to hash anything out while the wound's so fresh, but I can't hide from her forever.

"Hey. Please tell me you're in labor," I deflect.

"God, no," she guffaws. "I wish. I'm a house! How are you? Why don't you come over so we can talk?"

"I don't know," I say, surveying the jumble of fabric and thread in front of me, not to mention the many water glasses, plates of crumbs, and lone wine glass of the last day or so. "I'm sort of a mess, to be honest."

"Look, come over in your sweats, and we can just watch a movie or something." Lilia nudges me. "Plus, I'm bored out of my mind." She tells me her husband is off at the firehall now and her three-year-old is already sleeping.

"I'm really not good company."

"Dammit, Nito. You know that I actually care about you, right? I've seen the news, and I know you're dealing with a lot. Get your butt in the shower, wash your hair, put on some clean jogging pants, and get over here. We can wallow together. I'm super pregnant and could use a friend, too. You can vent, I can vent, or we can just watch some crappy Lifetime thriller and eat popcorn. I made pampushkies."

"All right, but only because you made dessert..." I say, pushing myself away from the sewing table in the guest room. "I'm warning you, I'm cranky."

"Join the club. See you soon." She hangs up before I can back out.

In the shower, my mind wanders to the *LA Times* article. Having avoided all things Revel Pointe for almost a week, I had decided it was time. It was a relief to me that the bridal story broke right away. One less secret to keep. But new emotions crept in.

For one, I am beyond pissed off at Grainger. I know he heard at least some of what I was so delicately trying to explain to my dad that night in his hotel room. I run through that conversation over and over, my mind playing tricks and wondering if I'd actually said their names out loud—Simon and Aurora, Gaspard's out-of-wedlock twins. But I reassure myself again that I had not because I never planned to. I've actually never said those names out loud to anyone, and the only person I had ever thought to say them to was James (and possibly Mick Reve). Grainger has called me a few times, but I blocked his number. He seems to have gotten the message. That or he's just too busy talking to anyone who will give him a platform.

My emotional seesaw sweeps back up to shoot my anger at James. What grown man stomps off in the middle of such a massive event, leaving his date behind? I start imagining what I'd say to James if I could. How childish it was to abandon me at the gala, just standing there, all eyes and cameras trained on me in the dress he bought me. He had no idea how I'd retreated into the library, found a nook in the east wing, and waited for my body to stop shaking. It was Henri who came to find me, asking if I'd heard from James, asking if I needed anything, and finally making sure I got home, helping me avoid the paparazzi through a side exit.

"He's not the easiest guy to know," Henri told me, and I knew exactly what he meant. "I know he thinks very highly of you. He's different around you." Henri said he could see James' armor coming down. That he was letting me in when he supposedly never does that. "You know his nickname, right? The statue? Well, he isn't like that with you. He was, I don't know, emoting and stuff."

Well, yippee for me, I think, turning off the shower. It means I get to deal with the fallout of an emotionally scarred, privileged man.

This is good, I think. Anger is easier to deal with than sadness, disappointment, and just plain missing him. And I do miss him. Not only do I miss his dry sense of humor, his weird hybrid accent, his smell, I miss the way he looked at me. Every time we were together, I felt like the best version of myself. Yes, my senses were more alive in every way with what I could only describe as elemental passion, but also my whole being felt calmer around James. I was more myself, the self I've always wanted to be with a man. I had never felt that way before. Screw him for showing me what I'd been missing.

I dry my hair, apply a touch of tinted moisturizer and cream blush just to look less defeated, and choose an oversized sweater and my only clean pair of yoga pants. I start to tell Dad I'm heading out for the night, but he's already passed out with his tablet on his chest, mouth open, in front of an old cop show.

As I slip on my fuzzy, warm boots, there's a quiet knock at the front door. My body goes cold. Another reporter? I almost don't answer it, but Dad comes alive on his recliner, on alert for unwanted guests.

"You going out?" he asks, sitting up.

"I'm going to Lilia's for a bit," I tell him. "But someone's at the door."

Dad pulls the lever on his La-Z-Boy so fast I think it'll launch him out of the seat. He stomps to the front bay window, peers through the curtains, and suddenly his shoulders drop.

"Go ahead and answer it." Dad doesn't look at me, but continues to watch the person at the door.

"Who is it?" I ask, grabbing the handle and slowly pulling the door open to reveal James Reve standing on my doorstep.

"Hello," he says. He appears sheepish and cold with his hands in the pockets of his stylish navy coat.

"Hi," I say, too stunned and confused to move or speak. James Reve—all that I knew of him from those dreamlike days at Revel—standing on my front porch in my sleepy Ohio suburb.

With an anxious look on his face, James runs a hand through his hair and drops his gaze to my feet. "First off, I came to say I'm sorry," he begins, his breath rising into the biting cold air between us. "I know it's not enough, but I'd like the chance to talk with you, to attempt to... explain myself."

I'm still too bewildered by this change of events, and when I don't respond, he goes on.

"I'll leave right now, if you want me to." He motions with his eyes behind him. "I told the car to wait, so... I'll go if..." Parked at the curb is a black SUV idling in the slushy snow.

My dad coughing inside triggers me to wake up and let James in yet I still have no words. The foyer feels cramped with James in it. I slip off my boots so we can head back into the living room where my dad stands frowning; however, Midwestern politeness takes over.

"Come in," Dad says gruffly.

Before James does so, he looks to me for approval, and I nod. My Midwestern manners also kick in, and I grab his jacket on autopilot. The three of us stand there in the dead space between the foyer, living room, and kitchen, not knowing what to do or say next.

"Would you like a drink?" Dad asks. "Water? Soda? Jack Daniels?" Finally, my brain says, *Yes, drinks, that's normal.*

As if to confirm his presence, I reach out and touch his elbow, just to steady myself. He looks down at where my hand rests and warmth flashes into his features.

"I'm sorry it took me so long to get here," he says.

Out of nowhere, I find my voice, and it's icy. "A text would have sufficed."

"Well, damn." James attempts a joking tone. "Text first, fly second. Noted."

"Did you take the family jet?" The biting tone in my voice surprises me.

"No, I..." James says. "I flew commercial, three flights actually."

Dad pipes up, breaking the tension. "Well, three flights calls for a whiskey, I guess."

Again, James waits for me to agree, and I turn to my dad. "Make that two."

Minutes later, I'm standing at the kitchen island with my dad, waiting for James Reve to explain himself.

"Have you seen the press about the library?" James finally asks.

"I have," I reply. "What does that have to do with me?" I'm finally starting to feel like I'm me again, in my body, and not floating above like an eavesdropping ghost.

My dad feigns a yawn and downs the rest of his drink. "That's my cue to call it a night," he says, even though it's pretty early. "Will you be staying with us?"

My body seizes. James Reve sleeping over in my childhood home? He senses my abject terror and shakes his head.

"I got a hotel room." James shifts his weight and asks to use "the loo." My dad points the way to the only bathroom in the house.

"You good, kid?" Dad asks. "I can stick around if you need me."

Tears spring to my eyes. I down my whiskey. "I'm good."

He says to holler if I change my mind, then kisses my forehead and saunters to bed. My text tone chimes in my purse, and I go to retrieve my phone, realizing that I've left Lilia hanging. I can't think straight, so I just type *James Reve showed up at my house. I'm freaking out. So sorry to bail last minute.*

Lilia's response is a row of surprise face emojis. Her next text is: *OMG! OMG! Punch him for me.*

I get three little pulsing dots before finally her last text drops: *You owe me the tea tomorrow. Brunch!*

I promise. I return.

I'm still not sure why James is here or even how I feel about it. I wander away from the kitchen and plop onto the sofa next to the glittering Christmas tree. We haven't had the heart to take it down. When James reappears from down the hall, he finds me holding my empty glass and staring into space.

"What are you doing here?" I ask him, as he sits on the sofa, leaving space so we can look each other in the eye.

"Attempting an overdue apology." He shifts, and I can't help but notice his chest flinch beneath his sweater. He searches my face, and I'm still unsure what to say.

"Don't you think we're past that?" The whiskey's making me bold.

He takes a sip and a deep breath, then looks me in the eyes and says, "Summer, I'm so very sorry."

"You left me at the gala," I say. "Alone."

His face falls, and he stares down at his hands. "I know. Damn, I know."

I'm not sure if it's the lighting in here, but his eyes go glassy. "I'm a shit, Summer. I'm terrible when it comes to relationships. Elsie says I'm so fortified that I'm basically a gargoyle."

"Made of stone and scary?"

"Exactly," James says, breathing out, shoulders slumping. "It's not good."

"No, it's not." My heart flutters fast. I'm still so attracted to him; it's distracting.

"I can't express enough how sorry I am for leaving you there. There were many reasons, personal shit, family history, that went into that split second decision. It's not an excuse, though."

"No, it's not," I say.

"Honestly, I stayed away thinking I was doing you a favor," he says, and I snort. "No, seriously. I live my life in a fishbowl. You've had some experience with it now. It's miserable. Not to mention how intense my family can be, the business, my *mother*. And I know I cost you the position at the library. I just felt like you'd be better off without me, without all—" He picks up his phone, gesturing with it. "All this."

"Listen, I always knew we'd go our separate ways," I tell him. "We never made each other promises. We never talked about what would happen after—"

"I know," he says. "It was complicated. It still is. I tried to deny how I was really feeling, but it's a losing game, Summer." He leans toward me, and I can feel my body want to be connected to his.

I wait to hear more, but he goes quiet again.

A huge part of me wants to forgive him on the spot and lunge at him, press my lips on his and melt into the bliss I know we're capable of, but that behavior got me into this situation. I need more from him. I also need to clear my conscience so I can sleep at night.

"I need to tell you something," I say and stand up to pace. "I tried to tell you earlier, but—"

"But I was amorous." James smiles wryly and shifts on the sofa, watching me.

"Yes, but I should have stopped you. First, I never told Grainger anything. I want to make that clear from the start." I cross my arms.

He nods. "Go on."

I hesitate. Where do I go from here?

"You can tell me anything," James says. "I know I have a temper, but—"

"A temper?" I say with mock surprise. "You?"

"Fair point," James says, sinking back. "I swear I will just sit here and take in whatever you have to tell me. No reaction."

I run my fingers through my hair and finally look him in the eye. "Okay, well... That night when we had dinner at your father's house and then we looked through some boxes in your father's office? Well, I found something delicate. Something your PawPaw wanted to find. A document I don't think your father wants anyone to see."

James holds his breath, not reacting. His brow furrows and his jaw clenches like he's holding back his beastly side. I take a fortifying breath. There's no turning back now.

Chapter Forty-Three

James

This is not where I thought the conversation would go at all. So Summer *does* know something shocking about my family.

"I swear, I haven't told anybody what I saw," she continues. "Especially not Grainger McCloskey. I saw his quote in the article, and I think I know what happened."

"Okay." I'm floored. I didn't want it to be true, that Summer was hiding something from me. Henri, Elsie, and Lucien assured me that douche Grainger was lying to save face, and I wanted to believe that. But it was there in writing, in the *LA Times*, and now Summer's confirming it's true. My throat constricts. I take another gulp of whiskey.

"The night before the gala, I went to ask my dad for advice, at his hotel. I told him I'd found some compromising Reve family documents, but that's all. I never said what was in them." Summer's words come flying out of her at a speed that's almost too fast to follow. "I only wanted his advice on how to tell you. More specifically, *when* to tell you because I knew it might hurt you. You had so much on your plate already. I almost told you that night, but then you had just come back from your mother's ambush party and we..." Summer peters out. I know what we did instead of talking.

"Summer." My voice sounds detached, but my body feels like hot lava. "What was in the documents?"

"Birth certificate copies and trusts for Simon and Aurora Mallory-Reve." Her hands go to her cheeks. "Your father's name was on the birth certificate." The look on her face betrays her utter worry.

I don't know what to say. I don't actually know what she's trying to tell me. I'm still piecing it together in my head. "Birth certificates," I state.

"They were twins, Simon and Aurora," Summer says meekly. "They *are* twins. Your older half-siblings, I think."

"Do you still have the documents?" I ask.

"I left them with Cricket, in an envelope for you marked 'Private.'"

"Wait, explain this one more time?" I ask. "You found documents in the boxes that were from my father's private office?"

"Yes."

"When you were with me?"

"Yes." Summer hugs her body tight, looking small and scared. There's a coffee table between us, giving us a wide berth. "When you went to the bathroom, or to get more wine, I kept looking. I found them in one of the boxes we were both looking through."

"And then my PawPaw interrupted us."

"Yes, and I didn't even quite realize what I was looking at, but I knew it was bad," Summer stammers. "And you had just said you couldn't handle any more family drama...and I didn't want to be the messenger, especially since your grandfather didn't share what he wanted exactly. But you have to believe me... I was going to tell you." Tears pool in her eyes.

"I believe you," I say. "I do."

"You do?" The worry lines in her forehead deepen.

"Yes." I finish my whiskey and immediately want more. Twins? More siblings? Now it's my turn to get up and pace. If this is true, that my father has twin kids out there, I need to know who knows. PawPaw must know. Does my mother? Ethan? I need to get back to Revel Pointe in case someone opens that envelope.

"When were they born?" I ask, not sure why this matters.

"1979." Summer gestures to my glass, and I nod. She crosses back into the kitchen, and I watch her through unfocused vision. When she hands me another two fingers neat, I notice she's watching me intently too.

"And the documents looked real?" I wish I could see them now for myself.

"Yes," Summer says. "Charity Hospital, Orleans Parish, 1979. There was a photo enclosed as well. Two women holding two infants."

"Who's the mother?" I don't know if I even want to know, but I guess I'll find out eventually. Another set of Reves to contend with. Tilda will be thrilled.

"Celeste Mallory," Summer tells me. I've never heard the name before.

"So my dad had two kids in 1979." I need to put the pieces together out loud. We drift back to the sofa and plop down. "That would have been before Wade and Ethan. What are their names again?"

"Simon and Aurora."

"Do you know where they are?" I ask.

"I don't," Summer says softly, carefully. "But maybe your grandfather does or wants to."

We're here in Summer's living room, and it feels so full of family warmth and love that I'm embarrassed by my own messy, fucked up family.

"I don't know why I'm surprised," I say. "Actually, I'm not." It's a factual statement. "It's my dad's M.O. You know his history: eloped with the first wife and cheated on her with the woman who would become his second wife, my mother, and then he cheated again with Yasmin."

Summer leans toward me on the sofa as if to console, but seems to think better of it and repositions herself closer to the arm rest.

"Why *wouldn't* there have been a kid, or two I guess, before Bambi?" I ask the ceiling.

"Bambi?"

"Yes, his first wife was Bambi," I say, recognizing the name's absurdity. "She died," I explain. "Complications in childbirth."

"Poor Ethan," Summer whispers. Her eyes are huge and glassy.

I want to close the distance between us, to hold her, but I maintain the space she's created. "Yeah," I whisper. "He mourns the mother he never had. I mourn the one I do." The words slip out, heavy but true. We're both quiet for a moment. "And you know what else is fucked up? I was born five months after Ethan."

Summer's face morphs from worry to pity, and I hate feeling pitied. I finish my whiskey. Tired from travel, from heartache, from secrets—sick of the Revel Pointe cistern. As if sensing my agitated state, Summer tucks her legs underneath her and curls into the corner. She doesn't deserve this rant. I'm not even pissed that she kept this from me. This information would have done me no good before the gala.

"I'm sorry I didn't give you the documents when I found them," she says as if reading my mind.

"I'm glad you didn't," I say. "Honestly. It was the right move."

Her whole body relaxes, and it makes me want to lay my head in her lap. She understood what I needed at that time. She was thinking of me, and that rearranges something inside me. I think about the photo of us dancing, her eyes shining at me, the feeling of being seen, of being loved. And me reciprocating. Jesus, I'm so in love with Summer I want to do something I've never done before, but that'll have to wait.

"I hope you mean that," she says. "Everything happened so quickly, I didn't know up from down."

She's been carrying the weight of this while I marched away in a huff and fled to Miami, pouting at all that had come to pass. I'm an ass.

"I'm so sorry I ran, Summer," I say. I want her forgiveness, and to kiss her more deeply than I ever have, but I have to wait. I don't want to assume she's longing for me too.

"Okay." Her voice cracks.

I set my glass down and slip my hands in my pockets. I don't want to do anything to spoil the settled feeling that has just come over us both. After what seems like ten minutes, I break the silence.

"I should probably go." I stand. I need to fix this mess I created and go back to the incredible thing we started, but it's not going to happen tonight.

She stands too. The wary look in her eyes spurs me to action. Words aren't enough. I need a way to show her I'm worth taking another chance on.

"Are you okay?" she asks.

"Yeah, right now, yeah." I want to say more, but I need to mull over the ideas flashing through my mind. I text the SUV driver, who is waiting in a parking lot down the street, and set my glass in the kitchen sink.

On a side table in the dining alcove is a candid family photo in a gold frame. They're all sitting at a picnic table next to an autumn lake. I drift over to the photograph and pick it up. There's Mitch, proud and waving, in his early forties, with his pretty wife, Isabelle. Summer, the youngest, perches at the end of the bench; though her back brace is clearly uncomfortable, she turns toward the camera wearing her beautiful smile anyway.

"Oh god, don't look at that," Summer says, coming up behind me.

"You have your mom's smile," I tell her. It lights up her face.

She pulls the frame away from me, tucking it behind her. "That's my peak awkward phase. Beyond awkward. My hair, my skin, my brace..."

"I think you're beautiful."

I can feel Summer holding her breath. I could kiss her now, but the idea forming in my mind, an idea that could mend the crack I shattered in this burgeoning relationship, is something I have to see through before I muddy the waters with easy physicality.

"Thanks," Summer whispers.

"Well, good night," I say and risk touching her elbow, reassuringly.

I move to the foyer. Summer retrieves my jacket. "Can I come back in the morning?" I ask.

"What more is there to say?"

"Please. Just let me have one more day."

She holds my gaze, searching my face, and whatever she sees there makes her shrug and say, "Sure, but I have plans in the morning. I'll text you when I'm free."

After I've checked into my hotel, I waste no time. In the car, I texted Reya Ghu, noting that I'm prepared to make a statement about the bridal deal and the gala incident. With the West Coast three hours behind, she'll still have time to file a short follow-up story for tomorrow's paper. Now I need to draft something brief and tasteful to clear up the wreckage I've caused—something that will show Summer we have a future.

Chapter Forty-Four

Summer

Lilia's eyes are nearly bulging out of her head when she enters Short Stacks, our favorite retro diner in town. She's texted me fourteen times this morning for updates, the last of which included her order of the candied bacon Benedict with a side blueberry short stack. She arrives at our table, flushed from the cold and ready for the hot gossip.

"YOU!" Her voice gives the older couple in the next booth a start. "You have been holding out on me, girl. I'll never forgive you." She removes her long puffy jacket and drapes it over her chair, revealing her large round belly under a stretched sweater. "Unless you tell me everything now. Like, ALL the details."

"It's so good to see you too, Lilia." I joke. She reaches across the table to squeeze my hand quickly.

"Yeah, yeah. You leave me with only breadcrumbs of info..."

"I'm sorry," I say.

"You can make up for it by telling me what the hell has been going on." She sits back. "Are you okay? What happened with James last night? I still can't believe we're talking about THE James Reve!" Her voice lifts again, and the old couple glances over.

I shush her, aware of how the mention of his name can perk ears, but no one seems to notice. "To be honest, I'm still sort of mystified by him and this thing between us."

"So there's still a 'thing' between you?" Lilia sounds like a child at a surprise birthday party.

"I don't know, honestly." I pause as our plates arrive and check my phone. No new text from James. He'd only messaged this

291

morning to say he'll be available this afternoon and that he would pick me up later.

"I want to know everything," Lilia says.

Over brunch, I go back to the beginning, right from our sparkly conversation in row eleven. I detail the dinner in New Orleans with Cricket and Lucien, our meeting in the dance hall, and the time we kissed in the oak grove. I give her the PG-13 version, omitting the clock tower orgasms, but I reassure her that James is beyond what I've experienced in that realm.

"You are killing me, Nito," Lilia moans with envy. "So now, what the hell happened with Grainger McCloskey?"

I give her the Cliffs Notes because I'm so annoyed with Grainger that I don't even want to give him air time. This brings her up to what she knows from the press. Of course she's read all of *The Secret Reveler* posts.

"For the record, I'm Team Revel library," Lilia swears. "I mean, what Reveler wouldn't want a Rose Red wedding gown, but not at the expense of preserving Revel history."

"I can't stand his mother for doing this to him," I blurt. There's a split second of worry that Lilia will spread this gossip, but then I remember it's Lilia. She's on my side. "You should have seen the hurt in his eyes. He just masks it as anger, but she used him and betrayed him. Her own son."

"I've heard she's ruthless."

"She's intimidating." I want to share more, but that would lead me into Revel twins territory, and I want to steer well clear of mentioning them by accident.

The server comes around with more coffee, but I'm caffeinated enough. I check my texts again, and there's one from James: *Pick you up at 1?* That's an hour from now. I reply with a curt *Yes*.

"I don't want to go home," Lilia says. "I want to hear more. Why don't we drive over to the school after this so I can grab more storybooks for Liam and you can keep feeding me details?"

As Lilia drives us to East Westerville, she peppers me with more questions about the memorabilia and of course about meeting Mick Reve. But my mind is clouded with thoughts of seeing James again.

At a stoplight, Lilia's phone lights up with a notification. She glances at it and freaks. Before I know why, she's pulling through the green light and into the pharmacy parking lot.

"New Secret Reveler post! New Secret Reveler post!" she says with such excitement that I'm afraid she'll induce labor. She clicks open the blog post and starts reading aloud:

"*Well, well, well, dear Revelers. You'll never guess who dropped your illustrious Revel blogger a line in the wee hours of night... None other than the very man in question, the handsome prince of the moment, Mr. James Reve.*"

Lilia's mouth drops open as she turns to me. "Did you know about this?"

"No, what does it say?" I almost scream back at her.

Lilia continues reading at breakneck speed. "*Don't worry, darlings, I know what you're thinking. The elusive, brooding James would never deign to comment in the gossip rags, but I did some super sleuthing to fact check the validity of his claim, and I can confirm the message I received came from THE man himself.*"

Lilia stops and smacks the steering wheel three times. I grab her phone to keep reading myself.

"*Here is his unedited, brief, but extremely enlightening missive:*

'*The Grand Revel Library will never become a couture bridal boutique. Revel Pointe may launch a bridal wear line, but it will never be housed in the library I built for my grandfather and his legacy. This was never the intention, and on my word, the beloved artifacts of Revel Pointe will be on display for all fans to enjoy very soon. The memorabilia was painstakingly uncovered by an expert team of archivists, including the brilliant Summer York. I can personally attest to Ms. York's professionalism throughout the project, as we worked closely together on several occasions. It was during this project that I developed feelings for her. Unfortunately, I hurt the woman I have grown very fond of. I only hope she finds it in her heart to forgive me."*

"WHAT?!" Lilia and I shout in unison.

We stare at each other in silence for a second. Lilia takes back her phone and reads it quickly again. "He's in love with you," she says.

"It clearly says 'fond of,'" I say. "That's hardly in love."

"Girl, you know I know Revel, and this guy hasn't said a peep until that *Times* article two weeks ago. James Reve saying 'fond' in public is basically code for 'in-love.'"

"It is not," I say, but I wonder. It's very out of character for James to reveal personal feelings to anyone, let alone to the world of die-hard Revelers.

"Holy shit, girl. This is gonna blow up online."

My phone vibrates, and it's a text from James: *I'm sitting in a car on your street. Let me know when/if you want to meet.*

I read it out loud to Lilia, and she squeals.

"We need to get you over there." She slams the minivan back into drive, and we're suddenly screeching into a parking lot like we're in an action-movie car chase. "I need to get you to the grand gesture location! No wait." She slams on the brakes. "Is your dad home?"

"I don't know." I shrug, bracing myself on the dashboard, trying not to hyperventilate. "Please stop driving like a cartoon character!" I laugh nervously.

"You can't have a grand gesture moment with your dad watching." Lilia turns down a residential street. We're nearly at our middle school. "Tell James to meet us at East Westerville. Yes, that's perfect. It's closed. Private. Romantic, full circle, grand gesture location!"

"A middle school is romantic?" I laugh at Lilia but grip the door and passenger seat as she weaves us through a neighborhood I've known all my life. "Slow down, we want to actually make it there alive," I say, feeling the excitement bubble in my stomach. I text James where to meet me, and he replies with a simple: *See you soon.*

James may have just declared his feelings for me to the world before he's even told me how he feels, and I only have a few minutes to decide how to take this.

Lilia and I beeline for the side door and unlock it.

Lilia narrates our next moves. "I'll just grab an armload of books for Liam and leave you alone when he arrives." In the silent tone of the dead hallways, I wait. My phone buzzes again, and it's Cricket: *Have you seen this yet?*

With this simple question is a link to another *LA Times* editorial written by Reya Ghu. My thumb can't swipe fast enough to scan through it. The story includes the same statement as *The Secret Reveler*, but Ghu has added her own color commentary.

"I spoke to James Reve on the phone last night, and I've spent some time with him at Revel Pointe, and frankly, he's a deeply serious man who seems to care about his family and his grandfather's legacy with a rare ferocity. Between the lines of his statement, I read a genuine commitment to seeing the library project through to its intended purpose. I also see his shrewd maneuvering to make a Revel bridal line happen, thereby keeping the peace with Tilda Olsen-Reve, the likely mastermind behind the proposed couture collaboration. But what's more interesting to me was the urgent and sincere tone when he spoke about Summer York. James sounded as if in solemn confession when proclaiming just how fond of Ms. York he's truly become. We may have watched him leave Summer at the gala, but we also witnessed their magical Christmas waltz. What we don't have at hand is what happened behind closed doors. Could this Revel Prince truly be falling in love?"

It's the second time this morning, hell, this hour, that someone has suggested James' feelings for me may include that word, yet I'm still guarding my heart.

Lilia bursts back through the double doors with an armload of books. I take some from her, and we head back toward the parking lot.

"Are you nervous?" Lilia asks. "This might be a super big moment."

"Or another super big letdown."

"I don't believe that," she says. "This has already been a once-in-a-lifetime experience. I don't think it's over. Unless you want it to be."

"I don't know what I want." Tears blur my vision.

"Look, I think that man is crazy about you. Gosh, he flew all the way here just for a chance to talk to you. And I know he's flawed, but we all are, Summer. James seems like he's a lot of wonderful things too. And you deserve everything."

I let the tears stream down my face now and nod, not fully grasping what she means. The sentiment 'you deserve everything' just feels like something people say in moments like these, but being deserving of a real love affair with James still feels like something that's not attainable for me. I'm not built for it.

Lilia hugs me and says into my ear, "You are amazing, and you deserve amazing things."

I try to take it in, as James' black SUV pulls into the empty school lot.

Chapter Forty-Five

James

Anticipation knots my stomach as I watch Summer and her friend emerge from the utilitarian school building. I'm laser beam-focused on Summer. I venture out into the cold to meet them on the packed, crunchy snow, searching for a hopeful expression in Summer's eyes, but she's so neutral and guarded I can't read her.

"Lilia Bilokur," says Summer's friend, offering her hand. She shakes mine vigorously.

"Pleasure to meet you," I say with a cautious smile.

"I have to tell you what a fan I am of Revel Pointe," Lilia says. I notice her Thumbelina earrings. "I've been three times. We're just waiting for this one to be fully potty trained before we go back." She pats her pregnant belly. "Such an enchanting place. I love what you've done to honor your family's legacy." She shrugs sheepishly, and it might be the loveliest exchange with a Revel fan I've ever had.

"Thank you," I say, genuinely moved. "I'm glad you love the park." I know we're both stalling.

Summer watches her friend with love in her eyes, and I'm dying to hold her. It's been too long.

"Are you going to give me the tour?" I risk asking Summer directly.

"Show him the library, Nito," Lilia encourages.

Summer nods and then hugs Lilia, promising her they'll catch up later.

Once Lilia is back in her minivan, Summer and I turn to each other.

"Nito?" I ask, suddenly apprehensive; there's so much I don't know about her. All of this may be crazy but I remain open. I've come this far. I need to see this through.

"It means *summer* in Ukrainian." She leads the way to a side entrance, and I hold the door open for her. I'm smacked in the face with the scent of pine cleaner. I never attended a school like this, only seen them on TV and films, which lends a sense of surreality. I'm suddenly hit by the realization that I might have come a long way to get my heart decimated.

Summer pushes through the heavy double doors, and then we're in a wide-open yet somehow still cozy library space. It feels like Summer, with its neatly labeled shelves, curated displays, and inviting color palette.

"I saw the articles," she says, circling away from me towards the front counter. It's warmer in here than in the drafty halls.

"I'm glad," I say. "After our talk last night, I felt the need to take a little of the narrative back. Take control of the gossip."

"Good idea." Her eyes chance a look at me, and I can tell she's still dealing with hurt or apprehension.

"Look, I wanted to say—"

"You made me feel like I didn't matter," she says and pauses. "At the gala..."

This guts me. "Summer, you matter the most..." I begin, but she holds up a hand, signaling for me to listen.

"One of us has to be the first to say what we really want," she says, taking off her hat and unzipping her coat. "Since we met, my heart and head have been at war. I feel like I've been tossed in the dryer, and I—"

I want to hear her out, but I know exactly what I want now, and I want to be crystal clear about it.

"Summer," I say, pleading with my eyes. "I was scared. When I ran, it's because I thought you betrayed me, but later I realized it was because you could really hurt me. And I've spent my life making it so no one ever could hurt me again."

Summer's jaw relaxes and her lips part in shock. She's so damned beautiful it hurts.

"I don't know how I'll ever forgive myself for leaving you at the gala like that," I continue. "And if I could go back and change that fact, I would. I would sweep you up in my arms and take you with me. Family and press be damned. Your happiness is the only thing that matters."

Light tears trickle down her cheeks, and I want to kiss them away.

"You should have talked to me." She sniffles.

"I know that now," I say, venturing a step toward her. "The thing I'm realizing is that I don't have a clue at how to love someone. Truly. I don't know what that looks like at all."

She looks up at me, wide-eyed, her eyelashes thick with tears. "What do you mean?"

"I mean just that—I think I always do the opposite of what someone needs or wants from me because I'm protecting myself," I say, almost confusing myself.

"From what?" She steps closer.

"From being sent away, from failing publicly, from being gutted."

"I get that—trust me," Summer pulls her long braid forward over her shoulder. "What do you want, James?" she asks finally.

"I want to make you feel as brilliant as you make me feel," I say. "I'm not sure how to do that and I'm pretty sure I'll fuck up again, but I want to be with you. I want to declare it to the fucking world. And I don't care if it's messy and complicated. I want you."

"How? You live in London and—"

"I don't care," I tell her. "We'll figure it out, damn it. Can I just hold you now?" I'm practically begging. "I need to hold you."

After a moment she nods, falling into my arms.

At once, I feel whole again, with her body pressed to mine. "I'm so sorry," I repeat into her hair.

"I forgive you," she says into my chest, then pulls back to look me square in the eyes. "I understand now, but please don't run again."

"I won't." This feels right, looking down into her loving eyes. I savor the moment a second more, then I lean down and finally kiss her.

Chapter Forty-Six

Summer

The waves of relief flood my bloodstream like sweet wine, giving me an instant high as James' lips press into mine, tender and slow at first, then harder and more urgent. The taste and scent and feel of him send a rush of warmth and pleasure to the center of my body. It's so all-encompassing that I never want to stop kissing him. He backs me up to the table, and I easily slide up onto it, sitting and wrapping my legs around him. I want him, all of him, every day, every night. I'm lightheaded with lust.

"We can't," I pant, pulling away from him. "Not right here."

Pushing him back, I hop off the table and grab his hand, yanking his arm to follow me. We wind through the shelves and rows of books. I lead him back behind the last stack, in the darkest part of the library, where the little emergency exit sign glows a soft red. We kiss deeply against the world history shelf, but I still feel myself hesitating.

I pull back from James and try not to sound desperate when I ask, "Are you going back to London?"

He shrugs, as his fingers slip under my sweater and caress my waist. "I'm not sure. Do you want to come to London with me?"

My chest booms with the force of a bass drum. "London? I'm supposed to just…"

He sees I'm serious and pulls back. He shrugs again. "The last four days were hell without you, Summer." James leans in and kisses me slowly, spinning me, my back pressing into the science books. Between kisses he rattles off options. "You wanna go back to Revel, I'll go back. Fuck, I'll move here."

"No, you wouldn't," I say, laughing into his mouth. "I don't even want to stay here." I pull away, surprised by my clear answer.

"You don't?" James asks, searching my face. "What do you want?"

In the quiet, I hear my own panting breath, and I know the answer is that all I want is to see if this thing between me and James has a chance. I can find a job anywhere. I can always come home to Westerville. But I've never felt this way for someone in my life. James' brows knit, concerned I'm going to say something he doesn't want to hear.

"Those four days were hell for me, too," I tell him, still scared to reveal my true feelings.

"I'm falling in love with you, Summer," he says. "Like I never have before."

"This is all new for me, too." I reach up and run my fingers through his thick wavy hair. "I kept telling myself I should just enjoy the fantasy of it all, that it was probably just a fling. But I fell for who you really are, in the quiet moments, when it was just you and me. That's what I want."

James nearly growls then, diving into my neck and lifting me off the floor. I wrap my thighs around his hips, slipping out of my long coat, and surrendering to the pleasure he so freely wants to give me. We knock stacks of books off the shelves, but I don't care. I'm where I want to be, entwined with James Reve. Except this time we're on the same page.

It happens quickly. We're ravenous for each other, barely undressing, needing to feel closer, finally dropping to the floor. As we cling to each other, coming together, each of us with full knowledge of how we feel about the other, I soar beyond the bounds of what I thought my body was capable of. How different sex can be with a man I know adores me as much as I adore him.

In the serene afterglow, using James' bicep for a pillow, I drift off into a placid reverie. Eventually, he turns to plant a kiss on my forehead.

"Where should we go from here?" he asks.

The fact that we're making this decision together fills my center with lust all over again. I tell him that the head librarian job at Revel went to Horace and that I'm planning to quit my job at East Westerville Middle.

"I'm a free agent," I say, sighing, surprised that acknowledging my current predicament is no longer freaking me out. "Not sure where I'll land."

"I'm in the same boat," James says, shifting to look me in the eye. "Remember our first conversation, when we met?"

"On the plane?"

"Row eleven."

"How could I forget?" I say. "You were so flirty."

"Pot, meet kettle." James smiles and caresses the curve of my hip. "I was thinking about how you've never seen a real castle."

My stomach bubbles with excitement. "Still never have."

"I think we should remedy that," James says. "Let's take a holiday. There's a job I'm planning to bid on in Scotland, near Edinburgh. I'd love some company in the drafty old land of kilts."

"Scotland?" My mind does somersaults. I have savings, and I have been working so hard, and we're still in that dead zone between Christmas and New Year. What could be the harm in indulging this handsome man who has just professed he only wants to make me happy? But this feels like more running away, and I hesitate. All our problems will be here when we return. *If* he plans to return. Could I really live my life so far from my family? And what about James and his family?

"What's going on in there?" James motions to my forehead.

"I'm asking myself all the 'what ifs' that you're ignoring," I admit.

"I'm not ignoring them," James says. "I'm just suggesting that we could carve out some time in a beautiful, ancient place to actually be together, to get to know each other better, away from everyone and everything."

"That does sound nice," I say, biting his shoulder gently. "Seriously, though. Some time and space away from all the complications might give us a new perspective. Either way."

"Either way?" James asks, lifting to his elbow. "Summer, I want to make things work with you. Whatever that means. If the opposite of running is sticking around and figuring it out, then that's what I want to do."

Looking into his lovely green eyes, I can see a genuine beginning for us.

"I'd like that," I tell him. "Let's go to Scotland to figure it out."

James leans down and gives me a deep kiss to seal the decision. "You're going to love it," he says. "Touring castles and walking the ramparts by day..."

"And hot hotel sex all night," I interject.

James groans. "I need this." He kisses me again, long and persistent. "I need you."

"Oh, all right," I tease.

"Besides," James says, rising to an elbow, and tracing my nipple with the tip of his finger. "You need to see where the saucy, treacherous Queen Isabella once lived."

I shiver beneath his touch and gaze, suddenly turned on again and ready to devour him once more. "This is going to be an amazing trip," I whisper before biting his earlobe.

"Yes...yes, it is," he growls. "Milady."

Chapter Forty-Seven

ONE YEAR LATER
Summer

In the late-morning quiet of our Edinburgh townhouse, I pace and fiddle with the Christmas ornaments in the fir tree we purchased at a village market yesterday. James and I argued over white lights versus multi-colored lights, and after a playful row that ended in living-room sofa sex, I won. Now our tree twinkles with red, blue, green, and yellow lights warming our place with nostalgic cheer. I'm just waiting for James to return from the airport, where he's gone to collect my dad for the holidays.

I return to my office off the kitchen with a view of the back garden, blanketed in a half inch of snow, to stare at my notes again. This fall, I started a Ph.D. program in History and Archival Sciences at the University of Edinburgh, and I've been considering the fictionalized diaries of Marion Angus, a lesser-known figure of the 20th century Scottish Renaissance, as a focus for my thesis. I originally wanted to pursue something from the 15th or 16th centuries, but I'm intrigued by the idea of a young woman so full of stories she wrote a serial for the local paper. In the new year, I'm planning a trip to the University of Aberdeen to view a collection of original correspondence between Angus and fellow writers.

I hear the oven chime in the kitchen. I rush over and carefully remove the sheet of ginger cookies I baked for Dad, wondering when they'll return from the airport. I wanted to go with James, but he insisted I should stay behind and bake my mom's holiday cookies so that Dad "would feel at home the moment he entered our place." James has been so supportive these past few months, with my arrival in August and the stress of returning to school life, I didn't question it. Plus, he was right. Between the real evergreen tree and the spice, the whole place smells like Christmas.

It all reminds me of last Christmas, which feels like three decades ago considering all that has come to pass since then. After a crazy-romantic New Year's vacation in the Highlands and an impromptu jaunt to Wales to visit more castles, James and I landed back at Revel Pointe. Before our whirlwind trip, the middle school principal and I had a heart-to-heart. I think she was secretly relieved to hear I wasn't coming back, as my presence would cause "a distracting environment for learning." Being briefly internet famous had its price.

Since James' official statement to the press about the library, which caused a fan frenzy, he had been in touch with his parents and the Fimura bridal company, and with Ethan's help, was able to broker a deal. The bridal couture boutique's new location is now Miss Maisy's Dance Hall. Instead of tearing it down, James created a design that honors the past while appeasing the Fimuras' aesthetic. Lots of baby pink. Inspired by the new design, the Fimuras named its first collection after James, calling it Devotion.

We also spent some time with James' grandfather, who seemed overjoyed to see his third oldest grandson fight for his family. At one dinner in Mick's cabin, he shared the story of his son Gaspard's past transgressions. The tale of Simon and Aurora was all that James and I expected it to be and more.

In 1972, after returning from Vietnam with internal injuries, plus broken ribs, collarbones, and left hip, Gaspard wasn't the same.

"He was listless," Mick recalled. "I didn't even recognize my own son."

He moved to New Orleans, enrolling at Tulane and drinking around the clock.

"We had to collect him from the gutter more than a few times." Mick explained how they set him up in rehab programs, and later, with positions at the animation studio that would only last a few months. One day, Marie received a letter from a young girl, Celeste Mallory, who worked at the ice cream stand at the Rag Tag Gameland in the park. She was only seventeen, still a senior in high school. In the letter she professed her love for Gaspard and revealed that she was five months pregnant with twins. When Mick and Marie confronted their son, he admitted to a relationship but denied he could be the father.

"It was shameful," Mick admitted. "Marie and I were distraught, but what could we do?"

It was the late '70s, but the blood paternity test did not rule Gaspard out.

"Marie met with Celeste and believed her. And I trusted my wife. But Gaspard was not fit to be a father. He was so full of anger and regret. And back then, the culture was so unkind to the soldiers returning home. We felt that Celeste and the children would be better off without Gaspard in their lives." Mick's blue eyes went glassy, delving back into those hard days.

Mick said he regretted the choices he and his wife made back then, and that he'd do things differently now. Back then, Mick and Marie helped the girl with medical care and set up trusts for the twins, Simon and Aurora. By then, Celeste, embittered by Gaspard's denial, cut off all ties with the family. It killed Marie not to be part of her grandchildren's lives.

"It hurt me too," Mick said. "Especially after you kids came along and I knew firsthand the joys of grandkids."

Marie sent gifts anonymously and watched them grow up from afar until she passed. In Mick's grief, Simon and Aurora receded from his concerns, along with everything else—his family, his work, his legacy. It was only recently, after Wade's death and Gaspard's stroke, that James' grandfather decided it was time to right the wrongs of his life and support the ventures of his grandkids, which included Simon and Aurora, and even their mother. Years ago, in that hazy time, he'd given the paperwork to Gaspard, who, by this time, had cleaned up his act and was running the business in Mick's absence. When Revel Pointe amassed the team of archivists, Mick worried the twins' information would come to light. He wanted to respect Celeste's wishes and not drag her children into the limelight.

James didn't care about how it might skew company succession if Gaspard's potential first children wanted a piece of the business, but it seemed wrong to keep this information from his siblings. PawPaw convinced him to give him some time to contact Simon and Aurora himself so that their wishes were understood before telling anyone else.

Between that time and starting my program, James and I had been living like nomads, sometimes apart and sometimes reuniting with intensity for weeks. I spent a few months at the Grand Revel Library as a consultant, working with Horace again, and six weeks over the summer back in Ohio with Dad. Life hadn't settled until James rented the townhouse just west of the city center and started work drafting the Art Institute project, to be built in the countryside next year. When I missed Thanksgiving, it started to sink in that I'd chosen my path with James. This journey in Scotland feels right, but I ached to be with my family for Christmas. That's when we made arrangements for Dad to come for a week.

I hear the front door open with a shuffle of boots on the foyer mat, and my heart jumps.

"Hello!?" I call, but I hear more voices than I'm expecting. Rounding the hall, I get my first glimpse of the guests—there's my dad, but also Gran, Kayla and her husband, John, and my nieces and nephew—all removing hats, shoes, coats, and dragging rolling luggage and backpacks. I'm speechless, and they all laugh at the shock on my face.

"Surprised?" Dad asks.

"Uh, yeah," I say, jogging down the hall for hugs. "It's gonna take me a minute. What the heck are you all doing here?"

"We're all surprised Dad kept it a secret," Kayla says, grabbing me for a ferocious hug.

"We took bets on the plane on whether you knew or not," Emma says.

"Who won?" I ask, feeling my face stretch with a mile-wide smile. Gran, Dad, and John raise their hands.

"We lost a buck each." Brody pouts.

"Don't worry," Kayla says. "I got you."

As I'm embracing my last family member in the cramped entrance, I finally lock eyes with my incredible boyfriend. James is as pleased with himself as I am. I'm only a tad bit annoyed he didn't tell me they would all be visiting for Christmas. I already shipped their presents.

"Well, we know James can keep a secret," Gran says loudly. "How'd you do it?"

"I'm a man of few words, Gran," James says, grabbing my hand for a squeeze.

As my family leaves their stuff and shuffles into the rest of the townhouse oohing and ahhing at the decor and the views, I turn to James.

"Thank you." I kiss him quickly and stare into his green eyes. "But where are they all going to stay?"

"I rented a house for them on the park," James says.

"My dad too?"

James nods, then pulls me close so he can lean into my ear.

"There's no way I can keep my hands off you for a week," he whispers. "And we know how loud you can get."

Heat floods my center as my neck tickles where his warm breath caresses my skin. I want to hop up into his arms and wrap my legs around his hips right there, but I'm distracted by the joy of watching my family make themselves at home in the cozy place that James and I have created together. Emma steals a ginger cookie as Kayla opens the fridge looking for wine. My brother-in-law and Dad check out the stone fireplace as Gran, Brody, and Vicky plop down on our comfy sofa, pointing to a few gifts already wrapped under the tree. Everyone talks over each other, and I couldn't love them more. As if it all couldn't get any better, it begins to snow and James whispers in my ear, "I love you."

EPILOGUE

The Secret Reveler:
A Blog Devoted to All Matters Reve

Something strange is going on at Revel. It's quiet. Too quiet. Not an iota of drama. Ethan and Marin are expecting their first child. Mazel tov. James and Summer are living their best Scottish lives in Edinburgh, far from the madding crowd (that's us, dear Revelers). The last time we saw our beautiful librarian and our beastly architect was at the opening for the bridal couture boutique, which of course was a smash success. It went off without a hitch—no historic snowfalls, epic fights, or stunning reveals. Boring!

Gaspard's been touring the world on a yacht, leaving Ethan and Tilda at the helm. Speaking of Tilda, word is she's working on something super hush-hush. All we know is Henri, her second son, has been called home from Croatia to do some special assignment, but the details are sparse.

Henri, seen here with his brother James at last year's Fete Noel gala, looks dapper in a tux, a far cry from his usual getup (no, that's not a picture of young Harrison Ford in Raiders of the Lost Ark, *that's Henri Freaking Reve, looking like an outdoorsy dreamboat as he replants trees in a Costa Rica rainforest).*

Let's hope he shakes things up.

The End

The Revel Pointe Romance Continues

Stay tuned for the next book in the Revel Pointe Romance series, *Cynda in the Swamp.*

Cynda doesn't love working in maintenance at Revel Pointe, but she sure needs the cash since her father died and divided the Foret land between his wife and daughter. The problem is that Cynda's stepmother wants to sell off her tract of the beloved land to none other than Tilda Olsen-Reve. When Henri Reve shows up on Cynda's land, their meet cute is explosive, literally. Shots are fired and sparks fly. Cynda will do whatever she has to do to protect the land her father loved, even reject the charming and privileged Henri. In this retelling of *Cinderella*, the heroine isn't about to wait around for a fairy godmother to make her dreams a reality. Let's just hope the prince doesn't stand in her way.

Did you love *Summer in the Snowfall*? Then you should read *Marin in the Moonlight*[1] by A.E. Merriweather!

Marin Vandersee cannot take another second of her overachieving family's disapproval and has escaped to her favorite place on Earth, Revel Pointe, the theme park mecca of the Revel Universe tucked along the Mississippi River just outside New Orleans. With the help of her costume designing, brilliant best friend, she begins work as Rose Red, her favorite Revel princess. Finally where her people are, Marin feels at home, surrounded by other Revelers and her dreamy co-worker, the actor Prince Roland. Marin quickly falls for him, but when she saves Ethan Reve, the interim CEO of Revel Pointe and notorious playboy, from drowning in the lighthouse moat, everything changes, and he offers her the job of her dreams.

---

1. https://books2read.com/u/47BNYg

2. https://books2read.com/u/47BNYg

Ethan Reve also ran from his family and Revel Pointe years ago, but a tragedy means he must take the reins of his family's multi-billion dollar park and entertainment company. To succeed, he needs to manage his grief as well as recuperate his bad-boy image. Drawn to Marin and recognizing her as a die-hard Reveler, Ethan needs her to finish his late brother's passion project, an immersive Island of Sirens experience. However, Ethan's power-hungry step-mother actively sabotages their project and budding relationship at every turn.

Together, Marin and Ethan must learn to trust each other while faking a relationship for the success of the project and their happily-ever-after in a race full of pitfalls to the deadline. Will their chemistry make this fairytale romance a reality, or will reality get in the way of their fairytale ending?

Read more at www.aemerriweather.com/newsletter.

About the Author

A.E. Merriweather is a pseudonym that represents three writers and friends. Combined, they have published short stories, articles, poetry, and scripts. They live in New Orleans, LA and would probably love your dog.

The first book in the Revel Pointe Billionaire Romance Series, MARIN IN THE MOONLIGHT, is available where books are sold. Look for book #3 in 2026.

Read more at aemerriweather.com/newsletter.